MW01530425

Jaya Nepal!

By

Martin David Hughes

Simi Books, Asheville 28801

© 2014
All rights reserved. Published 2014.

Editing by Kristin Thiel & Laura Garwood Meehan
Cover image by Vinnie Kinsella
Illustrations by Syaifullah Al Amin
Book design by Vinnie Kinsella
Printed in the United States of America.

ISBN: 978-0-9905784-0-6

All rights reserved. No part of this book may be reproduced in any form or by any electronic or mechanical means, including information storage and retrieval systems, without written permission from the author, except in the case of a reviewer, who may quote brief passages embodied in critical articles or in a review.

Contents

Contents

Acknowledgments

I HAVE A GREAT MANY PEOPLE TO THANK FOR HELPING BRING THIS NOVEL TO completion. Primarily, I thank the Nepali people for an incredible hospitality, genuine kindness, and indomitable spirit. The beating heart of this novel is the Nepali people themselves, and I am grateful for the warmth and compassion that I have experienced as a guest in the great country of Nepal.

I acknowledge all the people I've met in my travels abroad who have informed or contributed to the characters and story in this fictional work. There is a little bit of each of you in this novel, and I am grateful for having crossed your paths. Likewise, I acknowledge the contributions of the kind and considerate individuals who read and commented upon early drafts of the manuscript. The feedback you provided was invaluable and helped shape the final version of this novel.

A very special thank you to all the returned Peace Corps Volunteers (RPCVs) who provided insight and guidance about the Peace Corps experience, which is a volunteer experience unlike any other, and I am extremely grateful to have been the benefactor of your knowledge and wisdom. I specifically thank Steven Iams, a Nepal RPCV (N-196) who graciously and eloquently answered all my many questions about life in Nepal as a Peace Corps Volunteer.

I hold a special place in my heart for my two wonderful and talented editors, Kristin Thiel and Laura Garwood Meehan, who made countless improvements to the manuscript and provided incredible guidance and support throughout the entire process. I am deeply appreciative of your expertise and dedication in making this novel the best it could possibly be. Thank you, too, to Syaifullah Al Amin for creating the beautiful illustrations that appear in this novel, to Vinnie Kinsella for applying your excellent artistic talents to the novel's cover and interior layout, and to Jessica Glenn and Jessica Henkle, my gifted and passionate publicists. And another big thank you to the accomplished individuals at Open Door Design Studio, Marisa Falcigno and Shantanu Suman, for creating the novel's superb website.

Many kind thanks to my incredible family, especially my mom and dad, who have shown me unconditional love and support over the years. You are the stable foundation in my life and a tremendous source of joy and wisdom. Finally, thank you, dear Robyn. Thank you for reading the many iterations of this manuscript and gently, and with grace, offering your always-valuable thoughts and ideas. This book would not have been possible without your heartfelt support and encouragement. I love you.

Namaste, Nepal

<small>Bracing for impact, I walked toward the airport's final corridor,</small> the one that would spit me into the steamy Kathmandu morning. The flight from Bangkok to Kathmandu had been filled with business travelers clicking madly on computers, sleepy families watching a Bollywood movie on the overhead televisions, and attendants offering passengers spicy snacks and miniature cans of Coke. The airport was loud with announcements over the PA and swollen with Nepali nationals returning home after two-year work stints in the Persian Gulf. I suspected that the most comfortable part of my journey was about to end.

I slung my brown, weathered backpack over my left shoulder, took a couple of deep breaths, and strode confidently into an olfactory barrage. Thick pollution, human waste, and burning garbage mingled with jasmine-scented incense, sandalwood perfume, and cardamom, coriander, and cumin. You could wander the Indian subcontinent to its farthest margins — from the Hindu Kush to the Bay of Bengal, from the Maldivian archipelago to the Himalayan massif — but you could never mistake its unique combination of scents for anywhere else on the planet.

Above me, the outside arch of Tribhuvan International Airport was decorated with bas-reliefs depicting tantric acts and scenes of mutilation. Before me and beyond a swath of moist earth, the early-morning fog hung like a ghostly cloak around the bony shoulders of a cadre of men huddled behind a barbed-wire barricade: the final hurdle between First World and Third.

I understood, on some level, that it was now or never. I understood that if I weren't fully committed to the mountain-size task I'd been assigned, I should simply turn around and head back home. But I didn't turn around. Instead, I stood tall, accepted the challenges of the life I'd chosen, and took a giant leap of faith into the unknown. And that leap of faith was a rush like I'd never felt before.

The men, whom I understood from a customs officer to be the crafty pilots of taxis and three-wheeled boxlike vehicles called *tuk tuks*, appeared to stand in solidarity, united as brothers in a proletarian trade, yet simultaneously willing to slash their nearest competitors' tires for cab fare.

They looked restrained, even orderly, as they waited quietly behind the barricade and a group of six gun-toting soldiers dressed in purple fatigues. But I knew they'd be starved for business. The heaviness of the drivers' hungry, hollow gazes wrapped around me like leg-irons and slowed my progress down the cement exit ramp. I was buying time—one foreigner against a mob on its home turf, nervous about being taken advantage of—and the drivers knew it.

"Hello, sir! Hello, sir!" the cabbies shouted as they began to walk toward me, then alongside me. "Very nice taxi for you!" they added. "Friend, where are you going? Sir, I have cheapest and best taxi for you to be going in Kathmandu City! Please, sir. Come with me. *Come!*"

Then I noticed a short man, darker in complexion than the others and much younger, probably in his early twenties, zigzagging through the group of cabbies with nimble body contortions and urgent footwork. His flailing emphatic arm unlocked my nerves. "Mr. Creed! Mr. Creed!" he shouted. "Greetings, Mr. Benji Man Creed!"

But the other cabbies had closed in around me, cutting off all potential exit routes. Switching from his lilting English to what I assumed to be Nepali, the man who had called my name replaced his radiant smile with a frown that gave his slender frame more bulk. He tore into the drivers, chastising them, I suspected, for their aggressive and unruly behavior. The cabbies, sullen but not broken, regrouped to target another batch of fresh arrivals. The man's harsh treatment of the cabbies on my behalf endeared him to me just as his smile had.

8

"*Namaskar*. My good name is Madhu Prasad Patel," the man said, playfully bobbling his head from side to side. He pressed both of his hands together in front of his chest and bowed slightly in a gesture of salutation.

As he explained that he'd recently been hired as a driver for Peace Corps officials and that he also worked part-time in a small hospital in one of the communities close to Kathmandu, Madhu hustled me away from the mayhem and commotion of the arrivals area, past rows of squatting beggars with outstretched arms and gnarled amputations. He wore a brown polo shirt, tan slacks, and a pair of well-worn white tennis shoes; he explained that the weather in Kathmandu was uncharacteristically warm, even for late summer. Unzipping and removing my jacket, I followed him closely as we walked briskly toward the airport parking lot.

When we finally reached the lot, I was warmly greeted by a handful of Nepalis and Americans from the Kathmandu Peace Corps office. The three men and two women placed garlands of flowers called *mallas* around my neck and dabbed a red paste on my forehead. The paste, known as a *tika*, was a quintessentially Nepali way of welcoming me and introducing me to the country's customs, explained Madhu. Running a hand through his short black hair, he smiled, assuring me that that would not be the last tika I'd receive during my time in Nepal. His playful mannerisms and jovial nature immediately set me at ease, and after just a few minutes in the country, I felt as though I already had a close friend.

We all climbed into the Peace Corps van and settled in for the short trip from the city's outskirts to Kathmandu proper. From his position behind the craft's wheel, Madhu turned to me and said, "You are trusting me, *daai*? You are trusting me, big brother? I have been driving these streets for many years now with having only three major accidents!"

Three major auto accidents sounded like a lot to me, but then again, I hadn't seen Kathmandu's traffic. I assumed that Kathmandu's traffic was probably as insane as any other South Asian city. Besides, nobody else in the van, Nepali or American, seemed particularly concerned about Madhu's track record on the roads of Kathmandu. "Fair enough, Madhu," I replied. "Let's go!"

We tore away from the airport only to merge awkwardly with rush-hour traffic outside its gates. Slowly and with great patience, Madhu picked his way through the idling gridlock and noxious fumes spewing from the cars, buses, and tuk tuks piling into the city. His impeccable, straight-backed posture made it appear that he'd assumed a meditative position in the driver's seat. Not a bad way to cope with the heavy traffic, I thought, contemplating my own shift into half-lotus position.

I was tired after the prior day's long flight from San Francisco, despite the restful night's sleep I'd enjoyed at the Hotel Amari in Bangkok during my layover. I wanted nothing more than to crash, but the visual and auditory hyperstimulation of life outside the van was enough to keep my eyes wide open as I viewed Kathmandu for the very first time.

One of the first things I noticed about the city was the angular, almost haphazard layout of its streets. Its roads appeared to twist and wind like the roots of a strangler fig. I also noticed the architectural variety with each turn of the road as we advanced slowly toward the city center. A series of concrete buildings off to our right was painted and plastered with signs detailing the services offered within. Nepali script with accompanying English slogans marked the location of computer repair shops, car mechanics, banks, pharmacies, optometrists, and cybercafés.

I also noticed a blue-striped tent on the infield of a large triangular dirt field to our left, erected, perhaps, for a wedding, religious gathering, or political rally. I saw numerous roadside temples too, shrines both large and small, devoted to the Hindu gods Hanuman, Ganesh, Krishna, and Kali. I'd yet to get my bearings, but already a part of me felt comfortable in the hustle and bustle and turmoil of the sprawling South Asian capital.

A member of the Peace Corps welcoming party tapped my shoulder, pointed at my backpack, and said, "Benjamin, is this your only bag?"

"It sure is. Less clutter in my life, less clutter in my mind," I said, noticing that Madhu was flashing me a large, approving smile. Traveling lightly had become somewhat of a specialty for me, part of a concerted effort to reduce my worldly burden through a strict policy of minimalism. One of my life's biggest stressors was the dependency often associated with various material wants, needs, or desires. I wanted my time to be occupied by heady, important tasks and creative endeavors, not by the pursuit of material goods, although I often fell short of the mark. I was still a long way from realizing many of the ideals that captured my mind.

Most of the possessions I'd brought with me—apart from a few sets of clothes I'd stowed in my backpack—I was wearing, including a white T-shirt, a pair of blue jeans fraying at the cuffs, and a pair of ratty old Airwalks. My wardrobe, in conjunction with my three-day-old stubble, would have made even the lowliest official in the US government cringe. I had to admit that my appearance didn't exactly scream "capable American ambassador." But I couldn't have cared less about how I looked after so many hours of travel.

"So, where exactly are we going, Madhu?" I asked, shifting my attention from my backpack and its contents back to the Nepali capital's impressive sprawl.

"I am taking your fine and dandy self to Thamel, where you will be hotel living and spending your monies and your first few days in our beloved Nepal country," he replied. "There, in that Thamel place, you can be doing meetings with other Peace Corpses and big-time *bideshi* travelers from around the world."

We chugged further into Kathmandu's spellbinding embrace. The exhaust belching from countless two-stroke engines did little to mask other offensive aromas wafting through the inner city streets. Heaps of rotting organic debris and plastic waste lined many of the street's gutters, the byproduct, according to Madhu, of a massive, citywide sanitation worker strike. Cows, sacred in their heaving amplitude, feasted on the trash, while hoards of industrious children sifted through the mounds for valuable recyclables.

One of the cows, a massive bull, had mounted a nearby female and begun mating, its pounding penis sending shock waves through the female's fleshy hindquarters. The bull's large, sagging scrotum swung back and forth between its rear legs like the pendulum of a grandfather clock as it continued to thrust with urgency. "*Gaai!*" shouted Madhu, pointing at the copulating beasts. "Holy cows!"

Nobody on the street was paying much attention to the cows, except for two young boys who had inched close to the action and were whacking the bull's rump with a spindly branch. I presumed the mating of cows was a relatively common sight in Nepal, just as it had been in India when I'd visited there three years before. For many Westerners, though, especially those who'd grown up exclusively in an urban setting, the image of two large beasts mating probably would have been a real attention grabber.

Many of the things visitors found unusual or irritating about the subcontinent—such as the nonstop price haggling with merchants, the chaos and confusion of the streets, and the well-intentioned yet often inaccurate directions provided by strangers—were precisely the things I found most interesting about the place. I also loved that the forces of creation and degeneration were so apparent on the streets. Those most obvious images of *samsara*—that never-ending cycle of birth, life, and death—humbled me and gave me a renewed sense of appreciation for where I'd come from and the life I'd been given.

I also suspected that many of us who had signed on with the Peace Corps shared the common understanding that living in a place such as Nepal—or Botswana or Cambodia or Mozambique or anywhere else the Peace Corps was currently active, for that matter—meant we would have to accept things that were beyond our control while focusing on the duties defined by our posts. If people weren't willing to do this, if people weren't willing to admit their limitations and contend with the unexpected shocks, setbacks, and daily frustrations of life in the Third World, they would prob-ably be better off lounging on the white-sand beaches of Thailand. And that was the unspoken deal with the Peace Corps: you had to be willing to invest yourself in the lives of all members of the society in which you were placed while retaining your own individuality. You had to participate in your new neighbors' lives, but you also had to be yourself and exist as you did to show others how Americans lived.

I felt cautiously optimistic about my ability to rise up and meet the challenges I would inevitably face in my role as a Peace Corps volunteer, even though I hadn't yet made it through preservice training. I had already missed my group's two-day staging event in Seattle, but my parents, Peter and Linda Creed—themselves former Peace Corps volunteers—had done their best over the previous months to prepare me for the life that lay ahead. I was grateful for their support.

The streets of Kathmandu opened up as the morning's fog finally began to lift and rush hour traffic lightened, and we rolled more freely. Taking full advantage of the open blacktop with his deft weaving and clever accelerations, Madhu raced down Kantipath—a broad thoroughfare flanked by throngs of pedestrians.

We sailed past the Tundikhel parade ground, Ratna Park, and the Rani Pokhari—landmarks I recognized from the Nepali guidebook I'd studied so thoroughly before my departure from America. Then we turned left onto a new street, where we again assumed a snail's pace in deference to the seemingly random movements of cycle rickshaws and foot traffic. According to Madhu, we had arrived in Thamel, Kathmandu's tourist haven.

I chuckled at the crowd's energetic mingling as the van puttered through Thamel's narrow alleys. I watched from my position in the vehicle's front seat as countless Westerners haggled with merchants for reduced rates on souvenirs, while touts, the men enlisted by the enclave's major hotels to recruit new guests, did their best to fluster and confound the newly arrived. The *touts* targeted the young and the old first before moving on to more challenging prospects. I also saw begging mothers with sad eyes and sickly looking infants slung over their shoulders approach foreigners for money in a routine too practiced, too perfected, to be credible. The women's empty, outstretched hands and ropy, almost fibrous arms repeatedly moved to and from their mouths in exaggerated, well-rehearsed gestures designed to shame and embarrass.

I understood that poverty was a complex issue and that the act of begging was more than just artifice or an amusing sideshow put on by enterprising locals to entertain visitors from abroad. I did harbor feelings of deep sympathy for the beggars' plight, but I couldn't, in good faith, support the kind of practices, such as mutilation, baby borrowing, and child exploitation, that often defined the begging lifestyle.

I had been told by friends back home in Berkeley that Nepal's beggars were among the world's most formidable, that it would be difficult to stick to my principles and deny them the few rupees they requested. The beggars were living up to their infamous reputation, considering what I'd seen thus far on the streets of Thamel. I was thankful for the van's shelter for the moment, but I knew it would only be a matter of time before I too was on the receiving end of the beggars' persistent pleas.

Rolling down the passenger side window, I listened to the street's sounds as we cruised deeper into the heart of Thamel. The tinny whine of Nepali pop tunes mingled incongruously with the soothing sounds of Tibetan meditation music, both permeating the enclave's cramped corridors. The enclave itself was peopled with trekkers, stoners, buskers, and wandering minstrels, strumming their miniature harps. Many of the buildings lining the crowded streets in this bubble of imported Western culture appeared to be filled with the things well-to-do visitors from abroad typically revered about their lifestyles back home, including outdoor performance sporting equipment, baked goods, yoga studios, tea shops, and restaurants serving fusion foods, to name a few.

Through the glass doors of international dialing booths, I could see other Westerners placing phone calls, perhaps reassuring their concerned loved ones that they were alive and doing well on the far side of the planet. I knew that my parents were also expecting such a call, and I would place that call soon. Numerous karaoke bars, carpet stores, and shops selling Buddha statues rounded out the tourist district's commercial offerings. Each establishment was filled to capacity with patrons paying far too much for the luxury of living a Thamel lifestyle, I imagined.

I was unsurprised by Thamel, as seemingly every major urban center had its own tourist district. And I had little desire to linger in the city's tourist center when there was so much new country and culture to explore, but the haven did have an exuberance and a festivity bounding down its congested lanes and echoing off the decorative facades of its newly renovated shops.

We continued to creep through Thamel in the van, and it suddenly felt as though the umbilical cord connecting me to everything familiar—my family, my friends, my way of life—was being played out to its limit and was on the verge of being severed. I felt small and insignificant in that moment, even a little scared, but I tried to remind myself of the motivating factors that had led up to that very day.

My decision to join the Peace Corps and give twenty-seven months of my life in service had been a loud personal statement to the world about what America and Benjamin Creed should epitomize. After graduating from UC Berkeley with a degree in interdisciplinary studies, and after acquiring a two-year college degree in nursing, I'd felt compelled to hunt for opportunities that would define me as a human being and not simply reinforce the elaborate designs society had drawn up for me—even if those designs were well-intentioned and seemingly in my best interests.

Of course, my decision to join the Peace Corps had also come at a time when militant world leaders were, yet again, taking humanity down the path of war, death, and destruction, actions that had only served to galvanize my opinions and accelerate my departure from America. There was something else too, though: some other point-source of motivation to enroll in the Peace Corps that came from a place deep within, from a place filled with sadness that yearned for a chance at redemption and an opportunity to abolish lingering regrets.

Perhaps the most obvious reason for joining the Peace Corps was my desire to immerse myself in a foreign culture, to live among the people of the so-called Third World and intertwine my life with theirs. I understood that many of life's most important lessons could best be learned when a person lived alongside people from other cultures. I wanted to better understand the struggles and triumphs of Nepalis, so that I might be a more effective agent of change in the local and global communities. I also liked the fact that, through my work with the Peace Corps and the people of Nepal, I would have to learn to do more with less; I would have to find creative ways of engaging and collaborating with Nepalis without the benefit of limitless resources and technical skill.

I also felt a sense of urgency to do something important with my life, an urge my mother had dubbed my "inevitable, and devastating, quarter-life existential crisis." Acutely aware of my own mortality, I understood that there were, essentially, only three viable options for living life: we could do good, do evil, or do nothing at all. The latter two choices, of course, depressed me deeply. I wanted my life to be meaningful, and the fullest expression of a meaningful life, I thought—and still think—was to embrace option number one, bravely doing good work for good people. Service to others is one of the few healthy ways a person can face the fact that she or he is going to die. Service is the antidote to suffering.

Making a quick left turn, Madhu steered the van through a set of wrought-iron gates. He killed the craft's engine and coasted down a short lane before eventually bringing the vehicle to a halt. The sign at the gate had read *Kathmandu Guest House*—my home during my first few days in Nepal.

Saying good-bye to the staff from Peace Corps headquarters, I grabbed my backpack from the van and followed Madhu to the hotel's reception desk. He introduced me to the manager, a starchy man of few words, who quietly led me to my room at the guest house's rear.

Once I had settled in to his satisfaction, Madhu handed me a leaflet containing a list of the following days' activities. It contained a schedule for meetings and orientation sessions with various Peace Corps Nepal administrators, including the country director, the program and training officers, and a handful of other people associated with the organization. I was also scheduled for a round of vaccinations with Peace Corps medical. It would be a busy few days before our group of volunteers left for preservice training in Bhairahawa, a town near the Indian border.

"Mr. Benji Man Creed," said Madhu, standing to leave, "I am wishing you a most excellent preservice training and many successes in your posting. Maybe it is I am seeing your good self soon. Oh, and as the matter of principle," he added, "you must not be paying the drivers in this Kathmandu city too much for the car trips. I am telling it to your face right now: look for best in fiber, worst in driver. *Bujhnu bhayo?* Are you understanding this, boss? OK," said Madhu. "All the best with the rest, Ben-*ji!*"

I woke up hours later, hungry and drowsy. I rose from my bed and walked toward the guest house lobby in search of cheap eats and a breath of fresh air, but instead I found the pull of the streets too enticing to deny.

Leaving the hotel compound's seclusion and privacy, I followed a snaking procession of bodies away from the heart of Thamel. I glanced frequently at my guidebook for orientation, reveling in the exotic-sounding names of the local lanes, bazaars, and temples: Dharmapath, Gangapath, Bhagwan Bahal, Kasthamandap, and Asan Tole. These names were as foreign to me as the street side architecture, with its awnings and overhangs supported by ornately carved wooden struts that cast long, jagged shadows upon the dancing crowd.

I noticed pedestrians on the procession's outer edges meeting with considerable resistance from a series of vegetable vendors, fiercely guarding their right to the gutters. Foot commuters in the middle of the surging crowd enjoyed an almost easy passage, advancing at a steady rate relative to their peers on the margins, who had to skirt both the unsightly knolls of trash that had accumulated during the recent strike and the feigned blows of the territorial vendors.

The group's progression suggested we were heading toward Kathmandu's Durbar Square, one of the city's most famous historic sites. "Hey, man, what's going on here?" I asked a stocky young backpacker with a red fabric maple leaf sewn to his bag. "What are we celebrating?"

The Canadian, after adjusting his baseball cap, leaned in and yelled over the crowd's noise, "The Nepalis are celebrating the Indra Jatra festival." The festival, according to the Canuck, was an annual religious event that combined homage to Indra—the ancient god of rain—with celebration of a rare appearance of the young Kumari Devi—the living incarnation of a goddess. The Kumari would publicly bless the king of Nepal, an act that supposedly granted an air of legitimacy to the unpopular king's rule.

We soon reached the entrance of Durbar Square. The revelers quickly spilled into the large quadrangle, which resembled a life-size Hindu chessboard, its shrines and statuary at different stages in a game. Shouts of "*Jaya Nepal! Long live Nepal! Jaya Nepal!*" were deafening and delivered with fervor by the more outspoken and nationalistic crowd members. Many of the Nepalis wore elaborate masks and costumes and danced around the square in a celebratory fashion. Most of the foreigners in attendance had taken to the steps of the surrounding temples to snap pictures and soak up the totality of the incredible scene unfolding before their eyes.

I hoped the rest of my time in the country was equally as exciting. I got the distinct impression that festivity and celebration would play a more significant role in my life in Nepal than it ever had back home. I was grateful for the color, the emotion, and the pageantry of Indra Jatra, and I considered it an auspicious welcome from the country and its people. It was taxing to be in the middle of such a large crowd, but I also felt a rush of excitement. I was anonymous, and there were no expectations of me, at least not yet. And that was the sort of freedom that I loved. It was intoxicating, seductive even, and I lapped it up.

I had arrived in the square just in time to see the tiny Kumari—a living, breathing girl chosen to be the goddess's human embodiment—emerge from her brick house. As I watched, the young girl strode toward an enormous and lavishly ornamented wooden temple car, which she mounted with the help of several men. The juggernaut was then pulled around the square by a small army of devotees. The Kumari received her greeting from the king in exchange for her blessings and a ceremonial tika before her creaking temple car trundled away from the square.

The procession would make its way toward another temple, according to my guidebook, where a beer-spewing visage known as Seto Bhairab, or White Bhairab, would anoint a few lucky souls with a local rice beer called *jaand*—the frothy, fermented product of its horrible, fang-bearing palate. Wearing a headdress made of skulls, the glowering idol—hidden from the public at all other times of the year by a set of lattice gates—was apparently representative of the fearsome form of Shiva, one of the most important gods in all of Nepal.

I shifted my gaze from my guidebook to the action in the square and watched the Kumari's caravan, trailed closely by the large crowd, which had whipped itself into a frenzy at the thought of swilling beer from the mouth of Bhairab. Such an action, the Nepalis believed, would bring them good fortune throughout the coming year.

I followed the juggernauts and the crowd for a while until my growling stomach began to drown out the festival noises. I wanted to see the exceptional scene that was sure to unfold around the effigy, but the afternoon's excitement had drained my energy stores, and I needed to eat something substantial.

I quit the crowd in favor of food, and with the assistance of my trusty guidebook, I slowly worked my way back toward Thamel through the narrow, dust-choked streets of Old Kathmandu. Along the way, I searched for restaurants offering quality, sit-down fare and a private booth where I could collect my thoughts, but instead I spent most of my time fielding the queries of seedy drug dealers trying to broker a sale. "*Charas?* Hashish?" they whispered from the shadows of side streets. "Hey, man, you want smoke? Real cheap for your big wallet, huh?"

I examined the men's bloodshot eyes and their expressionless faces. They looked so out of it, so pathetically reliant on their uppers and downers. I waved the pushers away and continued toward Thamel.

Back on Tridevi Marg, I followed the intoxicating aroma of Italian home cooking to the doorstep of a busy eatery called Fire and Ice. Backpackers, expatriates, and well-heeled Nepalis alike came and went in droves through the restaurant's main door. A quick glance at the menu posted outside the restaurant's entrance revealed a variety of enticing entrées and a broad selection of sugary desserts.

I rubbed my belly in anticipation of the feast to come. I was then struck by a funny thought: I had joined the Peace Corps and come all the way to Nepal in search of something different—from customs to cuisine—and there I was, drooling over the thought of pizza and ice cream. *How unoriginal of me.* My mother, who'd spent two years in Nepal with the Peace Corps in the seventies, had told me that during my time in the country, I would become intimately acquainted with the Nepali dietary staple of *dal bhaat tarakaari*: lentil soup, rice, and curried vegetables. The dish would be eaten twice daily, she'd stated, so it was in my best interest to like it, and if I didn't like it, to at least make peace with it. I decided to indulge in Fire and Ice's North American comfort foods while they were still within easy reach.

I entered the restaurant and was greeted immediately by a thin, young waiter, who showed me to a small table. Upon the table sat a fragrant bouquet of flowers and a large jug of olive oil. The waiter introduced himself as Keshav Choudary; after making small talk, he explained that he had come to Kathmandu from the tiny island nation of Mauritius to pursue studies in mathematics at one of Kathmandu's fine postsecondary institutions. I was impressed by Keshav's ambition, and I was blown away by his language skills, which included fluency in at least seven different languages: Mauritian Creole, French, English, Hindi, Urdu, Bhojpuri, and Nepali. Keshav was a likable guy too, the kind of guy who'd be your friend no matter what language you spoke.

I watched the restaurant's happenings from my private booth, thankful to have a table all to myself. The privacy allowed me to process everything I'd seen and experienced on my first day in Kathmandu. It was true that I had never felt completely comfortable in situations where I was required to mingle with strangers, and that I had never been the sort of guy who would walk into a room full of people, loudly announce my presence, and then rally the group to join me in keg stands. But I wasn't a total loner either, and I usually got by just fine when I was around other people.

I shifted my attention from the restaurant's clientele to my Nepal guidebook, taking a long, hard look at the glossy map of the country. The country, longest along its east–west axis, looked like a whale beached between India and China, themselves two vast oceans teeming with life. The country was relatively small compared to its neighboring giants, but considering the extreme variations in altitude within its boundaries, I got the sense that I'd have more than my fair share of sightseeing to do.

Keshav delivered my whopping calzone followed by a dish of soft-serve ice cream. I downed both, paid my bill, and thanked the young waiter for his hospitality before leaving the restaurant.

Next, I strolled back toward the Kathmandu Guest House, crossing paths with a large group of well-tanned Australian backpackers who sheltered a pair of African men in their nexus. While the Aussies seemed easygoing and carefree, the Africans looked cautious, with preoccupied stares and furtive glances, and also somewhat aloof. Despite their stern expressions, they seemed popular with the boisterous crowd of backpackers, who encouraged all within earshot to join them at the Jump Club, a local disco, later that evening for a night of boozing and trip-hop dancing.

I wasn't entirely opposed to the idea, but I felt the overwhelming need to sleep, to rest myself before several long days of Peace Corps meetings and sightseeing around the Nepali capital. I was a tourist for now, but I was sure that that designation would change after the following day's orientation sessions and the informal Peace Corps welcoming party scheduled at a place called the Rum Doodle Restaurant & Bar.

N-199

I HAD BEEN HIRED AS A PART-TIME STUDENT EMPLOYEE WITH BEAR TRANSIT midway through my junior year at UC Berkeley. I drove one of their night safety shuttles—a service that ferried students home from campus at night. The program primarily catered to women who stayed on campus late into the evening for meetings, intramural activities, classes, or studying. Bear Transit provided them with a safe, reliable, and speedy means of getting home after dark.

I'd originally applied for the job to help boost my disposable income, but I quickly came to appreciate the value of the service and the camaraderie with the women who used it. My friends, of course, teased me relentlessly about the job, suggesting that I'd only taken the position to improve my odds with the ladies. It was true that, through the service, I'd met all sorts of interesting women, many from Africa, Asia, and South America, but it wasn't until I met Adriana da Rosa that I found a *driving* reason to show up for work each shift.

I had my nose buried deep in a city map of Berkeley the first time I met Adriana, busily planning my route for an upcoming shuttle run. "I hear you're a man who can make things happen," she said.

"Well, that depends on what you're looking for," I answered, continuing my mapping without glancing up.

"Well, here's the problem," she said. "I live just outside the shuttle's service area, and I've tried to get rides from you guys before, but nobody would ever take me. Some of my girlfriends who take the shuttle said you'd be working tonight and that you might be willing to bend the rules to help me."

"Normally we like to stick to the rules," I said, finally looking up, "but we might be able to make an exception." Any hesitation I might have had about breaking the rules melted instantly upon seeing Adriana. Simply put, she was the most stunningly beautiful woman I'd ever seen. Deeper than her kind eyes, beyond her cute, dimpled cheeks and her determined-looking chin, there was a certain quality about her; she exuded confidence and kindness, and she was polite, had an intelligent-looking face, and seemed like a gentle creature too.

It wouldn't have been a stretch to say that I fell in love with Adriana the moment my eyes met hers. The memory of those dark, sparkling eyes of hers—eyes filled to the brim with laughter—stayed with me for days after our first exchange. So did the image of her amazing body, which was thin with perfectly proportional curves that she seemed to neither flaunt nor hide. The possibility of spending even thirty minutes in her company was enough to make me report to work early the following shift.

I saw Adriana often over the course of the next several weeks. She planned her late nights on campus to coincide with my work schedule because she knew I would deviate from the van's set boundaries. We forged a fragile friendship during that time based largely around my willingness to help her, but also upon an unspoken mutual attraction, I believed. I could feel my affection for her growing exponentially during this time, and I wracked my brain for a way to spend time with her outside of work. Asking her out seemed inappropriate, considering how we knew each other.

Fortunately, luck was on my side. After dropping her off one night, I discovered that she'd forgotten several of her books in the van. Among them was her weekly planner. Taking note of her e-mail address, which she'd scribbled inside the front cover of the agenda, I wrote her a quick note letting her know that her books were safe with me and that she could pick them up during my next shift the following Tuesday. I also asked her out on a date. I was pretty sure I was overstepping my boundaries, but I went for it nonetheless. I was ecstatic when she wrote back and expressed interest in meeting at a local café for bubble tea and dessert, and I looked forward to our date with great anticipation.

The date was a great success, except for my having to ingest—and subsequently sputter through—the tapioca pearls in my bubble tea. We shared countless laughs and stories about our time at Berkeley, marveling at the fact that we had spent three years at the same college and hadn't once crossed paths that we knew of, until she'd begun taking the shuttle. I tried my best to make conversation, but I was so in awe of Adriana's beauty that on more than one occasion during the date, I found myself staring shamelessly at her angelic face. I couldn't seem to help myself, as there were just too many eye-catching details about her appearance that demanded my attention.

I loved the way that she parted her medium-length black hair in the middle of her forehead, pulling her naturally curly locks into a tight ponytail. I loved that she'd dyed a couple of light streaks into her hair, and the way that a few short strands tumbled down in front of her ears in wispy tendrils. I loved the way that her nose hooked downward, just ever so slightly, and I loved the fullness of her lips and her long eyelashes. I loved her creamy-brown skin too—skin the color of milky tea that seemed better suited for the beaches of the tropics than the moody climate of Northern California. And, of course, I loved most her dark-brown eyes, eyes sparkling almost black. They, above all else, belied her great compassion and integrity and captured my heart.

* * *

The first group of Peace Corps volunteers allowed back into Nepal after a multiyear moratorium due to political unrest and instability in the country, N-199, the 199th group of Peace Corps volunteers reporting for duty in Nepal—at least the ones who were still in attendance at the party—looked on from their chairs as silence settled over the Rum Doodle Restaurant & Bar in anticipation of the man's next story.

"So, you cats want another story, huh? Hell, *I'll* give you another story!" the wide-eyed character seated at the table's far end was shouting. The thirty something man from Los Angeles, encouraged by the small group's hoots of approval, pounded his fist on the table before standing and raising his hands for silence. We were perhaps all a bit flamboyant or cocky in our speech and mannerisms, but the ease with which he performed in front of an audience was unparalleled within the group and painted him as an extrovert's extrovert.

"Come on, Bronte," encouraged a studious-looking man in his late twenties or early thirties, who was seated at the table's opposite end. "Don't keep us hanging here!" He was dressed in woven hemp shorts, sandals, and a collared shirt with a checkered design. His curly brown hair was pulled back into a ponytail that reached halfway down his long, thin torso. Several thick books—including textbooks on quantum mechanics and particle physics, the *Mahabharata*, and the complete works of William Shakespeare—that he'd just bought at Pilgrims Book House were piled in front of him. Fingering his scraggly goatee, readjusting his glasses, and smiling, he added, "I don't know where you come up with these stories, but they're pretty amusing, if not a little unbelievable."

Bronte fixed us in our chairs, one by one, with his piercing eyes, which were slate gray and peppered with flecks of black around the edges. I'd never seen eyes like his before; then again, I'd never met anyone quite like Bronte James before either. Bronte had stated earlier that night that he was "50 percent black, 50 percent West Indian, and 100 percent gay." He wore his hair in a closely cropped Mohawk, and the sides of his head looked recently shorn by something like a Bic razor. He was average in height and muscular-thin in build. His attire consisted of a tight, black clubbing shirt, tapered jeans, and a pair of knee-high, black commando boots. He seemed comfortable in his own skin and more than a little self-assured. He possessed the kind of self-assurance a man might develop from playing the underdog his entire life. I also got the sense that he liked being seen as an original, as one-of-a-kind.

A crooked smile crept its way across Bronte's long, thin face. "So our ship's docked in port, right, and I'm on shore leave in Miami, and I'm hittin' on this chick in a club—mind you, this was back in the day when I was still swingin' both ways—when this punk-ass mama's boy pushes through the club's front door and swaggers past the bouncer like he's the king shit.

"He rolls over to the bar, orders up a few drinks for himself and his homies, and starts eyein' up my girl, who, I have to tell ya, had the finest

26

badonkadonk east of the Mississippi. Of course, all this time I'm thinkin', like, *damn*, who is this fool? Dude waddles over to my table after a while and tells me to get out of his way, like I'm some sort of nothin' or somethin'. I politely tell him that she ain't interested in his ass and that he ought to make like a leaf, if ya know what I mean. This gets him real upset, though, like, *crazy* upset, and he tells me all the things he's gonna do to the girl and all the things he's gonna do to me if I don't stop pissin' him off."

"So what did you say?" We all were wondering this, but it was the man called Manfred who voiced it, a look of curiosity etched on his face.

"Shit, Freddy Man, I can't repeat *everything* I said in the company of such fine and innocent ladies," said Bronte, winking at the two women seated at our table of six, "but, naturally, it contained many derogatory comments about his mama."

He stood firm behind his decision, despite the protests waged by the women, who insisted they wouldn't be offended by Bronte's comments about the man's mother.

"You're being sexist, Bronte," said one of the women as she plunged a straw into her banana *lassi*.

"Yeah, Beth's right," added the second, a trace of defiance in her words. "We can handle anything you can throw at us."

"Ladies, ladies, ladies," muttered Bronte, shaking his head. "One day you too may be mothers. For the sake of all that's good and decent in this world, I think it's best if we just let this one slide. By the way, Beth, I ain't sexist, just sexy." He tweaked his own nipples in jest. "Now, where was I? Oh yeah, the showdown. So, by this point, some of my friends are shootin' me daggers with their eyes, suggesting I might be wise to back down and let this burly dude have his way.

"Of course, then, I was one of the navy's best boxers in my weight class—super featherweight—so I felt as though I could take a few rounds out of him, if need be. So I get all up in his face, and we're starin' each other down, and it's gettin' all serious and shit, and then homeboy fakes a punch at me, poundin' his fist into his left hand, like, *BAM!* just to see if I'll lose my nerve. After that, we start pushin' and shovin', and he keeps tellin' me how he's gonna squash me like a damn bug. Before I know it, his homies are haulin' him away, and the bouncers are leadin' me through the club's back door, wondering if I'm loco or something. You have to understand that, until that point, I'd been away from the US for some time, and I'd never heard the name Mad Dog Malone. Lookin' back on it, I still think I could have whooped that boy's be-hind."

There wasn't a single one of us sitting around that table whose jaw hadn't dropped to the floor in disbelief. I couldn't believe that Bronte had had a run-in with Mad Dog "The Menace" Malone himself and had lived to tell about it. Even though I'd met Bronte for the first time only a few hours before, I could easily picture the squirrelly look in his eyes as he stared down the notoriously short-fused former heavyweight champ—and later, convicted murderer. Recovering from their initial shock, everyone burst into laughter at Bronte's daring feat.

"Holy TKO, Batman!" shouted Beth. Her freckled nose was scrunched up and her pale-blue eyes were narrowed into slits as she heaved with laughter. A quick, almost imperceptible snort concluded her laughter and was immediately followed by the onset of evenly spaced hiccups. Tucking her straight red hair behind her ears, Beth furrowed her brow and sighed loudly. "Ah, man, not again. This always happens when I laugh too much. Bronte, this is all your fault!"

"Is our poor little Beth Lewis sufferin' from a bout of hiccups?" teased Bronte, curling his lips into a frown and wiping a mock tear from his eye before taking his seat. "I heard that you can die from them, if they're bad enough."

"How could you suggest something so horrible, Bronte?" scolded the taller woman. The strawberry-blond, whose name was Laura Giffen, put her arm around Beth and cast a reproachful glare at Bronte.

"Look, Laura, girlfriend, between you and little Miss Beth, I get more grief than most married men. I get the feeling that opportunities to feed it back to you divas are gonna be rare, so I plan to take full advantage of 'em whenever they present. Unnh," he added, for emphasis, nodding his head emphatically and scanning all faces at the table.

"Hey, Beth, you should try pushing on your uvula, you know, that ding-ly-dangly thing at the back of your throat that looks like a boxing bag," I said, almost without thinking. "It sounds crazy, but in the past, I've seen that technique stop hiccups."

My fellow volunteers all looked at me with bright, clear eyes and curious smiles following my unexpected—and slightly embarrassing—little outburst.

"Benjamin Creed!" chirped Beth between her squeaky hiccups. "Where the heck did you come up with such a crazy idea? Only one full day in Nepal and already offering advice," she teased, before being rocked by another round of hiccups.

"No, seriously, if you push your uvula to the back of your throat and you hold it there for a ten-count, it's supposed to trigger some sort of reflex mechanism that stops your hiccups. You should try it."

"What you're saying is really interesting, Benjamin," stated Manfred. "I think I've heard about this phenomenon. I say we try it!" Manfred was clearly a man of science, and his words already seemed to carry considerable clout with the members of N-199. With degrees in mathematics and molecular biophysics from Harvard under his belt, he was the group authority when it came to all things scientific. But he was also a voracious reader and a perpetual student of philosophy, English literature, and religion. While he was an academic, he wasn't aloof and unreachable like many of the other intellectually gifted people I'd met. Manfred possessed a certain worldliness that I both envied and respected.

"But, Manfred," wondered Beth, "how am I supposed to hold the dingly-dangly thing against the back of my throat without gagging?"

"Maybe you can borrow Bronte's foot," a grinning Takahiro Yamamoto, the quietest and most self-effacing of all the group members, stated. When he spoke, Taka, as he liked to be called, spoke evenly and unhurriedly in accented English. Sizing up Bronte, he continued his sneak attack. "He so good at sticking his foot in his own mouth, isn't he, maybe he can help you too."

Taka, a volunteer from Japan via Seattle—and a *huge* Ichiro fan—could be counted on to deliver a few well-placed zingers every now and then, from what I understood. He looked tough with his short, stocky build, a look that was aided by his muttonchops and a white bandana over his shoulder-length black hair. A professional cabinetmaker, he had come to Nepal in the hopes of working with an in-country counterpart as a small-business development consultant. He also hoped to establish a small cooperative of woodworkers whom he would train in cabinetmaking and other forms of the craft.

It seemed clear that the group's dynamics had already formed. Jousts and jabs were exchanged frequently and without a hint of malice. Nobody in the group was immune to good-natured public ridicule and embarrassment, but poor Bronte seemed to be everybody's favorite target. However, as the group's oldest member, and because of his fiery disposition, Bronte easily sidestepped every joke, the lighthearted barbs bouncing off him like monsoon raindrops from a betel leaf. And he was more than capable of dishing it out whenever he felt like it.

Standing again, Bronte kicked his chair to the side, almost spilling his half-full mug of beer.

"The Emperor," Bronte muttered, placing his hands on the table's surface and staring down the cabinetmaker. "I should have known *you'd* be the one to cross me. In the navy, we learned that the Japanese are famous for their surprise attacks, ain't they, Sudoku?"

"Come on, Bronte," Laura said in all seriousness. "I have zero tolerance for your racial slurs."

"OK, take it easy, princess. Trouble in paradise? You premenstrual?" he asked, shooting her a sideways glance.

Her reaction did seem out of place, but she'd acted irritated all night. I wondered if something else was going on in Laura's life. Perhaps things at home weren't going so well, or maybe she was having a tough time adapting to her new surroundings. I understood from my parents that there was a surprising amount of stress and strain associated with life in the Peace Corps. My parents had told me that a person's breaking point could be reached much more quickly in a place like Nepal, due to the numerous strikes, bureaucratic snags, and other frustrations volunteers in the country encounter. Those who were normally self-possessed could snap for seemingly no reason.

Bronte, whose intuition perhaps told him that Laura was nearing her own breaking point, immediately backed off. He sat down and waved his hands at the Rum Doodle's decor. "Needs more tapestries," he mused.

"Guys, I'm out," Laura said. The Naropa University grad stood, straightened out the wrinkles in the sea-foam tunic of her *salwar kameez*, and said, "I just need to be by myself for a while. Thanks for the company. It was nice to meet you, Benjamin. I'll see you guys again tomorrow, OK?"

Beth jumped to her feet and escorted Laura out of the restaurant after we all said our good-byes. Returning to the table a few minutes later, Beth slapped Bronte lightly on the back of his head before reclaiming her chair. "Can't you recognize a girl in distress? Laura just broke up with her boyfriend back home. Their relationship had been totally rocky for a while, and it sounds pretty final this time," Beth explained.

I ached for Laura. I hadn't been in a long-term relationship for years, but my last brush with romance and relationships—yes, with Adriana—had left me completely exasperated and wary of the suffering that inevitably seemed to accompany love. I looked forward to my own Peace Corps experience as a time of great personal growth, an experience that would round out my education and help shape me into the person I wanted to become. I hadn't ruled out the possibility of finding love while abroad—in fact, I'd thought about it often—but my focus was, perhaps selfishly, on myself and my own development as a professional health care worker.

"Damn," Bronte said in response. "That ain't no good. Look, I didn't mean to get her all riled."

"I think we should all let it go," Manfred insisted. "It's nobody's fault. We all know Laura's strong. She'll bounce back. I'll talk to her tomorrow morning to see if she's feeling any better. I can't imagine how tough it would be to start into all this while trying to maintain a long-distance relationship. I'm grateful that Gloria and Samuel agreed to make the trip to Nepal with me. Having my family here in Kathmandu is going to be a huge advantage for me as a volunteer. I almost feel as though I'm cheating!"

Smiling, Beth patted Manfred on the back. "Ah, you're such a good guy, Manfred. We're all happy you're a part of this thing with us." Manfred returned her smile and humbly nodded his head.

I had to agree with Beth, even though I'd just met him: Manfred was a grounding force within the group. He was a man wise beyond his years, and he possessed the ability to lead and to make people feel good about themselves. Beth too, sage and confident in her own unique way, seemed to be the gel that held the entire group together. I looked at Beth and was suddenly moved by the feeling that we'd met before. She seemed too familiar, as though we'd known each other in a past life.

Her freckle-dappled face was home to countless laugh lines, especially around the eyes, and it seemed full of wisdom and kindness. I got the sense that Beth liked herself and was good to herself. She was rugged, in her own feminine way. From what I could tell, she was the type of girl who wasn't afraid to get dirty, earn a few bruises in her outdoor pursuits, and take a physical risk every now and then. I also got the sense that she was proud of that fact, proud that men respected her for what she could do and proud that most women didn't even attempt the things that she did. Her pride wasn't stifling or overbearing, though, and it wasn't driven entirely by ego either. Her pride was driven by the simple knowledge that she could do whatever she wanted, if only she wanted it badly enough.

Hip-hop remixes of Jack Johnson tunes blared loudly over the restaurant's speakers and kept the night's lingering patrons bopping to the beat. Large paper cutouts in the shape of what looked like Abominable Snowman feet were plastered to the Rum Doodle's walls. Former patrons had scribbled notes on them, everything from thoughtful poetic verses to advice on where to stay and what to do in Kathmandu. The signatures of Everest summiteers and other famous people were displayed in a prominent position behind the bar. The restaurant's decor wasn't really my aesthetic, but it did feel welcoming. Besides, if it was good enough for Jimmy Carter—who'd apparently dined there—then it was good enough for me.

"What's going on behind those dark-blue eyes, Baby Bear?" asked Beth, addressing me by the nickname she'd coined earlier that night after learning that, at twenty-five years old, I was one of the group's youngest members.

"I was just thinking that you haven't hiccuped for a while," I said.

A waiter cruised by our table at that very moment to let us know that the bar was closing and that if we wanted anything else, we should place the order. It was ten o'clock, which seemed early for last call, but Manfred explained that nightlife in Kathmandu, especially outside of Thamel, was quite limited. The vast majority of bars and restaurants in the country apparently closed their doors well before midnight.

The Rum Doodle would become the preferred hangout for the group's weekly get-togethers over the coming year. The restaurant was a place where we'd all spend plenty of time, share plenty of laughs, and drink plenty of beer. It was also the venue where we'd share with each other our most recent frustrations and triumphs—as well as the quality and consistency of our latest bowel movements, a common topic of conversation among Peace Corps volunteers around the world.

"Beer me!" shouted Bronte in response to the waiter's query. "And one more for Benjamin Creed, that punk-ass new trainee from Berkeley—my California brother!"

I could say with certainty that Bronte was one of the most unusual people I'd ever met. He was a spontaneous beatboxer and talented free-styler. He was loud, obnoxious, and more than a little abrasive. But he was profoundly unique, and I appreciated him for that alone. There was no doubt in my mind that Bronte James was a lover of life, a man who milked the maximum possible enjoyment from each day and each interaction. I also got the feeling that, in his over-the-top presentation, few ever saw his mile-wide kind streak, the compassion in his heart, or his desire to find his one true self.

Bronte had joined the Peace Corps in 2004 and was assigned to Nepal as a member of the original N-199 group, trainees who were set to arrive in the country in September 2004. Peace Corps Washington pulled the plug on operations in Nepal due to safety concerns over the Maoist conflict just weeks before their scheduled arrival in the country, evacuating all volunteers within the country and canceling N-199's arrival. Bronte had been reassigned to Bangladesh and had already served twenty-seven months with the Peace Corps in that country. Now in his second tour of duty, he was the only member of that original N-199 group to have made it back to Nepal with the Peace Corps.

Bronte hoped to work with a host-country national to coordinate recreational activities for street kids living in one of Nepal's urban centers. The main problems facing the kids, according to Bronte, who was already well-versed in South Asian street life, included tuberculosis and malnutrition, involvement in crime, substance abuse, and physical and sexual abuse at the hands of adults and other street kids. Some of the kids begged for a living, some scavenged from garbage heaps for items to sell, and some resorted to petty theft and picking pockets to scrape by. The vast majority of them sniffed glue as a means of escaping the realities of poverty and homelessness. I appreciated the severity of their situation, as I'd met many such kids during my time in India three years earlier. What Bronte hoped to do in Kathmandu, or wherever he was eventually posted, was extremely important and had major implications for the long-term well-being of those most vulnerable of Nepali citizens.

The waiter somehow seemed to already know Bronte well, or at least his bar needs. He waited still, even after Bronte had ordered my beer. "Taka? Freddy Man? Beth?" asked Bronte. "Can I interest y'all in a final round of spirits? A shot of Jagermeister, maybe? It's on me."

"Thanks, but I'm going to have to pass," Manfred said, shoving his books and a lengthy to-do list into his backpack before standing to leave. "Gloria's expecting me home before ten thirty, so I better shake a leg. I'll be on diaper duty for a month if I'm late," he joked. "And you know what you always say, Bronte," added Manfred, pausing in front of the restaurant's exit. "If the woman ain't happy, ain't *nobody* happy."

"Ain't that the truth," Bronte said, nodding his head in agreement.

Taka, saying that he'd already had too much to drink, took off about five minutes later, leaving Beth, Bronte, and me at the table as the restaurant's other patrons slowly trickled out into the dark streets of Kathmandu.

"So why exactly weren't you able to join us for the staging event in Seattle?" Beth asked—or I should say, despite her friendly undertone, probed. Only much later did I realize that I was being interviewed that first night at the Rum Doodle. My motivations for volunteering were being weighed and measured and my potential compatibility with other group members assessed, with levity at first and, now that the restaurant was a little quieter and the night was winding down, with more seriousness.

Because N-199 was such a small group—twenty-two trainees, all told—the ability to settle in quickly and bond with other members was crucial, I would quickly come to understand. I didn't know it then, but several members of N-199 would soon early terminate—or ET, as it was called in Peace Corps lingo—during their preservice training in Bhairahawa. One person would even have to be *wack-evac'd*, the term volunteers around the world used to describe an evacuation caused by a mental breakdown.

Beth and the others, even without this knowledge, were somewhat cautious about how the new arrival, especially one who had missed the staging event, would fare as a Peace Corps trainee. There was a mutual understanding among members not to get too close until I'd proven myself as an adaptable and dedicated individual, despite their offer of unconditional friendship.

"I was all set to join you guys in Seattle, but my grandfather passed away just before I was about to fly up to Washington," I said. "The Peace Corps was really hesitant about letting me miss the staging event, but they eventually agreed, and here I am."

"Well," Beth said, "I'm really sorry about your grandfather, but I'm happy that you're here with us here in Nepal. We all plan to work hard and play hard, from what I can tell. And we've got a bunch of ideas for fun trips we can take over the next couple of years, things like trekking, rafting, and safaris, not to mention Peace Corps talent shows—which I plan to coordinate, by the way—and a whole bunch of other really cool stuff. I think we're all going to find that we need little escapes from our lives as volunteers. It could be too easy to get caught up in the day-to-day grind of work, eat, sleep, repeat. We need to remember that we're in Nepal, one of the coolest countries on the entire planet!"

"As much as I hate to admit it," said Bronte, taking a large swig of his Tuborg beer, "our little vixen's right. The time you spend away from your post is just as important as the time you spend there—trust a brother who's done this before."

The clustering of volunteers in cities like Kathmandu, Bhaktapur, and Pokhara and in towns along the Tarai was a relatively new phenomenon for the Peace Corps in Nepal, according to organization officials. Volunteers historically had been sent separately to the country's remote regions to work alongside villagers on a variety of projects. In fact, since the Peace Corps had begun working in Nepal in 1962, most of the volunteer placements had been in rural settings, in venues far removed from the clamor and commotion of Nepal's major cities.

In those days, volunteers had been sent to places like Taplejung, Tumlingtar, and Lamidanda in the east, Mustang, Bajura, and Jumla in the west. Now, post assignments were severely restricted, and volunteers were being clumped together near the nation's most populated areas. Keeping volunteers in a handful of easily accessible locations, it was thought, would provide a measure of security should the political situation again turn ugly, however unlikely that was.

My mother had paid close attention to all developments within the country since her Peace Corps days, especially during those years of political strife leading up to the Peace Corps' pullout. More than once I'd found her crying as she read the heartbreaking news coming out of Nepal, then a nation riven by civil war. There was a time, I remembered, when it seemed as though bombings, torture, rapes, and extrajudicial killings were happening almost every day in the country. It was clear, according to my mother, that Nepal had changed considerably in the years since she'd served in the Peace Corps. She'd been frustrated by her inability to reach out and help again. Her concern for the people she'd grown to love during her two years abroad was palpable and reminded me what an incredible woman she was, how strong and compassionate and caring she was with family members, friends, and strangers alike.

I, perhaps selfishly, was happy about the clustering of volunteers. I hoped to be posted in one of the communities near Kathmandu, and if I got my wish, I'd have the best of both worlds, from what I understood. I'd be far enough from the city to get a taste of rural Nepali life, but close enough to feed off the energy of the city and my fellow volunteers. I'd be able to lead a double life, in some ways.

"So, Beth," I said. "I already know what Bronte hopes to accomplish here in Nepal, but what's your area of interest?"

"I worked as a guide for a river-rafting company in my former life, back in Montana," she explained. "I was based out of Bozeman, but most of our trips were run out of Glacier National Park. The people were great, of course, but life on the water was really what spoke to me, you know? Anyway, I knew that I wanted to join the Peace Corps, and I thought about how I could combine my passion for rivers with volunteer service overseas, and then, finally, it clicked! Maybe I could work alongside people in the developing world to help restore the health of their urban waterways. Of course, this is just an idea that's been floating around in my head. I won't know for sure what I'll be doing until my post is determined."

"Yee-haw! You go, girl!" shouted Bronte, slapping the rear flank of an imaginary steed as he galloped in his chair.

The rivers in Kathmandu and other urban centers throughout Nepal, according to Beth, were polluted with sewer runoff, industrial waste, and the products of human consumption, including soaps, shampoos, and motor oil. Cleaning up the rivers would be a huge task, but Beth was an ambitious person, and I didn't doubt she'd meet with success in her post, if that was in fact what she ended up focusing on.

"And what sort of volunteer work are Manfred and Laura interested in?" I asked.

"Professor Manfred," said Bronte, "is gonna be teaching some science and mathematics. It's kind of his thing."

"Rumor has it," stated Beth "that a group of monks at Kopan Monastery here in Kathmandu, not too far from the Buddhist *stupa* at Boudhanath, want to learn math and Western science as well as English and philosophy. We all think Manfred is the perfect person for that post."

The monks had definitely found the right man for the job in Manfred Little, if it were true that he was bound for Kopan Monastery. He seemed patient to a fault and excellent at explaining complex ideas in a straightforward way. He was eminently qualified for the position, too, with his multiple degrees and broad range of interests.

"And we all know that Laura's going to be doing something involving early childhood education," added Beth. "There are rumblings about volunteer opportunities in that field in orphanages here in the city."

"That girl will have the toughest row to hoe if she's gonna be workin' in orphanages, no doubt," said Bronte.

"How so?" I wondered. I'd never visited an orphanage, and I had no idea what kind of conditions the kids lived in or what struggles made up their lives. Bronte explained that many of the orphanages in Kathmandu and elsewhere throughout the country were filled to overflowing with children whose parents had been killed by the guerrilla warfare and violence that had rocked the country over the past decade.

"I've done some reading about orphanages in Nepal," said Beth. "I get the sense that orphanages here tend to be run like any other business and that, sometimes, the bottom line is more important than the kids' welfare. It's probably not like that with all of them, thank god, but I'm sure Laura will see her fair share of questionable practices if that's the work she ends up doing."

After Beth had finished speaking, Bronte stood up and stretched. He let out a loud groan that drew the bartender's attention. Bronte locked eyes with the man, smiled, and nodded as if to say, *How you doin'?* The skinny bartender, smiling coyly, then returned to the task of buffing the bar's surface with a dry rag. "I haven't had me a smoke in at least two hours!" Bronte stated with pride.

"Are you down to two packs a day yet?" said Beth.

"Close," replied Bronte, missing her sarcasm. "I feel as though I'm gettin' enough of that shit just from breathin' the air, ya know what I mean? I hadn't planned on quittin' while I was here, but *damn*, I says to myself, why not?"

We left the Rum Doodle after leaving a handsome tip for our waiter. Outside on the street, I watched Bronte light up a cigarette he'd bought from a local smoke shop and take a long pull on the skinny stick.

"Thanks for the warm welcome tonight, guys," I said. "I guess I'll see you both tomorrow at Peace Corps headquarters?"

"Promise us you won't spend any more time at headquarters than you've got to," said Bronte, suddenly sounding irritated. "The only reason to go there is to collect your mail. Too many damn headaches and too much bureaucratic bullshit, I can guarantee you that."

"Hey, which way are you going?" Beth changed the subject.

"I'm staying at the Kathmandu Guest House for these first few days," I replied.

"I'm heading that way," she said. "My guest house, Kathmandu Peace Guest House, is just on the other side of Thamel. I'll walk you home."

It was a nice offer, but I didn't want her to think I was incapable of making my own way through the dark streets. Besides, the guest house was just a stone's throw away. I fumbled for an excuse but instead came up with a confused look.

"It's no problem," she said, trying to set me at ease. "Really."

We said good-bye to Bronte and headed toward Beth's bike, which was chained to a signpost near the restaurant. The streets of Thamel seemed remarkably quiet at night, which was unexpected, given the insane noise and foot traffic that filled its narrow lanes during the day.

I noticed that the chain of Beth's bike lock was looped through the bike's frame and both tires. "It's a rental," she said, catching my glance. "I don't want to lose the deposit."

She undid the lock and fished the chain out of the bike's guts. Stowing the lock in a metal cage mounted on the bike's rear rack, she grabbed the handlebars and began walking the single-speed toward the Kathmandu Guest House. "You coming, Baby Bear?"

"I'm right behind you," I said.

I was curious about what Bronte had said only moments before. "What was that all about, with Bronte, I mean? There seems to be some friction between him and Admin."

"That's the understatement of the year," Beth said, laughing. "So here's the deal: while volunteers have their primary assignments, everybody's encouraged to take part in secondary projects too, things that don't necessarily have anything to do with the reason you came to Nepal. These secondary projects can be almost anything you think might benefit the local community. Past volunteers, from what I understand, gave health talks or built websites, latrines, or libraries. It really doesn't seem to matter what you do as long as it's helping the people of Nepal in some positive way."

"What does that have to do with Bronte and why he's so irritated with Admin?"

"Basically, Bronte got into some trouble when he was serving in Bangladesh. He helped form this group called the Shining Star Society and ended up threatened with deportation by the Bangladesh government. The country director intervened on his behalf, but he had to quit his work with the Society."

"The Shining Star Society? Deportation?"

"The Shining Star Society is a Dhaka-based organization that assists Bangladesh's gay male community," she said. "Bronte was teaching a lot of classes on safe sex and HIV/AIDS prevention, and he was also trying to create an umbrella organization to unite all underground gay rights organizations throughout the country. You have to understand that, in Bangladesh, homosexual acts can land you in prison for life. Some people have even been killed for their sexual preferences. Peace Corps Admin in Bangladesh made Bronte quit his work with the Society and apologize to the government, and he understandably got all bent out of shape. I don't think he's ever let it go."

I admired what Bronte had tried to do in Bangladesh, and I felt sympathy for his plight. But I could also understand the position of Peace Corps Admin. Peace Corps volunteers were allowed to serve around the world because various governments allowed us to be in their countries, and their concerns—justified or not—had to be our primary consideration. What we did on our own time, provided it was helping the community in some way, was our own business, but it also couldn't run contrary to the laws of the land.

Beth had spoken with several former Peace Corps Nepal volunteers, and she explained to me that the relationship between administrators and volunteers had, in the past, been like that of a parent and child. Admin set the rules, and volunteers often tried to break them. It was Beth's belief that Admin wanted to stay out of volunteers' business as much as possible, but there had been times when intervention was necessary, and volunteers had been disciplined for their actions. She also believed that, apart from the authoritative role it occasionally had to assume, Admin genuinely cared for every volunteer in the country, and that past volunteers, in turn, had loved the staff at Peace Corps Nepal headquarters.

I was glad to hear Beth's assessment of the relationship between volunteers and Admin, as it was in line with what my mom had already told me. I understood that there would be many challenges in Nepal, and I didn't want my relationship with the staff at headquarters to be complex or strained in any way. I wasn't a conformist, but I understood that those people made up my support team and that they would make my life easier if I played by the rules.

"So why did Bronte sign on with the Peace Corps for a second mission if he felt like organization officials were busting his chops so much?"

"Well, you'd have to ask *him* to get the true answer," said Beth. "But I think he genuinely loves volunteering. And he's career driven too, like a lot of us here. I also get the sense that he thinks his Peace Corps experience is going to be radically different here in Nepal. We'll see."

Hearing a vehicle approaching from behind, I turned to see the distinctive outline of a Nepali taxi—a white Maruti Suzuki—illuminated by the faint moonlight. The beams of the taxi's headlights caught the reflective tape on the back of Beth's metal basket and made it shimmer. As the taxi caught up with us, the driver rolled down his window, poked out his head, and offered a halfhearted sales pitch: "Hello, mister and missus. Taxi to get you home after whiskey?" Beth and I waved him on. The tiny car trundled by, gently rocking from side to side over the uneven pavement, and vanished into the purple shadows.

We resumed our leisurely pace through the heart of Thamel, both of us registering the faint smell of juniper incense wafting from one of the above-store apartments nearby. "You know what, Baby Bear?" Beth said. "I think you're one of the good ones."

"Oh yeah?" I replied, caught off guard by her unusual statement. I wasn't sure if she was referring to the members of N-199, who all seemed like "good ones" to me, or to something else.

"But there's something about you I just can't quite put my finger on," she added, pausing for effect.

"Really?"

"I think there's a dark side to you, and there's nothing more intriguing than a good dark side. I've got my eye on you, Baby Bear," she added before hopping onto her bike and pedaling an ellipse around me on the deserted street. For a moment, my consciousness zoomed out to watch us, happy amid the cement-walled shops, telephone poles bearing a decade's worth of paper flyers, and a cow plopped down beside a small mountain of earth.

I wondered what she meant. Didn't we all have a dark side? Didn't we all keep secrets? How was I different from anybody else? I was about to ask her what she meant, but at that very moment we came flush with the main gate of the Kathmandu Guest House.

"This is my stop, Beth," I said instead. "Hey, are you sure you're going to be OK getting home?"

"No problem, kiddo," she said. "But I'm glad to see that chivalry isn't dead. Oh, by the way," she added, standing tall on her pedals, the six bangles on her right wrist chiming lightly in the night air, "I plan to head up the N-199 peer support group. I want you to know that you can come to me if you ever need to speak with somebody about a problem you're having, either personally or professionally."

"Thanks, Beth," I said. "That's a really kind offer." I stood at the hotel's main gate, beside a fragrant jasmine plant vining its way up a trellis, and watched her small, wiry body peddle down the narrow street until she rounded a corner and rode out of sight.

The hotel's security guard, rising from his sleep, stood up, offered a groggy namaste, and swung open the compound's wrought-iron gate. I made my way toward my room, doing my utmost not to disturb the hotel's other guests.

I closed my bedroom door behind me and fell into bed. The night—and my first real brush with fellow members of N-199—had been good overall. It had also left me with much to consider, not the least of which was the merits of the Peace Corps' work in Nepal and the rest of the developing world. I knew that some people back home felt that the Peace Corps was simply a holding tank, an organization dedicated to distracting and pacifying an entire army of demanding idealists. Others felt that the Peace Corps was obsolete, that many of the countries in which the organization worked now had more than enough skilled workers to assume the roles American volunteers had filled for decades. Even among my friends and acquaintances back home, a good portion either hadn't really known what the organization did anymore or thought that the program had died out years earlier. Of course, others still believed that volunteering in a foreign country was a type of neocolonialism, and that volunteering itself was a self-righteous act with little to no benefit for those on the receiving end.

A person could debate the merits of the Peace Corps' agenda, or the role of development at all in the so-called Third World, but considering what I'd heard from fellow volunteers earlier in the night, it seemed clear that good things were about to happen in Kathmandu and Nepal. I was grateful that the Nepali government had allowed us to work alongside its citizens and learn from them, because that idea meshed with my own thoughts about how international development should work.

We, as volunteers, wouldn't be pushing ourselves on people. We wouldn't be telling them what was right and what was wrong. Instead, we were in the country to gain experience in the field, to learn about the culture, and to foster the exchange of ideas. There was an understanding among volunteers in Nepal that, because of their incredible spirit and their legendary generosity, the Nepalis would end up teaching us far more than we would teach them. That expectation grounded me in humility.

We were idealistic and naïve as a group, sure, but there was a keen awareness, at least among the members of N-199 I'd met, of what could and could not be achieved in our future posts. I also sensed that there existed among group members the idea that Peace Corps Nepal was somehow special, that even relative to Peace Corps groups in other developing countries, the program in Nepal was uniquely rewarding. Former Nepal Peace Corps volunteers had seemed to genuinely love their host country, according to Beth and the others, and I took that as a positive sign. Peace Corps Nepal: small in number, but mighty in spirit—a fact and a slogan that would quickly become the rallying cry of volunteers serving throughout the great kingdom of Nepal.

Nepali Pete

I LEARNED DURING OUR DATE THAT ADRIANA'S ANCESTRY WAS GOAN, HENCE the Portuguese surname of da Rosa. I could see the Portuguese influence in her features too; she looked almost as Portuguese as she did Indian. Both of her parents were originally from Goa, she explained, although her father had lived in Pakistan for many years before moving to San Francisco. It was there, in San Francisco, that her parents had met, married, and had three children: two girls and a boy. Adriana was the middle child.

I became fascinated by the customs and traditions she'd grown up with and had come to regard as routine. Her description of relatives' weddings, birthdays, and other significant events made the celebrations sound much more elaborate than the standard American versions. I was eager to learn more about her intriguing upbringing, even if she herself identified far more closely with the average American than the average Indian.

That night with Adriana marked the beginning of my love affair with South Asian culture. I was amazed that a person, even one I barely knew, was able to spark a passion in me for an entire region and group of people with whom I had essentially no shared history. But that was the power of love at work, and I wasn't immune to its motivational effects. I wasn't immune to its blinding effects, either, as I would soon come to understand. In the presence of Adriana, I was quickly succumbing to the staggering and occasionally paralyzing feelings of infatuation experienced by every young romantic. I couldn't seem to stop my mind from racing ahead to explore all possible details of our future life together.

But it was a bumpy beginning.

It was with great shock and sadness that I received an e-mail from Adriana following our date telling me she was already seeing somebody and that she was sorry if there'd been any confusion about her motivation or intentions. Her e-mail caught me completely off guard after the evening's high. I felt deflated, upset, even betrayed.

I would have normally taken that news in stride and accepted her word, but there was something about the way I'd felt around her, even in those few short hours together, that I was unwilling to let slip away. There was a certain chemistry between us—either real or imagined—that I'd never felt before. There was a connection that had led me to believe that a romantic relationship between us was predestined.

I didn't see Adriana again until the following week, when I drove her home in the night shuttle. I strategically planned my route before departing campus so that Adriana would be dropped off last, so that I could speak with her in private about the strength of my feelings for her. She seemed unusually quiet and withdrawn, however, so I broached the issue carefully once we were alone in the van.

"Look, Adriana, there's something I've got to tell you," I said, stopping the van just outside her apartment complex. Over the course of a few bumbling sentences, I told her how incredible it had been to spend time with her, and how shocked I'd been to receive her e-mail. At first she thought I was being facetious, and she refused to take my words seriously. Only after I'd poured my heart out to her a second time did she begin to comprehend the true depth of my feelings for her.

It was dark in the van, but I could still make out a confused, almost dazed expression on her face; it was the face of someone who, whether she wanted to or not, now had more to think about than just term papers and final exams. There was tension in the air too, a charged feeling that was less than confrontational but more than earnest. I didn't know what her current relationship was like, and frankly, I didn't care. I just wanted her to know the emotions that she'd caused me to feel. She thanked me for the ride and before climbing out of the van and walking slowly toward her apartment promised that she'd mull over everything I had just told her.

The energy it had taken to share my thoughts with Adriana left me feeling drained, but I was happy, at least, that we'd talked and that I'd made my feelings known. My delivery hadn't been smooth or graceful or eloquent, but I'd said what I needed to say, and that was all anyone in my situation could do.

* * *

The following day, my second full day in Nepal, was filled with Peace Corps meetings and passed quickly. I enjoyed meeting everybody at headquarters in Lazimpat and becoming acquainted with the building itself. I learned during a meeting with the country director—a man originally from New Hampshire named Mike Swenson—that the Peace Corps had sold the building when it pulled out of the country in 2004. Through a stroke of good luck, the organization had recently been able to buy it back and was still furnishing the sparsely decorated space.

Between meetings, I took a tour of Phora Durbar, a nearby property owned and maintained by the US government. Described by Mike as "several lush acres surrounded by reality" and by others as a country club, the oasis was typically reserved for diplomats and high-ranking military personnel and their guests. Peace Corps volunteers, according to Mike, were granted access to the compound under the stipulation that they didn't ruffle the feathers of higher-ranking government employees. Considering its restaurant serving American-style food, shimmering pool surrounded by deck chairs, and waiters serving mai tais and piña coladas, it was obvious that Phora was a little slice of paradise for volunteers accustomed to life in the trenches.

There had always existed a palpable friction between volunteers and those who felt more entitled, Mike noted. Volunteers' access to Phora had been threatened on numerous occasions, sometimes for things as ridiculous as a volunteer using a treadmill while a diplomat had been forced to wait. I imagined steam pouring from the ears of a fleshy, middle-aged Texan, a fresh white towel slung over his shoulder and a bottle of water all ready to go, while some hapless volunteer pounded the treadmill with his or her footfalls, oblivious to the shock wave being sent up the chain of command.

After my orientation sessions ended on my third full day in Nepal, I hired a cab and headed for Pashupatinath, the most important Hindu temple in Nepal. I asked the driver to drop me outside the temple grounds, and then I walked to the Bagmati Bridge to get a good view of the temple and the burning *ghats*. I was distracted by a tall, lean man fanning the waters below the bridge with a lengthy bamboo rod. He, along with six Nepalis, was engrossed in his task, his head bent low as he sifted through the water with the patience of, I imagined, a Bengal tiger stalking its prey.

"Hey, whatcha *doin'* down there?"

Glancing up from the Bagmati's bubbling black water, the shaggy man scrunched up his face and said in an unmistakable Cockney accent, "It's a veritable gold mine down 'ere, mate! A real bloody treasure trove of riches. Never once let me down in a pinch!"

The man returned to scanning and periodically probing the water's surface with a swiftness and economy of motion comparable to a Kendo master's. He clearly was hunting for something special in the murky depths of the sacred river, the holiest body of water in all of Nepal.

The man paused again, planted his staff in the muddy sediment of the Bagmati's belly, and straightened up from his crouched position. He cupped his hands around the sides of his mouth to amplify his voice and shouted at me, but with his thick, gravelly voice and accent, his words were almost impossible to decipher.

"I *said*, shake a leg, mate, and shimmy your arse down 'ere." His meaning finally reached me, his words reverberating off the bridge's steel girders like a round of mortar fire. "Now mind yourself on the slippery slope, lad, as she's bound to send you arse over tit if you don't watch yer step!"

I caved to my curiosity and headed toward the embankment's edge as the unkempt Englishman waded toward me. He reminded me of what Moses might have looked like before his parting of the Red Sea, due to his long white beard and the gnarled bamboo staff in his right hand. But the man was also proudly sporting a pair of purple Speedos and a *topi*—the small pillbox hat worn by older Nepali men.

His face was contoured like a map of the world, and it was as brown as dirt, with trenches and gullies carved deeply around his eyes. His eyes themselves were dark and disarming pools, the quiet backwaters of a weather-beaten and expressive exterior. A ruddy complexion swept his wind-whipped cheeks. His face was so dark and pruny from what had likely been years of subtropical sun exposure and only sporadic bathing that he could have originated from the Kathmandu Valley himself. On midline, the skin overlying his nostrils—the foothills of his long, slender face—rose from the plains to form a mountainous beak, a pendulous, pitted crag turned purplish from an excess of superficial veins. Several crusty dragons dangled conspicuously in the protruding nose hair.

I hated to think it, but it looked as though he should have died years ago, perhaps from a heroin overdose or a knife fight in some seedy dive bar, but he seemed cheery and energetic nonetheless. And there was something comical about him that immediately put me at ease. He seemed like a joker, or a storyteller, perhaps. I imagined he was a man who could bring farce and humor to almost any situation. His flagrant disregard for the social norms of Nepali dress seemed appropriate, as though he were somehow immune to the cultural conventions strictly obeyed by everyone else in the country.

The man climbed the river's bank and doffed his topi to reveal an enormous bald spot that shone with brilliant intensity in the midmorning sun. A mostly toothless grin revealed one of his principle vices: betel nut. The overconsumption of *paan*—a conglomeration of betel nuts, lime paste, and spices—had left his teeth in a sorry state of reddened rot, except for a solitary gold tooth that somehow retained its lustrous twinkle. About his paan habit, he would smilingly say, "No worse than anything else Old Pete's put in his body over the years, mate! Haven't kicked off yet!" He insisted that, while paan did have mild narcotic effects, it was a digestive aid and a natural breath freshener and that I ought to try it sometime.

Speaking with the bohemian character at close range, I decided that the effectiveness of paan as a prophylactic against bad breath was questionable at best, an outright lie at worst. I imagined his overpowering halitosis rising straight from his gut to wilt the surrounding vegetation.

The man vigorously shook my hand and introduced himself as Peter Cornelius Dalrymple, a British national living in self-imposed exile in the

Kathmandu Valley. Nepali Pete, as he preferred to be called, had come to Kathmandu with a small group from the UK in the sixties in search of spiritual enlightenment but had instead found his passion in cheap dope, or "wacky backy," as he called it. Nepali Pete believed he'd been living in the country long enough to cite Nepali as his official nationality, although he didn't hold any citizenship papers, and his tourist visa had expired decades before.

"You a furry, mate?" he asked.

"A furry?" I replied.

"Yeah, a furry. Ya know, a Sherman tank?" he croaked. "A ham shank? A septic tank? Oh, for Chroist's sake, lad," Nepali Pete bellowed, "are ya a bloody 'Merkin or not?"

"Oh, *American*!" I said. "Yeah, I'm from California."

"No bloody way! Me uncle lives in California. He's a true lemon curd, but he's a wealthy old twat, I'll give him that."

"So, Nepali Pete," I said, curious about his activities below the bridge, "what exactly are you *doing* out there in the river?"

"Lad, you see those funeral pyres blazin' away on them burnin' ghats upstream?" asked Nepali Pete, glancing toward the temple complex. "Once the bloody conflagrations 'ave burned down properly, the stiffs are dumped into this 'ere Bagmati, see, and their charred corpses are floatin' downstream till they reach an impasse 'ere below the bridge," he explained, pointing to the pool through which he'd just been wading. "I used to work this watery plot with me mates from back home, but over the last decade or so, all the bloody wankers 'ave either croaked or buggered off to England. Now it's just yours truly and his crew of Nepali gold diggers," he said, referring to the half-naked men who were searching what I now realized were corpses—charred, ghastly remains I found startling—for precious stones and expensive jewelry.

Pete stated that he'd long since spent his meager savings on Manali hash and tasty baked goods in Kathmandu. He was obviously at the tail end of his rope, burned out from a lifetime of frequent cannabis use and excessive sugar consumption. It was clear Nepali Pete would do just about anything to support his habits, considering his work in the Bagmati. But I had to give the guy credit: he had an interesting, if not incredibly successful, history of financial freedom based on his entrepreneurial skills and his innate ability to sniff out riches where others had not.

I looked upstream at the expansive Pashupatinath temple complex. I watched closely as temple attendants doused funeral pyres with buckets from the Bagmati, the cool water sizzling like bacon upon impact and sending white tendrils of smoke curling skyward. Votive offerings—lit by the loving hands of relatives of the recently deceased—floated past me downstream on thick cupped leaves, the candles' paths largely dictated by the whims of the river's current. The candles that weren't immediately snared by the overhanging brush flanking the river eventually floated under the Bagmati Bridge and past a large shantytown that trailed away from the temple complex along one of the river's banks like the tail of a comet.

Leaning on his bamboo pole for support, a talkative Nepali Pete explained how the tent city had come into existence. "It's a bloody travesty, mate. Those people, the entire bloody lot of 'em, are the salt of the earth. They're the finest kin a man could have, but it's a true miracle they survive at all, given the way the cards are stacked against those poor baahstaards."

I sensed that Nepali Pete shared an unbreakable bond with the shantytown's members. I didn't know who they were or where they had come from, but they had obviously affected his attitude and possibly his worldview. His concern for their well-being was touching, and it seemed to come from a genuine place, a place where the river of human compassion ran deep. I'd just met him, but I believed Nepali Pete to be a good man—odd, but good—and I made up my mind to befriend him and learn whatever I could from him about Nepal and its people.

His penchant for communal values and communism proper, I soon learned from Pete, had led him to establish a camp for landless laborers near the Bagmati Bridge in the late eighties. The tiny community—named Camp Cornelius, in honor of Pete's late father—had quickly expanded into a small urban slum that attracted many of the Kathmandu Valley's landless laborers, or *sukumbasis*—poverty-stricken men and women who toiled in odd jobs on Kathmandu's snarling streets. Nepali Pete, elected as head of the community on all matters foreign and domestic, apparently enjoyed great esteem among his peers. He kept a certain percentage of the profits from his Bagmati finds for the purchase of potent ganja, it was true, but a sizable chunk of the money always found its way back into the community in the form of quality building materials for huts, tuition fees for the children's schooling, or weekly visits from a local physician.

"It's no big whoop, mate," he said. "Say, brother, you ever heard Cat Stevens's song 'Katmandu'?"

"Sure," I replied, unsure where the conversation was heading. I studied Pete's face for clues, watching as his eyes darted around their sockets. I was sure that despite decades of drug abuse, there was still some phenomenal neural activity going on in the Englishman's brain.

"Well, I don't like to brag about me artistic talents," said Nepali Pete, puffing out his chest slightly before leaning in to speak, "but just between you and me, *I* was the bloody bloke who scribbled the lyrics of 'Katmandu' on the bathroom wall in that smoky teahouse in—"

Pete stopped abruptly, suddenly looking blank. He was somewhere else for a few seconds, perhaps back in the sixties. I grabbed him by the shoulders and gently shook him back and forth, eventually slapping him lightly on the cheek a few times. Pete vigorously shook his head before running a hand through his greasy hair and refocusing on his immediate surroundings. "Sorry, lad," he apologized. "Happens all the bloody time. A real pain in the arse, if I do say so meself."

I probably would have laughed if I weren't so concerned about Pete's health. His unusual mannerisms and quirky disposition were already bringing humor into my life. I appreciated the hardships of his situation, and I took him seriously enough, but he was a total comedian, a total ham.

"So what teahouse were you talking about?" I wondered.

"*Teahouse?*" he roared. "What are you blatherin' about now, mate?"

"You know, the teahouse where you wrote the lyrics for 'Katmandu.'"

"Oh, *that* teahouse," he replied. "Shit, mate, why didn't ya say so? It's near Asan Tole. It's where I've done some of me finest work."

It was clear, considering what Pete was saying, that he fancied himself a poet *and* a songwriter, the laureate bard of all things lyrical and expressive. He hawked up a loogie, which he then spat with extraordinary accuracy onto the back of a nearby monkey who was rifling through a small pile of garbage. The hairy creature turned to face us and hissed aggressively before bounding up the embankment to a perch well out of the range of Nepali Pete's bodily juices.

"You see, mate, after the song became famous, I wrote old Cat a letter," he said. "In the letter, I demanded a proper share of the royalties from his *Mona Bone Jakon* album, otherwise I'd go public and lynch 'im with the truth."

"So what happened?" I wondered, uncertain if I should believe a man who seemed prone to delusions of grandeur or, perhaps, confabulation. This story sounded particularly like a fantastic yarn, but I decided to believe him. Pete, along with everybody else, I realized, had one part of the world's story to tell, and regardless of whether it was fact or fiction, I listened patiently and with great interest as he detailed his part.

"Well, because I was living on the street and had no fixed address, old Cat's reply took yonks to reach me," explained Pete. "Eventually, a letter arrived for me at the British Consulate here in K-du that said that as long as I kept me north and south—me jabbering, flappy trap—shut and the secret to meself, I'd continue to get royalty checks in the mail. The checks are as small as nuts on a toad these days, lad, but the bloody things keep comin'!"

The compromise had apparently been a good one for Nepali Pete, netting him enough cash to prolong his dope habit for several decades. But the lack of formal recognition for his artistic talents seemed to weigh heavily upon him.

"So, mate, how long 'ave you been in Nepal?" Pete's ability to change the direction of our conversation without warning was mildly exasperating, but I did appreciate that it kept me on my toes.

"Just a couple of days," I replied. "I haven't seen much of the city, except Durbar Square here in Kathmandu."

"You 'aven't seen Pashupatinath?" he wondered, his voice filled with shock—and possibly disdain—at the fact that I hadn't yet visited his home turf.

"Not yet," I replied, hoping that my strange new friend might offer a personalized tour of the temple where funeral pyres roared at all hours of the day and night, the temple where holy men from all around the subcontinent gathered en masse to pay homage to Shiva.

From what I could see, Pashupatinath was a dark, creepy place, a place where the smell of ultimate finality perpetually floated on the breeze. It was a smoke-filled forum of death and decay, a showcase of human limitations and a testament to the impermanence of our lives. Inside the temple complex were fire, water, smoke, and steam, and there was something intensely organic about the experience of Pashupatinath that helped define the place too. At Pashupatinath, you could witness the timeless interaction of human beings with the elements of the natural world, an interaction punctuated by the knowledge that we would all, someday, return to the earth. That knowledge, that understanding that we were all going to die, while bothering me more than ever as I watched bodies being cremated on the ghats upstream, was the only sure thing any of us could expect from life.

"Living just downstream from the ghats, in Camp Cornelius, I've become quite familiar with the place," he confided. "And given that me health ain't what it used to be, I'll soon find *meself* on the burning ghats." He laughed, making light of his obvious joie de vivre—et mort. As though recalling his history of bodily abuse, he offered a chilling prediction of his inevitable demise: "I am bound to wind up on me back in a bloody pool one way or another, mate. Might as well be where scavengers like meself can make use of valuable resources." He pointed at his own gold tooth, which would eventually float down the Bagmati with his charred body and into the hands of a new generation of industrious Nepali gold diggers.

Wobbling, Nepali Pete rose from his haunches and swayed back and forth on his bowed legs—his cribbage pegs, as he called them—griping all the while about the pain in his arthritic knees. I watched curiously as he repeatedly moved his hands to and from his nose while he searched the bank for his belongings. Much later, I learned he did this not out of some spiritual routine or because of a nervous tic but simply because he enjoyed the smell of his own fingers.

Pete picked up a dirty white smock from the river's edge and finally preserved his modesty by donning the simple garment and shrouding his unsightly purple Speedos. "Right then," he said. "Let's not piss away the day, lad. There're plenty of things to see and do, and the clock's ticking." He tapped a wristwatch he'd no doubt recently lifted from a water-logged corpse. "It's jolly well time we took our walkabout, don't you think? Shall we off?"

A walking tour sounded like a great idea. We struck off along the narrow strip of land beside the river, heading upstream toward the large temple straddling the Bagmati. On our side of the river, directly ahead of us, a cremation had just gotten underway on the burning ghats. The family and friends of the departed stood stoically under a parapet as the body was consumed by the flames. Western tourists, conspicuous and invasive with their digital cameras, snapped shots of the solemn event from a nearby footbridge.

"I smell a bloody rat!" Nepali Pete's temper flared like the nostrils of an angry orangutan. Fuming, he ran toward the footbridge, wagged his fist at the tourists, and wondered aloud if they had no shame. "Why don't ya just snog right 'ere in public while you're at it, you shameless wankers, you merchant bankers and oil tankers!" His squirrelly glare and fist-wagging effectively mobilized the troop from their voyeuristic vantage point. "I've got a shotgun and a shovel, and ain't nobody gonna miss yer bloody carcasses. Now *sod off*, ya baahstaards!"

Nepali Pete's chastising, as harsh as his rebuke sounded, was refreshing. I appreciated the way he said what he thought, that he didn't hold back from voicing his true opinions. His willingness to speak his mind was a trait I'd witnessed in other Brits too. My own hesitation, perhaps due in part to my culture, to be honest with others in face-to-face confrontations and my preference instead to lie about disagreements to preserve the peace had always disgusted me. I was buoyed by Pete's lack of self-consciousness in his reprimand of the tourists.

"Chroist," grumbled Nepali Pete. "Can you Adam and Eve the gall of those feather pluckers, those Tommy Tuckers?" he said, using his Cockney rhyming slang. "It's difficult enough for families to see their loved ones singed to a bloody crisp, let alone have to bear the gawking leers of a grand assemblage of ass clowns."

Pete's blood pressure finally normalized, and he led me past a handful of small stone stupas, each containing a *lingam*—a phallic symbol representative of Shiva's creative powers. We ascended a set of broad steps and landed on a terrace that overlooked the entire temple complex. I watched as a *sadhu*, a Hindu holy man, entertained a crowd of tourists with a writh-ing cobra, which he let free to roam over a small, cobbled courtyard. Even from a distance, I squirmed uncomfortably at the reptile's spastic move-ments and slithery, unchecked wanderings, happy to have both elevation and distance on my side.

"With any luck, mate, we'll catch a glimpse of the Milk Baba."

"Who's the Milk Baba?" I wondered, hoping not to sound too igno-rant. With a name like that, I was sure the man had an interesting story to accompany his epithet.

"The Milk Baba is a wanderer, mate, a true ascetic, and a master of the sacred Sanskrit Vedic scriptures. Get this, mate," said a giddy Nepali Pete, tapping me on the shoulder several times in quick succession to hold my attention. "He's devoted himself to something called the Milk Austerity Path and has gobbled down nothing but milk for the past *thirrrty* years! And for twelve of those bloody years, mate, this bloke tramped around India. You wouldn't believe how popular he is, especially with the ladies! He's got a whole bloody harem of Western women to tend to his needs, I swear to you on me mother's grave. And he's been invited to flap his gums to followers all over the world. He's got more bloody stamps in his passport than you can shake a stick at, and he's also pretty damn good at the yoga, if ya ask me. Among holy men in Nepal, mate, he's pretty much the mutt's nuts."

As if on cue, a wiry, ashen-faced sadhu wearing bright orange garb and heavy dreadlocks emerged from a small hermitage near the riverbank. He quickly descended to the level of the ghats. There, on the Bagmati's banks, the guru situated himself in front of a large group of tourists and began contorting himself into advanced yoga poses, all the while invoking the mighty and mysterious counsel of Ram. The Milk Baba, a highly regarded expert on the *Ramayana*, the famed spiritual tome of India, followed a devotion to god along the path of *bhakti*, according to Nepali Pete. He was also wildly popular with the tourists, including some of the same tourists Pete had earlier scattered, who snapped countless pictures of the votary and left small donations at his feet, humble tokens of their appreciation for his spiritual guidance and yogic mastery.

There was something extraordinary about the Milk Baba, something so calming yet unnerving at the same time. In his face, I saw no searching, no angst, no sense of urgency. In his body language were the telltale mannerisms of a self-realized human being, mannerisms that humbly told the world he was beyond attachment and suffering. Pete assured me that he wasn't stoned either; the Milk Baba's current level of awareness was the result of years of intensive study and meditation.

The Milk Baba finished his ritual morning posturing and returned to his simple hermitage. I realized that I had felt an immediate connection with the milk-loving guru. I *knew* that I hadn't seen the last of the Milk Baba, that somehow he would find his way into my life as a spiritual guide and companion.

Nepali Pete insisted we continue our informal tour of Kathmandu. We followed the pathway past the Gorakhnath Temple before descending a steep hill that brought us back down to the Bagmati. From our position near the river, we could see the great stupa of Boudhanath, the gathering place of Kathmandu's Tibetan community, rising up on the horizon.

Pete led me through the backwaters of Kathmandu throughout the afternoon, along damp alleyways and dusty *chowks*, intersections that seemed hidden away from the advancing hands of time. I picked up a few simple Nepali phrases along the way, just enough to make some common requests and pose a few relevant questions.

Pete eventually led me out of the labyrinth and toward a great commotion rising up in the distance as evening descended on my third full day in the Nepali capital. I followed closely behind him and tried to mimic his loping, swaying gait, but the uniqueness of his walk was impossible to emulate. There was a strange forward bob to it, almost as though he were performing a subtle head bang with each lengthy stride. He didn't use his arms, either; the long appendages simply dangled against the sides of his torso. It was a goofy walk, a walk that Monty Python might have incorporated into their Ministry of Silly Walks, but it seemed to fit Pete and his personality to perfection.

The sounds of the raucous party grew louder and louder until the noise was almost deafening. Pete stopped abruptly on the edge of the gathering, and with the athleticism of a man half his age, and despite the degenerated condition of his knees, climbed a drainpipe to the rooftop of a two-story building, urging me to follow his lead. I was impressed and inspired by his agility, but I didn't know if I had the wherewithal to duplicate his deft moves. I had barely gotten my legs back under me after the jet lag, and there I was contemplating the vertical ascent of a rusty, jagged old piece of metal. But it was a day of letting go, a day of giving myself over to chance encounters and unexpected adventures, so I threw caution to the wind and started up into the Kathmandu sky.

Muscling my way up the pipe, I pulled myself over the edge of the gently sloping roof. I shaded my eyes to block the day's last rays—beams that slanted hard against my face and blinded me with their ocher intensity.

I struggled to orient myself to the rooftop's layout, as my eyes were still adapting to the light. Before I had much of a chance to get acquainted with my surroundings, however, I caught sight of a blurry object moving at top speed toward the rooftop's ledge. It was Nepali Pete, rushing straight past me like an all-star receiver heading for the end zone; he let out a piercing scream and launched himself off the building's edge and onto a nearby rooftop. "'Ave some of that, lad!" he yelled, after landing successfully.

I watched as he continued to leap from one building to the next with the deftness of a snow leopard in pursuit of its prey. "Stop arsing around, mate," he called. He insisted that his aerial acrobatics were completely safe and encouraged me to follow him. "Just blow a raspberry if you need a little extra lift," he chided. "It's piss-easy, really."

"I don't know if I can do this, Pete." I figured my odds of making the jump without plummeting to my death were better than average, but I was definitely no stuntman.

"That's a load of malarkey, mate. Don't be a ponce," he roared. "You jolly well *can* do it. Just remember to keep your pecker up and everything should be tickety-boo! If old Pete can do it, so can you!"

I took stock of my situation, laughing at its absurdity. There I was, stranded on a rooftop in a very foreign place with a burned-out hippie in purple Speedos and flip-flops encouraging me to soar through the air like a leaping lemur.

I had no choice but to trust my guide *and* my gut, so I took a running charge at the broad cleft separating the two buildings and vaulted myself into the Kathmandu evening. That long leap of faith was liberating and not nearly as scary as I'd imagined it would be, much like that first morning in Nepal, when I'd strode away from the airport into the relative unknown.

Seconds later, I landed squarely on the opposite rooftop, both feet finding their mark more easily than I had thought possible. Nepali Pete, laughing like a scoundrel, clapped his approval, whirled on his heel, and continued leaping as I tried to close the gap between us.

Pete and I slowed to a contemplative trot when we'd finally run out of buildings and could leap no further. We sauntered up to the rooftop's ledge and looked down upon a scene of utter pandemonium in the adjacent square. "Mate, welcome to the Durga Darshan Drive-in Theater!" Nepali Pete spread his arms wide.

"A drive-in theater in Kathmandu?" I said. I was philosophically opposed to the notion of cramming so many people and motorized vehicles into such a confined space, considering the reckless abandon I'd already seen championed by Nepali drivers. I was sure blood would be shed before the night was done.

"You'd think it would be a total bloomin' nightmare," agreed Pete. "But somehow it just works. I've come 'ere many, many times over the years, mate, and not once has there been a bloody fatality."

Motorcycles, autorickshaws, and tuk tuks all jockeyed for position in the square below, in front of a large, windowless brick wall. The vehicles' horn play was deafening, a shrill serenade to which Nepali Pete responded with a small jig, dancing precariously on the rooftop's narrow ledge. The massing block party of Nepali teens and twenty somethings filled in the cracks and crevices between the motorized vehicles as the square quickly became a standing-room-only venue.

The evening's movie, according to Pete, would be a Bollywood film entitled *Gangster*, starring an actor named Emraan Hashmi. Pete also explained that the Nepali crowd had a love-hate relationship with Bollywood films after a well-known Indian actor, Hrithik, supposedly made derogatory comments about his Nepali fans, comments that the actor adamantly denied having made. While the crowd jeered, Pete said they shared a hidden admiration for the stars' work—otherwise they wouldn't have shown up to the drive-in in such staggering numbers.

The film, a love story with an unexpected ending, relied heavily on the appeal of hit songs to carry the plot. I'd already enjoyed some of the film's tunes in cybercafés, restaurants, bars, and taxis in the short time since I'd arrived in Nepal. The soulful melodies took on a far greater significance now that I was familiar with their origin. Those songs would become like personal anthems to me over the weeks and months to come, and over the years, they would remind me of my time and experience in Kathmandu.

The film finally finished and the crowd began to disperse. Nepali Pete and I fled from our rooftop position, climbing down another rusty drainpipe. Pete flagged down the appropriate bus and climbed onto its roof via the ladder tacked to its rear, again encouraging me to follow his lead. "I'm right knackered, lad. Let's ride this bucket of bolts back to Camp Cornelius for some tea and crumpets." He smiled coyly as he elbowed me in the ribs. "And, mate, by tea and crumpets, what old Pete really means is rice and marijuana!"

The rooftop ride back to Pashupatinath and Camp Cornelius was a total rush. The fast-moving air that filled my lungs was noticeably cleaner than the air at ground level, where countless tailpipes poisoned pedestrians. I thanked Nepali Pete for being such an excellent tour guide. He'd shown me parts of the city I was sure few Westerners had ever seen, and he'd coaxed me along with just the right amount of enthusiasm and encouragement.

"Think nothing of it, mate," he shouted over the road noise.

He insisted he was at the end of his rope, but there was still plenty of life and mischief left in Nepali Pete, I was sure of it.

We approached the Bagmati Bridge, and Pete signaled the driver to stop by banging on the bus's side with his fist. We climbed down from the roof, paid our fare, and took off toward Camp Cornelius. After several minutes of brisk walking, Pete raised his arm and motioned for me to stop. "Mind if I drain me lizard 'ere by the side of the trail? Old Pete's swollen bladder can't wait till we get back to camp."

"No problem, Pete," I said. "You just do what you need to do."

"Right, then," he said, angling his body away from the trail. Pete turned to me again after a few seconds of silence and said, "Ya mind buggerin' off for a wee bit?" He cocked his head to the side and added, "It's me bashful kidneys, me tricky North and South Sydneys, see. I just can't dicky diddle when there're other blokes about, tha's all."

We regrouped after Pete had thoroughly doused the greenery, and continued walking for several more minutes until we finally arrived at Nepali Pete's shack. His shack, constructed from tin, plastic, and bits of bamboo, stood on the community's fringe; it was the closest structure to the bridge and the watery plot he and his Nepali recruits worked on a daily basis. I glanced around the hut and noticed a broom, a few pots and pans, and a pile of loot pilfered from Bagmati corpses that Pete clearly had yet to parse.

Nepali Pete began preparing the evening's lentils and rice. We sat down on a pair of wicker stools when the dal bhaat was finally ready and began feasting, Nepali Pete performing a shameless face-plant into his food before coming up for air. "It's no bangers and mash, mate, but beggars can't be choosers now, can they?" said Pete, between mouthfuls. Ravenous and seemingly lacking a satiety signal, Pete put his well-developed jaw muscles to good use. Three heaping servings later, he belched loudly and pounded his chest. He was a total beanpole, skinnier even than many of the homeless men I'd seen on the streets of Kathmandu, so where he stored all that food, I had no idea.

"Wha?" he said, catching my awestruck look. "I'm eatin' for two, ya know. I've got to feed me bloody tapeworm. I call her Sherri, by the way, after me ex-wife—both parasites of an unimaginable wretchedness! Ha ha ha!" he cackled.

Nepali Pete's incredible appetite, his inability to gain weight, his blatant disregard for hygiene—it all added up to a likely diagnosis of parasites. Most of the water he drank came out of a nearby tap, unfiltered, unboiled, and no doubt contaminated with monsoon runoff. I'd been religious about drinking only filtered water since arriving in the country, and the thought of hosting a twenty-foot-long tapeworm provided more than enough motivation for me to continue.

A small and curious group of sukumbasi children had in the meantime made the short hike upstream from the heart of Camp Cornelius to Nepali Pete's hut. The smiling boys and girls peered through the hut's open doorway and waited for Pete to beckon them inside. The children sat down on the floor. Pete introduced each by first name and gave me a brief synopsis of how their families came to be living in the encampment.

The appearance of the round-faced children stood in stark contrast to that of Nepali Pete. Unlike Pete, they were well-scrubbed, well-groomed, well-nourished, and well-dressed. They looked like the children of parents who'd given them much love. There was a tremendous amount of hope in their big brown eyes, and their proficiency in English was impressive.

I rose from my wicker stool and stretched after the kids had scampered back to their parents' huts, telling Nepali Pete that it was time for me to head back to Thamel. He wondered if I'd stay for dessert. "There's no better nightcap than a *bhang lassi*, mate! Won't ya stay a wee bit longer? I'm so bloody tired of gettin' stoned all by meself." The bhang lassi turned out to be a blend of yogurt and ice water that incorporated a marijuana derivative for mind-blowing effects.

I declined his offer but thanked Pete for his guidance and his company before heading toward the Bagmati Bridge, where I immediately flagged down a taxi.

"Where are you going, sir?" asked the driver, leaning his head out the window.

"I'm going to the Kathmandu Guest House," I replied. "In Thamel."

"Oh yes, I am knowing Thamel and that guest house very, very well. Please, come with me."

The driver looked anxious for business, but he had an honest face. I jumped into the taxi and we roared off toward Thamel. I stared out the taxi's window at nothing in particular, realizing that my days as a tourist were over. The following morning I and the rest of N-199 would be heading to Bhairahawa to begin our preservice training and our Peace Corps careers.

Pepsicola Townplanning

I DIDN'T HEAR FROM ADRIANA FOR A WEEK AFTER MY PROFESSION OF LOVE. I knew she was busy with her classes, but I'd expected at least some correspondence—a simple phone call or even an e-mail—after the way I'd put myself on the line. The silence and the waiting almost killed me.

When she finally did call me, she apologized profusely and expressed genuine interest in meeting whenever it was convenient for me. She had just come through an intense series of tests and assignments, according to her, and she now had more free time to catch up with friends and be social.

I knew that Adriana was a woman of integrity and would never betray the trust of her boyfriend—a loud yet charismatic guy named Manish Nair, who was well connected in the campus community—but for her to want to talk further meant there was a remote possibility she'd found a measure of truth in the words I'd spoken. It was a minor breakthrough, a little victory I could cling to with a renewed sense of hope until we next met.

When we finally did meet, she looked exhausted. She explained that things with her boyfriend had been rocky over the past couple of weeks and that she wasn't sure where they stood. Adriana said that their relationship was still in its infancy and that there were numerous questions dangling in her mind about where it all might lead. I could hear the doubt in her voice, but I tried to be impartial. I tried to simply listen to what she was saying and not offer the solution that seemed so obvious to me.

It was clear that she wasn't as happy as she wanted to be, but I was in no position to comment on the details of her situation. It just wouldn't have been right. So, instead, I listened.

We saw each other often over the course of the following term. My feelings for Adriana continued to grow during this time, even though she refused to let go of her troubled relationship. I'd been in love before, but the feelings I'd developed for Adriana superseded all my previous experiences. It was agony to see her cling to something that had so obviously run its course. I believed in my heart, right or wrong, that no other person in the entire world could possibly match my feelings for her; I would love her unconditionally and care for her for the rest of my life.

While driving the safety shuttle back to campus one night, I saw Adriana walking home with her boyfriend. The scene was so heartrending that I could barely keep the van between the lines. Seeing her with another man cut me deeply and sent me flying over the edge of rationality, down a long and twisted road of jealousy and resentment. I felt cheated, as though I'd invested my time, energy, and, most important, my heart, only to be left in the choppy wake of Adriana's personal life.

That night, I realized that if I valued something enough, and if I wanted it badly enough, I just had to go out and get it, whatever the consequences. Life would pass me by unless I put myself out there and made things happen. It was as simple as that.

I began actively pursuing Adriana after adopting this new philosophy, writing her and calling her on a regular basis. I made my intentions very clear to her, and while she still wasn't willing to end her relationship with her boyfriend, she didn't push me away either.

* * *

I slept late the morning following our group's return from Bhairahawa. It felt good to be back in Kathmandu after some time away. In Bhairahawa, we'd undergone extensive preservice language and cultural training. We'd lived with host families and adjusted to life in Nepal without many of the distractions and creature comforts to which Westerners are so accustomed. All trainees agreed that our immersion in Nepali society had been thorough and complete, if not a little exhausting. The group members, at least those who had made it through preservice training, looked comfortable and confident in their new lives as soon-to-be volunteers and goodwill ambassadors.

My new friends and fellow preservice training graduates had already begun to disperse. Most of them, like me, had been posted to Nepal's largest cities—Kathmandu, Bhaktapur, Pokhara—but a handful of volunteers had been sent to Nepal border towns in the Terai, such as Birganj, Nepalgunj, Biratnagar, Janakpur, and Mahendranagar.

The realization that today was the first day of my future suddenly cracked through my fatigue, and I jumped out of bed. I'd been assigned to a community called Pepsicola Townplanning, and I was scheduled to meet my host family and a key contact in the neighborhood, a man named Dr. Singh, later that day. I knew almost nothing about the community, except that it was located on the outskirts of Kathmandu and was home to a run-down Pepsi-Cola bottling plant.

I knew equally little about my new host family. The Peace Corps provided all volunteers with a monthly three-thousand-rupee stipend to help cover the cost of lodging, along with a monthly salary of eight thousand Nepali rupees, or about one hundred dollars. I wanted to continue my immersion in Nepali society, and so I'd opted to stay with a Nepali family for the duration of my service. I hoped that my new Nepali family was as eager to meet me as I was to meet them.

I had some time to kill before leaving Thamel for my post, so I decided to visit Peace Corps headquarters in Lazimpat. I left my backpack with the man at the guest house's reception desk and walked over to the embassy district. I touched base with Mike Swenson before spending some time thumbing through a book called *Himalayan Gourmet*—a cookbook containing recipes for dishes such as Sagarmatha roast pork, french-fried eggplant, and Yeti stew, which had been submitted by former Peace Corps Nepal volunteers—and scrolling through a database of project reports generated by previous groups. Two of the projects in particular caught my eye. One of them involved building latrines and the other, building smokeless stoves to help stave off chronic inflammatory conditions, such as bronchitis, emphysema, and conjunctivitis, which were endemic to Nepal.

Jaya, Nepal!

I stopped briefly at Pilgrims Book House on my way back to the Kathmandu Guest House to buy postcards for friends and family. I wrote words of reassurance to my parents to let them know that I was alive and well, words of thanks to my inner circle of friends who had gone out of their way to throw me a good-bye bash before I'd left America, and words of deep gratitude to a handful of professors at UC Berkeley who had lobbied hard in support of my decision to volunteer overseas with the Peace Corps. And on the back of one of the postcards—a postcard I couldn't send because I had no idea *where* to send it—I wrote the words I'd always wanted to say but had never had the opportunity to utter. I stuffed *that* postcard into my journal until I'd found the correct address or perhaps, if I were lucky, the elusive recipient for whom the words were intended.

I began to feel my stomach churn as I marched through the tourist district. What I was feeling at that particular moment was an overwhelming sense of self-doubt mixed with a fragile courage and a resolve to make good on cherished promises to myself and others. I wondered if other Peace Corps volunteers around the world had ever felt that strange combination of emotions. I suspected they had, but I still felt very much alone at that moment. I felt like a man without a family or a cause to cling to for support. I was caught in the no-man's-land between ideals and real-life experience, and I suddenly felt the overwhelming need to make a foothold for myself, to surround myself with the sort of people who could nurture me and fill the emptiness I felt in my soul.

I retrieved my backpack from the Kathmandu Guest House and made my way to Thamel Chowk, where I looked over a long line of white Maruti Suzukis parked next to the curb along Tridevi Marg. Despite the aggressive nature and occasionally shady business practices of Kathmandu's cabbies, there seemed to be a code of conduct they all followed to the letter. I'd only been in Nepal a short time, but I'd already gleaned a lot about the nature of cabbie-cabbie and driver-customer relationships.

Formal queues near the major tourist hubs—places where drivers would wait patiently for their turn to be first in line for paying customers—were respected and obeyed. If another driver tried to swoop in and steal the lead spot in the queue, the cabbies would band together to rout him out, rocking his car until he agreed to give up his passenger and move to the back of the line. Even at the airport, where the horde of drivers had tried in vain to sell me their services, I'd noticed a certain degree of respect meted out to those men who could broker a sale without the use of force or coercion, those whose selling techniques relied more on savvy than blatant harassment.

Even as it concerned the interactions between drivers and passengers, there seemed to be a certain code of behavior, a sliding scale of ethics used by the driver based largely upon *how* the deal between pilot and passenger had been transacted. If the passenger was suckered into paying too much, the best he or she could hope for, I understood, would be a lazy jaunt throughout the city that might or might not include a stop at a local teashop, all on the passenger's dime. On the other hand, if the passenger undercut the driver, paying him less than his services were thought to be worth in the context of Nepali society, the best that person could expect would be a cold, stony silence and a reproachful glare once the destination had been reached. If a passenger played the game well, though, if he or she bargained hard but left a sizable-enough profit for the driver, the passenger could invoke an unbending loyalty from the pilot.

On this particular day, I bargained hard with the lead driver until we settled on a reasonable fare of two hundred and fifty rupees. I threw my backpack into the backseat, climbed into the tiny vehicle, and hunkered down for what I suspected would be a jarring ride out of the city. Good drivers—ones who would treat you fairly—were tough to find, but if you found the right one and treated him well, he'd go out of his way to get you where you needed to go in a timely fashion, even if that meant occasionally putting a couple of the taxi's wheels up on the curb to pass a slower-moving vehicle. Drivers in Kathmandu routinely took great personal risks to their vehicles to make sure their preferred customers' commute times were slashed to the absolute minimum.

A glossy-paper version of Shakira pasted to the cab's ceiling looked down upon me. I had to agree with my driver, or whomever had invited her along: the pop goddess's pouty lips and sinewy thighs brightened what was otherwise a drab interior.

Admin had a policy of delivering every volunteer to his or her post, but I insisted on making the trip by myself, as it was just a short taxi ride to

Pepsicola Townplanning from the heart of Kathmandu. The driver, leaving the tourist district, bisected the roaring anonymity of Kantipath—the same broad boulevard I'd navigated with Madhu that first day in Nepal—and headed toward the city's outskirts. "It's a good day for driving, my friend," I said as we passed the fenced-in grounds of the international airport.

"Oh yes, a *very* good day for the driving, brother," the man agreed, craning his neck to glance at me. "And I am very, very, very happy for your businesses today," he insisted, momentarily lifting his hands from the wheel to crack his knuckles.

The driver swung left onto a side road not long after we'd cleared the grounds of the airport. The traffic on this road was lighter, and the air less polluted. I looked out the window and watched in awe as we sailed by a community in transition, a group trading its agrarian roots for the cement and steel of the city. I caught short frames of rural life far off in the countryside in the spaces between the concrete buildings. These images were snapshots of a life less cluttered by the material accumulations for which so many in Kathmandu proper seemed to be perpetually striving.

The asphalt gave way to gravel after several miles, and the pace of life slowed perceptibly. The nervousness that had been eating away at me began to dissipate. The driver geared down as we entered Pepsi Chowk—a small, dusty bowl ringed by fruit stands and bicycle repair shops—and executed a flawless U-turn before coasting to a stop. After I paid the agreed-upon fare, I looked up to see a smiling Madhu emerge from a nearby temple, to my amazement. I thanked the driver and waved him off before turning to greet my friend.

"I am hoping your first few months in our beloved country are being *very* good for you," said Madhu, looking pleased to see that I'd at least survived that early test and perhaps even more pleased that I'd been assigned to his community and healthpost. "But already it is, daai, I am missing you so very much."

"Well, Nepal's an incredible country," I said, appealing to the young man's sense of national pride. "And I missed you too," I added.

It hadn't been *that* long since I'd last seen him, and we barely knew each other, but given the sincerity of his words, I understood that he really had missed me. If just that period of separation had provoked such feelings of loss, how would he—and everybody else I would come to know—cope when it was time for me to leave the country for good? I wasn't trying to be full of myself or assume that my influence in the community would be anything more than superficial, but I had to face the very real possibility that my presence and my work might affect people on a deeper level, and that I, in turn, would be moved in ways I had never imagined possible.

Before I left America, many people asked how much I would be "interfering" in the locals' lives. The truth was, I planned to "interfere" a lot; that was the whole point. I planned to immerse myself in their lives and exchange ideas and customs with them. I thought and hoped that I might affect the lives of the Nepali people in some positive way, but what I never imagined, especially in those early days, was how deeply my own life would be affected by the citizens of Pepsicola Townplanning, and specifically the men and women of the Pepsicola Community Hospital.

My first impression of Pepsicola Townplanning was that the community was *not* beautiful, at least not beautiful in the way I'd imagined every corner of Nepal would be beautiful. It wouldn't be long, though, until I would come to see the place in another light. I would come to understand in the days, weeks, and months ahead that the neighborhood's charms lay not in its appearance but rather in the kindness and the compassion of its people. Physical beauty *was* there to be found, I eventually came to realize, but I had to look in the right spots.

"The good life here is being much quieter than in Kathmandu City," Madhu said, as though reading my mind. He started leading me away from the dusty intersection on foot. "We could be driving to the clinic, but you will be seeing that the bumpy bumpies are too bad for the cars."

The countless potholes dotting the earthen streets would have reduced even the most burly sport utility vehicle to a crawl. And I was glad we were traveling to the clinic on foot, because it afforded me a chance to soak in the details I otherwise might have missed, such as the rainbows of produce displayed in an open-air market, the meticulously groomed fields hemmed by narrow earthen walls, and a rough-and-tumble barber's shack, where young men from the community congregated.

After taking me on a long walk through the neighborhood, Madhu eventually led me up the front steps of a nondescript building, the Pepsicola Community Hospital. As we marched down a hallway, Madhu grabbed my wrist and veered left into a treatment room, where he insisted I wait until Dr. Singh and the rest of the clinic's staff arrived for the afternoon's shift. A long line of patients sitting quietly on a bench in the main hallway apparently also awaited the doctor's triumphant arrival.

The Pepsicola Community Hospital appeared to be a bare-bones affair, consisting of four rooms bathed in an ultramarine hue, a large washbasin, a dispensary, and a lavatory. Three of the rooms, including the one in which I was seated, served as examination and treatment rooms, and each contained a desk, an examining table, several chairs, and a bucket for vomit. There were no decorations on the walls, and although the rooms had two windows, both were guarded by a set of sturdy iron bars on the outside. Single light bulbs dangling from extension cords provided the rooms' only source of illumination, apart from the curtained windows. In one of the other exam rooms, according to Madhu, there was a small stash of emergency materials, including gauze, bandages, and thread for suturing wounds.

Conditions in the clinic were spartan, but the place looked kempt and hygienic. The clinic's minimalist look and feel suited me perfectly; it was medicine stripped down to its bare fundamentals. I was curious to see how Dr. Singh used the small hospital's limited resources to treat the public. He'd have to make those resources stretch if he wanted to help them all, considering the number of people queuing up to see him.

I felt good being back in a clinical setting after placing my nursing career on hold to join the Peace Corps. I hoped that the skills I'd gained in school would, in some way, be put to good use in the community. I also hoped that I'd be as helpful as the doctor needed and perhaps expected me to be, if in fact there was a role for me in the clinic.

I heard the droning of a motorcycle approaching the clinic only a few minutes later. Moving to one of the treatment room's windows, I peeled back the curtain and peeked through the iron bars, watching as a large cloud of dust billowed into the air behind a solitary rider clad in a fashionable pinstriped suit. The rider killed the engine, coasted toward the clinic's front steps, and removed his helmet, which he tossed to Madhu before straightening his clothes and spryly bounding up the stairs. The heavy footfalls of his dress shoes grew louder and louder as he came down the long hallway toward my room.

Dr. Singh, I presumed, flung back the curtain that separated the treatment room from the hallway, entered, and strode confidently toward me. He extended his right hand. "Damu Sankar Singh, MBBS." He shook my hand vigorously. "I'm *very* pleased to meet you, Benjamin. Would you mind if I called you Benny-*bhai*?" The doctor spoke in a clipped British accent.

"Yeah, I think that would be fine," I said, smiling at his unbridled enthusiasm. I liked him immediately.

"Well, you've come such a long way to join us here in Pepsicola Townplanning, Benny-bhai, so let's not waste any time. Let's get right to the heart of the matter, shall we? Mr. Madhu, please, send in the first patient!"

Mike Swenson had told me that the fifty-five-year-old Dr. Singh was an interesting man. He was the type of guy who could spontaneously burst into a lecture on digestive physiology, quizzing you on the function of parietal cells in the grand gastric scheme, and then only a moment later be reclined in a chair, grooving to the latest Hindi pop hits blasting from his mobile. I'd also been told that he had boundless energy, that even the younger doctors at Bir Hospital—one of Nepal's busiest hospitals—struggled to keep up with him, and that he was a man who supported the underdog and respected people who stood up for themselves. Some within the Kathmandu medical community had accused him of being blunt and overaggressive, but he was regarded by most as something of a phenomenon, a highly skilled practitioner who excelled in all aspects of his life.

He was a handsome man, too. His square jaw was chiseled and cleanly shorn, and his short black hair looked as though it had been recently trimmed. He had an athletic-looking body and a dignified bearing that made him appear taller than he was. There was a certain confidence in his overall body language, in fact, a collectedness that seemed cultivated from and refined by years of interactions with patients and colleagues.

Madhu, only too happy to oblige the doctor's let's-get-to-work mentality, assisted a portly woman and four of her family members into the treatment room. I understood right away that, in Nepal, a trip to the doctor was a family outing. Dr. Singh began questioning the woman about her chief complaint once she was seated and her entourage introduced. Nodding, Dr. Singh let the woman finish completely before translating for me that the postmonsoon rice harvest was in full swing in Pepsicola Townplanning, and that a grain of rice had somehow lodged itself deep inside her ear and was causing her considerable grief.

Dr. Singh, peering through his otoscope, noted that the woman's ear wax—or cerumen, as he called it—had staked a serious claim on its unexpected prize. The grain of rice would be almost impossible to extract, given its delicate final resting place, but he would try his best. Dr. Singh rummaged through his doctor's bag, producing an unusual assortment of probes and other devices.

Despite the woman's cries of "*Mommy! Mommy!*" Dr. Singh was merciless in his pursuit of the morsel. He tried several different styles of probe, but finally conceded defeat to the starchy nugget, calmly explaining to the woman that her condition was not an emergency and that she shouldn't be too concerned about her new companion. Time, along with some wax-softening ear drops, would eventually take care of it, he insisted.

As Dr. Singh was wrapping up the visit, a goat wandered into the treatment room. The creature bleated several times, swished its tail, and then plodded out of the room. Nobody else in the treatment room seemed to pay the goat much attention, but I found the chance encounter quite amusing. When I told the story to my Peace Corps friends the following week at the Rum Doodle, all agreed that I had experienced a "Peace Corps moment"—the type of moment that could not have happened to me outside of this place.

Dr. Singh released the woman from his care. The four family members gathered around her, their arms locked as though they were in a rugby scrum, and each took his or her turn with the otoscope to inspect the woman's ear wax.

The doctor and I paused in the hallway before entering the second treatment room. "What about an ear irrigation?" I wondered, thinking we might have been able to blast the grain of rice from the woman's ear with a strong stream of water then and there.

"I like your train of thought, Benny-bhai," said the doctor, "but we can't risk exacerbating this woman's condition with a fully inflated grain of rice. It would only increase her stress levels, you see. And we don't always follow protocol here. I've found that evidence-based treatments do not always produce the most meritorious results. Not to toot my own horn, Benny-bhai, but I consider myself a magna cum laude graduate from the school of practical experience!"

He was right, of course. We'd never get the woman out of the clinic if the ear irrigation failed and the rice morsel began to expand. There were plenty of patients to see, and we needed to get moving. And I trusted the doctor's clinical wisdom. He'd apparently been healing people for years using a unique blend of Eastern and Western healing techniques.

Following the consultation with the afternoon's final patient—who had a relatively mild case of indigestion—after a day that had progressed immediately from a trapped grain of rice to an ugly case of scabies and then maintained that level of seriousness, the doctor and I stepped out behind the clinic for a quick tête-à-tête.

"Given what you've seen here today in our tabernacle of unorthodox medicine, our healing house of empirical evidence," he said, "I think you can appreciate that we need an extra set of hands, if you're willing. Mr. Madhu has excellent phlebotomy and suturing skills, but we could use your help in triaging the patients and recording their complaints. We could also use your help in organizing and managing this tiny hospital, and we'd love to make good use of your knowledge of clinical nutrition, sanitation, and other basic health care information."

"Thanks for your openness, Dr. Singh," I said. "And in terms of helping out around the clinic, I'm just happy to do whatever I can to ensure everything runs smoothly."

"Good," he replied, nodding his head. "A piece of advice for you, though, Benny-bhai. I believe you will have the greatest collective effect in this community by staging public health campaigns with the help of Mr. Madhu. Can I suggest two issues you might address?"

"Absolutely," I said. "I welcome your suggestions."

"Excellent," he replied. "I've been trying for years now to get the community to switch from sticky rice to brown rice, not only because of the higher nutritional content but also to help stave off adult-onset diabetes. Diabetes has become a major health problem throughout Nepal, especially in the urban areas and in those of us over forty years of age."

It would take plenty of coaxing and cajoling to convince the residents of Pepsicola Townplanning to switch from white rice to brown, according to Dr. Singh. It would take a dedicated and focused effort to get people thinking differently, to get them to accept new ideas and break with tradition.

"Also, I'd be forever grateful if you can find a way to get more protein into people's diets." He gripped my shoulder and looked me squarely in the eye. "I think you'll quickly discover that, in a country like Nepal, every shred of protein counts. Yes, brown rice and protein should be excellent starting points, Benny-bhai."

The doctor's ideas were excellent, and I looked forward to getting out into the community to spread my message of optimal nutrition and its effect on human health. I reminded myself that, even at this early stage, I needed to be careful not to become consumed by something larger than what I could handle. In the past, I'd occasionally bitten off more than I could chew, taking on projects impulsively, only to end up feeling scattered, distracted, overwhelmed, and even resentful. I think the doctor must have sensed this apprehension, because he had phrased his ideas as suggestions, not demands. I was thankful for his prescience. It was clear, right from the start, that Dr. Singh would be my greatest ally and cheerleader in Nepal.

"I hope it's OK with you, Benny-bhai," continued the doctor, "but I have taken the liberty of setting you up with a Nepali language tutor, who will work with you several mornings each week. I think you'll find your Nepali language skills blossoming in no time flat with such individualized attention, which will help you immensely, both in the clinic and in the community. Language is the key that unlocks doors, Benny-bhai, especially here in Nepal."

Extracting a pack of cigarettes from the inside pocket of his suit coat, he withdrew a slender stick and set it smoldering with his butane lighter; only then did he say, "Do you mind, Benny-bhai?"

The look on his face was one of, *Try not to judge me too harshly; we all have vices.* I was shocked that Dr. Singh was a smoker, and I was immediately concerned for his health, but I also understood that it was common for physicians to smoke, even in the US. I gave the doctor a sympathetic nod after I'd recovered from my initial shock and said, "Of course."

"I've been trying to kick this pack-a-day habit since my wife's death, but the addiction's proven too strong."

Shifting my gaze from the doctor's cigarette to the parking lot behind the clinic, I noticed a white VW Bus had shown up there. It appeared to be in remarkable shape, given its age.

"By Vishnu!" said Dr. Singh, following my gaze, "I almost forgot. I want you to have my van, Benny-bhai, so that you're not hampered in your ability to give talks in the surrounding communities. It belonged to an old boyfriend of my wife's—until he abandoned her, and it, for the beaches of Goa. Now, I know your organization prohibits you from owning motorized vehicles, but Mr. Madhu has generously agreed to be your driver, as long as it doesn't conflict with his other driving duties or his work here in the clinic."

"Dr. Singh, are you sure?" I replied. "That's incredibly kind of you."

I was floored by the doctor's generosity, and I couldn't believe my good fortune. Madhu and I showed off my new wheels to my Peace Corps friends the following Tuesday night at the Rum Doodle. Bronte, in all his uniqueness, eventually christened the vehicle Stella'! as in, Stellar!—a name that, according to him, described not only the craft's appearance, but also the freedom it would afford.

"Why, think nothing of it," the doctor said after giving me the van. "I simply want to ensure that you have every advantage possible so that you might succeed brilliantly in your post. Now, follow me, Benny-bhai, if you would."

I hadn't expected everything to come together so quickly. I understood that the details of my post would be sorted out more thoroughly in the days and weeks to come, but I was glad for the doctor's suggestions and his willingness to bring me into the Pepsicola Community Hospital.

We slipped back into the clinic. The doctor insisted I follow him to the dispensary for tea and a formal introduction to the rest of the clinic staff. One of my first observations about Dr. Singh was that he never sat still. He was always shifting his position and trotting to his next destination. I knew he had a busy professional life filled with one commitment after the next, but I wasn't sure if the man ever relaxed. I also got the impression that he was a relentless self-improver, that he was the type of man who was motivated by the need to avoid feelings of weakness or dependency. I paused at the dispensary's entrance, but the doctor quickly ushered me into the room and encouraged me to take a seat among the half-dozen or so crew members, all of whom had apparently amassed for the occasion.

An awkward silence fell over the room as I settled in on one of the benches. When I glanced around to smile at my new colleagues, I was taken aback by the curious looks on their faces. Each crew member seemed to be processing my various physical features, their eyes immediately drawn to my short, dark brown hair—which was probably sticking up in a million different directions, as it usually was—my dark-blue eyes, and the fairness of my skin. They scanned my heart-shaped face for any salient features that might indicate my motivation, lingering too long, I worried, on the dark stubble of my perpetual five o'clock shadow. I felt self-conscious about my appearance, wishing I'd shaved for the occasion, but I hated shaving; the maintenance never seemed to end.

The crew continued to size me up, gazes pausing on my broad shoulders and my long, thin limbs. The medics and administrators alike also appeared to take a keen interest in my clothing, at the way I wore my snap-fastened shirt untucked and my shoes unlaced. They seemed particularly intrigued by the pair of Oakley knockoffs I'd hung from one of the front pockets of my shirt, unselfconsciously leaning in to see if the glasses were real or fake. I felt like a bit of a slob around the men and women of the Pepsicola Community Hospital, who were all well-groomed and put together. I felt like the dumpy American who'd come to the Third World to flaunt his superior tastes and culture only to realize that he was impossibly outclassed. There, in the dispensary that evening, I made a mental note to better my look. It would take time and a dedicated effort, but, at that moment at least, it felt like the right thing to do.

I shifted my gaze to a collection of unusual photos hanging on the cramped room's walls, hoping to slink away from the limelight. The photos, framed and protected behind glass, showed a man jumping from an airplane, a man firing the blast valve of a hot air balloon, and a man free-falling from a trestle, his feet bound with a bungee cord. It took me a moment to realize that Dr. Singh was the daring adventurer in all three photos.

Dr. Singh was the one who finally deflected the attention that was being heaped upon me. "I'd like you all to meet the newest member of our team here at the Pepsicola Community Hospital," he said, radiant in his pronouncement. "This is Benjamin Creed, a Peace Corps volunteer from America who's come to our community as a health volunteer. God willing, Benjamin will be with us for at least two years."

The doctor, turning toward me, continued. "Benjamin, let me speak for all of us here at the clinic when I say that we are *very* excited you've joined us here in this community. We'll do our best to ensure that your transition to life in Nepal is smooth and comfortable. Isn't that right, gang?" he said to the others, who bobbled their heads from side to side in agreement. Continuing, Dr. Singh began introducing my new teammates.

"You've already met Mr. Madhu," stated the doctor. "Mr. Madhu is my first-class, grade-A wingman. He handles all the most important duties when I'm not in the clinic, including manual disimpactions, breast pump demonstrations for new mothers, and the provision of rabies shots to dog-bite victims. I'd trust him with my own life, as you should with yours."

After this formal introduction, Madhu smiled broadly in the unassuming way I would come to know and appreciate over the coming months. The Tarai native, a shy guy with a serious penchant for polo shirts and dress slacks, would be one of my best friends in Nepal, I already felt it in my bones.

"To my left," Dr. Singh continued, "is the lovely Ms. Kabita Koirala. Kabita comes to us from the far western edge of Pepsicola Townplanning, and brings with her a refreshing style, charisma, and wit all her own, evident through her designer salwar kameez and shawl collections and the sharpness of her tongue. If you should ever need a partner for debate, Kabita should be your first choice," he insisted. "She's in charge of dispensing the medicines, keeping the supply log up to date, and ordering new liniments, demulcents, and salves for the clinic."

I smiled at Kabita after Dr. Singh had finished introducing her. She returned my grin and then quickly averted her gaze. She was young—younger than both Madhu and me—but she'd clearly already done well for herself. I didn't know it at the time, but Kabita's English was among the best in the group, and over the following months, we'd have many in-depth conversations about the similarities and differences between life in America and life in Nepal.

"Next is Mr. Arjun Thapa. Arjun was raised on unpasteurized goat's milk, as you might have guessed from his ample biceps and well-developed physique," Dr. Singh explained, flexing his own biceps for a visual demonstration of his point. "He's the clinic's bouncer, and he collects our fees."

"Whoa, whoa, whoa. Hold on a second, Dr. Singh," I said, but my gaze was on the tough-looking thirty-year-old who was fidgeting with the edge of the tablecloth. "A bouncer? Hired muscle? You're kidding me, right?"

"Oh no, Benny-bhai," Dr. Singh said. "I'm being completely serious. Our clinic is located in the rough quarter of Pepsicola Townplanning, didn't you know? There are many *goondas*, which you might call thugs, in this part of the community who'd like nothing more than to access our minimal, yet potent, cache of seminarcotic drugs. Arjun is our great deterrent, however, and we have no problems with thuggery as a result."

Arjun, who, I would learn, spoke with a weird click of his tongue and who possessed a strange shoulder tick, always kept quiet around me, probably for those reasons, as well as because he didn't speak great English. But his exuberant hand gestures and exaggerated facial expressions left little doubt as to the thoughts he was trying to express. He looked every bit the part of a Bombay mobster, with his slicked-back hair and his face full of scars, except we weren't in a giant city; we were in a place innocently called Pepsicola Townplanning, where small community hospitals needed bouncers to fend off militant addicts.

"Sitting beside you is Ms. Shruti Bhupani," Dr. Singh continued. "Weighing in at an auspicious 108 pounds, she may be tiny by Western standards, but let there be no doubt: Ms. Shruti packs quite the wallop when it comes to keeping the clinic in tiptop shape and 100 percent germ-free. She also makes the finest lemon tea in all of Pepsicola Townplanning, and that's a fact you can hang your hat on." Dr. Singh cocked his head to the side and shifted his gaze to the adorable child on her lap. "And the little sweet potato sitting on Shruti's lap is her lovely daughter, Annu, a pigtailed gossamer who's *crazy* for the color pink."

"Namaste," mother and daughter said quietly in unison.

Shruti, whose shiny black hair was pulled into a tight ponytail, couldn't have been much more than thirty. She was a pretty woman, and she had the loving face of a nurturer. Her nose, freckled and pierced with a small stud, was long and slender, and she wore an elegant *bindi*, a purely decorative dot no bigger than the eraser end of a pencil, low on her forehead. Instead of making her look sad or tired, the small creases evident in the skin around the edges of her eyes spoke of a mother's wisdom.

Annu was beautiful too. Her dimpled cheeks bookended a priceless smile. Like her mother, she possessed mocha-colored eyes, but the skin of her face was smoother and creamier. Her nose, while pierced and studded like her mother's, was slightly broader. A tiny bindi shimmered just above her eyebrows on the midline of her forehead.

"Shruti and Annu have prepared a room for you in their home," explained Dr. Singh. "I think that, in their company, you'll find that slice of the real Nepal for which every visitor to our country seems to be searching."

Every part of Nepal was the *real* Nepal, as far as I knew. I expected to see many beautiful landscapes during my time in the country, but I had no illusions that I'd find a part of the kingdom untouched by the hands of globalization. I'd already seen the extent of development in Kathmandu, and I knew how impoverished the country was. I'd already seen how the seemingly timeless traditions of the past merged awkwardly with the impatient ways of modernization.

I refocused my attention on Dr. Singh, who was still speaking. "Shruti-*didi* has made excellent preparations for your arrival, and she will keep you strong with twice-daily servings of dal bhaat tarakaari."

I smiled at Shruti and Annu and thanked them for their willingness to shelter me during my time in Nepal. They, in turn, broke their reserve and expressed excitement about getting to know me on a more personal level.

Dr. Singh spun on his heel and introduced the clinic's final member. "Sitting on your other side is young Mr. Rakesh Chandrabanshi. Quite frankly, we're not sure why Rakesh-bhai is here, but we like his company, and he occasionally brings us fresh *pakodas* and vegetable *momos* to snack on, so we let him stay!" Dr. Singh cackled as he playfully landed a kidney punch on the skinny man with the hooked nose. The young man somehow managed an awkward smile-wince.

I took the doctor's candidness and friendly demeanor as indicators of how our relationship would unfold over the coming months. I felt inspired to somehow make an even more unwavering commitment to the clinic and the community than the one I'd already made by becoming a Peace Corps volunteer. I wanted to achieve beyond what competency demanded. I wanted to impress Dr. Singh, to go above and beyond his expectations of me.

"And there you have it, Benny-bhai: the cast and crew of the Pepsicola Community Hospital. We're all very much looking forward to getting to know you and your American customs during your stay with us here in Pepsicola Townplanning.

"If it suits you, Benny-bhai, you'll kindly assist us here in the clinic, and I'll periodically challenge your knowledge of physiology and pathology in true professorial fashion. Your Peace Corps focus is on public health education, and I suspect a good portion of your time will be spent out in the community, delivering talks on the issues we discussed earlier. I might also suggest developing lectures on the importance of boiling water, burying human waste, and building chimneys for better ventilation. But all that, as you know, is up to you. Here at the clinic, we work from three o'clock to seven o'clock, Sunday through Friday. The days will be short, but the work intense and challenging; I can assure you of that. The toughest job you'll ever love, indeed."

I saw no indication of violent crime—or thuggery, as Dr. Singh had called it—during my first two weeks in the neighborhood, despite what he'd said and what Arjun's presence implied. My new colleagues and neighbors seemed friendly, grounded, and genuinely pleased to have a visitor from abroad in their midst. The outpouring of kindness was almost embarrassing.

But then, every quiet night I walked home from the clinic, my self-consciousness washed away. I would watch the men and women who worked the community's nearby rice fields settle in for their night's rest while their children, still full of energy, lingered in the paddies to play hide-and-go-seek. Traffic was almost nonexistent within the community, apart from a few businessmen on their Hero Honda motorcycles returning from a long day at the office. Often, from a radio somewhere within earshot, the enchanting sounds of a Hindi *ghazal* floated softly through the sweet evening air. Each night, my stomach fluttered with excitement as it sunk in anew that I was home.

I had learned even before reaching my post that Pepsicola Townplanning—also simply known as Pepsi—had received its unusual name due in large part to a dilapidated yet still functioning Pepsi-Cola bottling plant located close to the banks of the mighty Manohara River. Snaking its way around the neighborhood, the river formed natural eastern and southern boundaries around the otherwise rapidly developing community.

In the middle of the Manohara River, on extensive sandbars, sun-drenched sukumbasis wearing loose-fitting rags sifted silt through makeshift grates to eke out a living. Tenant farmers worked small plots of spinach, cabbage, carrots, eggplant, cauliflower, radishes, and rice near the bottling plant and waited for contractors to plow under their fields and plop a new housing development on top. As it was, the fields—each of which was no larger than the infield of a professional baseball diamond—merged awkwardly with the neighborhood's new houses in what resembled a patchwork quilt when viewed from on high.

Kathmandu's newest suburb had been nothing more than a giant rice paddy until just a handful of years before, according to Dr. Singh. The rate at which Pepsi was growing was truly staggering in a country where development typically moved at a snail's pace. It would be only a few more years, Dr. Singh thought, until there were no plots of land left for the farmers to work, their *zamindars*, or landlords, selling the ground from beneath their feet in favor of lucrative development contracts. I understood the developers' desire to get ahead, but it was sad and disconcerting that farmers were being pushed off land. It was hard to say who had more of a right to the land, but I understood that once a new, multistory concrete house had been built, that plot of land would be lost to the farmers forever. The idea of building designer homes in some of the valley's most fertile areas didn't seem very wise to me, as food security was always an issue in a place like Nepal.

Affluent families began moving to the neighborhood in search of a quieter and less polluted existence as the city of Kathmandu ballooned into the countryside. The new occupants constructed large houses built primarily of concrete and ambition—ambition for better lives for themselves, their aging relatives, and their young children. While the new houses' designs were collectively homogeneous and best described as blocky, boring, and grotesque in scale, families seemed to take particular pride in the vibrant color schemes they applied to their new dream homes' exteriors.

It was common, I learned, for several family members to unite in building these monstrosities, which often rose three or more stories in height. It only made sense for siblings and cousins to combine resources and share the financial burden of buying a plot, as the cost of land in Pepsi had skyrocketed with the city's expansion. The houses, once built, were often split into single-family units, the units' size depending largely upon the individuals' financial contributions to the buildings' construction.

The neighborhood took on the appearance of wartime Europe, as many of the new houses were still in various phases of construction. With holes in their exteriors still waiting to be patched and plastered, and long, pipe cleaner–like strands of rebar popping out of load-bearing columns on the uppermost floors, the houses looked like the recipients of a missile strike from an enemy combatant. Only the Buddhist prayer flags and banners flapping freely in the wind on many of the rooftops betrayed the locale as Asian, not European, circa early 1940s.

The neighborhood's social dynamic was a microcosm of the larger social fabric of Nepal. While class divisions between the rich and the poor were blatant, all those living within the community seemed strangely fine with their status and state of affairs. People, despite their situations, seemed genuinely content, as long as they had enough food to eat, enough work to perform, and relatively easy access to their friends and family. My impression, right or wrong, was that the struggles and frustrations of upward mobility didn't weigh quite as heavily on the minds of Nepalis as they did those of middle-class Americans, although many of Pepsicola Townplanning's newer residents came from wealthy backgrounds and were financially set.

The ground level in many of the new houses was reserved for commercial tenants, the sometimes sticky boundaries between commercial and residential zoning clearly not a contentious issue in Pepsicola Townplanning. The shops, or *pasals*, ranged from Internet dens to grocery stores and were how new property owners creatively raised the money to cover their monthly mortgage payments. Bulky padlocks on sliding steel garage doors—the kind of sturdy doors commonly seen in the bazaars and along the commercial thoroughfares of Asia—protected the shops from after-hours vandalism.

You could find orphanages, grade schools, car and motorcycle repair shops, a small produce market, a Hindu temple, and a stand selling freshly killed chickens within the neighborhood. A rectangular patch of nappy greenery in the middle of the community had been left undeveloped, claimed by Nepal's national football team as its rough-and-tumble home pitch and practice *maidaan*. It was possible on any given morning to watch the strikers hard at their trade in intrasquad matches. Usually a small group of boys co-opted a corner of the pitch to indulge their insatiable cricket cravings. Cricket, just as it was for young Indians, was more than just something to pass the time for Nepali boys; it was a way of life.

I could see the majestic purple spires of the Himalayas to the north on clear, cloudless days. At other times, a thick haze of pollution rendered the mountains impossible to see. While the pollution in Pepsicola Townplanning was lighter than that in Kathmandu, there was no escaping the stranglehold it had on the valley; there were just too many two-stroke engines spewing fumes into the air.

The neighborhood's grid of dirt roads were gouged and pockmarked with the holes and ruts left by lorries transporting building materials and fill to job sites. The potholes were so large that, following monsoon rains, I'd been told, you could easily float a small boat across their great expanse. They'd even been rumored to have swallowed small children, or so parents in the community had fibbed to their little ones to keep them out of mischief and harm's way.

It was on a well-beaten path around the community's perimeter that I performed my daily ritual: morning runs, my legs setting a brisk tempo for my heart to match. Farmers, shocked by the sight of a ghostly white apparition moving at top speed through their slumbering community, would often stop their work to stare. Soon enough, my once-private six o'clock ritual became a community-wide one, faithfully rousing a small gang of boys from bed to match my strides. The children's little arms and legs pumped like pistons as they huffed and puffed and struggled to stay by my side. "Hello, sir! Hello, sir! Where are you going?" I found their shouts endearing and knew they were fueled by a genuine and friendly excitement and curiosity.

While it's true that the enchantments of postmonsoon Nepal are manifold, of all the things that made me pause in lighthearted amusement, the aerial acrobatics of kites in the hands of those very kids and their friends intrigued me the most. Kite flying in Nepal is more than just an attempt to keep a piece of fabric in the air; it is all-out aerial warfare. Holding tightly wound spools that spun like well-greased prayer wheels, the kids played out their lines with incredible speed and dexterity so that, within less than a heartbeat, their kites seemed to be miles away, dancing with the clouds surrounding the craggy peaks of the Himalayas. Then the barefooted children, with a few deft moves of the wrist, would try to cut their mates' lines with their own, which were booby-trapped with an interesting assortment of homemade weaponry, from wads of sticky bubble gum to the crushed shards of old light bulbs. It appeared the ordnance was extremely effective, given the large number of mangled kites I'd seen hung up in nearby trees and draped over power lines throughout Pepsi.

The human members of the community all settled down for a restful night's sleep when dusk descended on the neighborhood, protected from the earsplitting roar of jumbo jets landing at the nearby international airport by a large earthen berm. Meanwhile, the neighborhood's four-footed residents, packs of roving, feral dogs, took control, picking fights with cows, water buffalo, and domesticated pets while ripping garbage bags to shreds and spreading their rotting contents around Pepsicola Townplanning. Shruti, overprotective of her new guest and tenant, made it very clear that I should always take a taxi right to her doorstep after late nights on the town. She believed that a juicy Westerner would be quite the prize among animals roaming the neighborhood. I appreciated her concern, and I promised her I'd be extra careful.

It was October in Nepal, and throughout the country, Dasain—Nepal's most significant annual festival—was in full swing. The fifteen-day festival is celebrated primarily in villages, but I could still easily spot telltale signs of it throughout Pepsi. For example, the residents erected on the football pitch a giant bamboo swing, its four thick, sturdy legs lashed together at the structure's apex. The community's children swung for hours in graceful arcs from the long ropes. A self-propelled wooden Ferris wheel called a *roti-ping* had been lodged in two neighboring trees. It was clear that Dasain was one of the children's favorite holidays, considering the squeals of delight emanating from them during their play.

The merrymaking was also evident within my new home, an unpretentious single-story cottage constructed of mud, orange brick, dung-caked walls, and polished earthen floors. Shruti planted a handful of barley seeds in specially prepared soil as an offering to the gods to ensure a plentiful harvest. She'd also deep-scrubbed the entire house to welcome the cleaner air of the postmonsoon season.

Her house was at least eighty years old, according to Shruti. Its humble appearance stood in marked contrast to the mammoth new concrete buildings popping up all over Pepsi. The use of concrete, Dr. Singh told me, was intended to showcase a family's wealth. In essence, then, there were *two* Pepsicola Townplannings: a concrete-and-plaster one for the new elites and a mud-and-brick one for the impoverished, longtime residents.

That year, my arrival was part of Shruti's festival cleaning. She and Annu had kindly rearranged their home to give me a whole room to myself, leaving them a single bed to share in what was not only their bedroom but also the kitchen, living room, and dining room. I felt more than a little guilty about taking up so much space in their house, but Shruti and Annu refused to consider another arrangement. I suspected that Dr. Singh, who had lived in the UK for a number of years while attending medical school, had passed some insight along to Shruti regarding the typical Westerner's expectations of personal space, which was a good thing, because I indeed craved privacy.

Not far from the house was a *charpi*, a latrine shared by several families. I quickly realized that cleaning the charpi, while ensuring the necessary standard of hygiene, was not to be one of the more enjoyable aspects of my life in Nepal.

The cold showers that I took on daily basis were, however, perhaps even more unappealing than cleaning the charpi. I had the option of sponge bathing with warm water in a stall behind the house, but I lacked the patience necessary to heat the buckets of water on the propane stove in Shruti's kitchen. It wouldn't be long, I imagined, until the Kathmandu Valley's chilly winter temperatures forced me to abandon showers in favor of less frequent sponge bathing.

One of the most wonderful parts of my daily life was listening to the fast-moving stream, or *khola*, rushing by Shruti's house. It served as both an irrigation source for the surrounding fields and a nightly tranquilizer for me, its calming gush faithfully lulling me into a deep and restful sleep, most nights.

My room, consisting of a bed, a simple desk, and a wicker chair, was located at the house's rear. Standing in front of the room's small rectangular window, I could look out over a field of crops worked by Shruti's brother, Achu Pahari, a part-time farmer, or *kisaan*, who lived in the house next door with his wife and their young daughter. I'd occasionally catch a glimpse of a cow or water buffalo meandering along one of the many footpaths that carved their way through Shruti's backyard.

Achu owned both of the houses and the land upon which they sat. This differed from many of the other farmers in the community, who paid a landlord for the privilege of working their plots of land. As the oldest—and only—son in the Pahari family, he had inherited the fields from his parents, and they were his to do as he pleased. I spoke with Achu on numerous occasions about farming in Nepal, and I realized early on that he was a different breed of farmer. He was running his biodynamic farm, he told me, "to take care of cosmic energy by using only strictly organic inputs." I wasn't exactly sure what this meant, but it seemed that he had the land's best interests in mind, and that sounded good to me.

He also had his sister's best interests in mind, doing his utmost to ensure that everyone treated Shruti, and Annu, with kindness and generosity. I was completely unaware of it during those early days in Pepsi, but I soon came to learn from Dr. Singh that devastating events had rocked the family.

Shruti's spouse—or *mister*, as husbands are commonly called in Nepal—Bharath Bhupani, a talented mechanic in a local auto repair shop, had simply vanished on Annu's sixth birthday, according to the doctor. Authorities thought foul play was involved at first, but after they investigated his disappearance, they ruled out any criminal connection. Rumors began flying around the community about what had happened to Bharath. Some believed he'd been kidnapped by Maoist rebels; others thought he'd disappeared into the Nepali underworld.

Rumors continued to morph over the following months, with some people saying that Bharath had taken another spouse in India, and others saying he'd renounced the material life entirely and gone on an extended pilgrimage. Whatever had happened to Bharath, he'd left his family in a real bind. Shruti and Annu probably would've ended up on the streets of Kathmandu if it hadn't been for Achu's graciousness.

The stress of not knowing what had happened to her husband or why he'd chosen to leave Pepsicola Townplanning had taken its toll on Shruti, according to Dr. Singh. She'd cried for months during that period of great mourning. Still, she was only in her early thirties, and she was a beautiful, vivacious woman. I got the impression that, if she wanted to marry again, she would have no difficulty finding an excellent mate.

Shruti, because she was still unaware of her husband's whereabouts and his true reasons for leaving, had not yet divorced Bharath on the grounds of desertion or neglect. My presence in her house had sparked minor outrage and drawn condemnation from conservative elements within the local community, people who felt that Shruti wasn't living up to the expectations of her station in life.

The more progressive thinkers within the community realized she could use the extra money a tenant would provide and had reached out to convince the others that there would be no real harm in letting me stay with her. One lingering loud exception, however, was nosy, opinionated Old Kumar, a cantankerous widower who lived just down the street.

The grizzled, ossified, and senile Kumar, who was stooped severely at the waist and who walked with a cane, blathered to anyone within earshot about how shameful and scandalous it was for Shruti to take another man into her house. Thankfully most people just ignored him, and he usually kept to himself. But every now and then, he'd fly into a fit of rage outside Shruti's house and bang his cane loudly on the door until his son, apologizing profusely for the old man's belligerent behavior, came to collect him. Old Kumar's language was coarser than the earth worked by the neighborhood's farmers, according to Shruti.

Situated in the middle of a small chowk in the village's center, not far from Shruti's house, was a stately *bodhi* or *pipal* tree, which I would come to affectionately call a people tree. The people tree was an exceptionally old and sacred fig tree under whose branches community members would gather to engage in *gaph garnu*, the chatting about all matters of daily life from local gossip to international politics. Lovers, executives, and shopkeepers all spent time under its broad, leafy branches during their leisure hours. The village drunk, Manmohan Bishwakarma, could often be found at its base, passed out among its twisted roots after a long afternoon of boozing. It was also there that Shruti would rendezvous with Amrita Thapa, Arjun's mother, for her daily cup of goat's milk after her ritual morning *puja* at the local temple. The calcium-rich drink, fresh from the udder, had been prescribed by Dr. Singh to help buffer bone loss as the diminutive Shruti advanced into her thirties.

After two full weeks in the neighborhood, I found that Pepsicola Townplanning was becoming my home, my community, and my base of operations. Pepsi was the place from which I would launch my search for something larger than myself. I would come to travel extensively throughout the country, but I could always count on that place as a retreat from the clutter and commotion of more chaotic venues. Pepsi was the place to which I could always return, a destination and a place of familiarity, all at once.

Winds of Change

LATE ONE WARM SUMMER NIGHT, BETWEEN SHUTTLE RUNS, I TOOK ADRIANA to Maxwell Family Field—a multiuse sports field in the shadow of formidable Bowles Hall and the towering Berkeley hills. We walked out to the middle of the empty field and stood in silence, facing each other under the light of a full moon. My heart beat wildly in anticipation of the question I was about to ask her.

"Adriana," I said, "if everything was different, if we'd met under different circumstances, would you be with me right now?"

"Yes, I would," she said, without a moment's hesitation. But her answer had come too quickly, and it made me wonder if what she had said was genuine or if she were simply trying to avoid hurting my feelings.

"Then what are we doing here, Adriana?" I asked, plumbing the depths of my deepest fears. "Why can't you and I just *be* together?"

She took a deep breath, pounded her fists against her thighs, and said, "Because, Benjamin, it's just not that easy, OK? I have more to think about than just my own happiness. I have to think about my parents' wishes and the future and…and…a whole bunch of other stuff, which I have very little control over. You have to understand that Manny's family helped my dad get established when he came to America, and my dad feels a sense of obligation to repay them for their generosity. I love my family, and I don't want to risk alienating them over a decision like this.

I know it probably sounds ridiculous to you, and it's not what I want, but it's just the way it is. I'm sorry that everything is so messy, Benjamin. I just hope you can understand where I'm coming from. I think you're an incredible guy, but you have to give me some space, OK? You have to let me sort things out before anything can happen between us."

It seemed that any hope of a romantic relationship with Adriana was slipping away after our full-moon talk. I knew she had plans to visit India on a month-long vacation with Manish and her family after she finished her summer session, which would complete her degree in public health. She had always been nearby since I first met her, and I feared that, in that month-long separation from me and with such proximity to Manish, she would be lost to me for good. Her business in Berkeley was almost done, and I wasn't sure if I'd ever see her again.

I fell into a state of inconsolable sadness on the day she was scheduled to leave for India, unable even to call her to wish her farewell. What I didn't know for several days was that, just moments before taking off, the plane's crew had to abort the transpacific flight due to a power outage at San Francisco International Airport, which in turn had forced the cancellation of the da Rosas' trip. I assumed she had taken off for a month-long holiday, but instead she was tucked away in her parents' home in Fremont, just fifty minutes from Berkeley. So when I received the e-mail from Adriana that read, *Boo! I'm here in Fremont. Want to hang out in SF?* I thought she was just playing around, pulling a prank on me from the other side of the world. I was overwhelmed with happiness when I read further and realized that she was serious. In fact, I had never felt so energized in my entire life.

The morning after receiving her e-mail, I stuffed my backpack with food and drinks, hopped onto a BART train in downtown Berkeley, and headed for San Francisco to meet Adriana. The sky was cloudless, and the thermometer hovered around seventy-five degrees. It was a beautiful summer day, a perfect day to share with the person I cared about most. While the waters of San Francisco Bay were placid that morning, my own stomach was churning with excitement at the thought of spending the entire day with Adriana.

* * *

I leaned back against the basket's railing and watched with curiosity as a long lick of flame leaped from the burner through the mouth of the hot air balloon's synthetic envelope to warm the surrounding air. Dr. Singh, dressed in a red jumpsuit constructed of natural fibers and sporting a pair of goggles, looked every bit the part of an experienced aviator.

I recalled the pictures in the clinic dispensary, laughing at the activities the doctor regarded as "routine." Skydiving, hot air ballooning, bungee jumping—it didn't really matter what he was doing, as long as it was adventure taken to the extreme. He had worked his way into his mid fifties, but he didn't seem to be slowing down. If anything, his appetite for excitement was growing, the others at the clinic told me, as he neared retirement age and found himself with more free time to devote to his passions.

I had never been much of an adrenaline junkie or thrill seeker, but the invitation to join the doctor for some ballooning over the Kathmandu Valley was too good to pass up. Still, now that the balloon—which had been ripped and patched in more than a few places—was the only thing keeping me from plummeting to my death, I felt more sober than excited.

I told myself to just relax and enjoy the ride, that this wasn't as extreme as some of Dr. Singh's other hobbies. I took a few deep breaths of the crisp morning air and settled in for the flight. I did look forward to spending time with the doctor in a venue that wasn't the clinic.

Over the burner's thundering roar, Madhu's voice crackled across our two-way radio, his words filling the basket with a cheeriness that felt incongruous to our on-the-edge situation. "Yes, hello? Testing, one, two. Testing, one, two. How do you be copying, Kathmandu Klipper? Over."

"We copy loud and clear, Mr. Madhu. Loud and clear. Over."

"Yes, hello again, daai. I am being in the bus now, with the Arjun. We will be keeping our big eyes looking up on your progresses, and we will be staying as close as possible. All the best with the rest. Madhu, over and out."

"Roger, Mr. Madhu. Over and out."

I could see the retired Chinese school bus pulling away from Nagarkot, a small resort town about twenty miles east of Kathmandu. Dr. Singh had long ago bought the bus from the city of Kathmandu to serve as a retrieval vehicle for his aerial outings.

The valley's floor was still largely bathed in the shadows of dawn, but I got a clear sense of just how expansive the valley was. I'd had an aisle seat on the flight into Kathmandu from Bangkok, which meant that I hadn't seen much of the country's scenery.

At the standard rate charged by local ballooning companies—around two hundred dollars per hour—I was having a morning of leisure costing close to the annual income of an average Nepali citizen. With Dr. Singh I rode for free, but knowing what well-heeled tourists paid for an hour of leisure highlighted for me the utter wealth disparity between America and Nepal.

"You have never known the true meaning of bliss until you have drifted gently over the countryside on the wind's whims." Dr. Singh smiled and seemed to become more tourist than pilot himself, once the altimeter indicated we'd finally reached our desired elevation. "Peace and quiet reign supreme up here, Benny-bhai. And smell that air! No pollution! Did you know that breathing the air in Kathmandu for one day is the equivalent of smoking three packs of cigarettes?" He turned to me, serious. "Let me be frank, Benjamin: the only way a young person can survive this city is to occasionally breach its boundaries, to blast off and get some fresh air in his or her sails."

On the horizon, the rising sun's rays lit on fire the upper flanks of the heaving Himalayan massif, including the breathtaking peaks of Melungtse, Cho Oyu, Gauri Shankar, and the all-mighty Sagarmatha. A band of lush green flora around the valley's rim played host to countless terraced fields, their jagged edges standing in stark relief against the foothills' rolling contours. A number of villages, each made up of a dozen or so red-tile-roofed houses, perched in the hills. And scattered throughout the valley, looking very lonely and isolated, were a handful of stone stupas.

Within the valley's boundaries were an abundance of cultural and architectural riches, not the least of which were its numerous UNESCO world heritage sites, its temples, and its strong Newari influence. Kathmandu was like a living museum; its relics were venerated by the devout and photographed by travelers from around the world. Not mutually exclusive

from its treasures, however, were the less savory aspects of its complex character, including pervasive sickness and disease, the nonstop badgering of an entire army of beggars, and the ongoing problems of air and noise pollution.

I shifted my train of thought, listening closely as the doctor began to speak again. "There are big changes on the way for the people of my country—your country now too, Benny-bhai." Nepali society was becoming increasingly homogenized as the hereditary caste system of Hinduism began to disintegrate, according to Dr. Singh. Unfortunately, although the caste system had been condemned by the government and shunned by progressives, discrimination based on its precepts was still an integral part of life in Nepal. The longstanding divisions among Brahman, Chhetri, Vaishya, and Sudra castes, according to the doctor, were still evident in the society's power structure.

Besides the social stratifications, there were self-defined ethnic groups, including the Magars, Rais, Limbus, Tamangs, Sherpas, Gurungs, and Tharu. One of the most prominent ethnic groups, based on their historical access to the centers of higher learning, wealth, and power, were the Newars. Newari art, architecture, and culture could be found everywhere throughout the Kathmandu Valley. This population, at over one million strong, made up roughly 5 percent of Nepal's national complement. The Newars, who practiced a form of Hinduism that incorporated Buddhist elements, had made a name for themselves over the centuries as talented farmers, artisans, and aristocrats. They were also believed to be the traditional inhabitants of the Kathmandu Valley. Many of the people I'd met in Kathmandu were Newari, including Shruti and Annu.

And thanks to Shruti, who was an incredible cook, I was coming to love Newari cuisine. The Newari diet incorporated meat from goats and water buffalo along with the standard Nepali vegetarian fare of greens, beans, and rice, the latter of which was eaten beaten or boiled. I hadn't felt hungry for a single moment since I'd moved into her house, and it wasn't unusual for Shruti to fill my plate two or three times after I really ought to have called it quits.

My astounding ability to consume food had impressed not only Shruti but also the entire community, most of whom were proud to have such a voracious eater in their midst. They seemed to take my prodigious food consumption as a huge compliment and a sign of respect for and acceptance of their culture. I also found it amusing how many of my neighbors in Pepsicola Townplanning knew exactly how many servings of dal bhaat tarakaari I'd had the night before, or how many *rotis* I'd consumed for breakfast.

Dr. Singh repositioned the gimbal and opened the blast valve. I watched as another searing quiver of fire shot upward. The prevailing winds largely dictated our path through the air. The plan, as best we could control it, was to head west and slightly north so that we'd skirt the grounds of the international airport and Pepsicola Townplanning while avoiding drifting too far away, into Bhutan, Burma, or Bangladesh, as Dr. Singh joked. The tentative set-down point was a large field on the far side of Swayambhunath, Kathmandu's monkey temple, at the valley's western edge.

"Can you see the exodus unfolding beneath you?" wondered Dr. Singh. "Countless men and women are returning from their home villages to swell the city's ranks now that Dasain's over. I've been told that you can see the migration from space, but I suspect this is simply the musing of a well-intentioned yet semideranged friend. But I digress."

Shifting my squint from pilgrims I couldn't see to Dr. Singh, I studied his face for clues to his past. A smudge on his forehead indicated his most recent past: on the tenth day of Dasain, Vijaya Dashamei, a community elder had blotted a red tika on his brow.

I looked down at the valley, at all the villages scattered within its margins, and thought about the people I'd met in my post thus far. I'd spoken with many young men around Pepsi who, along with their spouses and children, had been the first in their families to leave their villages and relocate to the city. Most of the men enjoyed the conveniences and comforts of life near the city and had found decent jobs to help pay the bills, but all shared a love for their villages. They also expressed disdain for recent increases in urban pollution levels, crowding, price hikes, scarce commodities, strikes, thefts, murders, kidnappings, and other unappealing aspects of city living. Each would have packed up his family and headed back to rural Nepal if financial considerations weren't an issue.

"So, Dr. Singh," I said, "how come you didn't go back to your village for Dasain festivities? I thought every Nepali had a native place that tugged at his heartstrings."

"My commitments at Bir Hospital make it very difficult to take a leave of absence when so many others are on holiday," he explained. "Besides, I've been living in Kathmandu for as long as I care to recall; surely you can understand my hesitation to leave the city. It wasn't always this way, Benny-bhai. But you must understand that I'm so far removed from life in the village that going back now would only expose me as clumsy and uneducated in the ways of my peers. I *do* feel the Nepali yearning to keep one foot firmly planted in the fields while the other strides into modernity, but I'm afraid the allure of creature comforts has hastened my departure from any agrarian roots I may once have had."

There was something odd about the doctor's response. I knew that he had plenty of pull at Bir Hospital and that he could easily have gotten a few days off if he wanted, and yet he refused to leave the valley to visit his native place.

"And what about your family?" I asked. "It seems as though the Singh name carries considerable clout here in Kathmandu."

He licked his chapped lips. "Benny-bhai, a man in this society is only respected if he lives up to the legacy of his forebears," he said. "For me, the only son in my household, there was little choice but to embrace the estate I had been entrusted with. My ancestors controlled vast tracts of land throughout the kingdom, and as the last in a long line of Singh men, I've become, by default, the principal beneficiary of their spoils. Now, my dear wife and I did not have any children, so there will be nobody—no family members, at least—to whom I can pass my estate." Dr. Singh paused, lost in thought. "You know, Benny-bhai, Margaret passed away many years ago, but I choose to remain unattached to any other woman out of respect for her memory. Her death affected me on the deepest possible level."

"I'm sorry for your loss," I said.

"Thank you, my boy," said the doctor. "I feel the burden of grief most acutely each year with the coming of Dasain. Those feelings of loss weigh so heavily upon me during the holiday that, without calculated intervention, I fear I would slide into an inconsolable state of grief and remorse. When I feel the telltale prickle of those emotions, that's my cue to get active, to do something that gets my mind off my suffering and rejuvenates my spirits. Ballooning is just the prescription to center a wandering mind."

Dr. Singh took a lungful of air in through his nostrils, expanding his broad chest fully before continuing. "Benny-bhai, I think you'll come to find that you'll achieve the highest possible quality of life when you engage your most meaningful passions at full speed, when you seek out those things that focus your creativity and your desire to serve humankind and make them the centerpieces of your life. Ballooning, skydiving, bungee jumping—these things are all well and good, but none of them would mean anything to me if I couldn't be a doctor."

"What do you mean, Dr. Singh?"

"What I'm trying to tell you, Benjamin, is that there's no greater pleasure in life than serving your fellow humans," he said. "It's the very *nature* of my Nepali brothers and sisters—the quality of their characters, to be precise—that compels me to heal their wounds and take up their cause. While it's true that a doctor doesn't necessarily have to be passionate about healing to be effective, it just so happens that I am one of the passionate ones. It's my great hope, Benny-bhai, that, through your interactions with the fine, upstanding citizens of Nepal, you will find a limitless supply of energy and passion to carry you through your life. It's my hope that simply by coming to know the moral fiber of these men and women, you will be *compelled* to continue working for good and just causes in this world."

I took a moment to let the doctor's words sink in. I appreciated the way he passed along his wisdom. He had vastly more life experience than I did, but he wasn't forceful or condescending, just encouraging and courteous. Every day that I was around him, I could feel myself changing in subtle ways. I had come to understand, even during what short conversations we had had during my time in Pepsicola Townplanning, that Dr. Singh was a man who believed deeply in the innate goodness of humanity. He was an optimist who looked past the obvious flaws and shortcomings to see only the finest qualities in his fellow human beings.

Dr. Singh lived in a country where corruption was the norm, but he refused to write anybody off, refused to believe that some people were driven only by self-interest and the desire for money, notoriety, and power. And he refused to believe that certain realities in life could make change for the better almost impossible. He did expect big things from the people around him, and he held everybody to a higher standard, but he was also quick to forgive people for their weaknesses and render assistance when they needed help or advice. Patience and compassion were more than virtues for the doctor; they were the rules that governed life.

The Kathmandu Klipper drifted steadily over the valley on a light breeze. Kathmandu's tortuous streets and the surrounding lumpy terrain made me think of the veins on the back of a gnarled, old hand.

The doctor tended to the balloon before focusing his attention back on me. I felt my defenses go up immediately, despite his casual attitude and relaxed posture. "You're not like your peers, you know. Very few would willingly have given up a charmed life in America to wallow in the trenches of Nepal. In case you haven't noticed," he said, pointing down at the city, "this is *not* an easy life for most. I've lived in the UK—I know what an easy life is! So, tell me, Benny-bhai, because I'm incredibly intrigued—of all the places you could have chosen, and of all the possibilities available to a young man in your situation, why did you decide to come to Nepal?"

I leaned my back against the basket's railing and folded my arms across my chest, taking a few moments to absorb and process the doctor's question. I often struggled to express my thoughts and feelings in the moment, but I wanted to get it right this time. The truth was, I had many reasons for joining the Peace Corps and coming to Nepal, but some of those reasons were more admirable than others. Guilt, loss, and the need for redemption were all mixed up with other, more politically correct reasons for volunteering. I did want to talk it all out so that I might myself fully understand, but I knew resolving my personal problems needed to take a backseat to the commitment I'd made to the Nepali people through the Peace Corps.

I also understood that the doctor would respect me no matter what I said—heck, he'd probably welcome my honesty—but he was still my mentor. He was still the man that I looked up to as a teacher and a role model, and I didn't want my motivation to seem anything less than focused and pure. The answer I gave him needed to validate his decision to invest his time, energy, and resources in me, while remaining as true as possible.

I looked out over the valley and tried to tread lightly. "Well, it was pure luck—or destiny, maybe—that I was chosen to serve here, but I guess I've always wanted to come to Nepal, to be dwarfed by the mountains and humbled by its people." I shrugged. "My mom once told me that Nepal's the kind of place where a person can find answers to the great questions of life. And there was just something so compelling about the idea of joining the Peace Corps and learning about life abroad." I threw in one more point, hoping to steer him far enough off course to change the subject. "Not to mention, after the last decade or so, America's got plenty of wounds to heal and a lot of ground to make up in terms of international relations. I figured a little diplomacy would go a long way."

"Ah, yes," he replied, looking dubious but refraining from pursuing the discussion further. "Good answers, all." He grinned broadly. "So, are you enjoying your time in our small community hospital, Benny-bhai? I do hope you are. It was my hope that, in requesting additional personnel for our busy little clinic and the Pepsicola Townplanning community, we'd attract an ambitious person like yourself. Before you were selected for your post, your Peace Corps country director, Mr. Swenson, assured me that all candidates would be vetted based on their interests and aptitudes. I must say, Benny-bhai, that your presence in the clinic has breathed new life into my work. You should also know that Madhu, Shruti, and everybody else at the clinic are very excited you're here with us in Kathmandu. Did you know that only a very small percentage of the Nepali population has direct contact with people from outside the country?"

I knew the doctor was right, although I didn't know the exact numbers. Only a small portion of Nepalis—excluding those with ties to the massive tourism industry—encountered people from around the world. The Internet had opened many virtual doors for people in Nepal, however, especially among those in the younger set, who were extremely tech savvy and exploited the resource for business and social networking purposes.

"You're the first of your kind to join us in Pepsicola Townplanning, and your presence in the clinic is mutually fortuitous, I think, as there is much to be learned on both sides, Nepali and American. Yes, Benny-bhai, your presence in the clinic and the community is our great cross-cultural experiment!"

Indeed, the staff peppered me with questions on a daily basis and poked holes in the most common cultural myths. Our exchanges not only provided information about what they saw as a very strange way of living but also gave them a chance to hone their English-language skills. In the meantime, they had, along with my official tutor, taught me an increasing amount of Nepali, such that most of our conversations in the clinic were now carried out in a strange verbal fusion of the two great tongues.

My understanding of the Nepali language, while improving each day, was still rather basic, but I felt liberated to be immersed in a new language and be able to speak with my kindhearted new friends in the way in which they were most comfortable. Despite my lean vocabulary, the Nepalis never missed an opportunity to praise me, and I loved them for that. I didn't deserve their high praise, but their encouragement kept me striving to learn more.

Dr. Singh inquired, "And what do you think of your duties in the clinic? Please, any comments would be greatly appreciated."

It had only been a relatively short time since my arrival in Pepsi, but my role in the clinic had evolved to the point where I, alongside Madhu, was taking patient histories and recording the findings from physical examinations. I had also organized and was about to conduct my first public health campaign with Madhu, an ambitious initiative that emphasized the importance of consuming protein and brown rice and also the three Bs: boil your water, bury your excrement, and build a chimney. The three Bs, if carried out properly, would help the residents of Pepsicola Townplanning ward off all sorts of acute and chronic disease.

But public health education involved more than simply talking, so I had petitioned the Peace Corps for funds to help residents build communal latrines throughout the neighborhood and smokeless stoves in the kitchens of many of the community's older homes. I called my initiative Charpis and Chimneys. The funding hadn't come through yet, but I hoped that very soon my extracurricular health and sanitation program would take hold and improve lives.

"The pace is just right, I think," I said, thankful for the doctor's guiding hand. "There's so much to learn."

"Yes, indeed there is." A look crossed his face, but before I could prepare, he switched back to the topic I had tried to avoid. "Not the least of which is how to better mask your answers to elude a lengthy explanation. Look, Benny-bhai, I know there is more to your presence here in Nepal than you're willing to admit. I *know* this. I sense a strong yearning within you to come to terms with something beyond your immediate ability to reconcile. I suspect your bashfulness and your presence here have much to do with a wound from your past, although this is simply conjecture. And, with all due respect, I suspect you're not even fully aware of how your feelings have guided your life choices." His body language wasn't exactly confrontational, but it did demand my attention. His chin lifted slightly and his head cocked, he seemed to say through his posture, *I know where you've been, so why don't you just tell me the truth? Why don't you just tell me the whole story? I dare you.*

Though startled by his keen powers of observation, I looked him squarely in the eye and smiled. He had, of course, hit upon the truth, and I was mildly annoyed by his ability to read me where countless others had failed. But I wasn't going to admit any of that. "Maybe some other time, Dr. Singh," I said. "It's a long story."

"Very well, very well." He chuckled softly. "You can't squeeze juice from a stone."

We continued to sail over the valley as the sun crept higher in the sky. "Benny-bhai, if you look in a southeasterly direction, beyond Tribhuvan International Airport—which is a no-fly zone for dirigibles such as the Kathmandu Klipper, by the way—you should be able to see some of the more prominent landmarks of Pepsicola Townplanning," the doctor said, pointing, "including the Manohara River, the football pitch, and the great Pepsicola pipal tree in the neighborhood's center. Do you see them?" he asked, pointing toward the landmarks.

I squinted and leaned out over the basket's railing. The neighborhood looked so small and insignificant relative to all of Kathmandu. But it was *my* neighborhood. Pepsi was the place where, with the help of the doctor and the clinic staff, I had carved out a small and fragile niche for myself.

I felt as though my life had a purpose there. I gripped the basket's edge with those thoughts in mind and tried pinpointing the exact location of Shruti's house, but we were too high up and too far away for my eyes to discern that level of detail.

Slowly bobbling his head from side to side, the doctor said, "The neighborhood has grown so drastically over the past several years, Benny-bhai. It's very different from the peaceful enclave it was a decade ago when I first began my post at the Pepsicola Community Hospital." There was a far-off look in his eye. He lived and worked very much in the present, and claimed as much, but something about him remained stranded in the past.

"You and I will have a serious discussion one of these days, Benjamin, about the merits and pitfalls of development and progress here in Nepal. Forgive me if my aesthetic beliefs prove unyielding brutes, but I'd take the ornate designs of the Newari architects and artisans any day, over the grotesque concrete monoliths popping up all over the valley. The use of concrete is, for me, a tangible symbol of the Third World's misguided notions about progress and its abandonment of traditional methods and values in pursuit of Western ideals. I believe wholeheartedly that we should be more discerning with our development decisions here in Nepal."

To a large extent, corruption at the highest levels—the inappropriate distribution and use of foreign aid and domestic resources—kept the country mired in a state of perpetual poverty. There was an incredible divide between a few relatively wealthy and powerful individuals and the impoverished masses, as in many other countries around the world. There wasn't much of an emphasis on social security either. Hundreds, perhaps thousands, of nongovernmental organizations, or NGOs, had popped up to help bring essential services to the Nepali people in the absence of social programs and easily accessible microloans for would-be entrepreneurs.

Madhu, who had been monitoring our progress from the chase vehicle, suddenly piped up over the two-way radio, sounding urgent. "Daai, weatherwallah is predicting high winds for Kathmandu Valley. Do you be copying? Over."

Dr. Singh, picking up the radio, said, "Tell me, how bad does it sound, Mr. Madhu? Over."

"Daai, tempest from the east. You must be coming down *immediately*. Over."

"Please, double-confirm," insisted the doctor.

"Yes, daai. A tempest. It is what I am saying," said the quaking voice on the other end of the walkie. The skies had indeed begun to darken, and the wind was now whipping up.

"My options are limited, Mr. Madhu. I wish I'd known about this development sooner. I'm going to attempt an emergency landing in Durbar Square. We'll meet you and Arjun there. Over."

I felt a rush of adrenaline rise from the pit of my stomach and shoot out to the tips of my fingers. The doctor's plan was logical, given the few choices available to us, but the odds of successfully landing in Durbar Square were not good. It would take extremely complex maneuvering—and much luck—to avoid people, buildings, and power lines during our set-down.

"Please be being careful for the healthiness of your fine and handsome selves," Madhu said unsteadily. "The market will be a-hustling and a-bustling at this most busy hour. Madhu, over and out."

"My goodness," said Dr. Singh, a rare look of concern etched upon his face. "You just never know when these pesky squalls will sneak up on you. I can assure you, Benny-bhai, that we do not want a tempest in our teacup. I'm going to bring us down quickly, and I suggest you prepare yourself for a bumpy landing."

Grazing the flat-topped roofs of Old Kathmandu with a swift wind at its back, the Kathmandu Klipper made a fast and furious approach into the heavily peopled square. "*Ke garne?*" shrugged the doctor. "What to do?" We were huddled together on the basket's floor to protect our faces from the whip and scratch of nearby tree branches.

"If you have any sort of spiritual tendencies," Dr. Singh said, his eyes twinkling with mischief as he gripped my shoulder and shook me lightly, "perhaps now would be a good time to fire off a prayer to the god of soft landings. I'm afraid there will be no champagne toast after this most deplorable of descents." And indeed, he was cradling a bottle of vintage vino he'd brought along for a postflight celebration.

We were headed for trouble, but I was thankful to be by the doctor's side. I somehow felt protected by him and his assurance that no real harm would come to us in the crash. He seemed so confident, even casual, in his assessment of the situation, and that was something I loved about him: he could handle almost anything with a cool head.

The Kathmandu Klipper blasted into the square between the Bhagwati and Shiva-Parvati Temples at breakneck speed. I risked a quick glance over the basket's lip to check our path and saw that we were heading straight for the Kumari Bahal, the young Kumari Devi's permanent home. The balloon cast an ominous shadow over the entire market as its bulbous bladder blotted out the remainder of the sun's golden rays. Startled shoppers looked up in horror as the penetrating, all-seeing eyes of the Buddha, which were sewn to the balloon, bore down upon them. A brown cow directly in our flight path laboriously rose from its haunches and lumbered away, tracking every inch of our rapid advance with its left eyeball, hairy and suspicious. A row of six produce vendors, our only cushion to soften the blow, tried in vain to shuffle their carts out of harm's way.

The balloon whisked past the tall, white columns of the Gadi Baithak to our left, past ladies selling jasmine tea, marigold wreaths, and sticks of juniper incense. I could smell the stench of ritualistic slaughter on the breeze, the blood of countless animals who had been sacrificed in the square during the festival of Dasain. I tried to block that awful reminder of death from my mind. Closing my eyes, I clenched my teeth and curled into fetal position in the cupped palm of the balloon's basket, bracing for impact.

We crashed headlong into the row of produce carts seconds later, the sickening sounds of wood splintering and plump melons being pummeled reverberating through our basket. Dr. Singh and I were bucked violently as the basket grated over the ground behind the still-advancing balloon. I could hear the shrieks of the produce vendors who had been struck and knocked to the ground, their carts destroyed and their small mountains of merchandise sent rolling in a million different directions. I couldn't see what was going on, but I imagined the scene in the square resembling a battlefield rather than a peaceful, early-morning market, with bodies lying broken and bleeding on the ground and mass hysteria gripping the observers. I hoped that nobody had been seriously injured.

When the basket finally lost its momentum and its destructive progression was curbed, it tipped over and spilled its payload onto a blanket of *brinjals*, their purple, spongy embrace saving us from the spank and sting of the street.

Gripping the neck of the unbroken wine bottle, Dr. Singh quickly rose to his feet, brushed a clump of lettuce off his head, and limped toward a produce peddler, who was clutching his throat with both hands; the doctor slipped twice on lemons that studded the ground around us. He applied the Heimlich maneuver, and a mouthful of melon shot from the peddler's gaping maw. The doctor gave the man, who was coughing uncontrollably, a steady series of blows on the back, I suspected both to quell his nonstop hacking and to win the favor of the surly crowd massing around us.

Bystanders began inspecting the carnage, sorting through the remains of the organic produce in the hopes of getting bargain-basement prices on damaged goods. The balloon's envelope, torn like a sheet of scrap paper, was draped neatly over a nearby taxi; the driver cautiously peeked out from beneath the fabric's folds while children tugged at its seams. From the looks of it, we'd narrowly missed a large section of bamboo scaffolding surrounding the multitiered Trailokya Mohan Narayan Temple. Skinny day laborers, hanging off the scaffolding, wagged their fingers at us.

Few people had been hurt in the accident, but a number of the men surrounding us looked extremely angry, as though they'd been personally offended by the mishap. I was worried their fractious attitude would spread, that mob mentality would overcome common sense and leave us nursing broken bones and bloodied faces. I'd heard of such things happening in other parts of the subcontinent. I got the feeling that if anybody other than Dr. Singh had been responsible for the crash, we probably *would* have been mobbed by the crowd and beaten for our blunder. The doctor carried such weight in the community, however, that once the men realized who was to blame, they simply backed off and left us alone. The commotion in the square began to die down with their departure.

After examining the other injured people, Dr. Singh limped toward me and assessed my physical condition. "Looks as though you've got a few bumps and bruises, Benny-bhai," he noted. "Are you in any pain?"

"My neck's a little sore," I said, slowly turning my head from side to side. "But I think it's just a strain. I'll be OK. How about you?"

"It would appear that I've wrenched my lower back again." He grimaced as he twisted his torso, first to the left, then to the right. "Just when I was convalescing from my chronic lumbago, there I go abusing myself again. I'm getting far too old for these kinds of impractical stunts!"

I heard our chase vehicle's screeching whinny as the doctor continued to berate himself for what he called a "Himalayan blunder." When they pulled up, Madhu and Arjun hopped from their seats and raced over to help right the toppled basket. Madhu then helped the doctor and me climb aboard the bus while Arjun gathered up the balloon's envelope and the bottle of Chianti.

"Mr. Madhu, please arrange for reparations to be made with these vendors," Dr. Singh said. "They mustn't be further inconvenienced. Please inform them that they'll have the full measure of my resources at their disposal to replenish their stock and repair their carts." Many other notable men around Kathmandu would have simply shrugged off their responsibility for the vegetable vendors' well-being. Dr. Singh had class and panache. He was a master of human relations, one of those rare people whose influence and impact in the community always seemed to live up to the reputation that preceded him.

After Madhu finished chatting with the vendors and loading the rest of the balloon's equipment, he climbed into the driver's seat, jabbed the key into the ignition, and sparked the bus to life. The doctor and I, still shaken from the accident, sat forlorn and embarrassed in our seats.

Smoke and Mirrors

I FOUND ADRIANA WAITING PATIENTLY OUTSIDE THE EMBARCADERO BART station. There, after lingering in an embrace, surrounded by the coming and going of complete strangers, we laughed for a long time about her family's harmless but inconvenient bad luck. I could see in her eyes that something had changed. But I was too afraid to ask if that something involved Manish. I was too afraid of getting my hopes up only to have them crushed by her answer.

"Let's have a fun day together," she said. "Let's try to suspend everything that's happened over the past few months and just start fresh, OK?"

We strolled north along the Embarcadero, past shops selling kitschy souvenirs and long lines of camera-toting tourists preparing to embark on guided tours of Alcatraz. I bought a pair of tickets to Angel Island at Pier 41. To be all alone with Adriana while the rest of the world was going about its business was a very special feeling. I felt as though the day was ours, that we somehow owned it. We were both young, full of hope, and free of commitments—at least I hoped both of us were.

We sat side by side on the grass and soaked in the sun once we reached the island. We talked openly and from the heart, about life, love, and the intricacies of being human, oblivious to the families, lovers, and drunks who periodically passed by.

We then hiked through eucalyptus groves and stands of Portuguese cork oaks and Monterey pines on our way to the top of Mount Livermore, the highest point on the island. We took in an incredible panoramic view of the Bay Area from the summit, including the San Francisco skyline, the Bay and Golden Gate Bridges, Mount Tamalpais, and Alcatraz Island. We could also see the Marin Headlands, Tiburon, Sather Tower—the bell and clock tower on the hilly campus of UC Berkeley—and numerous ferries arriving at and departing from the Embarcadero. It was an amazing view, made all the more special by Adriana's presence by my side.

Unzipping my backpack, I pulled out a bottle of red wine and two wine glasses, and we toasted the freedom of youth. We marched back down the gently graded earthen trail to the ferry terminal after we finished the bottle, just in time to catch the last boat home.

We landed at Pier 41, the alcohol still buzzing in our veins, and headed toward downtown. There we visited art galleries, strolled through the Castro, and shared a lamb curry at Pakwan in the Mission before it was time for Adriana to head home.

As we walked together toward the BART station where her mother would be waiting, she turned to me and said something that stopped me dead in my tracks. "I feel like I should kiss you." She waited several seconds and then spun on her heel and continued slowly toward the train station.

She didn't act on her proclamation, but I would never forget those words or the way she'd said them. I would never forget the mischievous twinkle in her eye, either—a look that wiped clean the months of frustration, confusion, and pent-up emotions, a look that offered the promise of something long-lasting between us.

It was as though that moment of palpable tension between us was the window of opportunity for which I'd always been waiting. And that's exactly what her words had been, in hindsight: an invitation to hold her close and let all the repressed love I'd felt for her flow forth in one passionate embrace.

I'd waited so long for her to reach that point of readiness, though, and I'd misread so many signals before that I had no idea if the time to kiss her had finally come. She hadn't said anything that would lead me to believe she'd broken it off with Manish, which in fact she had—something I would learn several weeks later—and I didn't want to do something that would make her feel uncomfortable. There had always been a barrier between us when it came to physical contact, a precedent Adriana had established and insisted I respect while she was dating Manish.

So I stood there, like an idiot, and simply watched her walk away.

* * *

It was November in Nepal and, like everybody else in the country, I was caught up in the celebration of Tihar. Tihar, the Festival of Lights, was second only to Dasain in the Nepali hierarchy of festivals. Hindus around the world celebrate it, but those in Nepal worship a select group of animals, including crows, dogs, cows, and oxen, for their religious significance and their symbolic importance to Nepali society.

Tihar, while many things to many people, is most universally about worshiping the goddess Laxmi, the deity responsible for wealth and good fortune—meaning, for the largely agrarian Nepal, a bountiful rice harest. It's also an opportunity for sisters to express love for their brothers by wishing them long, healthy lives and for brothers to give their sisters gifts or money in return. The fourth day of the festival also marks the beginning of the Newari calendar, when executives clear their accounts and hope for a profitable year to come.

I sat quietly on the Maju Deval temple's uppermost tier, sandwiched between a trinket seller and a pair of shy lovers bashfully holding hands. I stared down at the bustling Durbar Square, my elbows resting on my knees and my hands clasped together. The temple, a seventeenth-century beauty situated near the square's far western edge, drew the eye and commanded respect. It sported stylistic elements representing the country's two most prominent religions: a Shiva lingam for Hindus and a rooftop crown in the form of a Buddhist stupa. I'd spent many hours in that exact spot since my arrival in Kathmandu. If I was alone, which was most often the case, I'd practice my Nepali with anyone willing to chat; if no one was willing, I'd just sit there and watch the activity in the square while contemplating my Peace Corps role and the life-path I'd chosen.

My fellow Peace Corps volunteer Beth Lewis would occasionally join me, pleasantly snapping photos with her elaborate camera-and-tripod setup. She took some beautiful photos, based on the work she'd shared with me at the Rum Doodle. The photos were mostly time-lapse shots perfectly capturing the flux that defined the bustling Nepali capital. Her other photos, primarily taken during the peak market hours in the square, reminded me of the visual hyperstimulation of a Where's Waldo? puzzle. They captured everything from teenage boys holding hands to stray dogs scrounging for scraps of food and men selling speckled balloons and party favors to passersby.

The temple's uppermost tier was the perfect place from which to people-watch, as Beth and I had quickly discovered. We had seen everything from that vantage point, including motorcycle collisions; successful pickpockets; impromptu, cymbal-clanging parades; and somber funeral processions. Of course, if she'd been sitting in our usual and customary position on a certain morning not long ago, she would have seen an out-of-control hot air balloon blast into the square and ram a row of vegetable vendors.

The Maju Deval itself was a magnet for all sorts of people from around the city, and if we ever grew bored of looking out, Beth and I could just look around. Executives hammered out deals on the upper tiers of the temple, while at the shrine's base, at ground level, produce vendors and assemblers of marigold wreaths hawked their wares. The Maju Deval's steps were also a common meeting place for fashionable young Nepali couples, a place to see and to be seen. It wasn't uncommon for large groups of twentysomethings to gather there before heading off to one of Kathmandu's popular discos.

I loved observing the playful latter group, but of all the people in the square to watch, my hands-down favorites were the rickshaw pedalers. Mounted on their metal steeds, the pilots of Kathmandu's pedicabs fanned out from the Maju Deval's base looking very much like a phalanx of South Asian pedalers waiting to charge.

Some of the men were curled up napping on the narrow benches beneath their carts' protective awnings. Other pedalers stayed upright in their saddles, exchanging jokes and good-natured barbs with each other and any member of the general public who passed within earshot. "Let's rrrollll together, baby! Riiiikshaa, riiiikshaa!" they would singsong—in English—to pretty girls walking nearby.

For other potential customers, especially wealthy businessmen, the men would appeal to their senses of humor, asking questions such as, "How will you ever manage to keep your pants up with such a heavy wallet, sir? Let us save you the embarrassment of a bare-ass moment!" And to the men stumbling toward their motorcycles after last call in the bars of Thamel, the waiting rickmen could be often heard to shout, "After whiskey, driving risky, boss! Think of your missus!"

Though everyone rode from time to time, tourists were the most profitable passengers, because they wanted to meander or travel far, ask sightseeing questions, tip generously to assuage their Western guilt, or any combination of the above.

It was true that the stress and strain of a predominantly manual existence hung themselves like yokes around the men's necks and shoulders, but they possessed a certain camaraderie and entrepreneurial spirit I hadn't seen matched in any other industry in Nepal. In fact, the Third World spirit of survival that had already humbled me on so many occasions was never more evident than in the rickmen, or *rickshawallahs*, of Kathmandu. With their sinewy calves and their gaunt, hungry faces, they embodied the very essence of what it meant to scrap and battle and claw away at a living, and I respected them for that reason alone.

With that thought in mind, I bounded down the Maju Deval's steps and headed straight for the closest pedicab. My blood sugar levels were beginning to flag after rock climbing with Beth for several hours earlier that afternoon at the Pasang Lhamu indoor climbing wall, just off Ring Road to the northeast of Old Kathmandu. On Beth's recommendation, I decided to go to a local dessert bar and hookah lounge called Slice of Life Bakery, where she promised I'd find enough sugary treats to satisfy a whole army of taste buds. The chocolate cake, according to her, was world famous and shouldn't be missed.

"*Hajur*," I said, catching the rickshawallah's attention as I walked toward him. "*Tapaailaai kasto chha?* How are you?"

"*Malaai dheraai sanchai chha! Tapaailaai ni?*" he responded. "I am doing very well. You?"

"*Ho, Malaai ekdum raamro chha!*" I replied. "Yes, I'm also doing very well."

A large grin broke out on the man's face when he heard me, a bideshi, speak his mother tongue, and based on the exuberance of his response, it was probably even rarer for somebody to ask him how he was doing. He must have assumed I was more fluent in the language than I was, however, because he began speaking too fast for me to follow.

"*Bistaarai, bistaarai bolnuhos,*" I said, laughing. "Slower, slower, please. *Ma ali ali Nepali bolchhu. Mero Nepali raamro chhaina!* I only speak a little Nepali, and the Nepali I do speak is not so good!"

"*Khahaa chha?*" he said. "Where to?"

"Slice of Life Bakery *maaj laanuhuncha?* Do you know this restaurant?" I said.

"*Tkk chha!* Slice of Life Bakery *ekdum raamro chha! Aaunus!*"

By standing fully erect, his feet flat on the wooden pedals, the man imparted maximum leverage and torque into the cycle's cranks and cogs. It didn't exactly make for a blazing start out of the gates, but it did get us moving in the right direction. I found it almost hypnotic from my vantage point to watch the man sway back and forth, bobbing from side to side as he ground his trike's pedals, so it took me a moment to react after we'd coasted to a stop in front of Slice of Life Bakery.

Once I'd finally snapped out of my trance, I grabbed my backpack and jumped down from the rickshaw. I fished a wad of rupee notes out of my pocket and paid the pedaler our agreed-upon fare, plus a healthy tip. I shook hands with the man, stepped back, and watched as he again stood tall in his saddle and slowly swung the bulky craft back in the direction we'd just come from.

I strode with purpose toward the entrance of Slice of Life Bakery. I'd heard many rumors about the place—that it was, for instance, more than just a dessert bar and hookah lounge. In the cakeshop's dimly lit confines, according to Beth and others, mingled a crossroads of career criminals, thugs, pushers, and mercenaries, the occasional pair of young Nepali lovers, and a steady stream of adventurous backpackers.

Alongside stacks of cheesecakes, cannoli, truffles, and tarts of all kinds, a broad selection of cobblers, crumbles, and chocolate discs generously sprinkled with rainbow-colored nonpareils served as scrumptious window dressing. A fresh, unsliced chocolate cake took a place of distinction on the display case mantle. The cake had been the restaurant's signature offering since the sixties and seventies, when hippie travelers interested in exchanging everything from countercultural ideas to bodily fluids had congregated and commingled under the restaurant's roof. I knew I'd have to try at least one piece as part of my initiation into the sugary subculture of Slice of Life Bakery.

I went inside and sat down at a table that afforded a good view of everything going on around me. I kicked back and let the cakeshop's details soak into my brain. The Doors played softly from one corner; it was a spooky, down-tempo track. Cake-seeking patrons had stuffed all sorts of memorabilia from their global travels between the heavy, clear-plastic table covers and the scarred wooden tabletops. Snapshots, ticket stubs, and movie posters had been placed alongside business cards, journal entries, and personalized notes—all for the amusement of future sugar cravers.

At least four of the tables were "possessed," shifting within the room to befuddle customers, according to what Beth had witnessed and heard. The tables, hardwired into a switch beneath the restaurant's main counter, often shook violently or released a puff of fog into customers' faces as they hunkered over their desserts.

One of the tables had been programmed to slowly grow taller and shorter, such that it could creep up to a person's chest, and then, only moments later, be down around the person's knees. Another spun at a rate of one revolution per hour—a speed indiscernible to the human eye but one that rotated desserts and drinks far enough away from patrons to provoke serious vexation. The victims' embarrassment proved a reliable source of amusement to those already aware of the tables' subtle designs.

I surreptitiously glanced at the other people busily snacking away in the restaurant. I didn't see anyone I would immediately associate with the Nepali underworld. The scene was chill, it was mellow, and given everything I'd heard about the place, it was completely unexpected.

I placed my order with a young waiter and watched with curiosity as the boy passed the order to a Chinese man wearing a powder-blue leisure suit and matching tie. The man's long bangs were swept to the side of his face, and he moved in odd, whirling motions, as though he were dancing to a song different from the one playing through the restaurant's speakers. The restaurant's quirky maître d' set a large piece of chocolate cake on a plate and danced his way over to my table. He then bent low, bowled the plate toward me across the tabletop, and disappeared into the kitchen, speaking not a word.

I immediately buried my face in the dessert. The cake was rich, moist, and dense as a brick, a heavily iced wedge of heaven that lived up to all the hype. I tried to savor its various textures but instead found myself wolfing it down and ordering a second round. I dropped my fork after finishing that next slice and pushed the plate of crumbs away.

I lifted my head just in time to see a pair of shady-looking men enter the restaurant. Taking a moment to thoroughly scan the joint before continuing inward, the men exchanged a few indecipherable words before heading directly toward me. They asked if they could join me at the table, but then they sat down and made themselves comfortable before I'd even had a chance to reply.

The men weren't like other Nepali men I'd met. They were too polished, too ready to approach me without a formal introduction. There was something else odd about them. It took me a few seconds to clue in: in their body language, in their too-friendly demeanor and their way-too-slick approach, they reminded me of a pair of seedy gem brokers who had approached me over three years earlier, in Manali, in northern India. They looked insincere to me, and I hated insincerity; it was the personality trait I most despised in others.

The men were gem scammers, I was sure of it, representatives of an illicit industry that thrived along the subcontinent's major tourist thoroughfares. Together, often with the help of desperate Westerners, the men worked like a pack of wolves to bring down lone, unsuspecting tourists. They used a number of different tactics, everything from flattery to shame, to achieve their aim, which ultimately involved the sale of worthless stones for resale in the tourists' home countries—unsuccessfully, the victims would discover too late. Fortunately for me, I knew their strategies and their game, and I knew the men were not to be trusted. I might have felt threatened by the pair if I hadn't already seen how their kind operated, but all I felt was annoyance that they had targeted me.

The larger of the two introduced himself as Grishma and his partner as Binod. I shook their hands reluctantly, hoping they'd read my body language and lose heart. But no such luck, of course: they were professionals, and they wouldn't be easily shaken. The men offered to buy me another piece of chocolate cake.

"Sorry, guys, but I've really got to be going. I've got a big Tihar dinner tonight, and I don't want to be late," I said, and it was the truth. Shruti was busily putting together an epic feast to celebrate the Newari new year. The evening would be a large, raucous gathering of her extended family, according to her, and I was looking forward to celebrating with so many new friends.

The men insisted I stay longer, suggesting that they, as my new friends, had an offer that was too good for me to deny. "Brother, we'd like to make you a very rich man."

"Look, guys, I'm already a man rich in the ways of the world." I tried to be coy. "Besides, I make eight thousand rupees a month, which is more than enough to cover my expenses."

"Who needs the ways of the world when you could have fabulous material wealth?" Grishma persisted. "Why would you want to just get by when you could be filthy rich? Think about it. You could do anything you want. It's easy." Grishma spent the next ten minutes sweet-talking me before he cut to the chase. "You buy our gems for what amounts to pocket change for you, and then you take them back to your country for high resale. You could earn at least five thousand USD, no problem." After making his pitch, Grishma swiveled in his chair, placed an index finger to one nostril, and blew a stringy snot rocket onto the floor of Slice of Life Bakery.

The shop had come alive as late afternoon slipped into the early evening hours. A hazy cloud of hookah byproduct—the airborne remnants of molasses tobacco and fruits such as cherry, orange, and apricot—curled and wafted lazily down a pressure gradient created by the frequent entry and exit of patrons through the shop's front door. The aromatic blend of respired fog mingled with the exhaust-infused cocktail of the street.

"So why don't you guys just go overseas and sell the gems yourselves if the market's that lucrative?" I played.

"Please, brother, you must understand how the odds are stacked against us," pleaded Grishma. "We must pay a 250 percent tax on the export of all stones to North America. How could we ever survive without the help of our friends like you? Oh, Binod, look…it's Klaus Kieler!"

A large German with dirty-blond, shoulder-length hair—a man equally as greasy and repulsive as the two Nepalis—had conspicuously entered the restaurant at the peak of their spiel. The man, whose nose was bent from too many back-alley brawls gone wrong, sauntered over to our table at the insistence of Grishma and Binod, sat himself down, and shook hands with all before lighting up a cigarette. I wouldn't have trusted Klaus with my laundry, let alone anything requiring a substantial investment of money.

"This is our friend, Klaus," said Grishma. "He's had much success in selling his gems back in Germany."

I began rummaging through my backpack for my wallet.

"*Queeray!* Fucking whitey!" Grishma hissed and pounded the table with his fist as I stood to leave. My plate fell from the table and shattered on the floor.

Raju Shrestha, the restaurant's truly imposing owner, emerged through a beaded doorway behind the counter to address the commotion. "Who dares steal the Great Raju away from his beloved hookah?" Spotting the men, he cursed loudly and smacked his fist on the counter. He then deftly vaulted over the cash register and tackled the sleazy trio as they darted for the door, upending tables and spilling drinks in his aggressive pursuit. With Grishma and Binod secured bilaterally in headlocks, Raju applied the Boston Crab to the lanky German, viciously retroflexing the Caucasian's back and lower extremities to dangerous angles.

"*Schiesse! Schiesse!*" gasped a distressed Klaus as he slapped the restaurant's floor with a free hand.

"What am I telling you *kondo ko dulis* about the harassing of my customers?" barked a furious Raju, tightening up his aggressive lock on the Nepalis' necks. "*Mero nunilo gula chus, maa chiknes!*" he screamed. "Lick my salty balls, motherfuckers!" Even after Raju had thrown the men into the street, he kept after them, repeatedly kicking them in the seats of their pants to promote maximum public humiliation.

Raju reentered his shop, reorganized his shoulder-length black hair into a high ponytail, and began the task of bringing the restaurant back to order. He apologized profusely to his customers for the unanticipated fiasco, and he offered everybody a round of chocolate cake and sticky buns on the house. The peace offering was well received.

Beth had said Raju was highly respected on the local scene, for both his street smarts and his business savvy, and he was considered by many to be a sort of rough-and-tumble street philosopher. With his small hoop earrings and large, expensive-looking rings, he looked like a man perpetually aware of his image, but it was hard to tell if maintaining an image was his obsession or simply a way of life.

"Those rascally fellows are no good," Raju said, fixing me with a penetrating stare. "You must be aware of their low moral quality. Perhaps I can explain better what it is I am trying to tell you. I am owing this to you, at least. Please, come with me."

Raju led me around the same counter over which he had leaped just moments before. He then turned up the volume of the restaurant's sound system before parting the beaded curtains that led into his private lounge.

The retreat was larger than I had expected. A group of swarthy men reclined with several beautiful Nepali women on plush Moroccan-style cushions that flanked the cracked and peeling walls. Under the lime-green tint of the room's principal light source, the stylings of Pink Floyd provided a slippery slope aiding the men's descent into the clutches of a heavy heroin stone. A series of mirrors along the walls lent their own trippy vibe and allowed a person to keep track of the room's activities from almost any vantage point.

Raju led me to a pair of beanbag chairs in an unoccupied corner of the lounge. We were free to speak openly, the high-decibel music acting as a shield of silence.

"Bahraini molasses," said Raju, nodding his head toward a *chillum* he had prepared, I assumed, just moments before all hell had broken loose in the restaurant. "By far my preferred type of *shisha*. Here, you must take a draw."

I'd never smoked a hookah before, but I didn't want to look like an amateur in the eyes of the Great Raju. I put the mouthpiece between my lips and meekly bubbled the water pipe. Trying this ancient South Asian tradition had been on my radar for a long time, and I was glad for the introduction.

"Your first time?" The expressionless Raju could not be fooled. "You should have told me. I did not mean to make you feel uncomfortable." I was surrounded by a horde of dangerous men, I was sure of it, and Raju's main concern revolved around my lack of experience with the water pipe?

The cakeshop owner grasped his own mouthpiece and sized me up with what was quickly becoming to me his trademark penetrating gaze. "I am not a man for the pretense, so let me just say that I am often seeing you around Kathmandu, and if you don't mind me asking, Mr. Benjamin, I am being curious about your business here in the city? *Tapaai ke kaam garnuhunchha?*"

I was strangely honored that Raju knew my name, but his familiarity with my presence in Kathmandu left me feeling uneasy. "I'm a Peace Corps volunteer," I said. "I work in a small healthpost on the outskirts of Kathmandu. My friend Madhu and I periodically run public health campaigns in some of the local neighborhoods, and we'll be helping community members build chimneys and latrines." I observed a perceptible change in Raju's body language—an exhalation.

"Ah, excellent, my friend," he replied. "You are giving something back to our country. Let me be one of the first to thank you. *Tapaai kahaa basnuhunchha?* Where is it you are staying?"

"I'm staying in Pepsicola Townplanning, not far from the clinic that I'm working out of."

"Yes, I am knowing the healthpost you are speaking of now. It is staffed by first-quality people. Anyway, I was afraid you were here to make trouble for me, to bring the police down on me, but I should have known better." His deep voice was calm and unwavering. "As a volunteer with your Peace Corps, you are a welcome brother in our great country of Nepal, and a friend of Nepal is a friend of Raju. The chocolate cake will be provided to you free of charge from now on." He waved his hand in the air as though money were no concern.

"Well, that's a very generous offer, Raju," I said. "I'll be sure to take full advantage of it."

It wasn't unusual for people in Nepal to shower volunteers with gifts, food, or praise once they learned we were with the Peace Corps. Affiliation with the organization conferred almost rockstar status. Unlike tourists, who simply helped drive the short-term local economy, long-term volunteers were seen as having a vested interest in the lives of Nepalis and in the country's development. Peace Corps volunteers, for many Nepalis, were also a flesh-and-blood link to the one thing they all dreamed about, the one thing they all held sacred: the *idea* of America.

I found the attention embarrassing and overwhelming most of the time, but there were advantages associated with fame too, advantages that almost every Peace Corps volunteer used as leverage at one time or another with authority figures, embassy officials, or other lollygagging bureaucrats. The peoples' trust and affection weren't something most Peace Corps volunteers wanted to abuse, but there was a certain belief among members that we were entitled to a bit of a free ride every now and then. If that meant playing the Peace Corps card to speed up the bureaucratic process or strike a deal with a local shop owner, volunteers wouldn't hesitate to let their status in the country be known. Was it right? Probably not. Was it convenient? Absolutely.

I glanced around the room again and took a leap, asking Raju about the other men there. "You see that man over there, in the opposite corner?" Raju motioned with his eyes toward a character with a baseball cap pulled down over his eyes. "He's killed five men…this week. The balding man beside him, along with the two men examining cigars in the humidor, are responsible for the trafficking of young girls over the border into Indian brothels. And this man"—Raju shifted his gaze to a man passed out on a couch—"controls a ring of poachers that is driving the trade of rare pelts and highly prized organs."

Oh god, it's worse than I thought. I swallowed hard and tried to keep going.

"But these are all indictable offenses, Raju. How can you feel comfortable in the company of such men?" I said. "These are truly dangerous people." But that was the very worst path to go down. I was becoming emotional and heading into dangerous waters by passing judgment on the men Raju hung out with on a daily basis.

"You are right," he said, nodding his head slowly and leaning back in his beanbag chair.

"I am?" My voice cracked. "I mean, yeah, of course."

"It is true; these men are the worst of the worst," he admitted. "But do you know what, Mr. Benjamin? They are also understanding how the world has kept away from them the opportunities for advancement. You have *no* idea how far some men will go for a taste of what you might be calling a normal life, something that is not possible in Nepal through regular means. What these men have done, right or wrong, is sidestep oppression, and they are living like King Gyanendra right under the authorities' noses. There's a certain, how do you say, perverted element of justice in all of this," explained Raju. "You must be seeing this."

Raju was right: most of the men sitting in his private lounge probably had recognized the invisible, oppressive hand of structural violence and were combating it in their own ways, be they hard crime, corrupt business transactions, or black-market profiteering. The darkness and cruelty in their methods, however, sent a chill down my spine.

"But these men," I whispered to Raju, "are willing to ruin the lives of others just to get ahead. How can you make peace with these crimes?" My words were stern and, in them, there was a demand for accountability and a need for Raju to repent for the horrific crimes the men had committed. I needed a good answer from Raju, and I needed it immediately.

"Are you meaning to tell me that Western peoples have not made incredible riches off the backs of Third World laborers and resources?" he said, countering my question. "While the crimes these men have committed, and will be continuing to be committing, are severe, are they not simply expressing the desires that all men feel? I am asking of you what it is that is so wrong with a man's desire to live a life that is not poverty, illness, and hunger?

"I will also say this, Mr. Benjamin, because I am seeing it even in your own eyes, that even a good man, a Peace Corps man like yourself, has the possibility of some cruelty in his soul. So I am then asking you who it is who is worse: the good man who, fearful of his true desires, violently suppresses his fears, or the bad man who faces his fears head-on, recognizing that his desires are too powerful to be denied? The only point I am trying to make, Mr. Benjamin, is that sometimes we are too easily fooled by our own sense of righteousness, of what it is that is right and of what it is that is wrong. In Nepal, this understanding is not so easy, I think."

Raju had found a way to address my question without landing too firmly on one side or the other. On the one hand, he knew things were never black and white in Nepal. He knew that people living in abject poverty were justified, in many ways, in bending the rules to suit their needs. On the other hand, he didn't condone the crimes of his peers, or at least he didn't condone their crimes' severity.

His actions were particularly confusing, however. He had risked the reputation of his restaurant just moments before by chastising a few low-level thugs, while truly bad men—men who made life miserable for the masses—reclined in luxury in his private lounge. Both his extreme passivity and his extreme aggression made me uneasy.

On top of that, I found the veracity of his words disconcerting. *That whole bit about seeing the cruelty in my eyes? What was that all about?* It was as though he had looked straight into my soul and seen all the things that haunted me most. It was as though he had seen the damage I had done to myself and others in the past, damage I would never be able to fully repair. I wasn't sure if he was referring to those regrettable moments, or if he was referring to the possibility of projecting that cruelty onto others in the future. Either way, I found his assessment so upsetting that I resolved never to bring up the topic of morality with him again.

"I am liking you, Mr. Benjamin." Raju whipped the metaphorical tuk tuk we were on into a sharp turn. "The conversation, it is…stimulating. Now, *khaanaa khaanu bhayo?* Are you hungry?"

"Yeah, I guess I am," I said, amazed that my appetite had returned so quickly after gorging myself on the chocolate cake. "*Malaai dheraai bhok laagyo!* I'm very hungry!"

Raju stood and suggested we hit the streets for a bromantic evening stroll and some *pani puri* at one of the local food carts. The snack would tide me over until my big Tihar feast later that evening.

The blue hues of early evening smudged the city's shadowy recesses. A pair of young boys dressed in ratty jackets and yak-wool beanies squatted around an oil drum that served as a table for the popular Nepali board game they were playing, known as *bagh chal*, the moving of tigers. Another group of children was playing a game called *carrom* on chalk-marked tables. The game, a type of finger snooker, reminded me of crokinole, which I had often played with my grandfather when growing up.

We strode confidently through Durbar Square; I had one eye trained on the street and the other on the buzzing mecca of evening consumers. The shouts, shrieks, and hollers of bargaining shoppers and vendors pierced the evening air. There were porters and cabbies and beggars and palmists, as well as commuters on their Hero Honda motorcycles and men pushing portable peanut and ice cream stands throughout the crowd.

There were touts too, slithering their way through the massing crowd, diligently on the prowl for pale-skinned foreigners who could easily be coerced to stay at a local hotel, eat at a restaurant, or join a guided tour. I was immune to their advances with Raju by my side. The touts dared not enter our perimeter of personal space; doing so, they understood, would result in nothing less than a severe public beating by the hands of the cakeshop owner—a pound cake of an entirely different variety.

Raju insisted we visit a nearby temple complex called the Hanuman Dhoka before reaching the portable pani puri stand that usually parked somewhere between King Pratap Malla's Column and the White Bhairab. He wanted to make a quick votive offering to Hanuman, the monkey god of *Ramayana* fame.

Before entering the Hanuman Dhoka, the cakeshop's hulking owner paused to embrace members of a large gang of men wearing scowls and knuckle-dusters. The men quickly stood to greet him as a sign of respect and admiration.

The men looked strangely familiar, but it took me a bit before it finally clicked: they were the same men who had wanted to lynch Dr. Singh and me after our ballooning accident! It was a testament to the doctor's reputation as a leader in the community that our bodies had been spared a beating, but he wasn't here now. It seemed unlikely that the men would remember me, but I was nervous nonetheless. I felt as though they could sense that nervousness, that they could see the little beads of sweat forming on my brow.

The men's faces were pockmarked and scarred from a life of urban combat. Their arm muscles were knotted and balled like the burls of an old oak tree, and their blocky forearms were a morass of bulging, blue veins. I hadn't often felt threatened or intimidated by other men in Nepal, and now I had twice: when Raju invited me into his personal lounge, and now again with him outside the Hanuman Dhoka.

One of the men, after surveying me from head to toe, ripped off a string of Nepali grunts. Raju, wagging his head slowly from side to side, responded to the man with an equally cryptic round of Nepali. The whole group began to laugh after he spoke; while breaking the palpable tension in the air, it left me very curious.

"What did he say?"

"He is saying that he is thinking he could kill you in about three seconds," Raju said.

"Oh yeah?" I laughed feebly. I could feel my legs going weak.

"Yes."

"And what did you say to the group that was so funny?"

"I told him that you would be lasting at least *ten* seconds."

Inside the temple, Raju prepared *sindur*—a fusion of red vermillion dust and mustard oil—which he offered up to Hanuman. We left the temple when he'd completed his devotional obligations and walked the final few paces to his favorite pani puri stand.

I'd tried pani puri several times since arriving in Nepal, but I hadn't been too impressed. The pani puri from this particular cart, however, really hit the spot. Water, tamarind, chili, and bits of potato had been lovingly stuffed inside the rounded crisps to form bite-size morsels of pure bliss.

"You should not be taking pani puri from any other cart in Kathmandu," said Raju. "Everybody else uses dirty water."

I rolled the bits of chili and potato around in my mouth, smiled at the vendor, and complimented him on the quality of his food.

"Oh, thank you, thank you, sir! *Dhanyabad!*" He shoved another handful of the snacks in my direction.

Raju and I shook hands when we'd finished gorging ourselves and wished each other well. He then offered me the closest thing to a smile I'd seen from him yet.

I arrived back at Shruti's just in time to receive a tika and help with the meal's preparation. Cousins and uncles were busy stringing up tiny, multicolored blinking lights in the windows and doorways. In the living room, from which Shruti's and Annu's bedroom items had been moved, a large circle of women and children were manufacturing a batch of momos. Outside, on the narrow dirt track passing in front of the house, children riding bicycles zipped to and fro, waving long, fizzing sparklers at each other.

I considered Tihar a stand-in for Thanksgiving, given the two celebrations' temporal proximity. I'd never spent Thanksgiving outside the United States, even though I'd traveled quite a bit; this would be the first time that I wasn't able to celebrate with my family and partake in the traditional Creed family turkey, stuffing, and pumpkin pie, followed by some late-season hiking and canoeing at our tiny cabin in the Northern California redwoods. I felt incredibly blessed to be surrounded by such warm and welcoming people in Shruti's tiny home, but there was a vacancy in my heart that could only have been filled by closeness to my immediate family.

I spoke at length with Shruti's brother Achu and a handful of their male cousins while the rest of the food was being prepared. Relaxing on chairs now that they were done stringing up the blinking bulbs, the men passed a jug of water around, each man drinking from the jug without letting it touch his lips. This practice, which I'd seen performed often in Nepal, had always impressed me, not only because of its challenging nature but also because of the motivation that lay behind it: to place your lips directly on the jug's rim would be to pollute the water and render it *jutho*, or undrinkable, to others. On more than one occasion, the Nepalis had looked on in horror as I'd made jutho all sorts of communal serving spoons by letting them contact the food on my plate.

When dinner—a panoply of the finest Newari cuisine—was finally ready, we all sat down together in a circle on the living room floor. I, as an adopted member of the extended family, and as Shruti's honored guest, was invited to sample the food first; the women paraded countless dishes in front of me and scooped healthy portions of each onto my plate. "*Khaanus!*" they encouraged. "Please, eat!"

We had beaten rice, battered and fried goat lung, steamed buffalo blood and marrow, and *buff momos*. I had never been a particular fan of organ meat, but I found the Newari cuisine, which was famous for its use of all parts of the animal, to have exceptional flavor that teased the palate and encouraged multiple helpings.

Enhancing my enjoyment of the feast was the fact that the spread had been prepared in a newly renovated kitchen. Shruti had been the first person in all of Pepsicola Townplanning to receive a smokeless stove to help improve ventilation for her open-fire cooking. My Charpis and Chimneys initiative was gaining momentum on an almost daily basis, thanks to a generous grant from the Peace Corps Partnership Program. It was only a matter of time until the rest of the community would reap the associated health benefits.

A special goal of the project was to incorporate the community's women in the stove-building project. I suspected that many of the women—some of whom were illiterate and most of whom had phobias about learning—would be extremely hesitant to be involved, but I believed they would excel once given the opportunity. I knew these strong-willed women would take it upon themselves to help their neighbors build smokeless stoves in what would become a massive, snowballing effort to improve the community's health. The same was true with charpi construction, although the charpis would take longer to construct and would require more resources.

I set my plate down in front of me after the last dish had been passed around and assumed a cross-legged position. Shruti's niece, keenly aware that I had neglected her favorite snack, passed me a spoon upon which rested a spicy pickle. All eyes were on me to see how I'd respond to the offer; the men's, women's, and children's expectations that I would accept it were written on their faces with raised eyebrows and broad, encouraging smiles. I'd been in Nepal for some time now, but I'd never eaten a spicy pickle. Other Peace Corps volunteers had warned me about the Nepali pickle's smoldering potential. But the young girl had put me on the spot, imploring me with her eyes, and I couldn't squash her generosity.

I brought the zesty bite close to my lips and offered up a small prayer to my gastrointestinal tract for the sins I was about to commit: *Oh, poor alimentary canal, please forgive me for provoking your irritability through the consumption of this fiery and herbaceous curried pickle.* I shoveled the pickle into my mouth, right away sensing my body's utter rejection of the bolus careening down my throat.

Smiling as I swallowed, I gave the group a thumbs-up, a gesture that confused everyone until it was explained that, in America, the gesture was one of frank approval, not a sign of disapproval and disrespect like it was in some parts of Asia. The whole family cheered loudly at my endorsement after the confusion had been cleared up, and after I recovered from the shock of the spicy pickle, the festivities started back up again.

I thanked Shruti for the incredible meal after my third helping of food, and offered to help her with the cleanup. But she was an extraordinary host and refused to hear of it. She suggested that, instead, I should go for a short walk around the neighborhood to get some fresh air—but not too far away, she insisted, in case I should find myself alone and surrounded by a pack of rabid dogs. I threw on a hooded wool jacket that Dr. Singh had given me earlier that week, thanked the cooks again, and excused myself from the party.

Alone on the dusty street, under a November night sky lit from below by the blinking bulbs and wax candles of Pepsicola Townplanning in the throes of Tihar, I took a moment to breathe deeply and give thanks simply for being alive. I felt blessed that I had been given the opportunity to live and breathe and love my fellow human beings. It was one of those rare moments when life seemed easygoing and uncomplicated. I felt good, maybe better than I ever had before, and I began walking, ever so slowly.

I could hear the sound of a live band from somewhere on Pepsi's outer fringes. The band was playing a Nepali folk song, a song faintly reminiscent of the spellbinding tune of celebration enjoyed by the Ewoks in the closing scene of *The Return of the Jedi*. The music's magic stemmed largely from a soulful drumbeat being pounded out in a wide-open space, a beat that floated softly and melodically over the fields and fences of Pepsicola Townplanning to grace the ears of nearby residents.

The music was haunting, complex, and beautiful, and it seemed to represent a culturally deeper sound than any other music I had previously heard in Nepal. It was certainly different from the tinny, high-pitched pop music that bombarded us on the Kathmandu public transit system; that loud, obnoxious music was one of my all-time biggest pet peeves. Frozen in time, I closed my eyes and let this music wrap itself around me like a warm blanket.

The song finally ended. I turned and slowly made my way back to Shruti's brick house, a house that was symbolic of the people who dwelled within the community: solid, stable, and full of love.

I pressed my ear to the front door to refocus my senses before joining the family again and heard the distinct sound of a call-and-response session in progress. I poked my head into the living room and witnessed a lively exchange, a battle of the sexes involving all-out musical warfare between girls and boys, aunties and uncles, mothers and fathers. Two teenaged ringleaders, accompanied by the tabla and multiple acoustic guitars, led the exchange of good-natured barbs tossed back and forth. More raucous than I would've expected from such a culturally conservative crew, the teams brought forth countless rounds of gut-bursting laughter from both sides as the parents and elders lining the room's edge clapped and cheered.

The scene in the living room was everything about Nepal I'd ever imagined: family and food and music and laughter; multiple generations coexisting peacefully under one roof; and warmth and energy and a feeling of festivity.

Then I recalled something Dr. Singh told me on the day I met him, something that seemed so unusual to me at the time. He told me that in Pepsicola Townplanning, I might find that slice of the real Nepal foreigners were always seeking. This evening at Shruti's sure felt like the real Nepal to me, a place where family came first and food and festivity, a close second.

Standing on Higher Ground

"You look like a deer caught in the headlights! Come on, Ben, I can't keep my mom waiting. She'll worry if I'm late."

"Uh yeah, I'm coming." I tried to smile at Adriana, but my mouth felt frozen, my legs rooted in place, all of me under a spell as I realized with horror that I'd let our golden moment slip through my fingers, stupidly, for no reason. She had finally given me—us—the opportunity I'd been hoping for, and my lifelong inability to react spontaneously had ruined me yet again.

The biggest regret of my life, as it turned out, besides what I chose to make my last words to her, was that I didn't kiss Adriana that night in San Francisco. I often wondered later how different our lives might have been if I had just mustered the courage to embrace her—maybe that simple, yet heroic, act might have made a difference for us.

Adriana and I hugged formally and awkwardly under the disapproving gaze of her mother once we reached the BART station. Then she was gone, swept away into a world I thought was beyond my reach. Indeed, over the next several days, I was unable to reach her on the telephone, and she wouldn't respond to my e-mails.

Several weeks later, I learned through a mutual friend that Adriana had been too defeated and humiliated by my apparent apathy to listen to my message or read my e-mails. She purposely broke up with Manish the day before we met in San Francisco in the hopes that I would step up, according to my friend.

Her parents, while extremely upset by her decision, had told her that if I made a long-term commitment to her, they would accept her choice of partners, however begrudgingly. If a relationship did not develop between us, she would be obligated to reenter her relationship with Manish. That was the bargain they struck. Because I didn't make a move, because I hesitated and wasn't proactive enough, Adriana could not justify delaying her life any longer. She could no longer defy her parents' wishes, and she would have to marry a man she didn't love.

Suddenly, I was devastated for new reasons, beyond my own self-loathing. It just wasn't fair. Surely she understood how unjust it was! I wasn't a mind reader. How was I supposed to know the details of her situation if she never told me? The whole thing made me extremely angry. I was angry with Adriana for not being honest with me and for caving to her parents' demands. I was angry with her parents for being so dictatorial and not allowing her more leeway to make her own decisions. I was angry with Manish for having the dumb luck of being in the right place at the right time. And yes, I was still angry with myself, but now more so for all the wasted hours I'd spent falling in love with Adriana.

It felt as though I'd used up my entire life's allotment of love and longing on her. I was convinced in the heat of that anger that I had nothing left to give the world, that I had burned the last vestiges of energy and emotion I could apply toward another human being.

The more days that passed without communication between us, the more I could feel myself beginning to unravel, replacing open-mindedness, sensitivity, and compassion with criticism, contentiousness, and petty punitiveness. There seemed to be nothing I could do about the press of my emotions. In my anger, and with limited foresight, I did the one thing I came to regret more than anything else in my life: I wrote Adriana a letter full of verbal poison, of nastiness intended to cut deep. I told her that I hated her for the way she had refused to return my love for so long, for the way she had strung me along and made me believe that something more than simple friendship had ever existed for us. I told her that I hoped she never found love again or that she would be cursed by the same affliction that had drawn me to her: the curse of wholeheartedly loving somebody, only to be left battered and bruised in the end.

The things I said to her were so wretched that they would have made anybody lose faith in the goodness of others. Those venomous words and the emotions they no doubt stirred within her, I realized much too late, had the potential of spoiling future relationships for her too. Those words and emotions had the potential to rise to the surface at unexpected times and lash out with damaging consequences. I was full of regret that a trail of destruction was the one lasting thing—my legacy, essentially—that I gifted Adriana. The thought of it made me sick to my stomach.

* * *

Early in the week following Tihar, Beth and I boarded a Buddha Air flight in Kathmandu. We were bound for Lukla and the trailhead of the Everest Base Camp Trek. I was excited, not only because it was my first significant trip away from Kathmandu since preservice training but also because I was accompanied by my friend and fellow Peace Corps volunteer—and outdoor pursuits maven—Beth Lewis. She was a spelunker, a traceuse, an abseiler, and many other things that were about as hard to be as they were to spell. In short, Beth—the self-professed queen of the Tyrolean traverse—was the perfect partner for a multiday romp around the Khumbu region.

Beth and I had lobbied our superiors for the ten-day sabbatical. Admin didn't necessarily encourage volunteers to take vacations, but it wasn't hard to get away. We had easily persuaded Mike Swenson to grant us permission for a temporary leave of absence, citing the need for rejuvenation and a more well-rounded experience of the country. Dr. Singh, beside himself with excitement that I had booked a trip to the Himalayas, restructured the clinic's activities so that the usual volume of patients could still be seen, even in my absence. The other members of our small band of Kathmandu-based Peace Corps volunteers—Bronte, Manfred, Taka, and Laura—were preoccupied with various personal and professional activities in the city.

Of all the Peace Corps volunteers in Kathmandu, Manfred had most wanted to join us on our trip to the Everest region. With a young child at home and another on the way—news we had all just learned—Manfred was swimming in domestic commitments. His wife, Gloria, was incredibly understanding of the demands his Peace Corps post placed upon him, but she needed her man at home.

We were sad that he wouldn't be joining us, but we assured Manfred that he was making the right decision by staying with Gloria and his little one. Besides, there would be more opportunities for shared adventure to come, Beth had insisted. And that was one of the many things I liked about her: she was always trying to find a way to include all her friends in her adrenaline-fueled escapades. She was nothing if not welcoming.

The weather in Nepal's Solu Khumbu region— home to Mount Everest and the Sherpa people—was supposed to be crisp, clear, and inviting for the next ten days. Beth and I knew we would be joining the large crowds that flooded the Everest region in the latter part of the trekking season, but early November was one of the best times of the year to be in the mountains, and we were undeterred.

Beth, with her usual mix of foresight and generosity, had gone on a shopping spree in Thamel several weeks earlier, buying many of the essentials we needed for our trek. Being able to stay warm was of particular concern to Beth when it came to shopping for clothes and equipment for our high altitude trek. She suffered from a condition called Raynaud's disease that caused her extremities, especially her fingers, to become painfully cold at temperatures others didn't find troubling. Keeping her core warm was one of the keys to avoiding the onset of her symptoms, so she bought herself a pink puffy jacket bearing the corporate logo of the North Face.

Of course, like most items in the clothing shops of Thamel, the jacket was a knockoff, the logo unapologetically sewn onto what was otherwise a jacket constructed of lesser quality materials. But in this case, Beth had been impressed by the knockoff's ability to keep her warm, so she had bought one for me too, a large blue one with a detachable hood. She even gave them nicknames; hers was the Pink Puffer, and mine, the Blue Bloater. I found these nicknames amusing, not only because they described the jackets' appearance to perfection but also because those were the names Dr. Singh used to describe patients with emphysema and chronic bronchitis, respectively.

We landed in Lukla, on an airstrip 9,380 feet above sea level, on a bright November morning. We grabbed our bags from the luggage rack on the tarmac and took a moment to orient ourselves to our new surroundings. The long early-morning shadows across the valley were receding quickly from the mountains' flanks. The upper reaches of the mountains themselves were as bald and blinding as kneecaps and bathed in sunlight.

Straightaway, I noticed a large group of men standing shoulder to shoulder, watching us new arrivals with curiosity and optimism. The men reminded me of that first morning in Nepal, at Tribhuvan International Airport. I knew these men couldn't be cabbies, though; beyond the airstrip at Lukla, there were no roads—the terrain was simply too rugged and too remote. There existed only three ways of getting around from here on, all the way to the base of Mount Everest: on foot; by yak; or via a large, tapered, wickerlike basket, known as a *doko*, strapped onto the back of a Nepali porter.

"Pretty cool scenery, huh?" Beth smiled her big toothy smile. I hadn't told her that I had trained extra hard in the weeks leading up to our departure, just so I would be able to match her strides on the way up to base camp.

During the planning phase of our trip, Beth insisted that we would carry our own bags. She wanted to do an independent trek, which essentially meant we would trek by ourselves—without the assistance of a guide or porters—from one guest house to the next. Having taken care of herself and others in some of the most remote parts of the United States, she believed in and promoted the ideals of self-reliance and personal responsibility. She felt each person should own his or her burden and not pass it off onto others.

I respected her opinion, but I wasn't wild about the prospect of schlepping my seventy-liter backpack all the way up to base camp and back, not only because the task seemed extremely labor-intensive but also because there were a whole group of men—the porters—who made their livings off people like Beth and me. Denying them the chance to earn a fair wage for honest work felt wrong to me. I thought about the relationships I was cultivating with the rickmen of Kathmandu, about how strongly I believed in supporting them. I too had initially been reluctant to use their services, but ultimately it didn't seem right to let my own ego dictate another man's fortunes. Needless to say, this issue had been a point of contention between Beth and me, but in the end I had agreed on a two-day trial run without the porters' assistance.

I hefted my backpack over my shoulder and followed Beth away from the terminal, toward a trail leading into the heart of Lukla. Some of the independent porters were successfully hammering out deals with trekkers, while others, like the two men who trailed Beth and me, pleaded in vain.

"That is a too heavy packs for you, good sir!" one of the men exclaimed.

"Madam," said the other one, racing in front of Beth to get her attention, "my legs are strong as yak, you will see!"

The men were extremely persistent in their attempt to solicit work, but there was also a politeness and a playfulness about them that I liked. I wanted to hire them because they seemed more than capable and their energy was undeniable. I smiled at them, shrugged my shoulders, and gave them a look that said, *Sorry, guys, but this decision's out of my hands.* The men, looking confused, hung behind briefly, then collected themselves and marched back to our sides with renewed vigor.

"Where you go?" they wondered. "Sagarmatha? Sagarmatha, we know. Best friends, we are being, so many times have we been. Ohhh, Sagarmathaaa!" they sang in unison.

"Look." Beth stopped abruptly to address the porters. "We can get to Sagarmatha on our own. There's probably a lot of people here who could use your help, but we'll be just fine by ourselves, thank you very much."

"Others no good," one of the men responded, stamping his foot. He had high cheekbones and thick, bushy eyebrows that merged just above his nose. His eyes were big and brown, and the bangs of his short, jet-black hair were plastered to his forehead. "You are beautiful American woman," he said, poking the tiny, weather-beaten American flag Beth had told me she sewed onto her pack years before, during the Clinton administration's reign. "We are in loving with American woman, yes...and man, too, of courses. We are loving it for all of America, it is much true."

"Best to trek." His partner nodded. "No problems. Americans all coooool." He drew out the word while wiggling his head from side to side. "Your names, please?"

"Well, I'm Benjamin and this is my friend Beth," I said. "We're Peace Corps volunteers in Kathmandu," I added.

"Ohhh," they gasped. "Peace Course volunteers *ekdum raamro*! We are go with you now, for a few days, just a little bit only, no problem. Later, if you want hire, OK. If you still no want hire, OK too. OK?"

I didn't know how to respond. They wanted to hike with us for a couple of days even if we weren't paying them? We could still carry our own packs, letting them join us as friends might, but it felt almost as wrong to *not* let able-bodied porters carry our loads. *Jesus, Beth,* I fumed silently, *let's just hire them already.* I knew the men weren't trying to shame us into buying their services, that they genuinely wanted to walk with us, but to let them do that would make us look either cheap or foolish, or worse, both.

"Sure," Beth chirped, surprising me even more than the men. "That sounds like a great idea. It'll be good to have the company, don't you think, Baby Bear? Hey, guys, what are your names?"

"I am Bhimsen," said the man with the unibrow.

"And I am being Brother of Bhimsen!" the second man reported with enthusiasm.

The two men, while sharing many of the same facial features, had their own distinct looks. Bhimsen's brother sported a shabby-looking mustache and a small colony of hair on the end of his chin. His face was gaunter than his brother's and his hair was wild and untamed, standing at attention.

"OK, Brother of Bhimsen, what's your *good* name?" Beth asked.

"Janak," he replied, smiling shyly. "Janak Dhruba Kumar Karki III, to be precises."

Our new party of four stopped briefly in Lukla to pick up snacks. With our backpacks stuffed to the gills, we followed a long yak train leaving town. When the street widened slightly into a small market area flanked by stone houses with colorful wooden window trim, we slipped by the slow-moving beasts of burden. We then took off down the trail like projectiles fired from one of the local boys' homemade slingshots.

We put in a solid effort that first day, despite breaking often to accommodate Beth's impossibly small bladder, or tiny tank, as she described it. Her peeing, which occurred every hour on the hour, provided welcome rests, but was a source of great irritation for Beth herself, who loudly complained about the inconvenience of her own low-capacity plumbing.

During our breaks that first day, on the way up to Phakding with Bhim and Jan—as we came to call them—I looked on in amazement as dozens of porters passed us by, their necks locked rigidly in flexion under the stress and strain of their dokos. Their short, nimble steps on the uphills and their effortless glide on the descents left little doubt that they were sure-footed. But their baskets were piled so high with trekkers' gear or supplies for lodge owners that I still feared the men would lose their balance, topple over, and go careening off the trail.

The men's tumplines—the broad cloth strips drawn tightly across their foreheads or chests—helped optimally distribute their loads' weight, but there was something fundamentally vital about the porters' bodies themselves. I even witnessed a porter carrying an entire refrigerator on his back. I had no idea where he was going with the bulky appliance, but his incredible feat of muscular endurance left an indelible mark on my mind.

Later that evening, Beth and I sat around a wood-fire stove at a small guest house in Phakding and chatted about all things Peace Corps. We were tired, but the smell of the pines, the hard physical labor of the trek, the genuine kindness of these rural Nepalis—all were restorative.

"A lot of Peace Corps volunteers live for this sort of thing," Beth said, unzipping the Pink Puffer. "They live from one vacation to the next, I mean. Thailand, Laos, Cambodia, even Europe, for goodness' sake. I've heard of volunteers who spent more time vacationing than volunteering! The practice of 'stealthing,' you know, just leaving your site without asking Admin, is pretty common too, from what I understand. I'll be the first to admit that I enjoy little escapes, but gosh, it would be *too* easy to shirk responsibility, and we didn't come here for easy, if you know what I mean."

I agreed. The real action, the stuff that mattered to us most, was back in Kathmandu. I loved having free time for travel, stimulating conversations, reading, writing in my journal, and working on side projects, such as a field guide to traditional Nepali botanical medicines—but after we had immersed ourselves so thoroughly in our various Peace Corps projects, it suddenly felt odd to be detached from our labors of love.

"It hasn't always been easy getting things done so far," I admitted, pulling my chair closer to the stove, "but that's exactly what I expected. Besides, there's meaning in struggle. I wouldn't want it any other way."

"It seems as though everybody's doing OK," said Beth. "Bronte's done some great work with those street kids; Taka's cabinetmakers are starting to turn out some great stuff; Manfred's a total whiz with those monks; and even Laura seems to be coping better with her work in the orphanages. I think we're all just hitting our stride, if you ask me. There was a hell of a lot to learn at the start, and sometimes, even now, I have to remind myself that we're still new to this thing. I'm just so thankful y'all have stayed so close and easy to access. I know it's made my life *a lot* easier."

It was true that, as Peace Corps volunteers working and living in and around Kathmandu, we all spent much time together, but as much as we had seen each other, we spent the vast majority of our time alone. Dr. Singh directly oversaw much of my work, but there were still many instances when I could have shunned my responsibilities, disappeared, and spent entire days lying in a cabbage patch, if I so desired. There was a consensus among the members of N-199 that what a volunteer did when nobody was looking was the true test of mettle.

I switched topics, asking Beth what she thought of Bhim and Jan. It still seemed weird that they were tagging along with us just for the fun of it, but people did things like that in Nepal, I was coming to understand. Sometimes, there was just no telling the lengths people would go to get to know you. I, as a Westerner, often assumed that ulterior motives were at play, but I was beginning to let go of that paranoia and just enjoy the company and curiosity of others.

"What can I say?" she said, tousling her ruddy hair. "They're great guys, and they're probably great workers too, but I still don't want to hire them. It's nothing personal; I've just made a decision and I want to stick with it."

"Let's just give it another day, though, and see how we feel. We can reevaluate the situation if the boys are still with us in Namche Bazaar and go from there. Even if you don't want their help, I may. Don't take this personally, Beth, but I don't think that this trek needs to be a death march, and I'm afraid that's what it's going to turn into for me."

"Speaking of a death march," Beth said, and I laughed a little nervously at the transition, "did you hear what that porter said to me earlier today when I offered him a drink of water?"

"No."

"Well, I'll quote him for you in my best manly porter voice," she said, clearing her throat and furrowing her brow before continuing. "He said, 'Porter kidney, strong kidney!' and then blasted up the trail without stopping. Can you believe these guys? I mean, who doesn't think they need to take in liquids during a multihour hike? Especially at this altitude? I love this country, Creed, but sometimes I get so frustrated with the stubbornness I come across. Do you know what I mean?"

I was vaguely aware that certain myths existed within the portering industry, based on conversations I'd had with Dr. Singh. One was this idea that porters were invincible creatures who needn't pay attention to the common health concerns others faced on the trail. Trekking agencies often used this argument to justify denying their porters access to essential equipment and services, but the porters themselves, to a certain degree, perpetuated this stereotype. The reputation they had carved out for themselves was one of toughness and stoicism in the face of hardship and adversity, and while this reputation was grounded in truth and was earned, in the end it usually worked against porters and their desire for empowerment.

We awoke the next morning to steaming bowls of oatmeal and a pair of fried eggs prepared by our kind hosts at the Phakding Lodge, but there was no sign of Bhim and Jan. Beth and I just gave each other perplexed looks and figured that that part of our adventure had ended. After eating and repacking, we thanked the owners and set off for Namche Bazaar.

We bumped into Bhim and Jan not far up the trail, in a grove of cedars. They had been waiting patiently for us. "Good sleep, good sleep?" Bhim asked, his deep voice booming throughout the wooded grove.

"Oh yeah. We slept great," I said. "Thanks for asking. How about you guys?"

"A little bits cold, but OK it is being," said Jan.

"Where did you guys go last night?" Beth said. "You just disappeared on us."

"We found very good cave, not far, not far," said Bhim. "Best cave in all Nepal," he added.

"What do you mean by *cave*?" Beth's small, freckled face scrunched up in confusion. "You didn't sleep in an actual cave, did you?"

"Oh yes, madam. Cave living it is for Bhim and Jan only. No room for us being at guest house."

"That's crazy!" Beth said. "There was *tons* of room at the guest house."

"Yes, tons of room, so much of room, but not for porter Bhim and Brother of Bhim!"

Beth cocked her head and placed her hands on her narrow hips. It was clear we weren't going anywhere until we had gotten to the bottom of this. I wasn't entirely certain what had happened, but I had a vague idea—it was likely that Bhim and Jan either hadn't had the money to buy a room at the guest house or had had the money but because of their status as porters had been denied lodging.

I remembered what Dr. Singh had told me weeks before, that although people watched porters carrying incredible loads all the time, they didn't actually *see* the men. This invisibility was a form of discrimination or social exclusion that porters often faced. The doctor said porters weren't allowed to sleep in lodges and were often forced to find shelter in make-shift camps or caves. I was ashamed that I had forgotten this, that I had thought Bhim and Jan were snugly tucked away in bed when, in fact, they had been shivering themselves to sleep in some cold, damp cave. I explained my suspicions to Beth, and we agreed to find the boys some decent shelter that night, even if it meant smuggling them into our rooms after-hours.

The trail had wound alongside the Dudh Kosi, or Milk River, for the better part of the day prior, ascending gradually in elevation. This would change drastically, according to the porters, once we crossed the high suspension bridge not far from the Sagarmatha Park entrance station.

We rounded a bend in the trail and a rustic Nepali lodge came into view. An employee emerged from the lodge's front door, garbage can in hand. *Oh jeez. Here we go.* I wondered if Beth had seen the man too. He descended to the banks of the Dudh Kosi and, seemingly without a second thought, flung the can's contents directly into the river. I chanced a look over at Beth.

"Did you *see* that, Creed?" she raged, her face flushed and twitching with anger. "Where does that mentality come from? What is it about doing something like that that people think is acceptable? I've come to expect it in the city, but the Everest region, for goodness' sake? Is nothing sacred anymore?"

Beth charged toward the man. She tore into him about his behavior, doling out one of the worst tongue lashings I've ever heard. She challenged not only his nationalism and sense of right and wrong but also his manhood, which I think provided the most substantial blow of all. Bhim, Jan, and I eventually had to carry her back to the trail to let the man slink away to the safety of his lodge.

Beth wasn't the only upset one. I hated seeing pristine environments polluted with human-manufactured debris. But as a person from America, one of the world's principal garbage generators, I had no authority or right to chastise others. I understood Beth's anger, but there was a double standard about it that bothered me even more. And I couldn't see an answer that would fix both.

We continued with our upward march after Beth had simmered down. After only thirty minutes of uninterrupted ascending, we were sweating profusely. "*Dheraai thado!*" I gasped, and Bhim and Jan just chuckled. "This trail is so steep!"

Beth and I lowered our packs to the ground and stretched out on the side of a shaded slope. The forested hills in the distance looked like the bent knees of supine giants.

We were separated in age by just a handful of years, but Beth was like the older sister I never had. Shruti and I were also separated by about the same number of years, but in Shruti I had more of a mother; in Dr. Singh, a father. I had a little sister in Annu, and a brother in Madhu. The role of older sister, though, belonged solely to Beth, and I think she secretly cherished that designation.

Already a biological older sister, Beth possessed a certain tomboyishness, a rambunctiousness, presumably stemming from years of terrorizing her younger brothers. She was merciless in her teasing, and occasionally critical of the things I said, but our relationship had always been playful. Beth and I had already spent so much time with one another, according to Shruti, that we reminded her of two grains of sticky rice clumped together, a cute analogy that seemed accurate enough.

I usually played a song in my head whenever I was on a long-distance hike. That morning, it was "Standing on Higher Ground," by Alan Parsons Project, one of my father's all-time favorite groups. It seemed like a fitting song for the mountains, but what I didn't realize then was that the song would remain stuck in my head for the entire trek, the chorus looping repeatedly in my mind as I trekked up hill and down dale.

In a falsetto, a voice carefully selected to be maximally grating on Beth's ears, I began serenading her: "I see the world...and I'm looking from a high place...way above it all, stannnding on higher grou-ound..."

"Oh jeez," moaned Beth. "Please, for the love of God or Krishna or whoever it is you believe in, stop that!"

"I breathe the air...while they're running in a rat race...waaay above it all, stannnding on—"

"Hey, Baby Bear," she said, cutting me off abruptly. "Who sings that song?"

"Alan Parsons Project."

Beth rolled over to look me in the eye. "OK, let's keep it that way then, huh?"

"Very funny. But I've heard *you* sing too, and let me tell you, you're not exactly the next Alicia Keys."

"You haven't heard me freestyle," she said. "I've got mad lyrics!"

"Right."

"Wait, I hear something," she said. "Do you hear what I'm hearing?"

"Yeah," I said. "It sounds like a bag of hot air letting off some steam."

"No, no, I'm not trying to be funny," she said. "I think it's...yak bells."

The same yak train we passed on the outskirts of Lukla was advancing toward us at a steady and impressive rate. The yaks continued up the steep switchbacks with what looked like great ease, driven on by the ceaseless whistling and haranguing of their masters. One of the yak men threw a rock ahead of the herd to keep the jangling beasts moving in the right direction.

"Man, those yaks can really move!" I said, raising my eyebrows in astonishment. "I thought we dropped them long ago, but it looks like they'll beat us up to Namche. I should've asked one of the men if I could hitch a ride."

"Suck it up, Creed," Beth joked, punching me in the meaty part of my right shoulder.

"You want to trade packs?" I said, eyeing Beth's twenty-five-pound load with envy. "Remind me again why we need all this stuff." My pack held about sixty pounds. "And remind me again why we're not hiring porters."

"Own your burden, Creed." Beth giggled. "Own your burden."

"*You* own my burden," I shot back in juvenile fashion, rolling my bag toward her with my feet. "I'm going to sleep."

"Very mature. I guess that's why you're Baby Bear."

The unmistakable whistle of a porter approaching us from up the trail pierced the air before a heavily laden man rounded the bend. Suddenly, he caught his foot on a tree's root, stumbled forward, and tried to regain his balance. His stringy quadriceps muscles strained mightily.

He recovered momentarily, but he lost his footing again on a pebbly section of the trail. The porter's right leg buckled grotesquely, and he landed face-first in a cloud of dust. The oversize duffel bag he was carrying vaulted from his doko, landed, and didn't stop moving until several yards down the trail, where it snagged on a sharp rock. There was the sound of tearing fabric, and through the bag's new wound, several conspicuous items—items only a Westerner would think of bringing on a trek—spilled: a curling iron, a flare gun, and a bottle of Calvin Klein perfume.

Bhim and Jan, who had been resting a little ways from us, jumped to their feet and ran to the porter's side. Beth and I joined them. They spoke soothing words and tried lifting him from the ground. When that didn't work, Jan crouched on the ground in front of the man and told him to climb onto his back.

"Jan, what are you doing?" I wondered.

"I think he's going to porter him to that healthpost we passed a couple hours ago," Beth said.

"Would it be easier if we all helped carry him?"

"Not so easy, boss," replied Bhim, who was efficiently gathering up the loosed belongings and returning them to the torn duffel bag. He placed the bag back inside the man's doko before shouldering the load and adjusting it on his back to suit his proportions. "Too many, too slow," he said. "We porters are having strongest backs only. You go the Namche Bazaar. We are seeing you there tonights or tomorrow morning it is, OK?"

I dug through my pants pockets to come up with what I believed would be enough money for the man's care. I felt awful about not being able to do more, but we were a long way from help, and our first-aid kit wasn't equipped for that kind of injury. Beth, a certified wilderness first responder, offered her expertise instead of cash, but Bhim and Jan were eager to get the man to the healthpost and were gone before we could persuade them otherwise.

I wasn't sure what had just happened. The porters were usually so sure-footed. It must have been a momentary lapse of concentration, or maybe he was new to the trade and was carrying too heavy a load. The result wasn't good, whatever the reason. The porter had likely ruptured some ligaments and torn muscle. His recovery would take a long time, and he probably wouldn't be portering any time soon, a fact that didn't bode well for him and the rest of his family. With any luck, he was a single man and didn't have any hungry mouths to feed, but I knew the odds of that were about slim as a cricket bat's handle.

Beth and I regrouped, gathered up our packs, and set off for Namche Bazaar. We struggled against the punishing grade, but we managed to avoid any further incidents. We were so fatigued that, by the time we stopped for the night under a blue-black starry sky at 11,286 feet above sea level, we could barely speak. Even Beth, normally full of energy, was suffering silently, I noted. It was true that we had had a long, draining day, but it wasn't like her to be so quiet. *Maybe we ascended too quickly?*

"Man, I'm starving," I said. "I could use a good meal—how about you, Beth?"

I knew something was wrong when she failed to respond. Her appetite was usually bigger than my own, despite her petite frame. In fact, she routinely put me to shame at the Rum Doodle during our Tuesday night pizza and beer gatherings. I often wondered if she, just like Nepali Pete, had an intestinal parasite to feed. We slogged ahead over the final few yards to the village's entrance. I knew we desperately needed to find a quiet place where we could hunker down and lick our wounds.

"How about this guest house?" I stopped, puffing for breath, in front of the first lodge I saw. A sign in front of the lodge read, *Dharamsala International Hostel & Guest House.*

"Sounds perrrfect." Beth's words were slow and her speech slightly slurred.

"Hey, are you OK?"

"I don't know," she said. "I feel, like, kind of funny, I guess."

Anything other than an "absolutely" from Beth meant she was hurting badly. "Well, let's get you a room then, huh?"

"I think that that would be all right," she said, unstrapping her pack's belt from around her waist and loosening her grasp on her trekking poles. "Hate to say it…altitude's *really* kicking…ass."

"Maybe we should think about going back down? If you've got acute mountain sickness, that's the only way to get rid of the symptoms, unless you've got some dexamethasone handy."

"Nope. No dex," she said. "But I know the symptoms. I don't think that what I've got is that serious." I trusted her backcountry experience, but I felt conflicted about her assessment. She wouldn't be thinking straight if she was suffering from AMS. I decided to test her by having her walk heel to toe along a straight line on the ground. She passed.

"OK then, we'll stay," I said. "But if you get any worse, I need you to tell me. It doesn't matter if it's the middle of the night—just come get me and we'll pack up our things and start back down the trail. It's that simple. I'm pretty sure you managed to jam at least a couple heavy-duty flashlights into my pack," I said, laughing, "so no worries about the lack of light."

I took a moment to let my words sink in and then continued. "So here's what I'm thinking: if you're feeling better in the morning, we'll stay in Namche tomorrow, which will give us both the chance to acclimatize before heading up the trail. Capiche? Oh, and we're hiring Bhim and Jan to carry our packs once they get back from the healthpost."

"I never thought I'd hear myself say it," Beth said, "but I'm *so* over carrying a pack."

We checked in with the guest house manager and, after he explained the house rules and gave us a quick tour, we hauled our gear up to our rooms on the second floor. I escorted Beth to her room, where I was relieved to find a small group of Western women already sharing the space. I was thankful for the hostel's dormitory-style accommodations because I wanted somebody to be around Beth at all times to monitor her condition.

"I suppose you're still not very hungry," I said.

"Not so much. But I am feeling a little dehydrated. I don't think I've peed for at least two hours."

"Now *that* is serious. I'll go grab you some water."

"You *are* one of the good ones, Baby Bear," she said, her words taking me all the way back to the streets of Thamel, that night we first met. She said those words then too, and though I had given them plenty of thought since, I still didn't know exactly what she meant.

I fetched some water for Beth and then left her with her new room-mates, a trio of Australian trekkers. I backtracked down the hallway toward the room I'd been assigned, passing a fellow trekker who was accosting the hostel's only soft-drink machine. The infuriated man, clearly a victim of grand larceny, yelled, *"Achtung! Achtung!"* before landing several vicious blows on the machine's belly. I quietly slipped by him, hoping I wasn't sharing my four-person dorm room with such a loose cannon.

I wasn't. Three Nepali soldiers on leave from the British Army Brigade of Gurkhas paused their relaxed game of cards to welcome me and make room for my gear, clearing one of the lower berths on a set of bunk beds. It was brilliant how the bunk beds had been built into the room's walls, I thought. There was a tall personal storage locker at one end of the bunks for hanging clothes and packs and safekeeping valuables. The bunks them-selves, just like the berths in sleeper cars on higher-end trains, had privacy curtains and their own reading lamps.

Dumping the contents of my backpack onto the bed, I took a long, hard look at what I was dragging along behind me. I'd sworn myself to a life of minimalism, but I knew a person needed to be prepared for all possible eventualities while out on the trail. I didn't envy Bhim and Jan, who would be carrying our packs the rest of the way. We hadn't told the men where we were staying, but I knew enough about Nepal not to worry about a triviality like that—they would find us.

I finished stowing my gear and preparing my bed before excusing myself from the group of Gurkhas and heading for the reception desk to reserve a room for Bhim and Jan. I suspected that they would drop in shortly. I also left them a message at the front desk, telling them about Beth's condition and our mutual decision to hire them, if they were still interested. We would finalize the details of their payment the following morning, I said in the note. Beth and I would do everything in our power to ensure they received fair and equitable treatment at the various lodges in which we would overnight along the route if they agreed to carry our bags.

I grabbed a bite to eat at the lodge's restaurant. I then took an alternate route back to my dorm room, finding a quiet wing that housed several private rooms, suites, reserved for customers with thicker wallets and a greater desire for privacy than the rest of us. The doors of each of these rooms bore the names of famous people who had stayed in the lodge or who were publicly active in the Everest region. There was a Jimmy Carter room, a Sir Edmund Hillary room, and much to my great delight, there was even a room reserved for the Abominable Snowman!

I crept up the stairs to the second floor. I was looking forward to a peaceful night's sleep after such a brutal day on the trail, but as I rounded a corner, I came upon one of my roommates threatening the same pop machine that had provoked fits of rage from the German trekker. It appeared that the Nepali was another victim of the pop machine's maniacal grasp on small change. I paused to watch him kick the machine in several key places, including the coin slot, holding the blade of his fiercely curved *khukuri* at the ready, but nothing happened. It seemed the hostel's owners had done everything possible to create a relaxing environment, except service the second-floor pop machine.

I woke early the next morning to the Gurkha soldiers' vigorous nasal expectorations. The horking and the snorting and the spitting routine of every Nepali's early-morning preening was particularly awful in Kathmandu, where slimy boogers, through some magical process, turned into thick lumps of charcoal overnight. I had found the sounds disgusting and irritating at first, but after living in the Kathmandu Valley under a cloud of constant pollution for the past while, I had come to understand the necessity of the cleansing ritual.

I added a few of my own snorts to the nasal symphony and dressed quickly in my berth before flinging open the curtain and embracing the day. I felt completely reenergized after a good night's sleep, but I was happy that we had decided to take a rest day. I wondered how Beth had fared overnight. I stowed my gear in my locker and went to find out.

"Housekeepiiinng!" I called in a high-pitched voice, knocking lightly on the door. "Anybody in there?"

"Just me," Beth said. "The door's unlocked."

I opened the door and stepped into the room, happy to find someone who looked like good ol' Beth there. "Where did your friends go?"

"The Aussies? Oh, they left for Lukla early this morning. Trying to do it all in one day."

"Wow, that's ambitious. So, how are you doing?"

"Grrrreat! I feel so much better after that sleep, believe it or not. I think I was just tired last night. I guess it wasn't mountain sickness after all. I still kind of feel like a dog who just pooped on the carpet, though, if you know what I mean."

"No, I don't really know what you mean," I said.

"Well, it's just kind of embarrassing to feel so low after telling you how extensive my outdoor résumé was, that's all."

"Oh," I said, smiling. "No worries. We all have bad days. The most important thing is for us to enjoy the trip. We're not trying to set any world records, right?"

"Right," she said. "But, that being said, with another day of acclimatizing, I'll be rip-roaring to go!"

"I'm going to try to find Bhim and Jan and work out a few details with them and then maybe take a stroll around town. What are your plans?" I asked.

"My first priority is food," Beth said. "Then photography." Pointing out the window, she said, "The light at this hour is *incredible*."

We had arrived in Namche under the cover of darkness and hadn't gotten a good look at our surroundings. There was a certain unmistakable feeling, though, that came with being in the mountains. You didn't necessarily have to see them to know that you were surrounded by them, that you had slipped into an entirely different zone. The mountains' magnitude seemed to alter the way sound traveled, and even with your eyes closed or in the pitch blackness of the dead of night, you could sense their hulking presence.

"So maybe we should meet up later this afternoon for a plate of yak meat and some deep-fried Mars bars? How does that sound?"

"That sure sounds sparkly, Baby Bear," she said, smiling and winking at me.

I dropped down to the hostel's lobby and asked the receptionist if Bhim and Jan had checked in the previous night. She confirmed that they had and were staying in one of the rooms on the first floor. I was eager to see them, to find out how the injured porter was doing, and to see if they were still interested in working with Beth and me. Knocking on their door, I called cheerily, "Bhim! Jan! Are you guys in there?"

The door flung open. The men smothered me with hugs and shouted, "Oh, thank you, thank you, thank you, good sir! Thanks it being to you, we are having it the most excellent sleeps in the fine Dharamsala dormitory styles last night."

"Uh, think nothing of it, guys," I said, awkwardly returning their hugs. "How's our injured friend doing? Was he able to get some good medical care?"

"Oh yes! For your Yankee dollars he is getting it the *most* excellent of cares for the big fat swellings of his knee," said Jan. "He is such a lucky fellow, that portering brother, to be falling on his faces in front of such a generous bideshi."

"So, did the doctor tell you guys what sort of injury he had and how long it might take until he can work again?"

Bhim, wiggling his head, said, "Sprain-strain ligament rupture. Probably many, many weeks before it is he can again be working for trekking company. Maybe it is they will not even be hiring him because of his new tricky knee."

It wasn't a good prognosis. There was no such thing as worker's compensation for porters in Nepal. If there was one saving grace about the whole scenario, though, it was the fact that the trekking season was coming to a close. It was possible, with the right care and the proper rehabilitative therapy, that the man could return to the trails again in the spring and resume his position without his employers being the wiser.

"So, how did you guys find us?"

"By the words of mouth, of courses," said Jan, who always smiled enthusiastically when responding to questions.

"Bideshi always make it a good resting for themselves, a *very fine* resting, at Dharamsala Guest House," added Bhim, still wiggling his head.

"Well, I'm glad you guys found us," I said, "because we could sure use your help. Are you still interested in working with us?"

"Oh yes! We are barely sleeping on the fine guest house mattresses from the excitement of carrying your much-too-heavy packs!"

The porters and I hammered out the details of their salary and I paid them the day's stipend for food and other essentials. We then broke and went our separate ways.

Stepping out onto the cobbled street, I felt the chill of early morning already fading away under the high-altitude sun's intense rays. I could see shopkeepers preparing for a busy day of commerce in the remote, but of course popular, village.

I followed the winding lanes, looking for a way up, farther and farther up. I soon found a stone staircase that led me to a glorious vista overlooking Namche Bazaar.

The great snowy peaks of Kongde Ri, Thamserku, and Ama Dablam surrounded the tiered village of comely blue-and-green tin-roofed buildings. The village itself had been carved into the side of its own mountain, and though many of the slopes around the village had been completely denuded—the trees felled for firewood or building lodges for tourists—there was still an undeniable alpine charm to its rugged appearance. When viewed from above, the horseshoe-shaped village vaguely resembled a giant, majestic Greek amphitheater.

There was a large market area in the center of Namche Bazaar, just as there was Durbar Square in Kathmandu. I would learn that, by night, the mostly Tibetan vendors stayed close to their wares, taking shelter in tents ringing the market grounds. Not far from the market grounds, a stream's minor torrents churned a handful of beautifully decorated prayer wheels that spun off mantras of spiritual blessing. I saw more of those brilliantly designed wheels along the trail in the days ahead.

I loved watching their entrancing whirl and hearing their rhythmic squeak, but the motivation behind their existence moved me most. It was a quintessentially Buddhist idea—that, by placing prayer wheels directly in the current, a steady stream of blessed water with the power of purification would be carried to all creatures dwelling in and along the water. The water wheel was just one of many different types of prayer wheels used by Buddhists around the world to accumulate good karma. While the bulky stationary wheels and the smaller handheld wheels were the ones trekkers saw most often, there were other wheels, too, wheels powered by heat and electricity and wind. There were even digital prayer wheels—approved, of course, as the others were, by His Holiness the Dalai Lama—for those who worked all day on computers.

I met up with Beth, Bhim, and Jan at the hostel for an early dinner, so we all could turn in early that night. I wanted to be ready to rise at dawn for the hike up to Tengboche, home to one of the most well-known Buddhist monasteries in all of Nepal. We'd be able to move quicker than before, now that Bhim and Jan would be carrying our packs.

Barefoot and Pragmatic in the Kingdom

ADRIANA HAD OFTEN WONDERED WHY WE COULDN'T SIMPLY REMAIN FRIENDS, why I always had to strive for something more complex and binding between us. Then, I believed that a mere friendship would not be enough, that if an intimate relationship were not possible, there was no point in investing more of myself in her.

I knew I would always feel a rippling undercurrent of bitterness and discontent about what I believed not only could have been but should have been and that that would sour our future interactions. And that was not what I wanted for us. So, in that final letter to her, I told her that if I couldn't be her lover and her partner, I never wanted to see her again, that I hoped she would go away and not come back for a very long time. It was a juvenile thing to write, but I *was* a juvenile.

Three things happened after I sent the letter. First, Adriana did as I demanded. Not once did she attempt to contact me. She didn't return my letters, e-mails, or phone calls, and I even heard rumors that she had left the country for an indefinite amount of time. Almost as soon as I mailed the letter, I realized how much of a mistake it was. By writing those awful things to Adriana, I was betraying her trust in me. She had come to regard me as a reliable confidant over the previous months, and now, because of a few inconsiderate and hurtful words, she would understandably never speak to, let alone confide in, me again.

And that led to the second thing: I became depressed. The words I penned had the unintended effect of reducing me as a person, to the point where, even years later, I still hadn't recovered pieces of myself that were shattered and seemingly lost forever.

But something unexpectedly positive happened too. Even though she hurt me and I hurt her, I realized that part of me—a big part of me—still loved her. Even with the sting of ultimate rejection, on some level I was still happy. I was happy because I had experienced the positive emotions—the powerful and uplifting sensations associated with true love—that Adriana undeniably evoked within me. The care of a special woman gives a man strength and confidence, and even though she never told me she loved me, I had always drawn a significant amount of support from Adriana's presence in my life.

Those remembrances of Adriana—the hope, the optimism, and the confidence I had felt whenever I was around her—were my life rafts. Slowly, and much to my surprise, I began coming out of my funk, and with the encouragement of friends and family, before long I felt the desire to get my life back in order and make amends.

I had gotten to know several of her girlfriends quite well during our friendship, to the point where I regarded them as my own friends too. I began asking around, trying to get a sense from these women of whether I could reach Adriana to apologize for everything I said. But her friends were leery about telling me where she was, as though she had given them strict orders to keep that information classified.

Fortunately, one of Adriana's friends, Serena, finally divulged the truth: Adriana had abandoned her life in America, her marital obligations to Manish, and her domineering parents to volunteer in a hospital called Chota Sion in the Mumbai slum of Dharavi. Her decision didn't surprise me—one of Adriana's primary passions had always been health care in the developing world, and her degree in public health from Berkeley reflected that passion.

* * *

The next morning, our little troop of four souls gathered outside a local bar called the Yak Train—a suitable name because of the numerous yak trains passing through the village and also because of the long line of Western trekkers who vomited outside its doorstep after consuming too much *chang*.

"OK, gang, let's have a great day today," said Beth. "Drink plenty of water, eat when you need to, and for goodness' sake, learn a lesson from me and rest as often as possible. Has everybody got their stuff together?"

It was amazing to see the change in Beth's attitude since her brush with altitude-induced exhaustion. She was still the same old sparkly Beth—part cheerleader, part ringleader, part field general—but there was a more judicious tone to her words. She had processed her experience, and instead of trying to cover up the embarrassment with a bunch of excuses, she was allowing it to influence her decision making in a positive way. I realized anew how skilled an outdoorswoman she was.

"Bhim, Jan—where are your shoes?" Beth continued. "You were wearing them the other day. Look, we're not going anywhere until you guys put them on. I'm not joking."

"Oh, no joking, madam," said Bhim, his eyes wide and his face honest. "We are no wearing shoes for the long treks. It is being *very* bad for the feets and knees and hips and backs. We are no-wearing-shoes fellows for a very long times now. It is no problem." He furrowed his brow and added a little head wiggle for emphasis. His expression seemed to say, *What's the big deal, lady?*

"Are you kidding me?" Beth moaned her disapproval. "Come on, you guys, you're killing me here."

Bhim and Brother of Bhim, standing side by side in their matching high-water pants and ratty old sweaters, looked confused by Beth's emotional response. Clearly *we* were the odd ones for having our feet scrunched up and tucked away in thick-soled boots. And with their doko baskets loaded to the brim and secured snugly upon their backs, they weren't about to indulge what was to them a ridiculous request.

"Hold on just a second, Beth." I pointed at their flawless extremities. "Correct me if I'm wrong, but I don't see any bunions, blisters, or hammertoes, do you?"

Bhim's and Jan's feet, while dusty and heavily callused, were true podiatric miracles. I had never considered feet one of the more beautiful aspects of human anatomy, but *their* feet were. They had strong, sturdy arches; broad, flat forefeet; and incredible natural toe splay. Their toes were straight and had plenty of space between them, which was very different from the toes of a typical shoe-wearing Westerner, whose phalanges were daily mashed and mangled in one way or another. And their toenails—smooth, pink specimens worthy of the public eye—were fungus-free and fully intact. My crammed toes were suddenly envious of the porters' liberated feet.

"I'm going barefoot too!" I said, like a battle cry, and much to the delight of the brothers, who chortled their approval loudly.

"Don't be ridiculous, Creed." Beth rolled her pale-blue eyes. "You don't always have to prove that you're a man of the people."

"Watch me," I said, stooping to unlace my hiking boots. I wasn't sure how the experiment would turn out, but now I was committed.

It wasn't just their feet that impressed me; the porters' entire posture was impeccable. I admired their near-perfect structural alignment, their healthy, accentuated spinal curves, and their drawn-back shoulders and opened chests. It struck me then that posture was a crystallization, or a summation, perhaps, of all of life's emotions, moods, movements, and poses. Posture was the visual evidence of how a life had been lived; it was often the first thing you noticed about someone, and it said much about the sanctity with which people held themselves. The porters' posture was perhaps their only lasting reward from a life of nonstop toil on the slopes, flanks, and moraines of the world's tallest mountains.

On another level, I just wanted to *feel* the earth beneath my feet. It occurred to me, as I felt the dirt's coolness on the soles of my feet, that I couldn't even remember the last time I had been barefoot outdoors. It felt good to feel the ground's varied textures and temperatures. It felt as though I were rediscovering a part of myself I'd long since forgotten.

Less than ten minutes in on that first day, on the hike from Namche Bazaar to Tengboche, my feet began to ache, and I had to put my boots back on. I was glad I hadn't completely abandoned them at the guest house. I continued walking barefoot part-time over the next several days, expanding the time I went without footwear as the soles of my feet began to adapt and my foot muscles grew stronger and more resilient.

We paused several times throughout the day in front of stone walls, known as *chautaaras*, which had been built to such a height that a porter could turn around and rest his doko on the wall's ledge without unstrapping it or bending his knees. When they needed a break but a chautaara wasn't available, Bhim and Jan would place the narrow bases of their dokos upon the crux of T-shaped pieces of wood they carried with them in the baskets. The tool, which looked like the overgrown offspring of a cudgel and a slingshot, could also be used as a walking stick.

On the day's final climb, on the last push up to the monastery at Tengboche, our tired quartet joined up with a large group of surly young monks dressed in billowing red robes, running shoes, and bandanas. Some of the monks were listening to Discmans, while others, with the sleeves of their robes rolled up to their shoulders, flexed their muscles at us and showed off their homemade tattoos.

The sun was quickly setting behind the hills, and we followed the modern monks as fast as possible. We soon entered a wooded grove, through which we could see the summit of Ama Dablam in the distance, and came across a man reclining against a rock and picking a tune on his acoustic guitar. He was also gorging himself on goji berries, the Himalayan fruit of longevity and well-being.

"Howdy, partners," he said, his voice slow and shaky in the stereotypical way beach bums' voices are slow and shaky.

He turned out to be Johnny Pozzarelli, a rock climber from Seattle, who had come to the Khumbu for the region's incredible bouldering opportunities. "Have you cats seen my Sherpa, Dorje?" he asked. He put down his guitar, laced his hands behind his head, and reclined even further, his lion's mane of sandy-brown hair poking out from beneath his woolen cap. "He was *supposed* to show me where the best bouldering was in the entire frickin' kingdom, but man, Dorje split, do you dig? Now all I've got is this here guitar, see, and a pocket full of goji berries. Ah, *shhiiit*, it's all good though. I'm really diggin' this al fresco lifestyle, man. Yeaahh."

Johnny's guitar reminded me of something a friend had once told me, that men loved handling guitars because the act reminded them of handling the voluptuous curves of a woman's body. I didn't suspect that Johnny was any exception to this rule. With his looks and guitar, and unbelievably, a yoga roll sticking out of his backpack, he looked like the sort of hippie playboy for which some women might swoon.

His guitar also made me think of all the ridiculous things people brought with them on multiday or even multiweek hikes in the mountains. It was true that Beth and I had brought a lot of gear with us, but most of it was relevant in our day-to-day lives on the trail. It wasn't that a guitar was com-pletely irrelevant—it just didn't make much practical sense to carry around such a bulky item. It wouldn't have been my first choice as a trail compan-ion—but then again, as Beth would surely attest, I was no musician either.

"Johnny, did you really carry that guitar with you all the way up here?" I asked.

"Hells yeah, *brah*. Best damn friend I ever had. More loyal than that cat Dorje, I'd say. Pluckin' this six-string allows me to get in touch with my artistic side...ya know...like...deep stuff, man...real deep stuff. Plus, it gets me away from my money troubles. My climbing café back in Seattle's kind of tanking, man. Major bummer."

"Wait a minute!" Beth snapped her fingers and pointed at Johnny. "Do you mean Johnny Jangbu's Climbing Café? The one with the indoor climbing wall and bouldering cave?"

"That's the one, sweetheart. You've been, huh?"

"Yeah, a few times. It's a pretty rad place," said Beth, adopting the climbers' linguistic code.

"You should tell that to the bank," Johnny whined. "Johnny Jangbu's up to his huevos in debt. It ain't no way to live, all that stress and strain and shit, I'll tell you that."

"So, what are you going to do now, Johnny?" I said.

"Ah, shit. I don't know, brah. I'll probably just pack up my stuff and head back to Kathmandu. You know, do the 'du for a little bit and then head over to Thailand for some sweet beach action. Can you cats point me in the direction of Lukla?"

"Yeah, sure," I said, pointing to the trail we'd just ascended. "Just keep heading down the trail and follow the Dudh Kosi. You'll know when you get there."

"The dude, Kosi?" Johnny wondered aloud. "Sounds like a bodacious guy. What does he look like? Does brah play a guitar too?"

"No, dude, *dudh!*" I said. "Dudh Kosi, as in the river, not a brah!"

"Wait, dude, I'm confused. There's a river that's actually a man, who's going to show me the way back to Lukla? Faaar out, brah! I dig it." Johnny nodded his head to show understanding.

We arrived in an open, grassy field at the foot of Tengboche monastery thirty minutes later, our vision clear and our bodies and minds purified from the pain of the climb—or so I told myself. Smoke billowed into the evening sky from the chimneys of several guest houses situated at the far edge of the grounds. Yak-dung patties caked the walls of the houses like sand on feet after a midsummer's romp on the beach. Around us, on all sides, the magnificent, snowcapped peaks of the Himalayas made us feel small.

The whitewashed monastery was larger than I had envisioned and was beautifully appointed, its colorful welcome arch adorned with the iconography of Buddhist worship. The monastery—or *gompa*—had burned down in 1989, according to my guidebook. All significant relics, artifacts, murals, and carvings were lost. It wasn't the first time the monastery had been destroyed, however. In 1934, an earthquake had also caused serious damage.

The grounds were quiet and perfumed with the calming scent of juniper, but we'd been told that only two weeks before, the place had been buzzing during the annual Mani Rimdu, a three-day festival featuring the finest in Sherpa dancing and theater, celebrating the triumph of Buddhism over the ancient Bön religion.

Beth and I entered the dining area of one of the guest houses and found Bhim and Jan munching on heaping plates of dal bhaat. The porters had easily beaten us to Tengboche over the final section of trail, despite their heavier loads. We scanned the dinner menu and placed our orders with the cook before dropping onto a bench beside the porters. Thankfully, we felt wiped out by healthy exhaustion and not AMS.

"Good day, good day?" asked Bhim, shaking his hand over his plate to dislodge the sticky rice.

"Yeah, it was a great day," I said. "How about you guys?"

"Oh yes, great day it is being for Bhim and Brother of Bhim!" said Jan. "We are so happy for the works."

"You guys must be pretty tired," Beth said. "I know I would be."

"Oh yes, little bit, little bit tireds," Bhim said, after shoveling another giant plug of rice into his mouth. Bhim munched quickly, then swallowed hard. The bolus hadn't even reached his stomach before another handful had found his open mouth.

"You've got to slow down, brother, or else you'll get a tummy ache," I said, clapping Bhim on the back and smiling broadly.

"Porter tummy, strong tummy!" Bhim said between bites, to which Beth simply rolled her eyes and shook her head in disbelief.

Our brave little group again set off for higher altitudes the following morning, after a quick face wash and a hearty breakfast of oatmeal. Our goal this time: Pheriche—a small, windswept settlement containing numerous guest houses and restaurants. Pheriche, situated at 14,340 feet above sea level, would be a *real* test of our altitude tolerance. I wasn't sure how my body would respond to the challenge, but thus far I'd had no difficulty with the altitude, not even a mild headache.

We left Tengboche's peaceful grounds and immediately dropped down through a thick belt of rhododendrons before climbing to Pangboche, where we stopped for lunch. Everybody seemed to be doing just fine, despite the elevation gain. We stayed above the tree line for most of the day and enjoyed unimpeded views of the surrounding mountains and the trail up ahead.

We hiked steadily all afternoon, arriving in Pheriche shortly before sundown. A sweeping mass of clouds cloaked the entire region in a gray haze about twenty minutes after we found a lodge and checked in. From the window of the room Beth and I were sharing, I watched the clouds, amazed to see how fast the wispy walls of moisture sailed by, just barely skimming the ground's surface.

"They recommend an acclimatization day here in Pheriche," Beth said, putting down her guidebook and looking over at me from her bunk on the room's far side. "How are you feeling, Baby Bear?"

"So far, so good. I'm feeling pretty strong. How about you?"

"Me too," she said. "So I'm thinking that with Bhim and Jan carrying our packs, we might as well just head up to Gorak Shep tomorrow, spend the night there, then head up to base camp the following day. That would give us more time to check out some of the other side trips available," she said. There were a number of day hikes in the area she'd had her eye on for some time.

The plan was ambitious, but I liked it. An acclimatization day in Pheriche would probably be wise, but we were both young and strong and feeling fit. And I was excited to reach Gorak Shep—I imagined it would feel like the first true milestone of our trek. Gorak Shep, Bhim and Jan had said, was the staging ground where the ambitious gathered before their final push up to either Everest Base Camp itself or Kala Pattar, a small, nearby peak with incredible views of the surrounding mountains.

"OK, sure," I said, "but let's be smart about this. If we're feeling draggy or lethargic, let's turn around and come back down to Pheriche. Let's give our bodies a chance to speak for themselves."

"Deal."

Later that evening, I turned off the room's overhead light, crawled into my sleeping bag, and turned on my headlamp to make a quick entry in my journal. I opened the small notebook and a postcard fell out. It was a postcard I'd written on the morning of my first day in Pepsicola Townplanning, the only postcard I wasn't able to send that day because I lacked the necessary address. I'd almost forgotten about it.

The picture on the postcard's front captured a busy market scene near Tachupal Tole in Bhaktapur, and while it did speak volumes about the day-to-day lives of urban Nepalis, the image did little to prepare the recipient for the seriousness of the words printed on the opposite side. I wondered if the postcard would ever find the hands of the person for whom it was intended, or whether it would always remain tucked away in my journal, destined to waste away until both picture and message were completely unrecognizable.

Our quartet rose early the following morning, like we had on all previous mornings during the trek, ate a solid breakfast, and discussed plans for the coming day. Beth and I decided to send Bhim and Jan ahead up the trail, giving them a good head start. There was a massive, almost-vertical boulder field just above Pheriche that would require a significant amount of time and energy to scale. Beth and I, without the burden of heavy packs, were likely to fare better in the boulder field than the porters who, despite their great fitness and acclimated bodies, would move more slowly under the strain of their weighty loads.

Beth and I struck off about one hour after Bhim and Jan had departed the guest house. The walk was easier than either of us had expected. Many of the small streams that trickled through the meadow upon which we trekked had frozen overnight, their ice just thick enough to bear the weight of our bodies. But the boulder field was not far away. Beth and I squinted up, trying to pinpoint the small, dark figures of Bhim and Jan, but they were nowhere in sight. Either they had already cleared the field or they were hunkered down resting, out of view behind one of the mammoth boulders.

If I had been impressed by Beth's recovery from the hike up to Namche, I was completely overwhelmed by her climbing abilities in that boulder field above Pheriche. It was the most difficult part of the trek we had yet met, but she set and maintained an incredible pace. It wasn't just her aerobic capacity that impressed me or the fact that she was as tough overall as the soles of our porters' feet; it was also the grace and style she exhibited. She was as sure-footed as a mountain goat, that Beth, always choosing the most efficient line through the stony rubble.

I was just about ruined by the time we reached the top of the boulder field. I peered down through the rocky jungle gym we'd just ascended, and it struck me that I would have only this one opportunity to reach base camp. There was no way I would be able to muster the energy to climb through that boulder field again. Either I would succeed now in reaching my goal, or I would fail; it was that simple.

Beth and I crested a bluff just beyond the top of the boulder-strewn path to find an arid, lunar landscape filled with stones and awe-inspiring vistas. The area, roughly the size of ten football fields, consisted of soft, earthy undulations studded with boulders the size of suburban homes. Interspersed among the boulders stood hundreds of chortens, whitewashed conical cairns standing at attention, some of which were in serious disrepair, others that had recently been erected.

We continued up the trail to Lobuje after meeting up with Bhim and Jan, who had been resting behind one of the chortens after their own brutal ascent through the boulder field. Lobuje was the last major stop along

the route before Gorak Shep. There, at a guest house, we ate some food and rested briefly, and we refilled our water bottles using one of the portable ceramic water filters Beth had bought in Thamel. She had insisted we bring them with us to help reduce our use of nonbiodegradable plastic bottles and avoid two weeks of the runs from giardiasis.

Nobody was talking as we stepped back out under the clear, cobalt skies, despite feeling upbeat. We continued to walk in silence at a sustainable pace throughout the rest of the afternoon, to conserve as much energy as possible.

We reached Gorak Shep, a collection of drafty, noise-ridden hovels, by late afternoon. I was amazed to see a group of bright orange tents pitched between the buildings. *Must be members of an organized trekking party.* I was impressed by the group's willingness to sleep outdoors, exposed to the elements, at seventeen thousand feet above sea level, but I didn't share their enthusiasm for such rugged living, at least not in the high-altitude environment of the Khumbu. I wasn't expecting luxury accommodations at Gorak Shep, that much was certain, but a simple room and a bed would definitely bring comfort in such a cold and desolate place.

Our guest house was a haphazardly constructed building, and my private room consisted of four thin walls and a lumpy, stained mattress. Once I settled in, I sat down and thought about how well the trek had gone thus far. I couldn't believe how fast we had been able to move after hiring Bhim and Jan back in Namche Bazaar. We had covered a significant amount of ground in just three days' time.

I was happy we'd made such good progress up the trail, but part of me felt uneasy about going so high so fast. All four of us were young, healthy, and ambitious, but I sensed that sometimes that triad of factors could work against a person.

When the sun began to set, Beth and I threw on our puffy jackets and beanies and left the lodge. We headed for a small knoll situated behind the guest house, to a place where we could sit in silence and take in the grand views. I looked up into the blueberry soup—that purplish, high-altitude evening sky—and breathed deeply. We'd made it.

"I'm leaving for base camp super early," said Beth, breaking the silence with her matter-of-fact statement. "Probably around four o'clock or so. You in?"

"That's a little too early for me," I said, cringing at the thought of rising at that ungodly hour.

Beth had earlier stated that climbers, mountaineers, and other adventurers owned those early-morning hours, wherever they were in the world. She contended that, apart from people working graveyard shifts, outdoor enthusiasts were the only people who chose to be awake between two and four in the morning. If her stories were any indication, Beth's past had been littered with early-morning summit bids and predawn rafting launches, and she had made peace with those cold, raw hours long ago. Now, sacrificing the warmth and comfort of her down sleeping bag was the price Beth was willing to pay for a slice of trekking nirvana.

"Maybe I'll even climb Kala Pattar afterward to get some sweet photos of the Big Boy," she added, nodding in Everest's general direction.

It was extremely rare to get evening views of the big mountains, according to Bhim and Jan, because most days they were socked in from late afternoon on. It felt incredible to be in a place like Gorak Shep, a place where humans were never meant to live permanently. We were all just visitors in this strange, inhospitable, and frozen land. We came from all around the world for a day or two at most, snapped a few pictures, and then quickly retreated to more hospitable locations.

Beth and I headed back to the guest house for a quick dinner with Bhim and Jan after the sun set and the air took on a distinct chill. We sat around a potbellied stove in the dining area and tried to stay warm while the cook prepared our food.

"You are enjoying it, our fine services?" said Bhim, smiling at me from the other side of the stove.

"Absolutely," I said. "But I would enjoy your services even more if you piggybacked me up to base camp early tomorrow morning."

"No piggies in base camp," said Jan, wagging his finger at me. "Only porters and Western peoples it is there. Maybe yak, maybe yeti, but no piggies, OK, boss?"

I became aware of a subtle process rattling my physiology at some point between ordering the evening meal and sitting down to eat it. I knew there was a problem when I could only make it halfway through my plate of macaroni and cheese with tomato sauce, but I blamed my poor appetite on extreme fatigue and the blandness of the processed food. I excused myself from the group and instructed Beth not to wait for me the following morning. I would head up to base camp a few hours after her.

"We'll probably pass each other on the trail," she said. "Nighty-night, Baby Bear. Sleep tight."

I felt the gears of perverted biochemistry beginning to grind as I made my way to my room. I began to worry that I had fallen victim not only to AMS, but also to the pride and ignorance that consumed so many trekkers in their lofty quests. I was embarrassed by the possibility that I put my own health and well-being in jeopardy simply because I wanted to push myself harder and go higher and farther than I had ever gone before. I was embarrassed by the possibility that I had succumbed to Everest fever and the ambition of youth.

I was especially embarrassed because of the way I counseled Beth, a backcountry specialist, about the need for taking it easy, for going slower on our way up the trail. Here I had thought her ego was insurmountable, but it was my own ego that was refusing to budge to common sense. My pride, and a growing sense of fear, shackled me into a shameful silence, and I felt trapped. I tried to simply shrug it all off and sleep, hoping I would feel better in the morning. It wasn't wise, it wasn't rational, but I wasn't thinking straight either. I didn't know it at the time, but I was much further into the breakdown than I ever could have imagined.

The full measure of my symptoms took hold long after everyone else at the guest house had turned in for the night. Waves of nausea, a splitting headache, and feelings of impending doom—as though the angel of death itself would arrive at any moment to carry me off—gripped me in their merciless clutches. Feverish thoughts began rushing through my mind.

The worst part of the entire ordeal was that, in the back of my mind, I knew exactly what was happening to me. But that fear of the truth left me powerless to do the one sure thing that would save my life: descend. I lay awake in bed and cursed the blackness of night for being so unrelenting and, yes, black. The thought of having to get up in that darkness, tell Beth what was going on, and then walk all the way back down to Pheriche or one of the other lower-altitude villages in the dead chill of night was unpalatable.

The irrational part of me also believed that if I got up and left the guest house, I would be validating the existence of the condition from which I was suffering. So I lay there, awake in my sleeping bag on the guest house bed for what seemed like hours, all the while yearning for the safety and comfort of the Dharamsala International Hostel & Guest House, with its painted gables and deep-fried Mars bars.

The relentless ticking of a small alarm clock left behind by a previous guest counted down every second of those wretched hours. And as if that weren't enough, and just when I thought my situation couldn't possibly get any more complicated, Alan Parsons Project returned to stand on the higher ground of my consciousness with renewed vigor, the song's verses looping in my mind, over and over and over again. Progressive rock certainly had its place, but it wasn't above seventeen thousand feet and in the dead chill of night.

I did fall asleep at some point in the night, though, because I dreamed I was sitting in a Berkeley lecture hall, surrounded by peers. Then something unexpected happened: the entire floor of the lecture hall was stripped from beneath my feet like a tablecloth snapped out from under a set of carefully prepared china by a magician. I was left hovering in space as a feeling of immense panic overcame me. I experienced the distinct sensation that I no longer existed as a human being; I was a lost soul in an unending cosmos whose immensity I repeatedly failed to grasp, and I was gripped by a fear of the vastness of the universe. I tried to scream, but my efforts were muffled by the choke and smother of the dream world.

This strange, dehumanizing loss of what it meant to *be* scared me most, a loss of ego that weighed so heavily on me I couldn't even lift my head. I was a shell of a human being at that particular moment. I had no name, no history, and everything around me seemed fake or nonmaterial. It even felt as though my family members were not real, that all my shared experiences with them and all the love they had showered upon me over the years had simply been an elaborate dream, a figment of my imagination. It felt as though, after countless years of patient observation and minimal tinkering, somebody or something, some omnipotent and malevolent being, had all of a sudden decided to alter the parameters controlling the study of my life.

And then, without warning, I found myself alone and helpless near the summit of Mars's Olympus Mons, the tallest known mountain in the solar system, at 88,850 feet—over three times the height of Mount Everest. Standing near the summit, I prayed for a return to familiarity, but was instead lambasted by an enormous realization that overwhelmed me and knocked me off my feet.

I rag-dolled down the mountain's gentle slopes in slow motion, suddenly aware of the energy required to fully engage life as a human being. The thought of this effort, which seemed unsustainable and unrealistic, pulled me down even farther. When I thought I would die for sure, the spiritual guru and yogic master known to the masses as the Milk Baba appeared. The Milk Baba, with the agility of a true transcendental yogic flyer, helped me break free of the Martian atmosphere and float gracefully into outer space. Led by the galactic guidance of the guru's milky way, I drifted slowly toward the earth, tumbling head over heels all the way home.

What is my reason for existing? If I am such an insignificant creature in the grand cosmic scheme, then why do I bother to exist at all? I kept tripping over the notion that I had no say in whether I chose to be born into this life; that it was cruel to force a person into existence, then fail to provide them with the answers to life's most fundamental questions—two slaps in the face before a person even knew what was happening.

The Milk Baba and I touched down at some point in the early morning hours—meaning the nausea woke me. "Oh, shit!" I said, feeling the partially digested remains of the previous evening's meal churning in my stomach. I unzipped my sleeping bag and mustered the courage and the strength to step out into the room's freezing air wearing nothing but my underwear. I quickly threw on my warmest clothes, including the Blue Bloater, groped for a headlamp, and then made a punch-drunk stumble-dash for the squat toilet situated inside a tin shack roughly fifty yards away from the guest house.

I did my best to hit the porcelain target, but squarely placing six rounds of regurgitated mac and cheese on the bull's-eye is a tall order for even the most experienced vomiter. Some of the puke ended up on the cement slab surrounding the toilet, some found the shack's tin walls and my clothing, and some even found its way onto the ceiling. The overpowering toxic aroma of the lemon-scented restroom—rest*shack*—cleaner set me off again.

I eventually shuffled back to the guest house, grabbed a handful of anise seeds from a brown bowl in the lobby, and crunched on them to get the awful taste out of my mouth. I made the wise albeit long-overdue decision to gather my belongings and head back down the trail to a lower altitude. I was in rough shape, but at least I was vertical and no longer hallucinating or paralyzed by fear, the night's crisp air and the vomiting having purged my mental and physical self. Stuffing my day pack usually took no more than ten minutes, but that morning, as the first rays of dawn broke though the icy window pane, it took me almost an hour.

My pack finally ready, I stumbled toward Beth's room and banged loudly on her door. I noticed that somebody, probably ages ago, had carved a monkey into the wood. It occurred to me after several rounds of knocking that she was already on the trail heading up to base camp. I wasn't sure what room Bhim and Jan were in, and I didn't want to go banging on every door in the guest house to locate them. I found a pen and scrap piece of paper in my backpack, and I painstakingly wrote a note for Beth, telling her where I would be if she wanted to find me later that night or the following day.

I folded the piece of paper carefully, feeling its smoothness beneath my fingertips, before slipping the note under Beth's door. She would get the note later that day, after returning from her hike to base camp. I then made my way to the guest house reception counter where, through an extraordinary display of higher cognitive function, I somehow managed to tally my expenses in the ledger, make out my own bill, and find the appropriate amount of cash in my money belt to pay the lodge's owners. Once I did all that, I hopscotched around the bodies of porters and guides sleeping near the lodge's potbellied stove. I couldn't decide if the dining area, with bodies strewn haphazardly about, looked more like a war zone or some bizarre high-altitude slumber party.

I returned to the scene of the crime to wash away any remaining evidence of the previous night's sickness and light a stick of juniper incense—just in case the stench of the vomit was worse than the stench of the lemon-scented cleaner. I flushed the remaining vomit down the hole with a much-too-yellow stream of warm urine before staggering through the boulder fields above Gorak Shep.

My mind was finally calm enough to accept the thought that I would never get to see base camp. I had come all this way, expended an extraordinary amount of energy, and I wouldn't even reach my goal. That realization was of little significance at this point, though, given the state I was in. Survival instinct had set in, and nothing but descending really mattered. Besides, I reasoned, somewhat coherently, I could beat myself up about it later if I wanted.

Along the trail, I passed a number of large, organized trekking parties, who were all marching single file, their members spaced as evenly as a Nepali porter's toes, on their way up to base camp. I was so out of it that I didn't even exchange greetings with them. I just stared straight down the narrow earthen track, my gaze fixed on distant landmarks, like a cow coming home from pasture. Additionally, the egotistical side of me didn't want anybody to understand how ruined I was by the altitude—I was sure that any acknowledgment I could have managed would have been, at best, a strangled grunt. I was lucid enough now to feel the sting of humiliation over ascending too quickly.

I eventually made it back to Pheriche, amazingly with no further injury, considering I was at times doing more of a controlled fall than a downhill hike. I visited the trekkers' aid post there, where I bought a few packets of black currant–flavored oral rehydration salts. It was only matter of minutes before the combination of the lower altitude and the salts gave me the energy and motivation to continue on to Tengboche, where I reserved a private room and quietly continued my recovery from the previous night's horrors by sleeping, journaling, and reading.

I thought about how much my family meant to me, and how much they cared about me. I knew they had been with me, in some capacity, throughout the night's ordeal at Gorak Shep. This was especially true of my mother, who often had vivid premonitions of danger. I had long ago learned to believe in a mother's unexplainable bond with her child.

The next thing I knew, I was torn from my sleep by a loud commotion outside my room. The door swung open a few seconds later, and I yelped as a beam from a high-powered, industrial-grade flashlight, its intense luminescence irritating, yet vaguely familiar, blinded me. Also vaguely familiar was a small female voice behind the light that kept repeating my last name. "Creed, *Creed*, is that you?"

"Yeah, it's me. Who wants to know?" I went from asleep to awake without passing groggy and struggled to sit up on my elbows.

"Bhim, Jan, he's in here!" The light clattered to the floor and though I couldn't see anything but fireworks, I felt a big squeeze from Beth through my sleeping bag.

Bhim and Jan, apparently also happy to see me, followed suit with hugs of their own. "Oh, big brothers, we are too happy to be seeing you alives and well," said Bhim. "You are having it the *wak-wak*? The nausea?"

"Not so much right now, Bhim," I said, "but, yeah, I was definitely feeling the wak-wak this morning."

"I'm *so* glad we found you," Beth said, giving me another quick squeeze. "I found your note—which was pretty whacked out, by the way—after I came down from base camp earlier today. The boys and I walked all day trying to catch up with you."

"But the note said not to worry, that I'd just wait for you guys here at Tengboche," I said, feeling sheepish about my hasty departure from Gorak Shep and the concern it had sparked. "You didn't have to come down right away, you know."

"Uh, I hate to say it, Baby Bear, but your note was a *little* more cryptic than that." Beth grabbed the flashlight off the floor and pointed the beam at a small piece of scrap paper she held in her hand. "Let me read it to you, and then you'll understand why we wanted to find you."

Clearing her throat, she began: "*Juniper maybe Pheriche but shit. Beth, embarrassed. Sooo embarrassed.*" Beth looked up.

That was it?

"*Now* you can see why we were so worried. We talked to the doctors at the trekkers' aid post in Pheriche, and they said you had passed through earlier in the day. They weren't 100 percent sure, but they thought you were heading here, to Tengboche, for the night."

"Sorry for the scare," I said, now fully awake. "But I'm feeling a lot better now."

"OK, we've all got rooms for the night, so you just sleep tight and recover," she said, and I knew she had accepted my apology. "And for god's sake, Creed, don't you *ever* pull a stunt like that again."

"Deal," I said before rolling over in my sleeping bag and falling back to sleep.

We all set off together at a moderate pace for Namche Bazaar the following morning. The morning passed without event, and by early afternoon we were back in the unofficial Sherpa capital of the Khumbu region. In Namche that night, at the Dharamsala, the sounds of altitude illness—that repetitive hacking and coughing and vomiting—filled the evening air and became background noise. We returned to the trailhead at Lukla after a rest day in Namche, where we warmly thanked Bhim and Jan for their company, their enthusiasm, and their local expertise before paying them for their services. We would be sad to part with them.

Bhim and Jan found another trekking group, but its members weren't quite ready to leave yet, and I opted to keep them company while Beth went to the Buddha Air office to see about changing our departure date. "So, what will you guys do after the trekking season?" I asked.

"We are doing some farmings and making it a few crafts for sale," Bhim said, smiling broadly.

"I did it!" Beth called, strolling toward us. "I got our flight moved up to tomorrow. I'm totally stoked! Hey, Creed, did you tell Bhim and Jan about our little gift?"

"Not yet," I said. "I was waiting for you."

Beth smiled and put her arms around our guides' shoulders. "Well, beautifuls, we thought you guys could probably make better use of our jackets than we could. It's chilly in Kathmandu, but it's nothing like the Khumbu." We simultaneously unzipped our puffers and handed them over to the boys; Bhim received the Blue Bloater and Jan, the Pink Puffer.

"*Gulaphi!*" said Jan. "*Gulaphi monparrcha!* Pink it is my *favorites* color!"

While flashier and much warmer than Bhim and Jan's ratty old sweaters, the jackets weren't exactly the best fit. The Blue Bloater was a little big on Bhim and the Pink Puffer a little small on Jan, but it didn't seem to matter. The jackets would help them work later into the trekking season, thereby allowing them to earn more money to help support their families back home.

Beth and I had wanted to do something special for the boys, something beyond simply tipping them for their services, although we did that too. She came up with the idea of handing over our jackets after brainstorming over cups of hot chocolate during our rest day in Namche. She had heard about a clothing lending program for porters run by a Kathmandu-based NGO called Porters' Progress. What had started out as a single closet and a dozen jackets had blossomed into a program through which thousands of porters annually received warm clothing, essential equipment, and other protective gear.

Beth and I woke the following morning to find a dense fog shrouding the entire village of Lukla. The lodge owner, a friendly Sherpa man in his fifties, informed us that all flights to and from Lukla had been delayed at least one day, if not more. Beth and I, disappointed but resigned to our fate, spent most of the day reading and writing and hoping that the fog would lift and flights would run as usual.

But it was no use. The following day's weather wasn't much better, and it started to become uncomfortably crowded in Lukla as increasing numbers of trekkers arrived for scheduled but delayed flights out of the mountains. The frustration and inconvenience proved too much for some trekkers; there always seemed to be some level of dispute simmering to a boil or fizzling out between trekkers and local airline officials.

I too was eager to leave, especially because I'd given away my best source of warmth to Bhim. But nothing could be done about the weather, and I saw no point in punishing the airline officials for something beyond their control. The only other option, besides sitting tight until the weather cleared, was to hike all the way down to Jiri, a challenging, calorie-crushing, multiday walk from Lukla. Beth and I continued to wait.

The weather improved on our third morning in Lukla. Beth and I, because we had made reservations for the return flight so far in advance, and because of our position in the departure queue, found ourselves on one of the first planes back to the Nepali capital. We had both started to go stir crazy in Lukla and were happy to be in the air and winging back to Kathmandu.

I was excited to get back to Pepsicola Townplanning and reimmerse myself in my Peace Corps duties. It had only been a short time since I'd begun volunteering, but an ever-growing aspect of my identity was intertwined with my role as a volunteer with the Peace Corps—or Peace Corpse, as Madhu continued to call it. It was who I had become, a title and a lifestyle simultaneously.

More Than You Bargain For

ADRIANA'S DECISION TO WORK IN DHARAVI INSPIRED ME IN A WAY THAT, TO this day, I can't truly understand. There was something so *human* about her compassion for people she'd never met. Over the years, this shaped my life's work and my own curiosity about the world, but in those first few days after I discovered her whereabouts, I was overcome by the simple desire to get out there, find her, and make things right between us.

If shame is the leash that tethers us to our mistakes, then pride is the knife that tries to sever that leash. Both helped mobilize me. I said good bye to family and friends during the remainder of the fall term at Berkeley, and shortly after New Year's, with hope flying by my side, I headed for Mumbai and one of the most memorable experiences of my life.

I wasn't even remotely prepared for India. From the air Mumbai looked like a city on steroids, a sprawling mass of humanity spilling from the Arabian Sea to devour all inhabitable land in its path. This paled in comparison to what I experienced on the ground.

I had no sense of direction, no real way to orient myself to the city beyond a guidebook I had borrowed from a friend. I staggered toward the airport exit, my gaze repeatedly shifting toward and away from two security guards carrying semiautomatic rifles. I had never seen that kind of weapon in real life, and I felt my knees weaken momentarily before I collected myself, put on a brave face, and stepped out into a wall of heat, noise, exhaust, and sweat.

I almost expected Adriana to be there to greet me. Of course she wasn't. I had never felt more alone than I did in those first few minutes in Mumbai. It was late afternoon, and already daylight was beginning to vanish. I had no idea where I would spend the night, and I was scared, truly scared, for the first time in my life. I didn't know how to act or what to say; I didn't know how to speak the language; I didn't know anything about India or Mumbai, and I couldn't seem to make sense of anything I saw around me.

The first people I met in Mumbai were the taxicab drivers and their associated baggage handlers. I didn't know how to protest against the number of men who seemed to think I needed assistance: there was one to carry my bags to the car, one to put the bag in the trunk, another to close the trunk and bind its latch with twine—so that nothing could be stolen while the cab was stopped in traffic—one to open and close the passenger door, and finally, one to actually drive.

My recollection of that cab ride through Mumbai has always remained clear, because the environment seemed so alien. I was struck by the non-stop energy of the place, by the fact that the city showed no signs of slowing down as afternoon became evening and evening became night. It was then that I realized Mumbai was the type of place that never allowed strangers to get their bearings—there was no place to hide and no privacy to be had, not even for a person's own thoughts. In one city, you are exposed to the *world,* and if you didn't submit to the curious nature of its people and let yourself be viewed, you would probably spend your entire stay locked away in your hotel room, hating yourself for ever having made the trip. I didn't want to feel more isolated or sorry for myself than I already did, so I made a pact with myself, in that tiny, orange-topped Bombay Ambassador taxi, to feel the opposite.

I spent two days in Colaba, the city's tourist district, before I finally worked up the courage to go to Dharavi and find Adriana. I was extremely nervous, not only because it would be the first time I'd seen Adriana in months, but also because I'd never seen a slum before. I had no idea where to go or how to explain my presence there. I didn't know whether I would be welcomed as a guest or run out as an intruder. It had always been my understanding that the world's slums were almost impenetrable by outsiders, that slum dwellers viewed visitors, especially foreigners, with suspicion.

There were countless reasons to pack up and go home, to admit defeat and simply move on with my life, but the power of love and the need for redemption drove me forward.

I didn't find Adriana at Chota Sion Hospital. She had left Dharavi when she heard that I was coming to Mumbai and hadn't told anybody where she was going. I had come halfway around the world to seek redemption, so to turn around at that point would have been a monumental failure in my eyes. With the helpful guesses of her coworkers, I followed Adriana around India in vain over the following three months, through Jaipur, Delhi, Dehradun, Rishikesh, and Manali, through Lucknow and Varanasi and Kolkata. But I was always just a few steps behind.

* * *

I shivered my way through that entire first winter in Kathmandu, despite the proximate warmth of my friends at the Pepsicola Clinic and my fellow Peace Corps volunteers. At night, when the thermometer dropped to near-freezing levels, I shuddered to think of all the homeless people trying to survive on the city's streets without even uninsulated walls to at least keep out the wind.

Despite the cold, and despite my body's desire to hibernate for the winter, the months following my return from the Everest region were productive ones. Our usual Peace Corps crew continued to meet every Tuesday night at the Rum Doodle, and we even had the privilege of welcoming N-200, a whole new group of Peace Corps trainees, to Nepal early in the new year before they underwent their preservice training and were split up and dispatched to their posts throughout the country. I visited Slice of Life Bakery numerous times too, not only for the world-famous chocolate cake but also to hang out with my tough new friend, Raju Shrestha: cakehouse owner, hookah magnate, and street fighter extraordinaire.

I valued his opinion not because he was popular and well-known but because I thought we had a lot in common when I was at my best, which I usually was when I was with Raju. He was always encouraging me to become more of a leader, and he treated me with a high degree of respect. Raju's influence in material matters began to rub off on me as well, and I found myself heading to New Road—Kathmandu's trendy shopping district—on a regular basis. I had come to Nepal believing in minimalism as a matter of principle, but my time in the Peace Corps was convincing me that materialism was not such a bad thing. You could own good stuff and still be a good person—an idea championed by the Nepalis I met and worked with in Pepsicola Townplanning and elsewhere throughout Kathmandu.

Raju suggested a store called Deep's Sole to replace my shoes, footwear he considered baser than the dirt they walked on. Raju insisted that I would never find the shoe store on my own, as it was hidden away in Old Kathmandu, so I decided to ask Madhu to take me there.

Ashish and Pradeep Rai, co-owners of the store and brothers, were good friends with the cakeshop owner—in other words, I learned, their names were in his Rolodex. Raju didn't have time for people with questionable business practices, which seemed surprising, given the clientele he served in his private lounge. A person only had to mess up once to be out of his Rolodex, a shameful fate his contacts wanted to avoid at all cost.

The day finally came for my shopping trip, and I met Madhu at the clinic early that morning. "Today morning, *aaja bihaana*," said Madhu, climbing onto his motorcycle, "we will make a move to Old Kathmandu to find you your handsome new shoes!"

Admin had a strict rule prohibiting volunteers from using motorcycles. The penalty for such an infraction was severe: immediate termination of a volunteer's activities and an early trip home, a fate otherwise known as administrative separation. I had never heard of anyone being "ad sep'd" for this offense, but the threat was always looming. Admin had established the rule after a study revealed that an unusually high percentage of Peace Corps volunteer deaths were motorcycle related. I was taking a huge risk riding with Madhu on his motorcycle, but Stella'! was in the shop, and I was too impatient to use public transit. I also felt confident we would elude the Peace Corps' dragnet for unlawful motorcycle riding.

We finally reached Old Kathmandu. Madhu parked the motorcycle at the mouth of a dingy gully, as he called it. The alleyway's entrance, flanked by statues of larger-than-life Hindu deities, smelled strongly of ammonia, as though the city's homeless had consecrated the nearby gutters as their sacred lavatory. A sign forbidding the further passage of motorized vehicles was positioned conspicuously over the entrance to the corridor.

Madhu and I slipped through the narrow passageway into a labyrinth where shadows presided with authoritarian rule over all who dared enter. The walls, festooned with orange flowers for an upcoming Hindu festival, retained the damp sheen of an early morning mist. As we passed through the entanglement of public corridors and private gardens, I also saw women, young and old alike, stooped at the waist, brusquely sweeping the cobbled lanes in front of their dwellings. Their short brooms, made of tightly-bunched straw, sent dust devils swirling into the air, where beams of heavenly light punching through the urban canopy caught them and made them dance.

The lanes soon became narrower and more difficult to negotiate. I hopped over puddles of stagnant water and dodged piles of desiccated dog poop before eventually tumbling out behind Madhu into a crumbling multitiered indoor-outdoor commercial complex known as the Bishek Bazaar. I was amazed by how little space each shopkeeper had—most of the shops weren't much wider than the door through which their customers came and went.

The shopkeepers had little real estate to call their own, it was true, but they had all managed to set up aesthetically pleasing displays with high curb appeal, their bountiful wares spilling onto the footpath like beer from the mouth of the White Bhairab during the Indra Jatra festival.

It was clear, given the place's bustle, that the complex was a popular commercial hub, a place where Nepalis from all over the city came to satisfy their needs for textiles, clothing, and a whole host of consumer items. A familiar Hindi pop song blaring over a tinny transistor radio caused me to stop dead in my tracks as I passed one of the specialty shops—one offering Cuban stogies, Native American dream catchers, palm readings, and a broad assortment of Tarot decks. And then I was dancing, bopping out to the up-tempo rhythm and the heartfelt, soul-infused vocals.

I couldn't help myself. It was as though I just *had* to move my body to the music. I don't know what came over me at that particular moment. I was quite shy about dancing in public in the States, as I think most

Americans are. But there were many things that I found easier to do in Nepal, and dancing in public was certainly one of them.

The shopkeepers in the vicinity noticed my bopping. They crept to their doorsteps and furiously head-bobbled their approval, their gazes and grins locked on me in silent amusement. The conservatively clad men were all dressed in the traditional outfit of an older Nepali male and the symbol of Nepali nationalism: a white *daura suruwal* with gray *juhari* coat and topi. They quickly followed my lead, descending the steps in front of their shops with unexpected agility to begin dancing with me.

They were like tea leaves in piping hot water, those men were, raising their arms high in the air, twisting their wrists rapidly back and forth as though they were screwing in light bulbs. Some of the shopkeepers whirled to the music's beat, while others, smiling broadly, brandished imaginary guns that they hoisted to their shoulders, firing them repeatedly into the air. Still others shimmied their shoulders, shook their hips, and wiggled their heads, reaching their arms out to embrace everyone and no one in particular.

"What a silly you are, daai!" Madhu snorted after the song had ended and he had led me to the entrance of the Bishek Bazaar. With a huge grin, he added, "If you don't mind me saying it to your face, you are looking very, very much like Hindi film star with your most fabulous dancing moves. You are seeing the way those men are liking your style? They are thinking you are a hero for all Nepal!"

"I'm flattered, Madhu! And thanks for showing me the way here. Are you sure you can't stay a little longer?"

"Sorry, boss, but driving duties for Peace Corpse calls," said Madhu, slapping me on the back and retreating to his motorcycle.

I found the Bishek Bazaar's watchman standing just inside the mall's entryway. He was an older gentleman, dressed in a neat uniform, and he had a crook in his back rivaling that of Old Kumar from the neighborhood. "Excuse me, sir. Do you know where I can find Deep's Sole, the shoe store?" He scratched his head and took a long time to think about my question. Then he slowly and silently raised his *lathi*—his slender billy club—and pointed at a nearby store. I thanked the man, placed a twenty-rupee note in his palm, and strode toward the shop under the dying flicker of a bank of fluorescent lights.

"Welcome to Deep's Sole!" said an enthusiastic young man with a flat-topped haircut. "I am Pradeep Rai, coproprietor of this fine establishment, and this is my brother, Ashish."

I shook hands with the young men. Ashish was a stockier, shaggy-haired version of Pradeep. Both men wore fashionable outfits and shoes with fiercely tapered toe boxes.

"I'm looking for a great pair of shoes, guys, but I need to use the public urinals first," I said, my bladder beginning to spasm.

"Sir-ji, if you must urinate, please do so in our private bathroom. Much cleaner and better for you, I think," said Ashish.

Once inside the restroom, I was distracted by unusual sounds emanating through the wall. I placed my ear against the cement and swore I could hear the faint roar of a crowd, punctuated by grunting. The noises were distinctly masculine and distinctly aggressive.

I emerged back into the store intending to ask the Rai brothers about the strange noises, but they quickly presented me with a glass of piping hot black tea and insisted I sit down at the sales counter and tell them my unabbreviated life story.

"Please, brother, *chiya khanus; laz na maanus!*" Pradeep cajoled. "Do not be shy; drink your tea!"

I had learned that Nepali businessmen loved to sit and chat at length with their customers, especially foreigners, whom they could butter up for a larger sale. This gamesmanship could either be sinister or playful, depending on the context. I sensed nothing slick or shady about Ashish and Pradeep, though. They were young guys like me, and I got the sense that they were simply curious to learn more about life in the United States. They had heard many rumors about the country—some of which were true, most of which were false—and they wanted to know more about the luxuries, the freedoms, and the responsibilities of American citizenship.

We finally got down to the business of shoe selection and price haggling when the tea was gone and my guts were spilled to the brothers' satisfaction. The brothers, aware they had my undivided attention, paraded countless makes and models before me for inspection. They turned their tiny store upside down, trying to find not only the perfect style of shoe to suit my tastes but also the properly sized shoe to fit my relatively massive size-twelve feet.

The process was exhausting. But then Ashish, nervously closing one eye and holding a box at arm's length, cautiously opened the container's lid to reveal the most incredible shoes I had ever seen: a pair of brand-new, cherry-red, low-cut, size twelve Doc Martens, straight from England.

The Docs, which sported a robust, waxy, full-grain leather with an oily sheen, were the real deal, explained Pradeep. Performing a side-by-side comparison of the Docs with a pair of cheap knockoffs recently shipped in from China, he pointed out the most glaring differences between the two pairs of footwear. "Not even the finest and most talented *sarki* in all of Nepal could reproduce this kind of quality," Pradeep whispered, caressing the shoes.

While the brothers continued describing the shoes' attributes, and Ashish spit-shined and buffed them, a steady stream of patrons entered the store, only to disappear into the small room containing the squat toilet and never return. The duo took no notice of their patrons' peculiar behavior, as though their customers' penchant for communal toiletry—and contortionism—was nothing more than a routine fetish in a land of unexplainable customs.

"My friend, this shoe will not wait for you," Pradeep said, pushing for the sale. "Please, sir-ji, try them on and see how they feel."

Although the Docs were nicer than any shoe I had previously owned, they were no substitute for the bare foot. I thought about how good it had felt to go barefoot while trekking in the Everest region. I understood that my foot would be healthiest with no shoe at all, but fashion sometimes trumps function, Raju had said, and the Docs were unquestionably fashionable.

And so the haggling began.

The brothers played the game well, throwing out a greatly inflated starting price to test my bargaining savvy. They looked personally offended when I countered with an offer less than half their initial ask, but they eventually rallied with a counteroffer. I came to understand through our back-and-forth that they saw themselves as *shoe-shriners* and *soul-repairers*: a pair of evangelical deliverers who preserved the sanctity of individual footwear while encouraging their customers to atone for their worldly sins.

"Look, look, Sir-ji," said Ashish, showing me the price tag on the shoes, "our cost price: five thousand rupees, plus a small bonus for my brother and myself. Helping us will boost your karma and help free your soul! You can cancel all your past transgressions with a single transaction here today, my friend!"

"Five thousand rupees!" I said. "*Dheraai mahago!* That's *still* too expensive, guys."

I took a few seconds to mull over the boys' offer before asking them if I could test out the shoes in the mall's main corridor. The brothers nodded encouragingly and watched me closely as I left the store and started a lap around the mall's ground floor. *Five thousand rupees is definitely a lot of money.* In fact, it was more than half my monthly stipend from the Peace Corps. But when would I ever again find such a pair of shoes? I knew I *had* to pull the trigger on the deal, but I wanted a second opinion to validate my decision. I spotted a pair of stylish men in their mid twenties and flagged them down. "Hey, do you guys think these shoes are worth five thousand rupees?"

One of the men, appearing slightly annoyed, approached with a swagger. Coming face-to-face with me, balling his hands into fists, he looked me directly in the eye and held the stare for several long seconds. Then, without warning, and much to my relief, he quickly dropped to a crouch and began inspecting the Docs. He squeezed a shoe's heel, examined the sole, and tapped his knuckles on the shoe's steel toe.

Standing, he addressed me formally. "May I speak candidly?"

His question caught me off guard. I hadn't expected his English to be so prim and proper. In fact, there was barely even a hint of a Nepali accent in his words. I suspected, based on the crispness and the clarity of his speech, that he was one of those lucky few who had been sent overseas to study, possibly to the UK, possibly to Australia.

"Yeah, of course," I said. "Please do."

"Then let me first assure you that your fears of being swindled are unfounded. Those shoes possess a steel toe box and a reinforced shank. Their soles are first-rate, the leather is nicely buffed and unblemished, and their overall quality smacks of English craftsmanship and design. But let me now rebuke you for your skepticism of Nepali business transactions," chastised the well-spoken man, removing his glasses for effect.

Pointing a finger at the shoes, he said, "Whoever is selling you these shoes for five thousand Nepali rupees is barely turning a profit on them. I'd encourage you to put more faith in your fellow human beings. Five thousand rupees for these shoes is a discount in any part of the world, I assure you."

After I returned to the store and we sealed the deal with a handshake, Ashish said, "Sir-ji, we must tell you that never in our wildest dreams did we imagine we would sell these shoes. This pair of shoes, as far as we're concerned, is the material manifestation of our Lord Pedis, the Hindu god of fine footwear!"

"Well, that might be true," I said, "but I just can't believe I was lucky enough to find these shoes. If it wasn't for my good friend, Raju, I'd still be looking for a decent shoe store."

"Wait!" said an excited Pradeep. "Are you meaning Raju Shrestha, owner of Slice of Life Bakery?"

"Yeah, that's the guy," I said.

"Oh god," said a beaming Ashish. "Sir-ji, why did you not say so earlier? Raju is practically a brother to us, always looking out for us and making sure we have a steady flow of customers. Sometimes he even volunteers as a security guard at our events, making sure the right people get in and the wrong people stay out, if you know what I mean. Any friend of Raju's is also a friend of the Rai family. Because of your friendship with the Great Raju, sir-ji, and because you bought such a special pair of shoes here today, I now bestow upon you all the benefits and luxuries associated with the Rai family name for as long as you live in Kathmandu!"

I wondered what benefits and luxuries two struggling brothers operating out of a decaying mall could possibly enjoy.

"You must come with us now," Ashish insisted, putting the Docs back in their box and placing the package on the shop's counter. "Sir-ji, you *must* join us in a weekly ritual sponsored by our family. We are famous throughout Nepal for the parties we throw and the events we host in our private auditorium. You must come now and experience the festivities firsthand. Aaunus!"

I followed the brothers to the store's rear and watched with curiosity as they squeezed into the small private bathroom. I hesitated momentarily before joining them. Once the three of us stood shoulder to shoulder, Pradeep locked the bathroom door. and his brother removed the full-length mirror hanging on the wall. Behind the mirror was a small opening, a crack just broad enough to fit one person. The brothers, agile and bursting with energy, easily hopped over the squat toilet and through the hole into the pitch blackness beyond. They reminded me of Nepali Pete and how excited he had been to play Kathmandu tour guide so many months earlier.

"We must hurry if we are to catch the day's best matches!" I heard Pradeep call.

I pressed my body up against the hole in the wall and reached through to the other side with my right arm. The brothers hauled me the rest of the way through and then waited until I had regained my balance before leading me to a wrought-iron staircase plunging deep into a subterranean environment. I again heard the noises, and they were growing louder with each step downward. We soon entered what I can only describe as an arena, a damp, dimly lit, funky-smelling grotto filled to the brim with wildly cheering people.

The boys explained over the din that the members of their family were the original developers and promoters of the Nepali Underground Wrestling Federation, or NUWF, a passion sparked in their parents by a now-distant trip to the American Midwest, where they had fallen in love with professional wrestling. They also realized the potential fortune to be made from introducing this brand of athleticism and theatrics to the South Asian market. The shoe store was simply a front, a way to hide the proceeds generated from ticket sales to their weekly underground extravaganza.

There was something absolutely brilliant about the idea of professional wrestling on the Indian subcontinent. The melodrama of pro wrestling seemed like a natural fit in a land where pageantry, noise, and color were celebrated like nowhere else on the planet, in a land where heroes were venerated and villains vilified.

It wasn't the first time I witnessed the cultural repurposing of an imported idea. I loved the way Nepalis could take some grotesque aspect of American pop culture—even something as over-the-top as professional wrestling—and run it through a great cultural filter to create something their very own. Their ingenuity provided a refreshing take on many of the elements of my own society I had either shrugged off with indifference or disowned altogether.

"The authorities look very disapprovingly upon such unsanctioned events," said Pradeep, steering us toward a block of reserved seats ringside. "They are morally opposed to the wearing of spandex and the baring of flesh, but mostly they are jealous of the success of the NUWF, and they are angry because we refuse to pay them *baksheesh*, bribes. As for the people? Some enter through the store, but most find their way here through numerous underground access points nearby."

Spectators remained glued to their seats, despite the sewer's singeing aroma. A series of food carts served up spicy varieties of dal bhaat and barbecued meats while, behind what looked like a hastily erected beer garden, rats rafted down the working sewer's murky stream on unidentifiable globs of goo. A troop of yammering monkeys patrolled the rafters, hurling plastic wrappers and peanut shells down upon unsuspecting fans.

"As you will soon see, many of the stereotypes we have created for the NUWF are not exactly, how do you say…politically correct, but trust us: the wrestlers are *all* amazing athletes and they're *all* incredible actors. Just sit back and enjoy the show!"

I thought about what Pradeep said, remembering some of the larger-than-life professional wrestlers from my own childhood, who had represented almost everything I knew about different cultures. For instance, there was the Iranian wrestler known as the Iron Sheik, who used moves such as the Camel Clutch and the Iranian Drop to stun opponents and inflame the crowd. There was Boris Zhukov, an American-born character billed as Russian, who sported a furry *ushanka*, a hat like the Russian military wore, a bushy beard, and a red singlet bearing a much-feared logo: the hammer and sickle. And then there was Yokozuna, a Samoan American behemoth representing Japan, a supposed champion sumo wrestler who was managed by Mr. Fuji, another American-born professional wrestling persona portraying a foreign-born character.

As a young boy growing up in Berkeley, I met people of widely varying ethnicities, but for some reason, the muscle-bound professional wrestling stereotypes had been the most memorable and convincing ambassadors of exotic cultures. It took several years and plenty of intervention by my parents before I finally realized just how ridiculous those stereotypes were. And those stereotypes quickly went from merely seeming tasteless to being a little offensive.

Pro wrestling, by the time I reached high school, had degenerated into a seedy enterprise based largely on the promotion of a glamorous, unattainable lifestyle of excess, sexual promiscuity, and the commodification of women, all of which made those early ethnic stereotypes seem rather harmless. And maybe by highlighting the most glaring differences between cultures, professional wrestling had given the public some opportunity to poke fun at the whole idea of labeling people based on race, to look at the way the entire entertainment industry portrayed varying ethnicities and to say, "That's bullshit."

It only seemed fitting that, in Nepal, with its extraordinary number of cultures, classes, castes, and systems of belief, some extraordinary caricatures had arisen to make light of those differences. In Nepali professional wrestling, according to Pradeep, you got maximum glorification of ethnic stereotypes, minus the pimping, the drinking, and the not-so-subtle sexual innuendo that came to define professional wrestling in America.

We settled into our seats. The arena's lights suddenly dimmed, and from somewhere within the shadows, an announcer's voice boomed over the PA system. "Ladies and gentlemen, would you please welcome to the ring PALDEN...THE BUDDHIST...MONK!"

A lime-green spotlight cast its powerful beam on a burly Tibetan emerging from behind a large *thangka* about twenty yards from the ring. Palden the Buddhist, dressed in full monk attire, prostrated himself his entire way to the ring, one body length at a time, mumbling incantations, as his song, "Om Mani Padme Hum," blared over the loudspeakers.

The boys explained that Palden's path to the ring fell directly in line with Mount Kailash, so it was only fitting that, as a devout member of the Buddhist faith, he prostrate his way to the wrestling ring. A cohort of nuns placed butter lamps around the ring's perimeter, which the nuns lit only after Palden had circumambulated the ring several times in a clockwise direction.

Palden's opponent, already in the ring, was a dour-looking young recruit from the actual Royal Nepalese Army; he flexed and ceremoniously kissed his not-so-ample biceps in an attempt to egg on the crowd. It was clear that the pro-Maoist crowd favored the monk, considering the stern backlash the young man received for his antics.

I had consciously sidestepped the country's politically charged issues, though propaganda plastered Kathmandu. Peace Corps Nepal officials had counseled all volunteers to remain politically neutral, as there was little to gain by choosing sides—and much to lose. I understood that both sides of the conflict had valid points, but I also understood that both the Maoist rebels and the government troops had committed unconscionable human rights violations.

Palden situated himself in a corner of the ring, lit a stick of incense, and meditated for a solid ten minutes, during which time the crowd remained silent. When the time was right, Palden rose as though in a trance and turned his opponent into a Nepali pretzel. He finished off the match with what Ashish yelled into my ear was his signature move—a high-flying leap from the top ropes in half-lotus position. Helped by the optical effects of the arena's strobe lights, Palden appeared to hover momentarily in midair before landing on his opponent.

Next up was a tag team of Sherpa brothers, Lobsang and Norbu, from the Solu Khumbu region; they had cheekily dubbed themselves Porters' Progress after the famous local NGO of the same name. The brothers used their dokos to pin opponents while their goats wandered the aisles and nibbled on fans' pant cuffs. When they weren't busy demolishing foes in the ring, the two Sherpas took out their rage on anyone in the crowd they suspected of traveling to Nepal with a Japanese, German, or British tourist group. The spotlight shone on more than one pasty-legged foreigner as he was forced to carry oversize dokos of duffel bags stuffed with useless odds and ends up and down the entrance ramp until he was exhausted.

And then there was the Tout, a loquacious man whose body moved almost as quickly as his mouth. The Tout would snake his way throughout the crowd between body slams of his opponents, attempting to sell package tours before his opponent recovered. A true thorn in the side of fans and opponents alike, the Tout, the Rai brothers explained, prided himself on his enterprising ability to multitask incitations of mass aggravation.

The Merciless Mendicant used the audience's sympathy. He was a footless man who regularly defeated his opponents using bamboo crutches—tools whose use the NUWF had sanctioned based on the Merciless Mendicant's obvious handicap and his ongoing battle with a crippling disease of unknown origin. If the Mendicant defeated his opponent, according to my hosts, he would set up a booth from which to collect alms from appreciative or pitying fans, caring not which was their motivation. If he lost the match, he would still set up his booth. In his case, his character was also his reality, and he needed those donated rupees for his next meal.

Perhaps the most beloved character to make an appearance was a wrestler known as Shiva the Destroyer, or by his unofficial handle, Hindu Stan. Even though Hindu Stan hailed from the Indian side of Birganj—a grimy border town known for its industry and rapidly growing population—the NUWC's fans had long since forgiven him for being born on the wrong side of the tracks.

Hindu Stan had lost every match in which he'd ever participated, according to the boys, which only served to endear him further to his ample fan base. Hindu Stan's religious tradition called for prolonged periods of fasting. Lacking a reliable protein source in his diet, he never stood a chance against his beefier opponents, who heartily devoured rich meals of mutton and buff on match days. The crowd applauded his decision to remain true to his religious convictions.

The afternoon's main event pitted the current titleholder, a seven-foot-tall dreadlocked Israeli working under the alias the Foreign Hand, against a hairy man-beast known simply as the Yeti. The Yeti had on several occasions wrestled the incredible Israeli to a draw.

A hush fell over the crowd in anticipation of the final match. The lights in the arena dimmed. Then the arena exploded in a staccato wave of Israeli rave beats and pyrotechnics. A motorcycle's engine revved from behind one of the curtains as the thumping music reached a frenzied pitch. The Foreign Hand roared down the entrance ramp on a retooled British Enfield, popping a wheelie the entire way to the ring and filling the arena with the scent of exhaust and burning rubber, which the fans, accustomed to the street fumes, were seemingly not averse to.

The Foreign Hand's girlfriend and manager, seated behind him on the Enfield, hung on to her man with a viselike grip. Heavily tattooed and muscled, she was known by the crowd as the Foreign Object, as much for her cheeky assistance ringside—where she made good use of collapsible chairs and other items illegal in the sport to slow down and batter opponents—as for her distinctly feminine curves.

The pair dismounted after several triumphant laps around the ring. The Foreign Hand removed his helmet to reveal his thick, waist-length, dirty-blond dreadlocks and proceeded to head bang with ringside fans to the intense beats still pumping through the sound system. His lengthy locks suggested he had been out of the Israeli Defense Force for at least a decade. The giant Israeli sported knee-high combat boots, pink Spandex trunks, and a designer tie knotted with a four-in-hand, which of course played off the wrestler's moniker.

The Foreign Hand's pomp and ceremony now finished, it was time for the Yeti's grand entrance. A large cage containing the man-beast was wheeled out from behind a curtain and a harsh spotlight trained on the creature for all to see. The Yeti, balking at the obnoxious spotlight, exhibited textbook fear-avoidance behavior but could do little to avoid the exposure, given its neck, wrist, and ankle restraints. Four armed guards released the creature, taunting the Yeti with hunks of raw meat and pitchers of beer.

The Yeti grabbed an entire leg of buff from a nearby concessionaire and furiously gnawed it to the bone before hurling the leftovers into the crowd. The rampaging man-beast—a true Himalayan berserker—then took repeated swipes at nearby fans, mostly to strip them of their Tuborg beer, which it swilled with impunity.

The match proceeded much as had been anticipated, with the Yeti wrestling the Foreign Hand to yet another draw. The crowd had hoped for a native Nepali to reclaim the title, but it recognized the Israeli's phenomenal athleticism and showmanship with a loud round of applause.

The Rai family had done a great job building and promoting the league. They knew exactly how to use scripting to play off the crowd's emotions, vulnerabilities, and fears, and they knew how to put on a cohesive show too.

Ashish and Pradeep took me by the arm and guided me away from the ring as the Yeti was "tranquilized" and wheeled away in its cage, and the crowd started to pack up and move along. "There's somebody we would like you to meet," Ashish said.

The brothers led me down a long, musty corridor before they disappeared into a dressing room. I waited in the corridor for several minutes until the hulking frame of the Foreign Hand, now garbed in a long-sleeved cotton shirt over three-quarter-length cargo pants, emerged through the doorway. I was impressed by how little time it had taken him to gather his things after his match.

The wrestler looked me squarely in the eye and addressed me in a strong Israeli accent. "Ah, so you are the honorable man Ashish and Pradeep just told me about." His booming voice echoed off the nearby walls as he folded up his pink wrestling trunks and placed them, along with his bulky NUWF champion's belt, inside his duffel bag. "You are the one who bought the cherry-red Doc Martens! Despite my great stature, I too wear only a size twelve shoe. I had to choose between the Docs and the Enfield, which I bought for five thousand rupees instead," he said, slapping me on the back and smiling at the brothers. "Why don't you join my girlfriend, Shil, and me for a night out?"

"Sounds great," I said.

"Oh, by the way, my close friends call me by my real name, Yarone."

I said good-bye to the brothers and thanked them for being great hosts. Yarone, Shil, and I left the Enfield parked outside the bazaar and strolled toward Kathmandu's Durbar Square as the shadows of another Nepali afternoon grew long and tired. We retired to the funky confines of Slice of Life Bakery, where we were greeted by Raju, who was pleased to see that the Israelis and I had become acquainted. I had learned from Yarone on our walk that he and Raju were old friends and that they trained together weekly in Krav Maga—a hand-to-hand self-defense system used and popularized by the Israeli Defense Force—on the cobbled terraces of the Swayambhunath monkey temple.

Raju eventually retreated to his personal lounge. I was still having a tough time fitting together the various puzzle pieces that made up his life. His influence on people wasn't based on fear or exploitation, as it often was with other tough men. He was a business owner, he was active in the community, and he was devoted to his religious principles. He was all those things, and apparently he was also a gangster.

We munched on apple crumble and chocolate cake. Our thirsty trio also enjoyed several cups of delicious Turkish coffee, which we clinked together in celebratory fashion before taking our first sips.

"I covet all the desserts here," Yarone acknowledged. "But you must do more than simply *eat* the dessert; you must make love to the cake, like this." Closing his eyes, he finished off his slice of chocolate cake with an indulgent grin and a long, slow lip-smack. Shil, rolling her eyes, playfully pinched Yarone's ear.

I proposed that we share a puff. I was a relative newcomer to the world of the water pipe, but I couldn't think of a better way to foster a sense of cross-cultural exchange. Sharing a communal hookah, much like sharing pots of tea, opened up lines of communication among people who might otherwise not have spoken. I understood perfectly well the implications of its long-term use, but I wasn't such a square that I would deny the hookah's unifying effects for fear of the occasional, brief exposure to toxins and an unlikely subsequent addiction to nicotine.

We discussed many things over the course of the evening, from the impact of American foreign policy on the Middle East to the sage wisdom of Jewish mystics. I learned that the pair had been traveling off and on for the better part of a decade. When Yarone and Shil weren't bouncing from Brazil to Nepal to Bali, they were living it up back home on their kibbutz in Upper Galilee, at the foot of the Golan Heights.

I listened closely as Yarone and Shil described life in their agriculture- and tourism-based commune. According to Shil, their kibbutz was an intentionally planned community that combined the beliefs and practices of Zionism with those of socialism. I learned from Yarone that consolidation of communal living and farming practices in his country had sprung from the desire to create an entirely new society where exploitation no longer existed and all citizens would be treated as equals. Kibbutzing, according to Yarone, was the couple's great *mitzvah*—their good deed to the world—and their way of leading others by example.

As I watched them bubble smoke through the water pipe's basin, it struck me that there was something magnetic about the pair. Maybe it was their confidence, or their brashness, or their ability to insinuate themselves into the complex urban framework of Kathmandu that captured my attention. Or maybe it was their worldliness, that aura of unflappability that comes from having seen everything from war zones and battlefields to breezy banana plantations and beachside hammocks. They had a gritty sophistication about them that I appreciated and envied too. I also envied that they consciously refused to participate in the grind.

Raju emerged through his beaded doorway when it was time to close the restaurant. He wished us well, insisting we return soon to sample the mango cheesecake he was about to unleash on the public. He also confirmed his Krav Maga session with Yarone at Swayambhunath for the following afternoon before embracing the Israeli with an effortless series of rapid backslaps in that authentic, yet guarded, way in which tough men embrace.

A thoughtful critic and a dedicated strategist, Raju insisted that the Foreign Hand would need every ounce of preparation he could muster for his upcoming match with the Great Khali, a seven-foot-three, 420-pound international wrestling sensation and Punjabi police officer who was scheduled to appear at Sharma Slam in just under two weeks.

Sharma Slam was named after a group of sponsors from the local Brahman community and was billed as *the* Nepali underground wrestling event of the century. According to Yarone, as much as the NUWF fans recoiled at the thought of a non-Nepali like him wearing the champion's belt, the idea of a high-profile Indian celebrity breezing into town and stealing the league's top prize absolutely drove them insane. Of course, this all seemed rather amusing to Yarone, who laughed heartily at the crowd's fickleness.

The Israelis and I walked back to the Bishek Bazaar and made plans to get together after the hype of Sharma Slam had died down. Another friendship forged. I felt fortunate to be surrounded by so many interesting people from such a variety of backgrounds. There was a richness to the sharing and blending of widely differing cultures that I loved, and it was proof, at least in my mind, that I could drop into any country on the planet and find common ground with almost anyone. That knowledge gave me a cultural fearlessness I could carry with me always, and I was grateful for it.

I felt a light tap on my shoulder as I watched the couple roar away on their Enfield. Turning, I recognized the Bishek Bazaar's ancient, hump-backed security guard. He cradled a familiar package in his gnarled, arthritic hands: a rectangular, cream-colored box with a small note attached to the lid. The old man handed me the package, shuffled around a corner, and disappeared into the night.

I peeled the note off the box and stepped into the glow cast by a nearby streetlamp.

Dear Brother, in the afternoon's excitement, you forgot these in our store. It is our great hope that whenever you lace them up, you will think of your Nepali brothers, Ashish and Pradeep, at the Bishek Bizarre.

The misspelling of bazaar was no doubt a humorous coincidence, but the error seemed apropos, given the unexpected events of one of the strangest days of my life. I had definitely gotten more than I bargained for at the Bishek Bazaar. I thanked Lord Pedis, the Hindu god of fine footwear, for such a lucky find, and began the short journey back to Shruti Bhupani's roost and my life in Pepsicola Townplanning.

Shooting the Bhote Kosi

THOSE THREE MONTHS IN INDIA WERE AMONG THE MOST FRUSTRATING OF my life. Frustrating not only because Adriana refused to hear my plea for forgiveness but also because of the poverty I saw around me, hopeless poverty that seemed impossible to combat. I eventually returned to Mumbai, to Dharavi, partly because I hoped Adriana would stop running and return to her post at Chota Sion and partly because the slum was the only true anchor I had in the country. I had gone in search of Adriana to make amends for the things I said to her, and when I couldn't find her, I decided to help those she was helping because that meant being close to her in a positive, honoring way.

I worked with a local NGO to help deliver medications to street kids over the following three months, and I worked closely with members of the Kumbhar caste, those men and women of the Kumbharwada potters' settlement who toiled in clay pits and around communal, open-air kilns to create their earthen wares. I was even adopted by a family of potters, the Panchals, who were sympathetic to the battering my heart had suffered, and who gave me food and a place to sleep in their simple one-room house in exchange for my continued work in the slum. I was accustomed to the sterility and privacy of First World living, and I was hesitant at first about living in the slum, but the people's spirit and my realization of what they could teach me quickly won me over, and I stayed.

I was aware that my presence in the slum was unusual at best, offensive at worst. Most of my new neighbors loved having me around, but a few questioned my motivation and regarded my decision as foolish, given the great opportunities for advancement I had left behind in America. They encouraged me to return to my family and finish my schooling. They said it was OK to strive for a better life for myself even while knowing that others were leading tougher lives. Having access to opportunity was something that should be prized, they believed. So I decided I would return home. But I had also learned that it was a privilege to work side by side with members of the *zopadpatti*, as the slum was known.

As a privileged Westerner, all I had to worry about was apologizing to a lost love, whereas the people of Dharavi dealt with the constant threats of relocation and destruction of their homes, poor sanitation, infectious disease, and an arduous daily grind. I emerged from my experience in Dharavi a changed man, a person whose worldview was shaped for the better by his time in the slum.

The feelings that India, Dharavi specifically, provoked in me set in motion my search for something greater than myself, for a way in which I could contribute to the world and help relieve suffering. The path to the Peace Corps seemed illuminated, but it took a long time to get myself in a position where leaving home was a realistic possibility. I had to finish nursing school—which I began after my return from India and my subsequent graduation from Berkeley—submit myself to the lengthy Peace Corps application process, and then, out of the blue, drop everything to help care for my grandfather during his illness. I had begun to wonder if my heart was still committed to the people of South Asia by the time I was finally ready to leave home, about three years after my experience in India.

One thing that didn't change during that time was my love for Adriana. I knew in my head that I should have long since let her go. Many of my closest friends, especially the women in my life, had said I should have sent her packing immediately after the incident at the BART station, that she wasn't worth all the trouble and the heartache. And maybe I *was* a fool for continuing to love her, but she was lodged in my heart, and it seemed that not a day went by without some warm recollection of her. I often wondered about the life she was living abroad and the wisdom she had gained over the months and years since we had last seen each other. I also wondered if she had found a way to forgive me. Whether she had or not, I understood that I would probably never see her again, so I shifted my focus to the realistic, to something within my immediate grasp: continuing her work, which was now my own, with the people of Nepal.

* * *

The mists of a new day had barely lifted from Pepsicola Townplanning, but down on the maidaan, the neighborhood kids were already playing a scrappy game of cricket. The kids, most of whom I knew by name, and most of whom were Annu's friends and classmates, had also gotten to know me well. They no longer woke early to sprint by my side during my morning runs. That acceptance meant everything to me.

Joining them, I borrowed a cricket bat from the hands of a willing boy and, at the insistence of the kids, who had greeted me with squeals of delight, took my place in front of the makeshift wickets. The nuances of its rules still baffled me, but cricket was quickly becoming one of my favorite activities. Playing cricket on a regular basis not only educated me about the culture but also won me the kids' respect and their parents' approval. Nepal, like India, was crazy about cricket, and through constant exposure to newspapers, television, and the boys, I had come to know the names of all the greats.

I tapped the ground in front of me several times with the bat's blade and waited patiently for the young bowler—Santosh, who was roughly half my age and a third my size—to make his pitch. Santosh steeled himself, and when he was finally ready to deliver, he wound up and took a long charge toward me before hurling the ball at the wickets with his spindly right arm.

The ball found a hillock not far from the wickets and changed its trajectory, hitting me squarely in the scrotum as I helplessly flailed the bat in self-defense. Doubling over, I dropped to the ground. I writhed in pain, both hands cupping my wounded testicles, and a sick feeling rose from my stomach. I was in serious pain, but all I could think about was how ridiculous I probably looked to the kids. *God, how embarrassing.* I continued to roll around on the ground as the boys chirped and jabbered loudly in support of the miniature bowler and his ability to slay the neighborhood's pale-skinned Goliath.

Not one to quit, I slowly rose from the ground, kicked my nemesis hill to smithereens, and demanded an opportunity to redeem myself. The delivery skipped its way to the wickets, twisting and snarling as it arced earthward, then back toward belt level. I wound up and lambasted a line drive—what major league baseball players might have called a frozen rope—that sailed just over the young bowler's head and through the lower branches of a stand of bamboo to loudly smack the wooden shutter of a nearby house.

The woman of the house, one of the boys' mothers, appeared at the window to cast the entire group a disapproving stare and wag a scolding finger. I was the one holding the bat, but I got off lucky, as most of her fury was directed at poor young Santosh. She slammed the shutters tight again after her harsh reprimand. The boys then flocked around me, as though I were the next Tendulkar or Lara, and tried to persuade me to stay and play longer.

But I couldn't. I was on my way to meet the rest of the Kathmandu-based N-199 group at Mike's Breakfast in suburban Naxal, the staging area for our imminent two-day getaway. Thanks to the detailed planning of Ms. Beth Lewis, who had sunk considerable time into organizing the event, we were taking Stella'! up the Arniko Highway, toward Barabise, for a short rafting adventure on the Bhote Kosi, one of Nepal's steepest and most well-known rivers.

It was the end of October, and the weather throughout much of the country was warm and stable. The rivers of Nepal, filled to overflowing after the monsoon deluge, were at their best for running, according to Beth, who booked our trip weeks in advance to guarantee our spot. She had also somehow managed to talk the rafting company into letting her guide the trip, something that was normally forbidden unless the individual had previous experience on the river.

Fortunately for us, Beth *had* run the Bhote Kosi before, several months earlier, when she secured herself a last-minute spot on a raft of Korean tourists. Of course, I was sure her high-powered American rafting credentials were the main reason the rafting company bowed to her wishes—yet another example of how Peace Corps volunteers threw their weight around with local authorities. Again, it wasn't right, but such tactics were convenient and usually effective.

We had continued to gather weekly at the Rum Doodle, but we rarely participated in activities as a group outside the city, so the rafting trip felt like an especially good reason to bend some rules. The trip would serve as an opportunity for us to break free of our obligations, if only temporarily, and see parts of the country few of us had yet seen.

Mike Swenson, recognizing the importance of the trip, had fully supported our vacation. Peace Corps administrators had to be part diplomat, part authority figure, and part cheerleader. Life in a developing country like Nepal was challenging and full of daily frustrations, and if Admin didn't find a way to motivate their troops, volunteers could quickly lose their energy, feel alienated, and begin questioning the program's meaning and efficacy. Admin's job, which I didn't envy in the slightest, demanded both the patience of a saint and the wisdom of a parent.

After a short hobble from the maidaan, I met with Madhu and Sundar Pandey at Sundar's auto shop on the edge of Pepsicola Townplanning. Sundar had been slammed with work all week, but he had agreed to perform yet another round of repairs on Stella'! on his only day off. Sundar was engaged to the daring young Kabita Koirala from the clinic; according to the neighborhood mothers, he was not only a talented mechanic but also a fine catch of a husband. He owned his own garage, along with a motorcycle and a small car—the latter two possessions truly rare among Nepalis.

He was also a handsome young man, a man whose charming smile and chiseled features made him a good match for the beautiful Kabita. Their love for each other was obvious and true; the gushing Sundar would call Kabita at the clinic at least several times each afternoon to profess his undying love. Kabita, soaking up the attention, would simply smile and bat her eyelashes as she listened on her mobile.

Always a man of his word, Sundar had risen early that morning and carried out the necessary repairs. Stella'! was ready to roll when I showed up at his shop. "Nice work, Sundar!" I said, high-fiving the young mechanic.

"It is no problem, daai. I am loving it, your auto. It is *dheraai raaan-gichaaaangi!*" he added, rolling the *As* of the word *rangichangi*, which meant "colorful" or "multicolored." I chuckled as he said it, because *rangichangi* was one of my favorite Nepali words. Just hearing the word made me want to shimmy my shoulders and wiggle my neck.

And Sundar was right: Stella'! *was* rangichangi. She had been the recipient of a heavy bombardment of multicolored powder from the neighborhood's kids the previous spring, during the Festival of Colors, Holi. Monsoon rains had washed away most of the powder, but Stella'! had become a favorite target for the boys' nonstop pranking. Some people may have found the vandalism irritating, but I found it endearing. It was the boys' way of showing me how much they liked me. Besides, there was no real harm in it, and most Nepalis I met seemed to think that, with her ever-evolving technicolor dreamcoat, Stella'! looked rather hip. Even Dr. Singh, who had sheltered the Bus in his own garage for several decades, expressed his approval, stating that Stella'! was now far more psychedelic than she ever was in the seventies.

I paid Sundar with money Dr. Singh had given me for the repairs and hopped into the passenger seat. Madhu, who had volunteered to drive us all to the put-in, jammed the key into the ignition, and we roared off toward Kathmandu.

We stopped briefly in Lazimpat, at Peace Corps headquarters, so that I could check my e-mail. In their Internet room, I had written my first e-mail to friends and family back home, letting everybody know that I arrived safely in Nepal. It was almost a guarantee that, whenever I entered the room, I would find at least a handful of other volunteers in from the countryside for business or personal reasons. I found it pleasant to check letters from home among other volunteers, and it was my preferred place to send and receive electronic correspondence.

I pulled up a chair to an empty terminal, logged on, and began sifting through the mountains of e-mail in my inbox. I deleted most of the junk before reading letters and forwards from my mom and dad, my friends, and a few of the professors at UC Berkeley with whom I kept in regular contact. I eventually discovered an e-mail without a title tied to a familiar name: Serena.

She's back in Mumbai. You can probably guess where. Just thought you'd like to know.

I tried to process the words I'd just read. *Could it be true?* Blinking several times, I took another look, just to make sure I hadn't read something wrong. But there it was, clear as the postmonsoon skies.

My gut told me to follow up on the e-mail, but I shoved everything—all my thoughts, worries, hopes, and fears—to the back of my mind for the time being. I knew that I *should* mull over what I wanted to do with this news.

I was still distracted when I stepped out into the street, and I was nearly run over by a rickman carrying two male tourists. One of the passengers, wigged out by the close call, turned around in his seat and yelled, "Hey, watch it, asshole!"

I took a deep breath and then hurried over to Mike's Breakfast with Madhu, hoping that I wasn't too late. I entered the restaurant's inviting courtyard and immediately saw my N-199 pals chowing down on breakfast. The group spotted me, sent up a little whoop, and then returned to the plates on the table, which was nestled in a shady corner of the restaurant's peaceful garden.

"Dammit, homey, *where* have you been?" frowned Bronte, but he stood to give me a quick, heartfelt hug, not unlike the one Raju and Yarone exchanged at Slice of Life Bakery many months before. "We've been missin' your pasty-white Berkeley ass. Who's the only one of us with access to wheels in K'du? Who else is gonna drive us where we need to be goin'? We've gotta bust a move, my brother, for real! We've gotta get our raft on, you know what I'm sayin'?"

Bronte kept going while I helloed everyone else, ordered, and caught up with their furious eating pace. Being back in the present and out of my own head, I was keeping Serena's e-mail tamped down.

"Can you *believe* that bunk?" Bronte said. "Boy got us some sort of foul-tastin', watered-down, Japanese knockoff biz-natch that ain't got no rightful place in any self-respectin' American's cooler." The rafting company would provide the food for our trip, but we had left it to Taka to procure libations. He held up his end of the bargain, but his choice of brew was the source of much controversy within the group.

"You must try," said Taka, closing his eyes and bowing his head slightly.

"I. Ain't. Tryin'. Nuthin'. You *know* I love you, Taka-hee-ro, but you keep that piss away from me now, you hear?"

"Oh, come on, Bronte," said Manfred, wiping the corners of his mouth with a napkin. "I'm sure it will be fine. You know, that so-called Japanese beer was probably brewed right here in Nepal, so at least we're buying local. Besides, it's stronger than American beer."

"Say what now?" said Bronte. "*Stronger?* Guess we'll see about that."

The waiter brought our bill and handed it to me. "Finders keepers," Bronte said. I shot him a glance. "Don't be lookin' at me, fool." Bronte recoiled from the tab. "I's Edga'. Allan. *Po'!*"

"It's on me, guys," said Laura, reaching for the bill.

"Absolutely not," said Manfred, furrowing his brow and snatching the bill from Laura's hand. While one of the most progressive thinkers I knew and a major proponent of equal opportunities for the sexes, Manfred also had a traditional side to him. His moral compass forbid him to ever let a woman pay for a meal out, a fact that somehow managed to please even the staunchest feminists in our little circle of friends.

"Oh come on, Sugar Daddy," Laura teased and then turned serious. "I'm sure I probably owe you guys for something."

"No, I insist." Manfred raised his hand to signify that the argument was over.

"We'll shower you with drinks the next time we're at the Rum Doodle," I said, giving Manfred's shoulder a squeeze. "Hey, where did Beth run off to?"

"Our Chef de Mission, our rafting wonk, and the leader of our small band of Peace Corps adventurers is just doing a final gear check," said Manfred. "Let's go ahead and get our fine chariot all loaded up."

After we settled the bill and went out to jam our gear and supplies into the VW, we did a final stretch before taking our seats.

"Shotgun, bitches!" said Bronte.

"All right, so we're good to go?" I said, settling into the seat behind Madhu. "We've got everything, right?"

"According to the rafting company, most of the bulkier gear—like the raft, paddles, and life jackets—will be waiting for us at the put-in," Beth said. "The only thing we still need to do is pick up one of the company men near Barabise who's going to guide one of the other rafts."

"Sounds good. Now, did everybody remember to pay homage to Ganesh?" I pointed to a bobblehead of the elephant god that was affixed to the dashboard. Madhu's addition to the VW's interior decor bore all sorts of blinking lights and played a devotional tune if you pressed a button at its base. Along with the van's multicolored streaks and splotches and a garland of dried flowers Beth had long ago slung over the dashboard mirror, the plastic statue had been a big hit with the Nepalis, who appreciated my attempts to blend in and absorb the local customs.

I saw many of the same sights I'd seen countless times before as we puttered through Kathmandu, but then something unusual caught my eye. A homeless man, an amputee, seated on a castered platform on the corner of a busy intersection, held aloft a small boy. This wasn't that unusual in Kathmandu, except this particular beggar looked strangely familiar. Then I remembered where I'd seen him: in the Bishek Bazaar's basement the previous spring, at the event where I met Yarone and Shil. He was the wrestler fans had dubbed the Merciless Mendicant, the man who, despite all odds, routinely took on and bested able-bodied challengers in the weekly grudge matches arranged and promoted by the Rai family.

Our eyes locked momentarily before my gaze shifted to his child to see if all his limbs were intact. It was ridiculous, especially since the man's amputations, according to Raju, stemmed from diabetes and a life of excess, not from congenital malformations or trauma, as so many assumed. I felt tremendous shame and guilt, and I quickly turned my head away from the pair and back to the road. Even after a full year in Nepal, my eye was still drawn to the grotesque and the macabre.

Stealing my thoughts away from the wrestler beggar and his child, Bronte pointed out the window at a pair of teenage boys walking arm in arm and said, "Ahhh yeeah, now this is my kind of country, dawg; a place where men ain't afraid to hold another brother's hand in public. Look at that PDA! Now *that's* the stuff I like to be seein'. It ain't official, but in my opinion, Nepal's the gayest kingdom in the world, mothafuckas!"

Hand holding, hair tousling, and even gentle facial caressing were among the routine exchanges straight Nepali men carried out on a daily basis. It was odd that a society that tended to ostracize homosexuals, especially gay men, supported such obvious public displays of affection between members of the male sex. Clearly such actions weren't intended to be sexual, but to Bronte, they signified an underlying Nepali desire to express their feelings of brotherly love.

Bronte continued to squirm in his seat as we passed the bus terminal at Koteshwor and started up the Arniko Highway toward Barabise. He leaned his body far out the window, slapped the Bus's side, and encouraged Madhu to take to the curb to pass a number of slow-moving buses blocking our path. When he wasn't providing colorful commentary on various roadside attractions, he was mercilessly heckling other drivers and pedestrians in our way.

I glanced at the others in the Bus and saw that everybody was cracking up at his nonstop antics. It was impossible to be around Bronte and not be swept up in his wake. I had to admit that nobody else had ever made me laugh the way he did. He could be crass, and occasionally downright rude, but his ability to provoke laughter and entertain more than made up for any lack of social graces a social worker should have possessed.

Bronte hauled himself back inside the Bus and turned up the volume on his iPod, which sat alongside Ganesh on the VW's dashboard, just in time to catch the chorus of Seal's "Kiss from a Rose." He raised an imaginary microphone to his mouth, leaned out the window again, and began serenading nearby pedestrians, all of whom looked at him as though he were a madman.

"Ooo-oohh, the more I get of you, Nepal, the stranger it feels, yea-ah...and now that your rose is in bloom...a light hits the gloom on the...graaaayy...da-da daaa da da da da da da, da-da-da."

We motored steadily up the Arniko Highway, past Bhaktapur, Banepa, and Dhulikhel, stopping only once for Beth to relieve herself in a nearby ditch. We sang songs and told jokes to help pass the time. Not far from Dolalghat—a popular point of departure for those rafting the Sun Kosi River—we came parallel with the roiling, boiling Bhote Kosi. We stopped briefly at a roadside restaurant near Barabise to pig out on pyramidal puff pastries known as *tatosamosa*, or hot samosa, before collecting the rafting company's man.

We craned our necks to the side for the vast majority of the trip from the roadside eatery to the put-in below Borderland Resort, trying to size up the river we would soon be rafting. Its name, Bhote Kosi, literally meant "river from Tibet," and although many rivers in Nepal bore that moniker, *this* Bhote Kosi was one of the wildest and most well-known in the country.

Many of the river's biggest rapids—either class IV or class V, depending on the season and the river's volume—had been given unusual, yet somehow appropriate, names to describe their ferocity, according to Beth, including Sphincter, Ferret in Your Pants, Gerbil in the Plumbing, Frog in the Blender, and Carnal Knowledge of a Deviant Nature. Over the course of our two-day trip, we coined a few more: the Chiller Room, Bhagwan's Revenge, the Hole to America, and Shiva's Consort.

We soon arrived at the launch, where a raft and other essential equipment were indeed waiting for us under the watchful eye of a rafting company official. I noticed, as we unloaded Stella'! and consolidated our gear, that we weren't going to be the only ones on the river that day, as two other groups were also preparing to shove off: a reserved group of camera-toting Japanese tourists and a slightly more rambunctious group of young Israeli men with scruffy beards and headbands pinning back their long, bushy hair. For safety purposes and maximum efficiency, Beth said, the rafting companies always ran their trips with two or more rafts.

I peered into the VW's rearview mirror and slathered a healthy dose of sunscreen onto my face. I had noticed over the past few months the emergence of countless freckles on my forehead, due in large part, I believed, to the great number of hours I had spent outside constructing charpis. Mine didn't have so many freckles as to rival Beth's forehead, but there were enough to make me conscious of the fact that I needed to cover up more often.

After we all thanked Madhu for driving us to the put-in, Beth called, "OK, all you river-rafting divas and debutants, gather 'round for a little rafting-safety tutorial. The first rule of rafting is *always* wear your life jacket and helmet when you're on the water. Make sure all your straps are snug and secure, so they don't slip off when the going gets rough.

We don't want any cracked coconuts, if you know what I mean. Second, keep your life jacket on while we're scouting rapids from the riverbank. You never know when you might trip over a root and fall into the river. Third, keep your carcasses, including all your gangly appendages, inside the raft, unless I say it's OK to dangle them over the edge, like when we all take turns riding the bull."

"Excuse me, Beth." Manfred raised his hand politely.

"Yes, Little?" Beth replied, placing a hand above her eyes and squinting against the bright sun.

"What, precisely, do you mean when you say, 'riding the bull'?"

"Excellent question, but I think it will be easier to explain when we're on the water," she said, smiling broadly before she continued. "Fourth, *never* tie a rope or a strap that's connected to the boat around any part of your body. If the raft flips—and with Bronte in the boat, there's a better than average chance that it will—this could kill you. And last but not least...YOU'VE GOT TO HAVE FUN, SPARKLIES!" she screamed, pulling out a fully loaded pump-action water gun from one of the dry bags and soaking us all.

A brief skirmish ensued as we wrested the gun from her small hands and turned it upon her. From out of nowhere though, a smirking Laura appeared with a second water gun and blasted our backs relentlessly until we let go of Beth. I had no idea where Beth and Laura had found water guns like that in Kathmandu.

Taka, Manfred, Bronte, and I regrouped, divided, and went after the girls. The girls' squealing quickly drew the attention of the Israelis, who bantered among themselves in Hebrew before putting out their cigarettes and shoving off from the shore, right in the wake of the raft full of Japanese tourists. It was shaping up to be quite a trip.

Beth continued her safety spiel once we were on the water and settled into the raft. "If this rubber bus does flip, here's what I want you kids to do. Number one, do not—and I repeat, *do not*—panic. Number two, do your damnedest to hold on to your paddles. Number three, swim toward the raft, if possible. Number four, if you can't reach the raft, assume the whitewater swimming position—you know, face up with feet at the water's surface and toes pointing downstream—and don't try to stand until you're in calmer water either,

just in case you snag your foot on a rock or something. Finally, number five, breathe deeply and just try to enjoy the ride. Does everybody understand?"

We all nodded our heads. After receiving a crash course in paddling from Beth, we set off down the Bhote Kosi to either master the river or meet our maker. None of us, except for Beth, were sure which one would happen first. Beth had insisted we all use paddles, saying it would promote a greater sense of teamwork. She could have taken us down the river using only her steering paddle, but she wanted us all actively involved in the success of our venture.

Situated at the raft's rear, she called out instructions as we stared down our first major set of rapids: Gerbil in the Plumbing, a class IV. "James, pull harder, you big, strong, strapping man! Chicken Little, for goodness' sake, stop evaluating the river's fluid dynamics and put your paddle in the water! Laura, come on, girl, show me what you're made of! Taka, put down that Japanese beer and get serious about this! Baby Bear, make sure that that life jacket's secure and try not to drown on us, OK?"

As goofy as I was sure I looked, I was glad to be wearing a helmet—not because I was worried about capsizing but because it provided a measure of protection against Bronte, who was seated directly behind me, and his wild flailing. I felt his paddle contact my helmet at least three separate times during our descent.

"Dude, you've *got* to watch that paddle," I told him as we stood on the riverbank during one of our breaks. "It's starting to give me a headache."

"Uh, sorry, dawg," he replied sheepishly, before suddenly growing defiant. "But I ain't ever done this shit before, so cut a brother some slack, huh?"

We gritted our teeth and battled hard when we continued to plow through the frothy rapids. In a quiet pool nearby, both the Japanese and Israeli rafters floated. It was clear they had been waiting for us to run the rapid, to see how we would fare in the tricky class IV water.

The two other groups' body language and dispositions couldn't possibly have been more different. While the long-haired Israeli men reclined shirtless in their raft, dangling their legs over the edge as they lazily smoked their cigarettes, the Japanese tourists, in their sun hats, were busily snapping photographs with their waterproof cameras and looking disappointed that we hadn't swamped the raft during our fast-paced descent.

Beth pulled us up alongside the Japanese raft. "*Konichiwa!*" greeted Taka, standing in the raft; he was sporting a white bandana with the red, rising sun featured prominently on his forehead like a giant tika. Before the tourists knew what hit them, Taka was flying through the air toward their boat. "BANZAAAAI!" He landed on the raft's edge and hopped up and down, doing his best to flip their boat, or at least incite mass hysteria among the crew. Bronte and Manfred, taking their cue from Taka, playfully brandished the girls' water guns and began spritzing the Japanese tourists in earnest. The tourists, confused and apparently unsure of how to respond, sat paralyzed in their boat. Laura, getting in on the action, filled a bailing bucket and threw great gulps of river water up into the air; it was as if it were raining only above the tourists' raft.

The tourists eventually snapped out of their zombielike state and meekly tried to splash us with their paddles. When that tactic failed to have its desired effect, a small group of the men banded together to oust Taka from the boat, shoving him backward over the raft's edge and into the Bhote Kosi. The Japanese men then reseated themselves and began paddling like mad while the women in their boat exhorted them to paddle faster.

"Gosh," said Beth, once they had floated downstream a few hundred yards. "I don't think they knew we were just joking. I guess they've never been on a river-rafting trip. This stuff happens all the time; it's practically expected."

"They will live," said Taka, climbing back into the raft.

I glanced over at the Israelis who were still floating peacefully in their raft. They'd been amused by the excitement, but the expressions on their faces seemed to say, *Don't fuck with us.*

One of the Israelis spoke to us as our rafts drifted closer together. "You Americans are always making such trouble. You have too much free time. Would you like to smoke some pot?"

Beth politely declined the offer on our behalf before maneuvering the raft downstream. She then pointed to a series of minor rapids ahead and encouraged us to ride the bull.

"You still haven't told us what that means," said Manfred.

"You see that short strap on the raft's nose?" said Beth. "Go to the front of the raft, sit down on the nose, and let your feet dangle over the front while you straddle the strap. Hold the strap with one hand

and keep your other hand free to wave in the air, and ride that rapid like a rodeo cowboy riding a bucking bronco, partner! YEE HAW!"

Bronte was the first to try riding the bull. He grasped the strap firmly with his right hand and rode the rapids like a champ, hooting and hollering and calling for more. It was only after Manfred insisted he share the experience with others that Bronte relinquished his hold on the strap and assumed his position behind me.

Riding the bull proved too much for Manfred. He tried repeatedly to stay upright, but even with constant encouragement from the group, he was unable to do so. With each rapid we descended, Manfred was bucked violently backward, his entire torso sometimes disappearing deep into the raft's nose while his long, skinny legs stuck straight up in the air like two lodgepole pines. We all tried our hand at riding the bull over the course of the trip, but few of us ever matched Bronte's enthusiasm or form. Even fewer of us matched Manfred's pitiful performance, however; it quickly became the stuff of Peace Corps lore in the months and years to come.

We passed through a series of drops, eddies, and whirlpools over the course of the afternoon. We skirted narrow canyons and slalomed our way through extensive boulder gardens. We didn't see the Japanese or the Israeli rafters for some time, and I wondered if we would be sharing a campsite with them later that evening or if they had decided to press on to the final take out at the dam just above Lamosangu.

We found both groups, plus a handful of others, at the campsite later that afternoon. The Israeli boys, having already erected their tent, sat in camp chairs around a small bonfire, smoking joints and drinking Tuborg beer. The Japanese tourists, whose trust we had shattered, eyed us suspiciously from their camp near the edge of a small clearing, and made no attempt to interact with us.

We found a patch of level ground and began setting up our own camp. We formed a bucket line to help speed things along, a human chain stretching from the raft almost to the campsite itself. Through this we passed gear quickly and efficiently from one person to the next until the raft was practically empty. Out came the dry bags full of food and camping supplies, out came the first-aid kit, and out came the cooler containing our foul-tasting Japanese beer.

My next job was to filter water for drinking. I headed to a secluded part of the riverbank after collecting my filter and a large, brown bailing bucket—which bore cartoon stickers of a sacred cow and Hanuman, the monkey god—and a copy of the *Himalayan Times*.

I found a comfortable place near the river's edge, dropped the filter's uptake hose and nozzle into the river, and began pumping. I watched closely as river water was drawn up into the filter's outer casing and then squeezed through the ceramic core to create a narrow stream of giardia-free liquid that dribbled into the bailing bucket.

Filtering water was a strangely fulfilling pastime for me. Its marriage of simplicity and effectiveness helped me relax and slip into a contemplative state. Caught up in an almost hypnotic trance, I thought about Serena's e-mail from earlier that day.

"You look happier than a pig in poop!" Beth startled me, taking a seat beside me as I continued to rhythmically pump. She had tucked a fragrant jasmine flower behind her ear. "I've got a pair of socks and a ball of string in my dry bag if you think that would amuse you too," she teased, bumping me with her left shoulder before setting a thermos of lemon tea down beside me.

"Look, I'm just a simple person, Beth." I smiled at her. I stopped pumping for a moment and rolled up my newspaper, noting the distinct difference in texture between the inky and non-inky parts of the page. "What can I say?"

Beth was the first to speak after a moment of shared silence, a moment during which we both sat looking out at the fast-moving river. "So, are you enjoying yourself, Baby Bear?" she asked, drawing her knees up to her chest and wrapping her long, skinny arms around them.

"I'm having a great time," I said, digging my bare feet into the riverbank's soft earth.

"Oh, that makes me so happy. *God*, I *love* the river," she said, slowly shaking her head from side to side. "I can still remember the first time I ran the Middle Fork Flathead back in Montana. I think that's my favorite river, you know."

"So, what is it about the river that you love so much?"

"I don't know. I think it's the challenge of reading and studying the water's patterns, or maybe it's the fact that, when you're on the water, you can only move as fast as the river itself, which is a good life lesson, I suppose. Are *you* moving at the speed of the river, Baby Bear? I don't think you are, at least not right now anyway. You seemed a little off today. Is everything OK?"

Beth's intuition, like her bladder and her appetite, never failed to impress me. I wasn't prepared to discuss the details with her, but I was happy to have somebody to talk to about my conflicted emotions. She pulled her purple beanie down over her ears and sat there, looking at me with eyes that knew something others did not, perhaps with eyes that knew I had already hurt a good woman. I thought it was incredible how, even though people could grow and change over time, the regrettable actions of their pasts always had a way of catching up with them. It was incredible how the suffering we caused to others managed to come back to haunt us when we least expected it.

"You know you can always talk to me. What's said between us stays between us," she added, placing a hand on my shoulder.

I trusted her, but again, I wasn't willing to share that particular part of myself with her, and I knew she wouldn't be offended by my reticence. She tried to be intimately involved in her friends' lives, but she was also a person who recognized and respected people's right to privacy—that much I had come to know about Beth over the past year. She was eager to listen and offer suggestions, but she was also acutely aware of the boundaries people set, and she knew enough not to pry into the matters others guarded fiercely.

I continued pumping and filtering river water as a series of questions formed in my mind. "Hey, Beth. Do you remember that first night we met at the Rum Doodle?"

"Sure," she said. "Like it was yesterday."

"You told me that I had a dark side to me. What exactly did you mean?" I searched her face for answers. Beth, Raju, Dr. Singh: they all suspected that a side of me that rarely showed itself lay somewhere beneath the surface. They were the only ones who had been able to look beyond my calm exterior to see, immediately, the brooding of a young adult.

"The good ones—and you *are* one of the good ones, Baby Bear, I'm more convinced of that now than ever—always have a fundamental

SHOOTING THE BHOTE KOSI

understanding of what it means to be truly cruel. That's just how it works. You can't be as good as you are without knowing the opposite pole. I'm not saying that *you* are cruel, but I think you know what I mean. Something *had* to have happened to you along the way that caused you a tremendous amount of suffering for you to do what you're doing, to invest yourself as a volunteer here in Nepal. Either you discovered something that enraged you or you're trying to make up for something that you did. Or maybe even both; I don't know.

"All I know is that, at the heart of it, something happened to *all* of us that made us angry about the state of things. Something upset us so much that it caused us to look for meaning in other areas of our lives. I'm not usually one to be motivated by negative emotions, but I do believe that that anger, when harnessed properly, can be a beautiful thing, and that it can be used for the purposes of good. That's why I think you have a dark side to you, Baby Bear. It's because you're so devoted to the Peace Corps and so interested in improving the lives of Nepalis that I can see not only the true measure of your humanity but also the true measure of your anger. Am I making any sense?"

"Yeah," I said into the bailing bucket. I pursed my lips and slowed my pumping. "You're making perfect sense, Beth. You nailed it."

"Whatever it is you're working through right now, just stick with it," she encouraged. "Just let it pass. We've all gone through tough times."

"Well, that's just it, Beth," I said, stopping my pumping and looking her squarely in the eye. "That's the problem. I don't know if I have enough patience to just let it pass. You have to understand that there's this *thing* inside of me that's eating me up, and if I don't deal with it the only way I know, I'm not going to be much good for anything."

After a few moments of silence between us, Beth, who usually felt the need to fill pregnant pauses, took a deep breath and said, "In the spirit of sharing, can I tell you something, Benjamin?"

I immediately felt my defenses go up, not sure what sort of bombshell she was about to drop. I knew she wasn't afraid to take a verbal risk, that she would share almost anything that was on her mind if she thought it relevant to the conversation's context.

"Please do," I said.

"On this very day, exactly sixteen years ago, I gave birth to a beautiful baby girl."

I dropped the filter into the bailing bucket.

I realized, as I looked at Beth, that her tears were tears of joy, or relief perhaps, and not tears of sadness. My instinct was to embrace her.

I held her in my arms, her head buried deep in my chest. I felt extremely privileged to have been the one in whom she'd confided. I suspected that none of the others knew, including Laura, and I understood that, on a fundamental level, the trust she'd placed in me had created a bond between us that would last for a lifetime.

That confidence in me, that unwavering belief that I would protect her privacy at all costs, reminded me that life was all about the small, crucial moments when we held the fate of another human heart in our hands. The gravity of those moments helped us become better human beings, helped us grow and develop into something eminently more aware and respectful of the lives that swirled around us. All we had to do was recognize and appreciate those moments for what they were, to cherish the role of confidant and stay true to that unspoken promise.

"Where's your daughter now?" I asked, unsure if it were the appropriate thing to say under such circumstances. "Shit, I'm sorry, Beth. I hope I'm not upsetting you."

"No, it's fine," she said, straightening up as I released her from my embrace. "Really, it's fine. My only real choice, when she was born, was to put her up for adoption. My parents—who were completely crushed, by the way, especially my dad—offered to help raise her, but it wasn't the right decision. I made a mistake in getting pregnant, Benjamin, but that didn't make it any easier to hand her over to her new parents."

"No, I don't suppose it would," I said, trying to imagine what a pregnant belly might look like on such a petite frame.

"There have been so many times when I've thought about all the things I've missed out on as a mother. Her first words, her first day of school, her first high school dance. She's probably just starting to date boys now," Beth said between sniffles. "Part of the agreement when I gave her up for adoption was that I couldn't have any contact with her. If we were ever going to talk, *she* would have to be the one to initiate the dialogue. Her parents said it was OK to send her pictures and a video, but it's been years now, and I haven't heard anything from her, and I think that that's what rips me up the most."

"Where's the father?" I asked, again hoping not to sound too insensitive or nosy.

"Mexico City," she replied. "At least that's where he was five years ago. I've lost touch with him completely. His name's Jesus, of all things. He was a seventeen-year-old exchange student at my high school in Bozeman."

"You've got to watch out for those exchange students," I said, teasing her. "Especially the ones claiming to be the Son of God."

"Oh, so *now* you tell me," she said, returning the needling with a good-natured laugh. Then she said, "I've been watching you for a long time now," but I didn't realize at first that she was abruptly changing the subject. "I can tell that you're in your element here. The Nepalis are instantly attracted to you because you've got this easygoing way of communicating with them, and…your inner light…it just shines so brightly! There's no judgment or pretentiousness in your dealings with the people, just an 'ease of being' and an authenticity of character that they pick up on and respond to with joy."

"Umm," I said. "Your daughter?"

"Now, I know your default mode is solitude"—Beth continued; she had moved on—"that you'd prefer to spend most of your time by yourself if you could, but your interactions with the Nepalis seem fluid and effortless. You have this 'universal' sense of humor that people find attractive, and *that's* incredible, Baby Bear. I think that, without even trying, without even being conscious of it, you cut out a lot of the filters that normally exist when two people from such different cultures try to communicate. You drop your filters and they, correspondingly, drop theirs. It's an instant heart-to-heart connection, don't you see?"

"Wow, Beth," I said, having started to really listen to her. "I'm…flattered."

"You should be, Baby Bear," she said. "I've been trying to figure out your secret for some time. But, see, that's the thing: there *is* no secret; it's just who you are! Look, Benjamin, plenty of people can *respect* other cultures, but I think you're able to transcend even *that* level of intimacy and meet the Nepali people in a pure and honest place. For somebody who lives in his head most of the time, you have a *heart* that understands how unnatural it is to build barriers between people. What I'm trying to say, Baby Bear, is that you've got a really big heart, and I'm glad, so glad, that you're my friend. And you really *care* about what goes on here in Nepal."

I was blown away. I hadn't realized just how much I'd changed since my arrival in Nepal until she said those words. I was also touched by Beth's desire to spell it out, to make me see that I'd made some important gains in the personal development department.

Beth and I hauled the buckets back to camp after I finished filtering the water and plopped ourselves down around the roaring bonfire. We congratulated Eagle Scout Manfred on a job well done. Chef Laura, piling our plates high with piping hot dal bhaat tarakaari, made sure that nobody went without several helpings. Dinner, everybody agreed, was the day's high point. Along with the fruits of Laura's culinary skills, we nibbled on Swiss chocolate and swilled Japanese beer with reckless abandon.

"We're living in true suckling-pig style," sighed a happy Beth. Having gorged herself, she lay smiling, bloated, and semiconscious on her back near the fire.

We recounted the day's highlights, laughing heartily. As the night progressed, Bronte suggested that Taka take the Japanese tourists a peace offering of cigarettes and alcohol. Taka staggered toward the group of tourists and proceeded to offer a heartfelt apology, only to be rebuffed and scolded for his role in the day's minor fiasco.

Returning, Taka said, "They are…uninterested…in our gifts." He slumped back down into his camp chair.

"Damn," snapped Bronte, "them tourists sure got their ugly on, huh?"

"It would seem so," said Manfred. "It would seem so."

That night, we all slept like logs.

The following morning, after we ate a hearty breakfast of fried eggs and banana pancakes and packed up our camp, we again followed the Japanese and Israeli rafters onto the Bhote Kosi for the final descent to the take out.

We floated down the river for a bit before entering a series of challenging rapids that apparently had been too difficult to read from upstream. "Oh, shit!" yelled Beth. We somehow managed to spin the boat sideways in a last-ditch effort to correct our wayward path before plummeting over a steep, almost vertical, pourover into a large souse hole, where we were quickly drenched by massive backrollers. The raft capsized under a back-roller's oppressive weight, sending all members of N-199 into the roaring current, a gigantic natural washing machine that ran us through several spin cycles before forcefully ejecting us.

"To the raft, swimmers!" said Beth.

We reoriented ourselves to the river and let the current take us down-stream once everybody was finally accounted for and clinging to the raft. In an eddy tucked away behind a medium-size boulder, not far from the site of our flip, sat the Japanese rafters, their waterproof cameras out and their memory cards surely full of shots of our snafu. I couldn't shake the feeling that we had just paid our dues for our behavior the previous day.

Blessings of the Doctor

THE CLOUDS ABOVE PATAN'S HARI SHANKAR TEMPLE EFFECTIVELY BLOTTED out the day's remaining rays, turning a dark day into a wet, miserable evening. My mood, in many ways, mimicked the weather. I had finally worked up the courage to speak with Dr. Singh after several weeks of relentless struggle and procrastination. I was finally going to tell him that I had decided to leave the Peace Corps to chase an impossible love.

I shivered and blew warm air into my fisted hands as I impatiently waited for a break in the weather. I watched men and women dash for cover as the rain grew more intense. The women in particular, in their colorful salwar kameezes and shawls, caught my eye. The women of Nepal were beautiful, with their long black hair, slender figures, and light-brown skin. They floated gracefully through the streets of Kathmandu with a certain elegance and sophistication. Besides their obvious beauty, they carried themselves impressively, paid attention to their posture and ornamentation, to their bangles and earrings and other accessories, and how those accouterments enhanced their already striking features. The young Nepali women always seemed so put together, even if they were just going to the local market to buy eggs or produce.

Sometimes, watching them, I got the feeling I could fall in love with all of them, if only the circumstances were right, and if only I weren't holding out for something else, for the love I'd longed for but never known. I was amazed how quickly my priorities changed when a sliver of hope was dangled in front of me, when I was faced with the possibility of realizing my most genuine, heartfelt longing.

But there was a problem with my logic, and I knew it. Even if I went to Mumbai and found Adriana, there was no guarantee she would even speak to me, let alone have the desire to pick up where we'd left off so many years before. I also had no idea what the years had been like for her, whether she was seeing somebody else, was engaged or married, or even if she had started a family of her own.

The experiences I shared with Adriana and the feelings she provoked in me were some of my life's watershed moments. But I had to consider the possibility that our experience represented only a tiny blip on her radar, that everything that transpired between us had not been nearly as profound for her as it had been for me.

These were all equally likely possibilities, but my biggest concern was that she still harbored feelings of anger and resentment toward me, and that, like myself, she had never been able to find the closure or res-olution that grants peace of mind and the ability to move on with life.

Despite all these worries, my belief in the fundamental human need for reconciliation was strong enough to cause me to quit the Peace Corps, which was no small feat, given how closely I had come to identify with the role of volunteer. That decision said something about the esteem in which I held her or, perhaps, about the sheer magnitude of my own youthful optimism. Either way, sacrificing my future with the Peace Corps, while drastic, was a measure I was willing to take if it brought me closer to the one I loved.

I could have waited to travel to India during a break from my Peace Corps duties, but the holidays were still a long way off. And I knew I couldn't wait that long to see her, based on the sense of urgency I felt within. I also didn't know how long the trip would last or how long Adriana would be in Mumbai. I didn't know if she had returned for good or if her time in Dharavi was temporary. All I knew was that I couldn't risk miss-ing my window of opportunity. Now that I'd made my decision, I had to reach her quickly.

I slipped from my covered hiding place when the hammering of rain-drops on nearby roofs eased and sprinted down an alleyway toward the nearest chowk. I hoped to find a warm taxi to chauffeur me to my final destination: the estate of Dr. Singh. Before I had taken one hundred paces, however, the sky crackled with tremendous ferocity and released its soaking payload onto the backs of those of us foolish enough to challenge its fickle nature and gross indifference.

I, along with a dozen or so Nepalis, quickly found shelter under the banner of a textile merchant who was conducting business as usual, despite the plummeting barometer. A group of vocal Tibetan carpet manufacturers on the building's second floor busily labored away on their planar designs, executing with perfection the stunning precision of the Senna Loop method.

I waited another few minutes before leaving the relative safety of the textile merchant's stoop to join a group of children in the street. I playfully kicked some water in their direction and then hurried on toward the nearest chowk. Even with the rain, it would be rude to keep Dr. Singh waiting.

I reached the chowk and was surprised to find scads of Maruti Suzukis parked alongside a nearby curb. It seemed odd that, on an evening such as this, the drivers would be starved for work. I hopped into the closest cab, gave the driver the address of Dr. Singh's home, and settled in for the ride.

"Three thousand rupees," said the driver, smiling a sly smile.

"Are you *kidding* me? *Forty* bucks?"

Then I understood why so many taxis sat idle in the rain: the cabbies were trying to hijack the public's wallets. I should have seen it coming, but I also couldn't let the drivers turn the screws on me. Disgusted, I climbed out of the cab, slammed the door, and regurgitated Madhu's advice from over a year earlier: "Look for best in fiber, worst in driver."

I wound my way to the nearest tuk tuk stand and resigned myself to a cramped journey to Dr. Singh's house. But with a price tag of only twenty rupees, at least it would be affordable.

The tuk tuk stopped for me several blocks from Dr. Singh's estate. I wiggled my way through the mass of warm bodies, paid the fare collector—a teenage boy sporting a mullet—and marched toward the Singh residence. Dr. Singh's spacious, Rana-style house was located in New Baneshwor, and was unlike anything else I'd seen in Nepal. His home was an island of tranquility in the heart of New Baneshwor, a neighborhood home to professionals, government officials, and prominent executives.

It was true that Dr. Singh employed a whole army of attendants, but this wasn't because he was lazy or vain or felt important enough to be waited on but instead because there existed the very real possibility that the men and women in his employ might starve to death without the job. He hand-selected his assistants based not only on their loyalty and qualifications but also on their financial need. Dr. Singh wasn't a man who believed in handouts, but he did believe in honest work for honest pay, and so he surrounded himself with dedicated employees and treated them well.

I had also come to learn from the crew at the Pepsicola clinic that the doctor was a generous land owner; he took far less of the profits from his tenant farmers than he rightfully could have. The doctor enjoyed great esteem among the farmers who worked his family's ancestral lands, due in large part to this generosity. His approach to business was unusual in a country where even the relatively affluent understood just how close to poverty they themselves were, where wealthy men tried, often successfully, to keep their tenant farmers mired in a state of perpetual poverty and subservience through all sorts of questionable business practices.

I followed a long stone wall to the compound's front gate. Countless shards of colored glass cemented along the top of the wall looked like the spiky ridges on the back of a prehistoric animal.

I whistled a tune to wake up the security guard and waited patiently as the man roused himself, checked his appointment book, and unlocked the compound's gates. It took me a moment, once inside, to orient myself to the courtyard's layout. Daylight had long since vanished, but I was keenly aware of the dense foliage shrouding the expansive grounds. I could hear only faint street noise beyond the compound's walls. Rhododendron leaves, soggy from the night's earlier cloudburst, grazed my shoulder and left their dewy deposit in broad swaths upon my wool jacket as I approached the front stoop.

I bent over and sniffed a potted jasmine plant after ringing the doorbell. Its pleasant aroma helped soothe my frayed nerves, but its calming effects were temporary. I was extremely concerned about how my decision would be received by the man who had breathed life into my Peace Corps experience. I feared disappointing my family, my fellow Peace Corps volunteers, and the people of Pepsicola Townplanning, who had so graciously absorbed me into their community and had given me a life in Nepal.

I hated the idea of losing the Peace Corps volunteer title too; that designation was something I had always felt proud of, something I had used during the previous year to show the world who I was. It was a badge of honor that I wore with distinction. I knew I would feel empty without the title, and that my self-confidence would take a big hit. My decision to terminate would be viewed as a personal weakness by my fellow volunteers. I couldn't bear the thought of the criticism I might face. I could already feel myself trying to mask my sensitivity to that criticism, so as not to appear weak.

I realized, standing there on Dr. Singh's porch, that my singularity of focus was simultaneously one of my greatest strengths and one of my greatest weaknesses. It was what had allowed me to throw myself into my work with the Peace Corps, to devote myself solely to working alongside Nepalis on various projects, and then, once a new, more compelling idea lodged itself in my brain, instantaneously shift my priorities and head off in an entirely different direction with equal enthusiasm. I reached for a small parcel that I had stowed in my pocket. The present felt more like a peace offering than a just-because gift, given the circumstances of my visit, but I hoped it would ease the news I was about to deliver, for me as much as for the doctor.

An attendant, a sprightly Tamang man from the hills, soon appeared at the front door. He immediately ushered me into the foyer and handed me a towel with which to dry my soggy head. When I'd toweled off to the man's satisfaction, he gave me a lemon tea and led me down a long hallway lined with beautiful works of art depicting various animals of Nepal, including yaks, elephants, rhinos, water buffalo, monkeys, and cows. A stick of juniper incense, which had almost burned to its base, sent a powerful plume of smoke toward the pressed-tin ceiling.

The physician, according to his attendant, was busily penning his memoir in his private study but was eagerly awaiting my presence. The man paused just outside the den, knocked lightly on the door, and clicked it open once Dr. Singh had called out his permission.

Dr. Singh looked up from his work as I entered. He removed his reading glasses and smiled. "Hello, Benny-bhai," he said. "I'm glad you made it here safely."

The doctor appeared to be at peace, surrounded by shelves of books that reached from floor to ceiling. Apart from a hoary shock that graced the part of his short, black hair and a small purplish scar over his left eyebrow, his appearance—despite his smoking habit—bore none of the tiredness that plagued so many of his contemporaries. His eyes, shifting from me to a plush lounging chair opposite his bureau, encouraged me to sit down and make myself comfortable.

"I hope I'm not disturbing you," I said, settling into the chair.

On the wall behind the doctor, bearing down on me like a squadron of hellcats, hung a formation of oddly sized degrees, diplomas, and certifications—a shooting gallery of the doctor's life's work on display for all those invited into his den.

"Not at all, not at all," he said. "I've just been reliving the adventures of my youth through the writing of my memoir. I don't feel as though I've aged a single day, although perhaps in my later years, I've grown a little wiser," he added, chuckling.

"Oh, Dr. Singh, before I forget, I brought you a gift," I said, pulling the parcel from my pocket.

"You did? Why, Benny-bhai, there was certainly no cause for it, I'm sure," he said, his trademark humility trickling through every word.

I placed the parcel squarely in front of the doctor and said, "To cure what ails you."

Dr. Singh, unwrapping the present, smiled, leaned back in his chair, and slowly clapped his hands.

"Brilliant, my boy, simply brilliant! *Dheraai Raamro!* Jack Daniels, the elixir of life, will live *here*," said the doctor, picking up the bottle and placing it at his right side. He opened the bottom drawer of his bureau and extracted two shot glasses before pouring each of us a shot. "To good health and long life!" he cheered.

"To good health and long life," I echoed, downing the shot in one quick gulp.

The doctor slammed his glass down on the desk, cocked his head, and looked me square in the eye. "So, what brings you to this part of Kathmandu on such a cold and blustery night?"

"Well, Dr. Singh, as you know, it's starting to get chilly here in Kathmandu and I think I could use some warmth, you know, the kind Jack Daniels alone can't provide."

The doctor chuckled. "Perhaps you do want to escape the cold," he said, "but I sense a deeper yearning in your appeal, Benjamin. I've noticed a change in your mood recently. Why don't you just level with me and tell me what's going on?"

Initiating the conversation with Dr. Singh proved to be one of the hardest things I've ever done. I immediately felt the desire to trivialize my needs, to make it appear that what I was about to say was not of great significance. But I remained strong and true to myself by bravely pushing forward with my words. They were slow to come, though, and when they did, they weren't nearly as eloquent as I had wished they might be. But not once did the doctor stop me to add a comment or insert criticism. He just took it all in, and when I was finished, he sat back in his chair and looked toward the ceiling, seemingly into the twinkling brilliance of the chandelier.

After what felt like an eternity of silence and thoughtful contemplation—in this moment of anxiety and vulnerability, my Western fear of quiet had returned—Dr. Singh finally spoke. "It seems this Adriana had quite the effect on you," he said. "Her loss affected you deeply. Please, tell me more about this intriguing young woman."

Dr. Singh, while listening to my description of Adriana, appeared lost in another train of thought. It then struck me that he was staring at a photo of his deceased wife that was sitting on the bureau. The photo, several decades old and yellowing at the edges, was a snapshot of a time when many of the cruel realities of life weren't even a glint in the physician's eye.

Slowly, and with great effort, Dr. Singh pulled himself back to the present. "Your timing is uncanny, Benny-bhai," the doctor sighed. "I was just writing about my wife, Margaret, when you arrived. You must know that I too chased an impossible love. There are great parallels in our stories, you know."

I listened patiently over the next hour as the doctor described the life he'd shared with his Margaret, who had died twenty-two years earlier after a lengthy battle with ovarian cancer. The decision to marry Margaret—a poor hippie from the UK—had directly contradicted the wishes of his mother and father, who had arranged a marriage that would have increased his family's land holdings considerably. Dr. Singh, banished from his village for his bold defiance, had traveled to Kathmandu, to the anonymity of the city, to begin his life with Margaret.

"Dr. Singh," I said, once his story was complete, "I'm so sorry about your wife and that your family was so closed to the idea of your relationship with her."

"Your condolences are appreciated, Benny-bhai. Fortunately for me, most people are wrong about most things most of the time. My decision to marry Margaret was the best decision of my life. They say that great minds discuss ideas, mediocre minds discuss events, and small minds discuss people. In my village, I was surrounded by individuals who talked about people and not much else."

Dr. Singh, waylaying my fears of being judged unfavorably for following my heart, added, "A young man in your situation should never be dissuaded from following his heart. Now *that* would be a real tragedy. And try not to be so hard on yourself, Benjamin. Look at all that you've achieved during your time here. By getting the community to switch from sticky rice to brown rice, you accomplished something that I, in over a decade of trying, have never been able to do."

Persuading the community of Pepsicola Townplanning to embrace brown rice *had* been a monumental achievement. Maybe the doctor was right. Maybe I would leave more of a lasting impression on the community than I'd originally thought.

"Why, during your time with us, you've accomplished two years' worth of work in the span of one!" he said. "And how many more homes in the community now have smokeless stoves in their kitchens? How many people now use the latrines on a regular basis and no longer suffer from parasites? I can tell you that the incidence of intestinal and respiratory ailments has sharply decreased in Pepsi since the inception of your Charpis and Chimneys program. And how much wiser is the community when it comes to proper nutrition and the spread of infectious disease? No, you shouldn't feel bad about your decision to leave, Benny-bhai. In fact, I'm surprised you waited as long as you did before coming to me."

"But what if everything backfires, Dr. Singh? What if nothing turns out the way I want it to?"

"By Vishnu, Benjamin, if you're going to make a mistake, make a *really big one*, and be proud of it!" said the doctor. "Look, people travel in search of love all the time, Benny-bhai; it's certainly nothing to be ashamed of. Now it's time for you to right the wrongs of your past, to vanquish those lingering regrets and move forward with your life. In your absence, you will be missed—don't ever think otherwise—but the spirit of friendship and cooperation you've fostered here with us will live on indefinitely. Sometimes, a person's legacy is even more powerful than their immediate presence," added the doctor, always cogent in his delivery. "And always remember this: a candle loses no light when it passes its light on to others."

Swimming with the Naga

THE NEXT MORNING, I FOUND MYSELF WATCHING IN HORROR AS A TOPPLED tuk tuk's front wheel spun dangerously close to an injured man's head. The man, whose motorcycle lay bent and broken at his side, clutched his right collar bone and moaned in pain. Pulsing rivulets of blood streamed down his forehead and pooled in and around his eyes.

Discombobulated passengers tumbled into the street from the tuk tuk itself. The women composed themselves more quickly than did the men, flogging the ejected driver with their purses and shopping bags before regrouping on the curb to rearrange their salwar kameezes and touch up their makeup.

The scene, though chaotic, was not without its heroes, as complete strangers dropped what they were doing or leaped out of their own vehicles to comfort the distressed with words of support, help people to the sidewalk, and direct traffic away from the crash site. "My goodness," I overheard one of the women on the sidewalk exclaim in Nepali. "This is the third time this month this has happened to me."

The accident, while serious, was not the first such smash I had witnessed in Nepal. Like most of the other accidents I'd seen, the blame lay with the tuk tuk's driver, who had allowed the craft's rear wheel to creep up onto the curb and then swerved too sharply back, overcorrecting and clipping an unsuspecting motorcyclist.

"Somebody with a mobile, *please* call an ambulance!" I said, rushing to the motorcyclist's side. I wished that somebody with more experience in trauma care had been present to assist, but I could already feel myself entering crisis mode, drawing on the calm strength I'd honed in nursing school. I peered into the man's eyes. He was confused, disoriented, and going into shock. I braced his neck and applied gentle traction while instructing several onlookers to find a blanket.

Somebody offered bandages, which was a nice gesture, but they were of little use because the man's helmet was still on his head, shielding his laceration. The amount of blood squirting from his head was unnerving and made me question the helmet's efficacy, but even minor head wounds bleed a lot, so I had hope. I began asking the man questions in Nepali to keep him from slipping into unconsciousness. Already confused about what had happened, the poor man seemed hopelessly thrown by the fact that a white guy was asking him questions in Nepali about what he'd eaten for breakfast that morning.

Before long, I caught a whiff of ammonia in the air. I looked down and saw a dark patch spreading from the man's groin across his thigh. I felt in that moment as much urgency to protect the man from the embarrassment of urinating on himself as I did to stop his bleeding. I asked one of the onlookers to continue applying light traction to the man's neck while I stripped off my shirt and wrapped it around his waist.

The decision to use my shirt to hide the pee stain had been instinctual, but the more I thought about it, the more I realized what a supreme privilege it was to preserve a person's dignity in a situation where there was absolutely no dignity to be had. To recognize those moments of extreme vulnerability in the lives of others and come to their aid was the very definition of being human, was it not?

The paramedics arrived about ten minutes later and took control of the situation, to my great relief. One of the paramedics pulled a spare T-shirt from his bag and handed it to me before patting me on the back. "Nice job, boss," he said, smiling. The T-shirt, small even by Nepali standards, was skintight and exposed my bellybutton. On the shirt's front was a splashy image of Darth Vader. *It's still better than wandering around Kathmandu barechested.* I picked up my backpack and headed toward Lazimpat on foot.

I watched from the footbridge near Ratna Park, the city's principle transportation hub, as a steady stream of traffic passed underneath. White Maruti Suzuki taxis, bullock carts carrying sacks of rice led by weary-looking horses, and the private sedans of the wealthy all battled bicyclists for road supremacy. I couldn't see it out there in the throngs of oncoming traffic, but I heard the sputter of an idling tuk tuk waiting for a slender opening through which to swerve into traffic.

The tuk tuks' sickly bleeps countered the blares of the buses. The mournful wail of an ambulance chimed in periodically, as did the sirens of police cars and other emergency vehicles. The cheeky scooters darting around pedestrians sounded like cats retching up hairballs while subcompacts offered up a sad rendition of the classic roadrunner greeting: "Meep, meep!" And somewhere out there in the tangled, twisted, and snarling traffic, a lorry made its presence known through a booming multinote announcement: ♪♫♪♫♪

Drivers honked at pedestrians, cyclists, and beggars on wheeled platforms as they cleared cows, mothers with suckling infants, and roadside temples by mere inches. Drivers honked at those who were slower; they honked at those who were faster. Drivers honked because somebody or something was there to honk at, and they honked again, just because they could. I got the feeling that if nobody else were around, if each vehicle were somehow the only one on the street, drivers would honk anyway, just to see if the horn still worked.

I was due at the Indian embassy in Lazimpat at eight o'clock. I was already behind schedule, because of the accident. In the past, Peace Corps Nepal volunteers had been given Indian visas upon entering Nepal, to help speed evacuation in the event of a natural disaster or political strife. Members of N-199 were not so fortunate. The visa process could take hours, I'd been warned. The key was to show up early, establish a place at the front of the line, and hope for the best.

So I continued over the footbridge, past men and women selling watches and wallets on the cheap. Beggars with cupped hands and no feet strategically situated themselves at the far end of the bridge, hoping that a few coins from generous passersby would find their way into their cracked and weathered palms. I had stuck to my principles during my time in Kathmandu and rarely given alms to street kids—as they were often used as pawns by adults—but for amputees and the victims of polio and other crippling diseases, I could always find a few extra rupee notes in my pockets.

I hailed a taxi when I reached New Road. The ride, normally straight-forward and stress-free, quickly turned into a hellish affair. The driver, a young man with sharp facial features and a lead foot, took me on a twisting trail through the backstreets of Kathmandu, hitting two dogs, a chicken, and nearly maiming a drunk man who lay passed out in a gutter. I'd already seen enough bloodshed for one day, and I wasn't sure how much more I could handle.

"Hey, man, slow down!" I said. "*Bistaarai haaknus!*" I assumed a spread-eagle position in the backseat, bracing myself against the Maruti Suzuki's rear doors. "*Hos garnus, bhai!* Be careful, brother!" My words seemed to shame the young man into returning the car to the main drag, where he impatiently worked his stick shift to seamlessly reenter the thread of morning traffic.

A large queue had already formed by the time I reached the embassy's gates. A sheet of paper bearing the Indian government's official seal was making its way through the massing crowd, and by the time it reached my hands, over forty names and nationalities were scribbled on it. There wasn't a whole lot to do while I waited for the embassy to open, so I amused myself by watching a group of monkeys in the nearby treetops and making up stories about the other travelers.

A humorous moment—a moment known only to me and a handful of other travelers with Nepali language skills—occurred while I was waiting in line. A taxi carrying a middle-aged American couple drove up to the embassy gates. The tourists exited the taxi, and the husband slammed the rear door behind him, catching the attention of the driver.

The driver, like many other drivers in the city might, became irate because of what he perceived as unnecessary abuse to his vehicle. Speaking Nepali, he chastised the man for his egregious act. The husband, thinking he'd done a poor job of closing the door, and in an attempt to restore his manliness and set the matter straight, reopened the rear door and slammed it even harder than the first time, which really got the driver fuming. In a huff, the driver snatched his fare from the husband's hand, hopped into his taxi, and sped away. The husband and wife, innocent and bewildered, simply stared at each other in disbelief. I felt bad for the couple, but I couldn't help chuckling to myself.

The embassy's heavy steel gates finally swung open, and our group was directed toward a moderately sized open-air waiting room, where we again took up our positions in the queue. A mulish official told us the application process would involve two distinct phases: in the morning, we would submit our applications and passports in the hopes of reaching the second phase, which involved returning later in the day to recoup our documents after the application had been approved and processed. In other words, attempting to acquire a visa for India would be a whole-day ordeal, and there were no guarantees that any of us would be successful.

I could already feel the frustration bubbling within, but I kept a calm exterior. More than once that morning, I contemplated giving up and coming back another day, but I understood that the whole frustrating process would just have to be undertaken again. There was no real choice except to wait.

The hours crept past. I befriended a young Korean couple, Seung-Bin and Shin-Young Park, who had been traveling throughout Asia for seven months already, and a potbellied Irishman by the name of Roger O'Malley. Roger had come to Nepal for some sightseeing but would soon be heading to Rajasthan for the annual Pushkar Camel Fair. But not everyone in the crowd was patient and friendly.

At one point, a brazen Chinese man holding a stack of fifteen passports and applications cut in front of the entire line. The queue, on hair-trigger alert for such unacceptable behavior, immediately balked, letting thoughts and opinions be known through reprimands of varying intensity. The man, seemingly unfazed by the verbal battery, stood his ground while pleading with an official to process his ample stack of visa applications. Several members of the queue began clawing at his jacket to tear him away from the booth's window.

Of all the enraged people in the crowd, it was tiny Shin-Young Park who voiced the loudest dissent. "Hey, be a man!" she said. "Do the right thing. Go to the back of the line." Charging to the front of the queue, she engaged the man in a boisterous yelling match that quickly brought security guards onto the scene. "SHUT YO FACE! SHUT YO FACE!" screamed Shin-Young in response to the man's haughtiness. "I give you good reason to shut yo face!" she added, putting up her fists, her eyeballs bulging.

The man, shamed at last by the severe public tongue-lashing doled out by a ninety-pound ball of fury, and at the security guards' insistence, slunk to the back of the line, where he sulked momentarily before storming out of the compound. Roger fired several parting shots at the man as he left the embassy's grounds, suggesting several vulgar ways he could process his stack of visa applications.

After five hours of waiting, I finally reached the processing booth. It took all of two minutes at the booth to hand over my application and passport. The official instructed me to return at the end of the business day to retrieve my freshly minted multiple-entry visa.

I struck out toward Thamel and Fire and Ice, only too happy to leave the compound. I was scheduled to meet Bronte for lunch. He and I had decided on Fire and Ice so we could touch base with the Mauritian transplant I had met upon my arrival, Keshav Choudary, perhaps the friendliest waiter in all of Kathmandu and the unanimous favorite of N-199. I turned off Kantipath onto Tridevi Marg and soon spotted Bronte playing hacky sack with a group of Rastafarians in front of Fire and Ice.

"S'up, B?" Bronte called. "Nice shirt. Hey, where've you *been*? I've been waitin' for you, dawg."

"Uh, around," I said. "Doing...uh...stuff." I hadn't told anybody else about my imminent departure from Nepal, apart from Dr. Singh and Mike Swenson. It would be impossible to tell Bronte about my morning at the Indian embassy without going into great detail about my decision to leave the Peace Corps. I wanted to tell my fellow volunteers, but only when the time was right.

"Hey, Bronte, how did you meet those Rastafarian dudes?" I asked, changing the subject as we headed toward our usual table inside the restaurant.

"Who? Those Ethiopian brothers? Shit, Berkeley, we goes waaay back. Met 'em at Burnin' Man back in the nineties. We been tight ever since."

"Wait, you've been to Burning Man?"

"Hells yeah. You ain't been? *Damn*, boy, you been missin' *out*!"

I knew many people from Berkeley who'd attended the eight-day art-based festival. Their experiences among fellow artists and freethinkers in the Nevada desert had always piqued my curiosity. I was sure that Burning Man wasn't my scene, but I was glad that such an event existed, and that it provided a creative outlet for some of the country's most inspired artists.

"I have to admit, the whole burning effigy thing's a *little* scary for a black man, but *damn*, I ain't ever been able to express myself like I have out there in the desert," said Bronte.

"Nice to be seeing you!" Keshav approached our table from the kitchen. "My favorite customers!"

Keshav was a hip-looking guy. He'd trimmed his sideburns thin and they came to a sharp point just in front of his earlobes. His mustache and soul patch were no less manicured. His expensive-looking vest matched his expensive-looking dress pants, and he wore a light blue dress shirt under the vest, with its sleeves rolled up to his elbows. Around his neck, he wore a designer tie, but instead of placing the tie under the collar, he'd looped it outside like a necklace; its knot was directly in contact with the skin of his throat.

Keshav took our orders, tucked his pen behind his ear, and put his hands on his hips. "Tell me you are still going to the match tomorrow." He was referring to an international football match between his home country of Mauritius and the Nepali national team, a match that was to be played on the team's home pitch in the heart of Pepsicola Townplanning. He'd been excited about it for weeks and, at his insistence, I'd agreed to attend.

"Of course," I said. "I think Manfred's coming too."

"Bronte?" Keshav prompted.

"Pepsicola Townplanning ain't no place for a civilized man like myself. It would take some *serious* cash to get this boy out that way for anything, 'specially a damn soccer game."

After we finished our entrées, and after Bronte indulged in two rounds of soft-serve ice cream, we made our way back to the street and the Rastafarians, who were huddled around a tinny transistor radio, listening to what sounded like a play-by-play of a running marathon. They beckoned us into their inner circle without hesitation and encouraged us to stay for the race's exciting conclusion.

233

On the radio, a short intermission marked a break in the race coverage, and the station spun Bob Marley's "Redemption Song." The song finished and the commentator resumed his play-by-play with the nerve-wracking news that Haile Gebrselassie, the Rastafarians' hero, had fallen slightly off pace and was struggling to regain his world-record form.

"Man, I don't know if he's going to do it," I said.

One of the Rasta men smiled at me, looked up at the sky, and raised his palms to the heavens. "No prob-lem," he boomed. "Jah weel provide. Rrraaaasta-far-eye, my brother." The rest of the men, nodding their heads in approval, echoed his sentiment before returning their attention to the race.

Gebrselassie fell short of the world record, though he won the race handily, and the Rasta men were still delighted. I wanted to hang out with them longer, but I needed to get back to the Indian embassy. I thanked the men for their kindness, said good-bye to Bronte, and headed back down Kantipath toward Lazimpat.

Arriving at the compound ahead of schedule, I was pleased to see that I was one of the first in line to collect my visa and passport. But when I reached the official's booth, I was informed that my application had not yet been processed and that I should stand to the side. I watched with growing concern as countless other foreigners met with the same fate, all belly-ing up to the window only to immediately be cast aside unapologetically.

The situation soon turned ugly as people who had expected the after-noon to go more quickly and smoothly than the morning began to snap. One by one, each unleashed vengeance on the nebbishy official behind the glass. Another official, a man clearly more experienced in the handling of irate travelers, quickly stepped in and screamed, "I do not suffer fools gladly. All of you, TO THE BACK OF THE LINE!"

Nothing more exciting than continued grumbling happened for the rest of the afternoon, and eventually my visa was stapled into my passport and the book returned to me. I took that as a good sign, and I worked up the courage to go to the Pepsicola Community Hospital and break the news that I was leaving.

The news came as quite a shock to the staff, who, with tear-filled eyes, tried to persuade me to stay. The men and women of the clinic weren't the only ones with tears in their eyes, I must say.

Madhu and Shruti took the news hardest. They'd been my closest Nepali friends, apart from Raju Shrestha. The staff and I talked late into the evening until it was time to part ways. They put on brave faces and did their best to mask their emotions, but they were good, honest people who lived by the compulsions of their hearts. Based on the sadness in their eyes, I could tell their hearts were heavy with a sense of impending loss. My heart was heavy too, and to alleviate the crushing weight of separation, I spoke hopeful words to the staff about my eventual return to Nepal, although I had no idea when that might be.

Pepsicola Townplanning came alive with excitement in anticipation of the rare home football match. The groundskeepers had done their best to level the problematic hillocks dotting the playing field, the same mounds that, only several weeks earlier, had turned a bowl from the young Santosh into painful consequences for me. The groundskeepers would have cut the grass too, had the stray water buffalo and venerable cows of the neighborhood not already devoured most of its weedy greenery. A small rice field in the maidaan's northwest corner—where the local kids often played hide-and-go-seek—had been harvested and filled in.

I made my way to the pitch from Sundar's garage, where Stella'! was getting a tuneup before her departure for India. Volunteers shuffled along the field's margins, sprinkling white incense donated by a local vendor to demarcate the pitch's outer boundaries. The national team, according to local gossip, had blown its chalk budget earlier in the season when it hosted Bhutan. The event's announcer, Mr. Tashi Man Singh, a local radio celebrity, issued a lighthearted appeal to fans over the PA system, instructing spectators to avoid smoking within ten feet of the volatile aromatic incense. Should the powder be set ablaze, he warned, the game would have to be called due to the hazy smokescreen it would surely create.

Fans from across the city arrived twenty to a tuk tuk. Maruti Suzukis taxied high-ranking Nepali dignitaries to their private seating near midfield, while a raucous group of foreign tourists hopped off a bus at the pitch's southern end. An impromptu drum circle heightened the massing crowd's excitement, as the feverish pounding of the *maadal*, a popular Nepali folk instrument made of leather and wood, wafted over the heath and sounded the tribal call to battle.

I had never witnessed anything quite like the scene unfolding before my eyes in the entire year that I'd lived in Pepsicola Townplanning. It was as though the entire city of Kathmandu had descended upon my sleepy little community. I was never one for big sporting events, but I found myself getting caught up in the excitement of the day's match, happy to be a part of something that was so important to so many people. But there was another emotion mixed in there too, and it took me a moment to figure out what it was.

Part of me felt territorial about Pepsicola Townplanning, I finally determined. Seeing other foreigners in the crowd made me uneasy. I was the only Westerner living in the community, and I'd never expected to share the place with other Westerners, even if it were only a once-in-a-while occurrence. Such emotion was common among Peace Corps volunteers, but I had never expected to feel it as strongly as I did. My reaction to the other Westerners demonstrated just how attached to the community I'd become and made me sad to think about everything and everyone I would soon be leaving.

I took a seat in the sea of Nepali red and blue, spotting several colorful Mauritian flags fluttering throughout the crowd. One came into my immediate peripheral vision. Turning slightly, I came face-to-face with Keshav Choudary, who was fully decked out in pro-Mauritian swag, including a T-shirt bearing the slogan: *Mauritian Football: Refusing to Go the Way of the Dodo since 1681.* It had been at least two years since he was last home, and I knew that he longed for the tropical climate and the extraordinary natural beauty of his native place. He had described on several occasions how the salty smell of the prevailing southeastern trade winds had never failed to make his stomach flutter, claiming there was excitement in the Mauritian air.

Working his way through the crowd not far behind Keshav and standing almost a good head taller than everybody else in the stands, was none other than Mr. Manfred Little. I hadn't seen my Peace Corps friend since he'd returned from his Vipassana retreat about two weeks earlier, and I was eager to hear about his experience at the meditation center. He warmly embraced both Keshav and me before taking a seat next to me.

"It's a lovely day for football, gentlemen," he said. "Should be quite a tussle between these two titans!"

"Welcome to Pepsicola Townplanning," I said. "I'm glad you were able to make it."

"Between Gloria, the kids, and the monks at Kopan, my free time's been shaved down to a mere sliver, but I'm happy to be here. And speaking of the monks at Kopan, they're building a new sand mandala. You should stop by and check it out; it's going to be quite stunning."

The realization that I would never see the completed mandala hit me hard. The mandala, which would be painstakingly built over the course of several weeks only to be destroyed upon completion with one sweep of the hand, was representative of my time in Nepal. I had spent months working in the community, getting to know the people while engaged in my various Peace Corps activities, and with one decision, I was about to decimate everything I'd worked so hard to achieve. Dr. Singh's assurance that the legacy a person left behind, the feelings he stirred in the people around him, was equally as important as his physical presence in a place filled me with peace, and I clung to it.

"So, Manfred," I said, "how was your Vipassana retreat?"

"One of the toughest things I've ever done in my life, Benjamin," he said, pushing his glasses up the bridge of his nose. "It's a rewarding experience, though, and I highly recommend you go at some point and try it for yourself."

All eyes were upon the head referee, Chin-Hua Sohn, from Korea, as punters from both squads trotted onto the field.

"We are waiting for a most famous celebrity in all of Kathmandu to arrive for the ceremonial coin toss," Keshav explained.

Seemingly on cue, I heard the familiar rumble of a retooled Royal Enfield motorcycle and then saw the dust cloud the bike was whisking high into the air. Accelerating, the Foreign Hand popped a wheelie as he deftly weaved his way through the minefield of potholes on the road surrounding the pitch. Ever the performer, the Israeli took several celebratory laps around the maidaan, waving and pumping his arm in the air. He had unequivocally won the Nepalis' respect and admiration after defeating the Great Khali at Sharma Slam so many months before.

The Foreign Hand parked his bike at midfield, dismounted, and placed mallas around the necks of players from both sides.

The captain of the Nepali team was a young man named Bishan Biswas, a second cousin of Shruti's who had visited her house on several occasions during my stay in Pepsi. I could see Shruti and Annu proudly looking on from their seats near the foreign dignitaries' booth when Bishan's name was announced over the PA system.

The Foreign Hand plucked a shiny new rupee coin from the back pocket of his fatigues and asked the Mauritian captain, Jacques-Désiré Periatambee, to make the call. "Everest or Nepal map?"

"Everest."

After working the crowd for applause one final time, the Foreign Hand flicked the coin high into the air. He bent down to get a closer look at the coin before bellowing, "Everest it is!"

Players from both sides retreated to their respective positions on the pitch. The Foreign Hand signaled Mr. Tashi Man Singh, who immediately pulled forward in his red Maruti Suzuki, upon whose roof the PA system sat. The Israeli reached through the car's open window, borrowed the announcer's microphone, and proceeded to sing rousing renditions of both the Nepali and Mauritian national anthems—in Hebrew. The appreciative crowd loudly applauded. Once the anthems had been sung, the Foreign Hand mounted his bike and tore across the field to the foreign dignitaries' booth, leaving a substantial rut on the playing field in his wake.

The Nepali squad, dressed in red, looked hungry for their first international win in some time. The Mauritians, in their white shorts and white jerseys, seemed both cohesive and carefree, despite their lower international ranking.

The Nepali offense was led by a pair of Africans, the same men I saw floating around Thamel when I first arrived in Nepal. They were clearly celebrities, but they always seemed to keep to themselves except for a small group of friends. I'd heard plenty of stories about the men and their business outside of soccer over the past year. Some people thought they were drug dealers, and others thought they were African spies; in actuality, Dr. Singh told me, they were political refugees from Nigeria, and they were fine with keeping their personal details unreachable behind the protective shell of the Nepali national football team.

The teams exchanged jousts and charges on the pitch in the hopes that their well-placed corner kicks and fancy footwork within the six-yard box might net them a goal or two. Neither squad had drawn blood by halftime, however, and we fans were becoming restless yet again.

Players returned to the maidaan and action resumed after we'd been treated to the up-tempo stylings of Nepali punk band Rai Ko Ris. A corner kick was awarded to the Nepali squad. Captain Biswas waited patiently near the corner arc until his team members had arranged themselves in front of the Mauritian keeper; then he sent his cross into the melee of attackers and defenders.

As the ball scribed a crescent toward the net, one of the Nigerians, who was lining up for a header, stumbled on a hillock missed by the groundskeepers and crumpled to the ground; he writhed in pain, grasping his ankle. A worried hush fell over the crowd. The head referee blew his whistle to signal a break in play as team members from both sides carried the injured footballer to the sidelines.

"Do we have any doctors in the stands, folks?" crackled the PA. "Any doctors at all? If so, we could use your assistance on the sidelines!"

My heart thumping, I waited. Surely Dr. Singh was in attendance. But when nobody seemed to be moving to help, I dutifully stood up and made my way down to the sidelines, followed closely by Keshav and Manfred.

The Nepali trainer peered up at me from his squat next to the Nigerian with a look of great concern on his face. "Maybe fracture?"

I fished through the trainer's bag and found a tuning fork. I set the fork buzzing before placing it on several key anatomical landmarks around the injured man's ankle.

"Any pain with this?" I asked the man, first in Nepali, then in English, unsure which language he knew better.

"No pain," he replied in English, looking on with curiosity.

I had the man attempt to move his ankle, but the swelling of the tissue surrounding the joint was already too significant to allow much pain-free movement. I figured he was suffering from a moderate ankle sprain, and I called for a bag of ice.

"We'll have to act fast if we want to ensure a quick recovery," I said.

The injured Nigerian looked me in the eyes and said in a deep baritone voice, "Please, do what you must."

I applied the ice to blunt the pain and found a roll of stretchy tape in the trainer's bag that I could use on the ankle to help stem the swelling, promote fluid drainage, and provide postural support. Amazingly, I also found a bottle of anti-inflammatory medication in the trainer's bag; I gave it to the Nigerian with explicit instructions on how much to take and how often to take it.

Now that the injury was taken care of, I couldn't help but linger a while on the unusual buildup of scar tissue that stretched from just below the man's kneecap to his ankle. The wounds, long since healed, had received countless stitches, stitches apparently applied in haste, given their uneven spacing and asymmetrical appearance. The Nigerian, catching my concerned look, was quick to speak. "We were the lucky ones."

"What do you mean?"

"It is very difficult to describe the horrors that Albert and I escaped from," he said. "My name is Danny Kobani, and that is my cousin, Albert Mitee, out there on the field," he added, pointing to the well-muscled forward zigzagging around opponents. I had been so absorbed that I hadn't noticed that play had resumed. "We fled to Nepal from the Niger Delta two years ago to escape persecution. As you can see," he said, looking down at his shins, "we did not leave soon enough."

"My god," Manfred murmured.

"Have you ever heard of the Ogoni Nine?" Danny asked, his eyes growing large.

I was familiar with the story of the nine members of the Ogoni tribe who, in 1995, had been tried on trumped-up charges of murder and executed at the hands of the military dictatorship led by General Sani Abacha. I remembered my parents discussing the execution of the activists, all critics speaking out against the environmental damage and theft of resources by multinational oil companies in Ogoniland and throughout the Niger Delta. The executions had brought international scorn and outrage against the Nigerian government.

"Both Albert and I are Ogoni." Danny directed his comments to the bag of ice he continued to press to his injured ankle. "We were heavily involved in the movement for the survival of the Ogoni people."

Danny said that many of the men in the Ogoni Nine were close family friends, besides being generally good men dedicated to halting the illegal extraction of wealth from Ogoniland. They tried to make sure that some of the profits from oil revenues flowed back to the Ogoni people and not just into the pockets of multinational corporations and corrupt officials.

"I was only young when the men were executed," said Danny, "but I was old enough to recognize the righteousness of the men's cause."

Though Keshav hadn't said a word since arriving on the sidelines, he was listening intently to Danny's story. Nigeria and Mauritius were separated by thousands of miles, and Keshav's first ancestors had been from India, but there was a silent solidarity between the two Africans that spoke far louder than words.

"Constant corruption, repeated oil spills, violent repression, abject poverty: *this* is the legacy of Big Oil in my country," said Danny, his deep voice wavering momentarily. "Albert and I became quite vocal about our disapproval of the way the government handled its affairs. In return, our village was destroyed and we were tortured by the authorities. The scars you see on my legs are nothing."

"So, how did you guys get out of the country?"

"Albert and I fled by sea from Port Harcourt to Lagos under the cover of darkness." Danny said he and Albert stayed in Lagos for a while and tried to maintain a low profile, but they both played football in the Nigeria Premier League and were relatively well-known in the capital. The military government's men caught up with them, and the threats against the footballer's lives and the lives of their families started again. Their only choice was to leave the country, to find a place where they could be safe and where their limited funds would last.

"Nepal was a good choice," Danny said. "With the help of a longtime family friend, Dr. Moses Ohanyido—a physician from Lagos with a professional connection to a very big man here in Kathmandu, a very influential man—we were able to arrange our flight and our visas to Nepal."

I remembered suddenly that I could start taping his ankle. While I did so, I mentioned to Danny that I'd occasionally seen him and Albert around Thamel.

"The Aussies!" said Danny, smiling broadly. He looked across the field into the large crowd of spectators, picked out his cohort, and waved. His personal cheering section responded immediately to his acknowledgement, sending up a loud round of hoots and hollers.

The action heated up back on the field as the clock counted down the match's final minutes. Each side came close on numerous occasions, but neither team had scored. From his position within the foreign dignitaries' booth, the Foreign Hand exhorted the Nepali offense to organize one final, determined attack.

Just when it looked as though neither team would score, Albert received a brilliant lead pass from a Nepali midfielder. He proceeded to undress two Mauritian defenders with his fleet-of-foot maneuvering and unparalleled moxie, weaving around them like an aggressive tuk tuk driver on Kantipath during rush-hour traffic. He closed in on the Mauritian goal and punted a laser beam that skimmed just over the maidaan's surface. The Mauritian keeper appeared to have it, but at the last moment, the ball found the same sandy hillock that had sidelined Danny. Its trajectory altered, the ball sailed past the keeper and into the open net.

When the referee blew his whistle for the final time that afternoon, Nepal laid claim to its first international football victory in many months. The win wouldn't budge the team too much from their unenviable position of 152nd on the FIFA world ranking table, but it would give the residents of Kathmandu and Pepsicola Townplanning something to talk about for a long, long time. The Nepali squad's fans, waving their red and blue double-triangle standards, were beside themselves with excitement.

Players from both sides exchanged jerseys in a gesture of international friendship. Because neither team's budget could truly allow for such an extravagance, the players immediately returned their opponent's jerseys and waved to the crowd. Danny invited us all—Keshav, Manfred, the rest of N-199, and me—to the large party that had been organized for both teams at the Rum Doodle later that evening. It would be part celebration, part going-away party. I threw Danny's arm around my shoulders and helped him hobble across the field into the capable hands of the Aussies.

I was heartened to see so many familiar faces at the Rum Doodle that evening. Besides Danny, Albert, and the rest of the footballers, Beth, Taka, Manfred, Laura, and Bronte had all made it out for the festivities. I also bumped into Raju Shrestha as I was milling about in the crowd. He had come to the Rum Doodle bearing gifts of Bundt cakes and rum babas he had prepared at Slice of Life Bakery.

"Benjamin, you are like a brother to me," said the cakeshop owner, handing me a miniature Bundt cake before leaning in to speak over the noise of the bar. "If we are not seeing one another again, I am wanting you to know that your friendship has been very important to me."

"Yeah, Raju," I said, surprised by the candid nature of his comment. "You've been like a brother to me too." Raju excused himself, rounded up his posse of tough-looking men who were sitting at the bar, and left the Rum Doodle.

I wondered how he knew that I was leaving Kathmandu. I was aware that news traveled quickly in Nepal, but there seemed to be no logical explanation for this. Eventually I chalked up the unusual occurrence, like so many others during my stay in Nepal, to being a cultural quirk that I would never fully understand.

I joined the rest of the Kathmandu-based N-199 crew at our usual table and began drinking. The alcohol was a cowardly way of masking the pain and embarrassment I felt about the announcement I was going to make, and I knew it, but I needed it to help loosen the screws in my tongue.

Toward the night's end, long after I lost track of how much alcohol I'd consumed, I stood up on my chair. "For the fine ladies and gentlemen of N-199, an announcement," I slurred, swaying. My mind and vision spinning like the wheel of a careening tuk tuk, I raised my half-filled glass of beer toward the ceiling, sloshed its contents on my shirt, and continued my speech. "Benjamin Creed, friend, colleague, and all-around grrrreat guy, is leaving the Peace Corps."

Whereas moments before there had been laughing and joking, everything at the table skidded to a halt.

"In honor of Baby Bear's Peace Corps service, we must all get completely and hopelessly shit-faced," said Beth, breaking the awkward silence with her emphatic declaration.

"Indubitably," said Manfred, reaching for the nearest pitcher of beer.

I climbed down from my chair and, after fielding dozens of questions from my comrades, slumped back in my seat and let the pent-up stress I'd been feeling for weeks slowly slip away. My friends even told me that, in my situation, they would make the same decision.

Bronte, who had disappeared after my pronouncement, suddenly came storming through the entrance of the Rum Doodle wearing nothing but a giant American flag and a feathered fedora. "OK, bitches!" he said, "Get your asses out into the street. It's high time we did done some skinny-dippin' in the ol' Rani Pokhari, you know what I mean?"

Somehow—could it be the liquor?—the thought of splashing around naked in a giant tank of water in the middle of Kathmandu suddenly seemed like a great idea. I had wondered what it might be like to swim in the Rani Pokhari ever since I arrived in Kathmandu, but I never imagined that I would be doing it naked and on a somewhat chilly night with my fellow Americans.

"How very First World of us," said Manfred, referring to our plan to supersede Kathmandu's bylaws and do as we pleased.

We regrouped on the street after we paid for our drinks. The street itself was relatively quiet, save the occasional backfiring of a taxi. We ran at full tilt down Kantipath, hooting and hollering and taunting the great, sleeping city of Kathmandu with our playful shouts.

About halfway to the Queen's Pond—the English name for the pool—we stopped momentarily for Beth who, after drinking too quickly at the bar and overextending herself on the run, ralphed several times onto the sidewalk. She insisted that she felt much better after throwing up, but we all continued toward the pond at a more sustainable pace.

Despite the warnings issued by Manfred, who insisted that the *naga*—a serpent deity locals thought lived in the tank—would get us, we all climbed the fence surrounding the pond and stripped down to our birthday suits under the cover of darkness. "Bombs away!" yelled Bronte, dropping his flag and performing a textbook cannonball into the tank's murky depths.

The water, chilly at best, helped sober me up, to the point where I felt almost sheepish about our little coup on Kathmandu. I tried to savor the moment though, because I knew it would be the last one we would all share for a long time. After a few more minutes of floating in the tank, and after a shameful group attempt at synchronized swimming, we hauled our bodies out of the water and threw on our clothes. My friends wished me success in my journey, and they insisted I stay in touch by e-mail. The members of N-199 each took a turn embracing me before they, as a group, headed back toward Thamel and the continuation of their Peace Corps lives.

It then occurred to me: I was free. I no longer had any obligations to fulfill, I had no more grant applications to write, and I no longer had any limitations on where I could go and what I could do. Thus, on to India, on to Adriana and the possibility of something greater than freedom: redemption.

India Bound

EARLY THE FOLLOWING MORNING, I LEFT PEPSICOLA TOWNPLANNING AND Kathmandu and headed west for the border at Sunauli under bright-blue skies and with the promise of new adventures on the horizon. I sipped water from my Nalgene bottle and donned a pair of sunglasses to shield my bloodshot eyes. I relaxed into my seat as Stella'! dutifully chugged out of the Kathmandu Valley toward the plains. I would be in India by nightfall, if all went well.

On several occasions, I spotted the ghastly wreckage of local buses that had somehow run off the road, over a ledge, and into a deep ravine, their charred remains indicative of a gruesome fate for all those aboard. Other vehicles lay nose-to-nose in the middle of the road, their windshields missing and their headlights busted, victims of a head-on collision from earlier that morning, no doubt. As horrific as those images were, and as much as they helped keep my wits sharp and my eyes on the road, what I mostly felt was irritation over the presence of an impossible number of exhaust-belching lorries plying the roads.

The dump trucks, carrying fill and other building materials to various development sites throughout Nepal, crept along the mountain roads at a snail's pace, stopping often to check their brakes and occasionally rearrange their loads. The trucks were almost impossible to see around, and they traveled in packs too, which made passing risky and condemned me to a morning of excessive tailgating and impatient honking. *Horn OK Please* was painted on the back bumpers of many of the many of the—admittedly brilliantly decorated—lorries, and *Horn OK Please* I did use many times.

The congestion and pollution on the highway stood in stark contrast to the surrounding area's natural beauty, and it reminded me of the less appealing aspects of development that inevitably seemed to accompany economic growth in places like Nepal and India. I remembered a conversation I had with Dr. Singh not long before I decided to leave the Peace Corps, about development in Nepal and how the need to build and expand and be viewed as powerful in the eyes of the world often superseded all other ambitions.

A freethinking man with progressive politics and nonsectarian religious views, the doctor tried to promote sustainable development in Nepal, which made him a champion of the people. He was celebrated in the greater Kathmandu community for his ability to tackle the tough issues with compassion and sensitivity. He strongly believed that more women needed to be involved in the decision-making process too; only once the voices and ideas of women were heard and incorporated into the mix would an era of enlightenment and prosperity grace the country and its people.

I could feel the air getting warmer by the time the road flattened out and the lorries began to disappear. I welcomed the Tarai's heat, much like I welcomed the opportunity to put my past indiscretions behind me and start fresh with Adriana. My mind had come to associate heat with both Adriana and Dharavi, and the rising barometer gave me butterflies in my stomach.

My evening arrival in Sunauli came not a moment too soon. Stella'! had developed a disconcerting thump at some point during the afternoon's ride, and I was afraid she would give up the ghost long before I ever reached a repair shop. I hated the thought of using the money Dr. Singh had given me as a parting gift—which was enough to last for some time, if I was frugal—for repairs, but the last thing I wanted was to be stranded in a seedy border town known for its disreputable, transient clientele and grimy conditions.

I crossed into India after changing my money and after the border guard had examined my documents. I then headed for the state-operated guest house suggested by my India guidebook and parked Stella'! in front. To my surprise, the place was all but deserted; I had expected more guests, given the level of traffic that flowed across the border. But then again, Sunauli was not a place where most people were inclined to linger. It was a bent and broken place, from what I'd been told, home to pimps and pushers, pickpockets and prostitutes. Most people arriving there immediately hopped on a bus and headed toward more appealing destinations.

I took a moment to explore the cavernous building before checking in. I found the space aching with loneliness and neglect. Its decaying facade and seemingly nonexistent staff gave it a spookiness too. If I had only listened to my intuition, if I had only had more confidence in my gut reaction to the place, I might have chosen to stay elsewhere that night, but I was tired and in an unfamiliar place, and I didn't have the energy to look at other guest houses.

I tried repeatedly to summon an employee, but nobody greeted me at the reception desk. Finally I took one of the keys hanging on a rack behind the desk and let myself into a room. I would square up with the receptionist in the morning, if there was one then.

There wasn't much to my room other than a bed and a bathroom, but the terrazzo floors were clean. I dropped my backpack on the floor, pulled back the covers, and prepared for sleep.

An explosive sound wrenched me from my peaceful slumber. I was sweating and disoriented and at a complete loss to explain the commotion outside my door. I heard women shrieking and men shouting, along with the sound of a door being kicked off its hinges. I also heard a heavy thud in the room next door.

I threw off the covers, ran to the door, and flung it open. The noise that had roused me from my sleep was *not* a Maoist bomb, as I'd first imagined, and it wasn't the innocent incendiary clap of a firecracker left over from Tihar either; instead, it was the report from a gun that had been fired in the room next door.

I stood frozen in my doorway and watched as two hulking men dragged a limp body across the rough cement. The man they dragged, whose face was hidden by their bodies, looked to be bleeding badly, the victim of a fresh gunshot wound to the thigh. A trail of blood oozing from the wound marked the trio's hasty retreat and captured the footprints of a team of paramedics following closely behind. I barely had time to think, however, before my attention was diverted to the room next door, where the violent sounds of forced restraint pierced the damp evening air.

I watched with disbelieving eyes as an overweight, balding Indian man wearing only a sarong and a set of handcuffs was paraded past me down the corridor by a team of armed men. "*Bhenchod!*" the man yelled repeatedly, wheeling to spit at his captors, his face twisted into knots. His aggressive posture was quickly softened, however, by a salvo of vicious licks from a lathi-wielding police officer. For a moment our eyes met, and I saw a flicker of recognition on his face. He looked strangely familiar to me as well.

I grabbed my pants and shirt from a nearby hook, threw them on, and stepped out into the cleared corridor. I peeked inside the room next door and saw a small group of young Nepali girls huddled together on the bed. An older woman was draping a blanket around their shoulders and urging the girls to get up and follow her. They passed me without a word or a glance. I turned back toward the narrow courtyard and saw a man slumped on a plastic chair, smoking a cigarette. His thin red tie dangled loosely around his neck, and his hair was in a serious state of dishevelment. Scanty moonbeams bouncing off nearby palm fronds gave the man's face a ghostly radiance.

"Hey, man, are you OK?" I said, approaching him slowly from the side. "You don't look so good."

"No problem," replied the skinny, mustachioed man, bobbling his head gently from side to side. He tapped the butt of his cigarette on the arm of his chair before straightening up and pointing to a nearby wicker stool. "Sit."

The man introduced himself as Sabin after I had introduced myself. "Many apologies, friend—we were not expecting such a bad time tonight."

"What do you mean?" I asked. "Can you tell me what happened here?"

"The police arrested a very bad man, a real zero."

"What for?"

"Sex trafficking," he said in a solemn tone.

The Indian and Nepali police had been tracking the man for some time, according to Sabin. The man, accused of recruiting and smuggling hundreds of girls from Nepal into India, had finally been caught red-handed during the evening's sting. Sabin insisted that without the help of an inside man, the police never would have caught him.

"And now poor Raju Shrestha has paid a major price for his efforts," Sabin said.

Sabin's words felt like a white-hot knife piercing my chest. "Wait, do you mean Raju Shrestha, owner of Slice of Life Bakery in Kathmandu?" I asked, frantic with worry.

"And part-time undercover agent," said Sabin. "Yes, that Raju Shrestha."

Of course! That's where I'd seen the Indian man before: in Raju's personal lounge in Slice of Life Bakery. All the contradictions that had bothered me about Raju were suddenly explainable. Then I remembered his odd comments to me at the Rum Doodle the previous evening, his comments about how, if he never saw me again, he wanted me to know how much he appreciated my friendship.

Pride welled up inside me. Raju was a hero. He was willing to lay down his own life to save the young women of Nepal from the horrors of Indian brothels. I was inspired by my friend's courageous actions, but I feared for his life after the vicious gunshot wound to his thigh.

"Is he going to be OK?" I asked. "It looked like he lost a lot of blood."

"God willing," Sabin said. "Paramedics think flesh wound only." Sabin explained that Raju would be rushed back to Kathmandu, where he would receive first-rate medical attention at Bir Hospital.

Relieved, I finally let down my guard. I was unsure why Sabin had been so willing to confide in me, much like the Nigerian footballer Danny Kobani, or Raju, in his private lounge so many months ago. It was unusual, I thought, for somebody in his position to share that kind of information with a stranger, but then again, I couldn't possibly hope to ascertain the status of his mental state. And maybe Beth *had* been correct when she described my ability to connect with Nepalis.

I suddenly realized how tired I was, but the thought of spending another minute in the guest house made my stomach turn. The thought of Nepali women—over two hundred thousand of them, according to Sabin—working as sex slaves in Indian brothels was unbearable. I wondered how many of those women had been infected with sexually transmitted diseases. I could only imagine that their lives were a living hell, and that, once they were absorbed into the system, there was little hope they would ever escape.

"My apologies, Sabin," I said, snapping myself out of my funk, "but I forgot to ask you what your role in all of this is."

Sabin dropped the butt of his cigarette on the courtyard's lawn and stamped it out with his right foot. "I am working for an organization called Maiti Nepal," he said, leaning back in his chair and crossing his legs. "We are based out of Kathmandu." Sabin described his organization's work not only to stop the flow of trafficked women between Nepal and India but also to create a home and a nurturing environment for the survivors of trafficking, who often had nowhere to go for care and support after their horrendous ordeals.

Creating such an environment was an especially important task in Nepal, where, Sabin insisted, there existed a strange culture of exclusion that kept survivors mired in a state of perpetual depression. When the survivors of trafficking tried to reenter Nepali society, he said, they were often shunned by family, friends, and the greater community, who would rather cut ties with the women than bear the shame and embarrassment associated with somebody who had worked in the sex industry, regardless of whether that work was forced or voluntary. The victims continued to be victimized by their own supposed support network.

"A very, very sad reality," he said.

Sabin also told me that traffickers targeted all levels of Nepali society in their attempts to recruit young women and girls for sex work. The women, unaware that they were bound for prostitution, believed they were being recruited for lucrative, high-paying jobs in India. Even a prominent politician's daughter had been lured away with the consent of her equally fooled parents. The only groups who seemed relatively unaffected by trafficking were the poorest segments of the Nepali population, due in large part to their long-held and deeply rooted suspicions of anyone promising an easier and more economically profitable life.

"The girls who were rescued here tonight, Sabin, looked young," I said, after a few moments of silence. "They couldn't have been much more than ten or twelve years old."

"Most highly prized are the young ones," he said. "They fetch maximum money."

How disgusting. I knew that young virgins were highly prized in the sex industry, but ten years old, for Christ's sake? "So what will happen to those girls?"

"They will be sent back to their orphanages in Kathmandu after receiving counseling," he said.

"They were orphans?"

"Yes, orphans; no mother, no father. Easy targets for traffickers," he said, shaking his head from side to side.

I was sure life as a prostitute in an Indian brothel was about the worst possible situation a girl could find herself in, but the quality of life in a Kathmandu orphanage wasn't great either. If anything, conditions in their orphanages had probably driven the girls to escape. Easy targets, indeed. I'd visited several Kathmandu orphanages with Laura over the past year, and they stood out in my mind as symbols of hardship, misfortune, and in some cases, neglect.

Between my recollections of life in the orphanages and the evening's happenings in Sunauli, I was reminded that Nepal was a country with many problems. It was true that there were many things about Nepal that I loved, but there were some truly horrible things that happened there too, things I tended to gloss over because I was so often blinded by the kindness of the people I knew.

I was amazed by the lengths people would go to climb out of poverty, the evil acts—like sex trafficking, for instance—they would consider committing if the ends somehow justified the means. On the other hand, I'd never personally felt the sting of poverty. I had never been in a situation where my future seemed bleak and the path to prosperity long and twisted. I believed in my heart that I would struggle and struggle until I finally made good, but maybe I too would be tempted by shortcuts to wealth. Maybe I too would be weak in the face of an easy way out. Maybe I too would be easily corrupted.

Sabin stood up and shook my hand after he'd finished his second cigarette, and he apologized again for the night's commotion. I watched his image merge with the night's shadows until he disappeared on the far side of the moonlit courtyard. Only once he was gone did my fatigue overcome me. I walked back to my room, locked the door, and fell into bed.

I saw no evidence of the previous night's struggle when I woke the following morning. Raju's blood had been scrubbed from the hallway, and the door that the police kicked in had already been replaced. The government-run guest house looked completely different in the daylight. It looked friendlier and better cared for than I'd assumed it to be the previous night.

After a quick shower, I gathered my gear and headed for the main lobby. There, the receptionist greeted me and asked me if I'd enjoyed my stay.

"Uh...I don't really know how to answer that question," I said, shocked that the man seemed so genuine in his interest. Perhaps he wasn't aware of the sting.

I loaded my gear into Stella'! and left Sunauli in a hurry. Buoyed by the disappearance of Stella'!'s odd thumping noise, I drove at a relatively fast clip through the northern reaches of Uttar Pradesh until I reached the city of Lucknow, where I stopped to eat.

Midway through my meal of lentils, rice, and chapatti, I was approached by a man wearing only a loincloth. I knew the man was a Shaivite, a follower of Shiva, based on his ash-smeared face, the three horizontal lines painted on his forehead, and the begging bowl and trident he was carrying. He sported a lengthy beard, but I could tell he was not old, as his skin was smooth and fair. He sat down beside me to watch me eat after gently setting his trident and bowl on the table.

I offered the man some of my chapatti, but he refused, seemingly content to watch me devour my food. Then something unusual happened. A swarm of butterflies appeared and circled the man's head and body. The holy man seemed completely unaware of the butterflies, and when I pointed them out, he simply laughed.

It didn't take long for me to discover that the sadhu spoke Nepali. I asked him where he was going. "Gujarat," he said, adding that he wanted to visit several holy sites there. I got a crazy idea as I finished the last of my lentils. *Maybe the sadhu would like a lift to Mumbai!* It would bring him closer to Gujarat, and his presence in the Bus, along with that of the butterflies, would keep me company.

The words were barely out of my mouth before the holy man had climbed into the passenger seat and fastened his seatbelt. It was clear that he was keen for a road trip, and that knowledge boosted my spirits. There was nothing like having a companion while traveling; somebody with whom to share conversation and, possibly, if he were up for it, the driving.

I felt the first rumblings of pain in my gut about an hour outside of Lucknow. I knew almost immediately that I was going to be sick. I'd been sick in India before, during my first trip to the subcontinent, and I still remembered how awful that experience was. Because there were usually so many people around, and because access to private toilets was not always guaranteed, a sick person in India was forced to forfeit personal pride. It wasn't unusual for people to vomit out the windows of buses or to defecate in front of complete strangers in an open field.

I pulled to the side of the road and headed with haste to a nearby field, where I could squat behind a mud-and-stone fence in relative privacy. At some point during the process, I realized I'd forgotten my roll of toilet paper in Stella'!, but it was too late to turn back, so I simply carried on and searched for a suitable replacement in my immediate vicinity. Fortunately, I found a large leaf that was perfect for the job, and after cleaning up to the best of my abilities, I felt not only a sense of relief but one of gratitude for having avoided detection. "Here's to radical self-reliance!" I said, before burying the leaf under a nearby stone.

To my shock, I found the sadhu hot-boxing Stella'! when I returned to the Bus. The holy man, smiling impishly, held aloft the roll of toilet paper I'd left on the dash. He then burst into hysterical laughter and began wrapping his head so that he resembled a mummy. *What a character.* I opened his door to air out the van.

Fearing a proximity high, I waited at least ten minutes before climbing back into the Bus and resuming our journey. We made good progress that first day, and by the time the day was over, we'd made it well into the Indian state of Madhya Pradesh. I offered the sadhu the small Therm-a-Rest mattress I'd brought with me, but despite my best efforts to persuade him otherwise, he insisted on sleeping outside, on the ground, at the base of a large nearby banyan tree. The butterflies loved banyan trees almost as much as they loved their human companion, according to the holy man. I suspected that the tree was in distant second place. Whatever chemicals his body was producing seemed to attract the butterflies and keep them satisfied in ways I couldn't possibly comprehend.

I stretched out on my air cushion on the Bus's roof. My thoughts quickly turned to Adriana and my imminent return to Dharavi. I gazed up at the stars and tried to form a mental picture of what our first interaction in years might be like. To Adriana, and with the great expanse of the cosmos as my one true witness, I spoke the following words: "I've loved you since the moment I met you, and I'm sorry for the pain I've caused you. You can't possibly believe me, but I'll continue to love you until the day I die." In that grand moment of reckoning, there existed only the swirling of the stars and the beating of my own heart—a great cosmic drummer pounding out a rhythm that was steady and true.

I woke up the following morning feeling better about my decision to leave the Peace Corps than I ever had before. The holy man and I piled into Stella'! after a quick meal and continued our westward journey. We passed through many towns and villages over the next few days, and I tried to get a sense of whether India had changed since my last visit. My conclusion, based on my observations of life, was that India *had* changed, and had changed considerably. Or perhaps it was *I* who had changed over the years.

The sadhu and I paused for a brief rest in a Maharashtrian village before our final push into Mumbai. We sat side by side at a scenic overlook—he with his trident, I with my journal.

I climbed back into the Bus after our break and rummaged through my bag for a snack, but instead found a gift from Shruti and Annu that they'd surreptitiously placed among my belongings. The gift was a framed photo of mother and daughter, a photo that captured to perfection the beauty and kindness of their angelic faces. *What a treasure!* I placed the picture on the dashboard. The holy man froze upon seeing the picture. There was a squirrelly look in his eyes. He tried to look away, but his gaze kept returning to the photo of Shruti and Annu.

"Ah, jeez," I said, realizing I must have left my pen at the overlook. "I'll be right back, OK?"

The holy man was gone by the time I'd retrieved my pen from the lookout and walked back to the Bus, and so was the picture of Shruti and Annu.

"Sonofabitch!" Then it dawned on me: could the holy man have possibly been Bharath Bhupani, Shruti's estranged husband? Something deeply instinctual told me it was him, that I had just spent several days with the man who abandoned two of my closest Nepali friends.

The Homecoming

I FINALLY REACHED MUMBAI. IN THE YEARS SINCE I WAS LAST THERE, I HAD forgotten just how crazy Island City traffic could be, and there were numerous times I wanted to abandon Stella'! and hire a taxi. As traffic closed in around me, as the cheeky little ambassador taxis maneuvered into my blind spots and a small army of subcompacts tried to box me in, I became a "right proper rogue," as Nepali Pete might have said, running red lights, speeding whenever I could, and cutting off pursuing vehicles to reach my destination in the shortest possible time. I'd never driven so fiendishly in my entire life, but then again, I'd never driven in Mumbai toward my one true love.

The aggression I used to navigate Mumbai's streets sapped my strength, and by the time I reached Chota Sion Hospital in the heart of Dharavi—the community that had shaped and molded me into the person I'd become—I no longer had the energy to feel nervous about meeting Adriana. I checked my appearance in the rearview mirror, took a big swig of a lemon drink I'd bought the day before, and popped a handful of anise seeds into my mouth as a natural breath freshener. I hopped out of Stella'! and headed toward the hospital.

I stopped several nurses as I walked the hospital's floors and asked them about Adriana and where I might find her, but nobody seemed to understand what I was trying to say. Many of the nurses spoke only Hindi and were unable to decipher my strange mix of English and Nepali. But even the ones who did speak English weren't able to answer my questions. I sat on a windowsill on the fourth floor to think about my next move, frustrated by my inability to immediately locate Adriana.

The expansive slum splayed outward around the hospital's base in concentric rings. Many of the houses were roofed with either corrugated steel or purple tarps, which made the shantytown look like a giant checkered quilt when viewed from above. Tall, skinny chimneys poked through the blanket of roofs and pumped out a steady smoke that curled skyward in the still heat of midafternoon. Along earthen lanes forgotten by most of the city and ignored by mapmakers, half-naked children played cricket, pausing occasionally to set off bottle rockets that exploded through the din of jackhammers and other construction machinery.

I felt like a voyeur from my vantage point high above the slum. Everywhere I looked there was life: a woman hanging up wet clothes to dry on a clothesline, a man placing freshly spun clay pots in a kiln to bake, a child rolling a rusty bicycle rim over the parched ground with a long stick, a cow munching on a pile of garbage along the main drag. I had no idea how many people lived in the slum, but it numbered in the hundreds of thousands, possibly a million. It probably would have seemed like hell on earth if I hadn't already spent time there, if I were only just seeing it for the first time. There was something absolutely heartbreaking about the slum's appearance, at least to outsiders. But for those who knew the people living within its boundaries, there was something profoundly comforting about the place too.

I'd always found it difficult to explain to people back home, but there was a beauty about Dharavi that an outsider could never see. For me, it was the radiant colors of the crumbling concrete buildings, the ingenuity of the residents who forged complex lives out of almost nothing, an audacious and aromatic jasmine plant baking in the sun that refused to die, and the glow of the children's complexions and the twinkle in their dark brown eyes that helped define the slum's beauty.

It was true that the slum was crowded, smoky, and hot, but it was a clean place, almost—clean in an earthy sort of way. Garbage and raw sewage and black water were problems, but people did their best to create a livable environment for themselves and their children, which, given the extraordinary density of the place, was no small feat. The people themselves, always neat and impeccably dressed, carried themselves with pride and distinction.

I gripped the iron bars surrounding the window. A sickening feeling began to rise from the pit of my stomach. *What if, somehow, she knew I was coming? What if Adriana ran away again?* I stood. If I thought the slum was charged with so much energy, perhaps I could find some answers there.

The slum was not a place for the claustrophobic, I thought, as I spread my arms and touched buildings on both sides of the narrow track. A network of electrical wires and phone cables—a veritable Hydra of coils and cords—writhed like a giant ball of snakes overhead, each reptilian cord slithering away from the nest in tortuous fashion to visit houses in the general vicinity.

Around me, shacks built from tin, plastic, concrete, bamboo, and mud yielded dozens of children who began to follow me as though I were a pied piper. Those who weren't grasping my hands stroked my forearm hair or ran ahead up the path to do a spastic little dance for my amusement. Most of the kids were too young to have any recollection of my first visit to Dharavi, but the fact that I was a complete stranger didn't appear to dampen their excitement or affection.

Despite the slum's outwardly rough appearance, and although domestic abuse, infant mortality, and illiteracy were alarmingly common within its borders, it was still a place of great hope, and nowhere was this hope more evident than in the children's eyes. That mischievous sparkle in the eyes of Dharavi's kids had stayed with me long after I returned to America, and seeing the slum's children for the second time reminded me how vital and playful they were. Nowhere else in the world had I seen such healthy-looking and beautiful children. They may have been confined to a place the greater world had rejected, but that hadn't stopped most of them from having a play-filled childhood.

I spotted several used condoms on the ground, and though disgusted, I was strangely thrilled that the slum's residents were taking the message of birth control seriously. I knew that Adriana had worked with them on that very issue, and those condoms were the tangible evidence of her efforts.

I shifted my gaze from the ground and stole glances into the houses I was passing. Most of the houses had dirt floors and hazy interiors, but some also had an unexpected assortment of amenities, including big-screen TVs, washing machines, and microwaves. It was clear that at least a portion of the slum population was thriving, and I was happy to see that prosperity was finally gracing the residents of Dharavi with the conveniences of modern living.

I began recognizing faces as our little troop traipsed by the potter's open-air kilns. Names began to form on my tongue as I exchanged greetings with the men and women from that most familiar part of the slum. "Sanjay! Sarita! Mahmoud!" I said. "Namaste!" Many of the people I greeted, however, had aged so much in the four years since I last saw them that I barely recognized them. The sun, the pollution, and the tough physical conditions of life had aged all of them prematurely.

I found Mud Panchal chewing on a hunk of jaggery and sunning himself on a concrete step leading to a small communal laundering hole deep in the heart of Kumbharwada. The last time I'd seen Mud, he had been a gangly fourteen-year-old struggling to grow a mustache and stay out of trouble. Now, from what I could see, he'd grown into a young man fully capable of sporting a mustache and breaking the hearts of many. Lying on his side, watching the activities of the laundering hole, the misunderstood middle child of Hari and Aiesha Panchal feigned interest in his younger brother's attempts to keep afloat an alabaster figurine in a boat hewn from Popsicle sticks and candy-bar wrappers.

In the fetid laundry pool, in what resembled a postapocalyptic scene, thin-limbed men and women dressed in rags flogged articles of clothing against flat stones rising just above the water's surface. The workers, most of whom hailed from the state of Andra Pradesh, received about ten cents for each item of clothing washed. Few envied them their profession, but the quality of the *dhobis'* work was almost legendary throughout Mumbai and gave them both notoriety and a reputation to uphold.

"Namaste, Mud!" I said, sitting next to Mud by the pool. I waited for the spark of recognition to flicker in his eyes, as the children escorting me pulled him to a seated position.

Mud squinted his eyes, scratched his head, and looked me squarely in the eye. I could tell he was mildly confused by what he saw because his face twisted into a knot and his head tilted to the side. "*Achchha!*" he finally said, his eyes growing large. "It's *you*, Mr. Benjamin-ji! It is really *you*!"

He clasped my hand in his and shook it with jubilant gusto until my wrist became sore and I had to gently pull it away. "That's quite the hand-shake you've got there, Mud," I said. The look on Mud's face was one of genuine excitement. "I like your mustache," I added, pointing to his hairy upper lip.

Bobbling his head from side to side, he stroked his mustache. He had a big smile on his long, lean face. "Total lady killer!" he said in a flat voice, before bursting into laughter. He put a hand on my shoulder and added, "In all my dreaming, *yaar*, I am not seeing you here in Kumbharwada again. Mummy and Daddy gonna be a real pleased! Come," he said before standing and hauling his brother, Malik, from the pool.

I was chomping at the bit to ask Mud if he had seen Adriana, but I didn't want to appear rude or desperate. Figuring out Adriana's whereabouts was of the utmost importance to me but spending time with the Panchals was important to me too. After all, Mud's parents had so selflessly taken me into their home four years earlier, and few days went by without some thought of them still. I was indebted to them for their hospitality, and I was excited to see them again after such a long time apart.

"How are things at home, Mud?" I asked as he led me toward his father's pottery den.

"Not so good, yaar," he said, pulling a comb from the back pocket of his jeans to groom the puff on top of his head. Apparently there had recently been a major falling out between Hari and Mud's older brother, Ramesh. Hari pushed Ram so hard to finish school—so that he might eventually become a doctor, lawyer, or engineer—that Ram had finally cracked. Unable to cope with the stress and his father's expectations, he had left Dharavi to join a small troupe of circus performers passing through the city. The two hadn't spoken since that day.

I remembered Ram Panchal as a stubborn guy, a do-it-yourselfer bent on forging his own path in life and not the path selected by his father, however well-intentioned. I wasn't surprised that Hari and Ram had become estranged, but it was too bad. I knew Hari would be deeply wounded by such a betrayal, but I also respected Ram's decision to make his own way in life.

"Daddy has not stopped spinning since Ram left," said Mud. "All day he sits at his potting—or should I say, pouting—wheel, waiting for Ram to return and beg his forgiveness. I swear, yaar, he thinks he's Gandhi or something with all this passive-resistance nonsense." It became widely known that the only way Hari would move from his wheel was if Ram quit the traveling caravan and returned to Mumbai to continue his formal education. Mud explained that the clay pot was a fitting symbol for the emptiness Hari felt in his heart.

"He is even now taking food at the wheel and has hired local boys as peons," said Mud, picking up his baby brother and placing him on his shoulders. "So crazy is he, yaar, that last week he even had a pit dug beneath his potting stool to swallow up his motions!"

We finally reached the entrance to Hari's simple, one-room workshop. I chuckled at the words painted on a small placard situated just above the door: *Hari Potter: Terra-Cotta Warrior.*

"Daddy has diversified," said a serious Mud, mistaking my good-natured laughter for confusion. "He is now making terra-cotta products, and has even perfected the art of vanity pottery."

"Vanity pottery?" Now I was perplexed.

"Yes, come, see for yourself," he said, lifting Malik off his shoulders and placing him on the ground. "But first," he said, bending low to speak to his brother, "why don't you tell our cousin-brother who your favorite superhero is being?"

The boy, though shy at first, was eager to please his older brother, and he quickly embraced his moment in the spotlight. "I like Superman, Batman, Spiderman, but my best hero of all is...*Hanuman!*" he squeaked, holding aloft his monkey figurine. *Cute.*

I followed Mud behind Hari's workshop to a small courtyard where his finished works were stored before shipping. I immediately understood what Mud had meant by "vanity pottery." There stood countless life-size effigies of famous Indian personalities. Standing alongside a scale replica of Amitabh Bachchan, the great Bollywood actor, was a clay statue of cricket sensation Sachin Tendulkar, fully glazed with acid gold. Film stars Sanjay Dutt and Shahrukh Khan—each draped in bubble wrap and propped against a nearby fence—were ready to ship the following morning, according to Mud.

"That's incredible," I said, running my hand over Amitabh's neat little goatee. "How does Hari make these effigies?"

"Trade secret," said Mud, smiling.

I shook my head in amazement at Hari's talents and followed Mud back to the workshop's front entrance. I could hear the chatter of children and the creak of the spinning wheel before my eyes adjusted to the dim light inside. My eyes eventually adjusted, and I watched as young boys and girls trampled a lump of blackish clay to prepare it for the wheel; others provided the potter with the sand and grog necessary to give his current piece its required hue and texture. Another gang of kids in a separate corner of the room slathered slurry, a sloppy mixture of clay and water, onto a pushcart that would eventually be wheeled to the potter's side. A final group of kids stood in waiting, ready to deliver any finished pieces to the nearest kiln for firing. And one child, perhaps the unluckiest of all, stood by the potter's stool ready to sprinkle a handful of wood chips into the pit below when Hari's bowels forced a movement.

Three teenage apprentices hovered around Hari, studying his every move with great curiosity. Just above the revolving wheel, on a crooked wooden beam that helped support the building's low ceiling, sat the autographed photos of Hari's celebrity customers.

"Muddy, is that you?" warbled a voice from within the crowd. "Come, Muddy," the man said. "*Come!*"

I caught my first glimpse of the bearded and bespectacled Hari when his apprentices stepped aside. It was obvious, seeing him hunched over his spinning wheel, that nonstop exertion had taken its toll on his body; his physical degeneration was evident in the forward crook of his spine, the frailty of his arms, and the swelling in his ankles.

"Daddy," said Mud, massaging the knots in his father's shoulders, "you'll never guess who's come to visit!"

"Unless it is Lord Krishna himself, I'll remain steadfast at my wheel!" spouted the cantankerous Hari, who then craned his pencil-thin neck toward the clay piece on the turntable.

"It's Benji-ji!" said Mud.

Hari turned his body slightly and greeted me. "*Arre!*" he said. "How wonderful to have you with us again, Mr. Benji! I'd rise to give you a proper welcoming, but I'm afraid my leg bones have fused in this twisted position."

"No problem, uncle," I said. "Your acknowledgement is welcoming enough."

Several of the children fetched stools for Mud and me at Hari's insistence, placing them opposite Hari and his wheel.

"Please don't think me rude," he said, continuing to work on his piece. "You understand my predicament, don't you? It is my sworn duty to protest my crackpot son's foolish, foolish choices. He knows that the only way he can stop me from spinning is to return home and pursue an honorable career. Is that too much for a hardworking father to ask? And besides," he added, rocking gently from side to side to find a more comfortable position on his stool, "what does a potter's son know about the performing arts anyway? *Bandar kya jaane adrak ka swad?*"

Mud, leaning toward me, translated Hari's words. "It is meaning, 'What does a monkey know of ginger?'"

"My relatives," said Hari, his bald head wobbling slowly from side to side, "came to Mumbai from Gujarat, from the Saurashtra peninsula. Potters all, they were proud and talented people. These days, many boys are leaving Kumbharwada and Dharavi to become carpenters and diamond cutters and members of the merchant marine. These professions should not be compared with those of a doctor, lawyer, or engineer," he sniffed, "but they would have sufficed. Instead, our most high and mighty Ram ran off to pursue a lucrative career in juggling, of all things, with a two-bit performing arts caravan. It is as though he is embarrassed by his own heritage." Hari harrumphed. "Yes, well, now we are embarrassed by him. I swear to Lord Shiva himself, if I ever see that boy again, I'll give him one tight slap for all the suffering he has caused me!"

Mud rose from his stool and disappeared into the shadows of the pottery den. He returned a few moments later, handing me a tattered workbook. "Guest register," he said.

I'd completely forgotten about the guest register Mud had had me sign during my first visit to Dharavi. I was pleased that the Panchals had kept the book for so long. I flipped through the pages and found my name, country of origin, and e-mail address. I'd also penned answers to questions about my greatest likes and dislikes, my thoughts on hope and sadness, and my political viewpoints. Under the question, "What is love?" I'd written, *Baby, don't hurt me...don't hurt me...no more.*

A young boy dropped a hunk of fresh clay onto Hari's spinning wheel, and I realized it was probably time to say good-bye, at least for now, and leave the master to his work. Conversation trickled off, and the workshop returned to its usual bustle and clamor.

Mud and I left the pottery den and set off through the slum to visit more old friends. We made plenty of stops along the way, drank a lot of chai, and shared many laughs. We even visited Padma Sanghavi, the young woman Mud had been wooing for quite some time.

Padma, with her shy demeanor and fair complexion, was generally regarded as the most beautiful and most eligible woman in the Kumbharwada potters' settlement, a graceful lotus flower who cut an elegant figure in her bright salwar kameez. Her brother had recently married, which meant she could now court a partner, much to Mud's great delight. I watched the two interact. It was clear that they were enamored with each other, and it was only a matter of time until Mud popped the question.

So busy were Mud and I that first day that I had little opportunity to ask him about Adriana. I lay in bed that night, inside the concrete-and-tin house belonging to the Panchals, and felt safe and cared for. I felt hidden away from the craziness of the outside world. My mind wasn't completely at ease, though, far from it. *Why didn't Adriana want to forgive and forget? Why didn't she want resolution of the pain and suffering I was sure she felt?* Of course, my mind assumed the worst in those dark, torturous hours.

Morning eventually came and, with it, the hope of a new day. After a hearty breakfast dished up by Aiesha—who always kept me as full as the water in her large *matka* jar—Mud and I headed for the Mahim Railway Station. He had some errands to run for Hari, and I'd agreed the previous day to accompany him. Mud halfheartedly kicked at a plastic bag floating lazily through the thick Mumbai air as we waited for the commuter train to arrive. A light breeze wafting over the nearby train tracks quickly brought the bag to life, its handles folding inward before rapidly shooting outward in an action that resembled a frog's kick in a boggy marsh.

"Free plastic," said Mud, swiping at the bag with his right hand and catching it. "Gucci!" he added, bobbling his head from side to side. "Bonus!"

"Nice!" I said, congratulating Mud on his lucky find.

Plastic was revered in the slum. It formed the roofs, walls, and floors of many houses, and almost everybody in the slum owned at least one special plastic bag used for toting goods. The more a bag stood out—in other words, the larger and more vibrant it was—the more chic the owner appeared to friends. I'd seen teenage girls on numerous occasions flaunting plastic bags bearing the brand names and logos of companies like Chanel, Tommy Hilfiger, and Calvin Klein. The bags never contained products from any of those illustrious companies but were used instead to demonstrate awareness of and appreciation for higher-end goods.

We continued to wait for the commuter train to arrive, and I finally summoned the courage to ask Mud about Adriana. "Hey, Mud," I said, "do you remember when I first came to Dharavi? Do you remember the girl I came to see?"

"Adriana-didi?"

"Yeah, Adriana-didi. Has she been around lately?"

"I got a sighting of her not long ago," said Mud. "But it has been a few days since she was last around."

No. No, it can't *be true.*

The fact that Adriana had seemingly disappeared again so close to my arrival in Dharavi told me everything I needed to know. I felt my spirit crumbling like a clay pot under the foot of a mighty elephant, and I recoiled at the feelings of rejection I'd felt so many times before. A deep and penetrating sadness enfolded me in that moment of realization, and I knew that all my sacrifices had been for naught. I'd gambled and lost.

Mud clicked his tongue in sympathy after I'd explained the situation and said, "So much *pataoing* you did for her, Benji-ji, and nothing to show for it in the end. So sad."

It *was* a sad situation and one that left me feeling without a physical sense of home too. I supposed I could always go back to Kathmandu and look for work, I could stay in India and wallow in self-pity, or I could go home, get a job, and move on with my life. Unfortunately, none of those options seemed particularly compelling, at least not while my pain was so raw and my anger so intense.

Mud, perking up from his position on the bench, cupped a hand around his ear and strained to hear something off in the distance. He listened attentively for a few seconds before grabbing my arm and leading me back into the slum.

"Where are we going?" I said. "I thought we had errands to run for Hari!"

"Errands later," said Mud. "Party first."

Only after we'd crossed the railway tracks and entered the slum near a busy shawarma stand did I hear the distinct, funneled reverberation of a bullhorn. My first thought was that a political rally had sprung up somewhere within the neighborhood, but Mud assured me that municipal elections were still months away. I was still reeling from the news about Adriana, and I had little interest in chasing after a party, but I followed Mud over the narrow footpaths back to the potters' settlement nonetheless.

It wasn't long before we came upon a boisterous twelve-piece marching band. Within the band, cymbals clanged, trombones throbbed, and flutists fluted. A young man held aloft by the hands of a growing assemblage of slum residents crowd surfed toward us as the band's fife and drum reached a frenzied pitch.

"My god, yaar," said Mud. "It's Ram! He's come home!"

Most of the settlement's residents had, in a matter of moments, quit what they were doing and filed into the alleys. Women, normally shy and demure, unabashedly shook their hips, jangled their bangles, and fanned the air with complex and mesmerizing hand movements. Several of the more daring men attempted old-school Western dance moves, including the sprinkler, the funky alien, and the running man. One of the men even performed the worm, to which the crowd responded favorably. The unrehearsed choreography, the irrepressible smiles, and the crowd's unparalleled animation would have made a Bollywood director swoon.

Even in my state of grief, I was happy that Ram had returned. I was happy for Hari and Aiesha that their prodigal son had come home from afar and seemed ready to make amends for his rebellious ways. Hari talked a tough game, but I knew he'd be elated.

The street party slowly wound its way throughout Kumbharwada, pausing occasionally near a few of the open-air kilns, where several unlucky pots, recently dried and fired, were hoisted into the air and smashed on the ground in celebratory fashion. Rice rained down upon the crowd from second-story windows. Wooden spoons, now being circulated throughout the crowd, were used to feverishly bang a broad assortment of pots and pans.

The entire procession eventually reached the doorstep of Hari Panchal's pottery den and came to a grinding halt. The music stopped, and Ram Panchal, a short man with dark-rimmed glasses and a crooked nose, was gently lowered to the ground. Hari, with Aiesha by his side, was carried to the doorstep by his teenage apprentices on an apparatus resembling a Sudan chair. The crowd that had formed held a collective breath as father and son locked eyes for the first time in weeks. Hari silently embraced his son, tears of joy streaming down his cheeks. He then grasped Ram's shoulders and bobbled his head from side to side as he struggled to find the appropriate words.

"My boy, why have you returned?" he said, tears streaming down his face.

"I should have listened to you, *pita-ji*," said Ram. "My future is here, in Mumbai, in school."

"But what of your troupe?" said Hari, a look of grave concern upon his face. "Was that not the life you were seeking?"

"Circus is dying, Daddy," said Ram. "Performers are like endangered species, practically."

Hari took a moment of silence to honor Ram's decision. He then said, "Tonight we celebrate the return of my son! No expense will be spared!"

That evening, after we feasted and welcomed Ram back into the fold, I took an autorickshaw to Chowpatty Beach and walked, alone, along the entire length of the crescent-shaped seawall. I had no idea what I was going to do with my life now that my worst fears had come true, now that Adriana had shut me out of her life for the final time, as I had accepted it. Nearing the end of my walk, I accidentally bumped into a short, white-haired man who was tying his shoe. "Oh, I'm sorry, sir," I said, apologizing profusely for my clumsiness.

The man stood up, and I instantly recognized his face: I'd spoken with him during my first trip to Mumbai in almost the very same spot, I was sure of it. Then, he had invited me to join him at his club, the Bombay Presidency Radio Club, located close to the Taj Mahal Hotel and the Gateway of India. But when I mentioned this to the man now, he seemed confused and didn't remember our first meeting.

I was shocked that, in a city of roughly twenty million people, I would bump into a person I'd met years earlier in almost exactly the same location. Then again, coincidences like that were almost commonplace on the subcontinent. I recalled my recent journey across India in the VW Bus with the man I believed to be Bharath Bhupani and the timing of my visit to Dharavi coinciding with Ram Panchal's return. The chance encounters offered me a glimmer of hope that I might somehow stumble across Adriana in Mumbai.

I stayed in Kumbharwada several more days. Hari took Aiesha away for a short holiday as a way of repaying her for the trouble he'd caused during Ram's absence. I decided to wait until their return before heading to Kathmandu, so that I could say good-bye and thank them for their hospitality.

"Daddy's in such a good mood," said Mud the day after his parents returned from their trip. "He's even regained the full use of both legs!"

It was true. After the incredible number of hours he logged at the spinning wheel, Hari looked to be on the mend. He had even moved his spinning wheel outside so that he might get more sunlight and air. Hari and Aiesha had many stories to share about their short vacation, but Mud and Padma had a story all their own to tell: they were engaged to be married! What only one week before had seemed like the pinnacle of Hari's suffering had given way to immense happiness and joy for the head of the Panchal clan. His oldest son had returned home from afar, and his second in line had claimed the most prized woman in Kumbharwada as his bride-to-be. Life had taken an upswing for the Panchals, and although I was still feeling extremely hurt by Adriana's snub, I was warmed by their upbeat spirits and their genuine excitement for the days to come.

Hari, with his usual mix of persuasiveness and caring, convinced me that I too should spend a couple of days in Matheran, where he and his wife had so successfully vacationed, to let the hill station's cooler air clear my mind before returning to Kathmandu. It would be a two-hour train ride from Mumbai, and if I wanted to park the Bus in his cousin's garage a few miles away, I was more than welcome to do so. No motorized vehicles were allowed in Matheran, which was part of its appeal.

I left a postcard with the Panchals before leaving for Matheran. The postcard was to be given to Adriana if she ever returned to Dharavi. It was the postcard I'd written in Kathmandu before my first day in the Pepsicola Townplanning community, the postcard that I had never been able to send. I hoped it would eventually find its way into her hands, that she would finally understand how sorry I was for the things I said. But in the back of my mind, I knew there was a good chance she would never get it, and that thought broke my heart yet again.

At the train station, surrounded by the entire Panchal family, I wished them all a heartfelt good-bye. It was considered bad luck in India, as it was in Nepal, to issue a decisive statement of finality, as though doing so would somehow invoke everybody's worst fear—death—so I compromised with a farewell that hinted at an eventual return. "Until we meet again," I said. "Until we meet again," they echoed.

"May Bhagwan bless you and keep you all the days of your life!" Hari added.

The train ride to Matheran, while hot and crowded, went by quickly and without incident. I switched to a narrow-gauge train at the Neral Junction station, situated near the mountain's base. It took a long time for the toy train to climb the steep grades, but when the train finally came to a rest, I stepped out into an India the likes of which I'd never previously known.

The air in Matheran was still and silent, apart from the chatter of disembarking passengers and the sounds of birds and other animals frolicking in the jungle canopy. I breathed in the sweet jungle air. I was shocked by the lack of pollution and the complete absence of artificial noise. There were no taxis or autorickshaws or scooters, and people moved about on foot only. Given the amount of time I'd spent in Indian cities, I hadn't believed Hari when he said such a place existed in India. But there it was, right before my eyes.

I strolled along on a red dirt path before ascending into the heart of Matheran, which consisted of numerous sweet shops and restaurants. I set off to find a guest house after a quick bite, following the signs for Juhu's

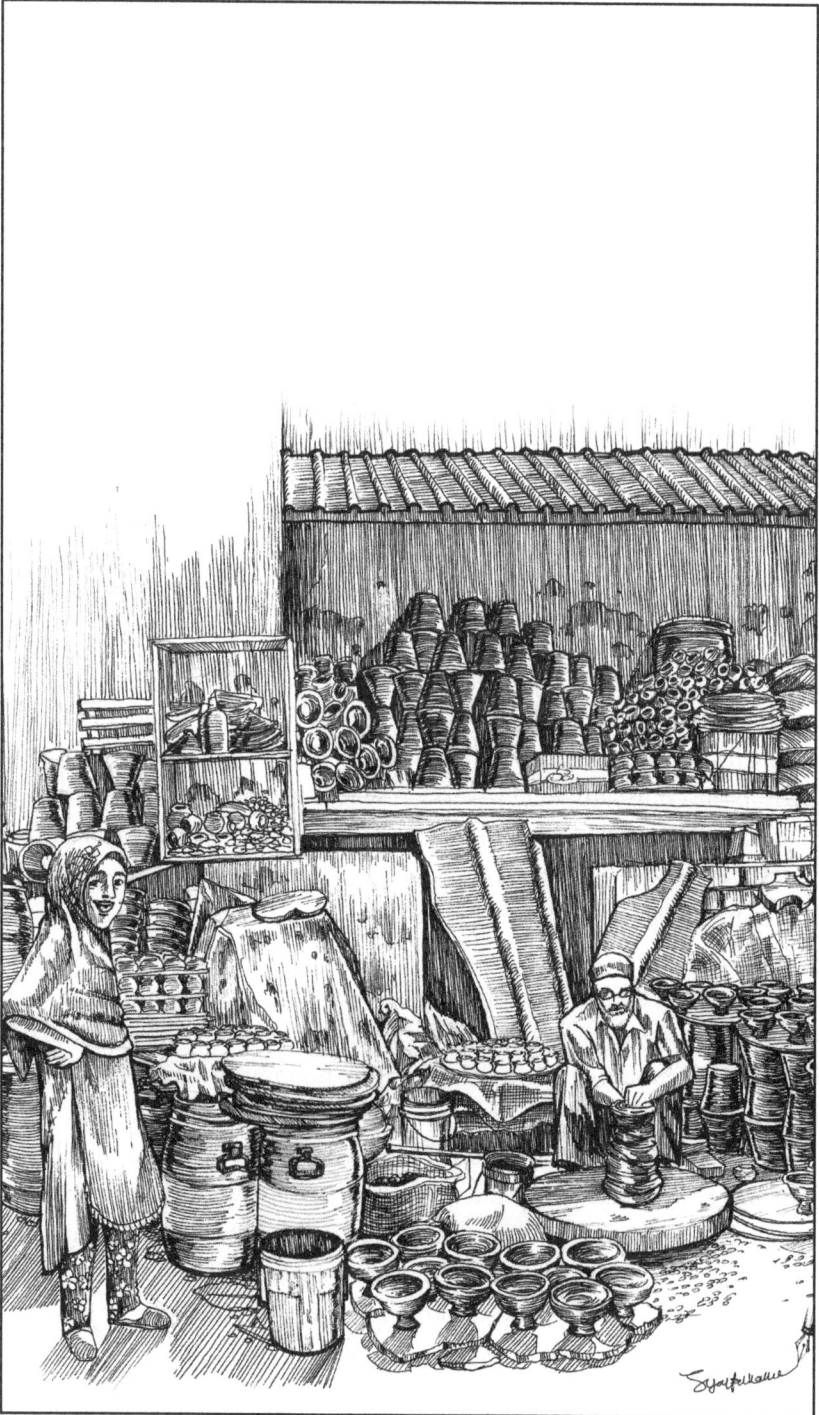

Jungle Retreat, a guest house my guidebook had given rave reviews. I eventually came upon a large bungalow set in a grove of bamboo. I checked out several of the rooms after conversing with the raisin-faced woman at the reception desk, and I decided to stay. The clean and brightly tiled rooms were highly appealing, as were the privacy and tranquility of the place. It seemed like the perfect venue to rest and recuperate.

I sponge-bathed my sweaty body in my private bathroom and then lay on the bed to rest. A thunderous noise rained down upon the guest house's tin roof, though, not long after I drifted off to sleep. Confused, I dragged myself to the door of my room. I peered into the guest house's central courtyard and saw a well-muscled, pop-eyed, half-naked Indian man shaking his fist and cursing at a group of surly monkeys who were beating the guest house's tin roof with their hands. The monkeys, in response to the man's cursing, immediately bared their fangs and ceremoniously presented their skinny bums while jabbering away from the safety of their lofty perch.

"Ma-ma-monkeys!" said the crazed man, his bulging eyes squirrelly with anger as he continued to wag his fist at the simian invaders. "Wuh-wuh-why do they torment me-me-me so?" The man, stalking back and forth in the courtyard, held a wooden switch in one hand and a growler of moonshine in the other—the switch as a weapon to be used against the monkeys if he got within striking distance, the moonshine, presumably, as a source of consolation if he didn't.

It took the man a few seconds to calm down, and it was only after the monkeys flung themselves into nearby trees that his indignation melted and he acknowledged my presence. "My-my-my name is Juhu Dhumal," he said, little comets of saliva shooting from his mouth as he spoke. "Wuh-wuh-would you like some moo-moo-moonshine?"

Juhu, barrel chested and Buddha bellied, invited me into his palatial dwelling, a newly built house that stood next to the guest house's main bungalow. He poured me a glass of his home brew and explained that he and his older brother, Bhupendra, were co-owners of Juhu's Jungle Retreat, though the women of the family—his mother and sister, especially—did most of the work. Juhu took great pleasure in showing off his marble floors and his big-screen TV, and he explained to me that his greatest task in life was to sire as many children as possible, the latest of whom was with a woman from Romania who had visited the guest house just over one year earlier.

"The foreign wuh-wuh-women, they come here, and wuh-wuh-when they see what Juhu has to offer, they nev-nev-never want to leave!" According to the thirty-five-year-old, in the not-so-distant past, he had worked as a gunrunner, dope dealer, and organizer of petty and large crimes alike for a mafia don in the Bombay underworld. To me, he looked like a run-of-the-mill thug burned out from the adrenaline rush that, I suspected, accompanied so many of his nefarious deeds.

Juhu explained that Matheran had always been a place of safety for him, a place where he could lay low until stormy seas in Mumbai settled. Bhupendra had also been heavily involved with the mafia but had recently given up the gig after falling ill with an undisclosed disease. Juhu's older brother was now confined to the king-size bed in his own extravagant house. The brothers, retiring to a life of relaxation in Matheran, had bought the guest house with their blood money several years before and now lived off the revenue from tourists like myself. Business at the guest house had been good, Juhu explained, despite the monkey insurgency.

Insisting I drink more moonshine and share a cigar with him, Juhu tried his best to convert me to his easygoing, lethargic lifestyle, but I politely declined and excused myself, saying I was still tired from the trip from Mumbai and needed rest. Juhu stood in the doorway of his house and watched me as I strolled back through the courtyard. He then stammered, almost apologetically, "Guh-guh-god willing, that pa-pa-pack of wild ma-ma-monkeys will not return tonight."

I woke the following morning to the songs of exotic birds in the jungle canopy. I stepped from my room into the softly lit guest house courtyard and saw a fit-looking woman in her late twenties rolling up her yoga mat near an artificial waterfall.

"Good morning," I said, yawning and stretching my arms toward the sky.

"Hello-ji, how are you?" she said, the stud of her nose piercing glinting in the sunlight. "What's your name?"

"I'm Benjamin," I said, pressing my hands together and bowing slightly at the waist. "Namaste."

"My name's Mina. Mina Kaimal. It's a real pleasure meeting you, Benjamin-ji. You are staying here at Juhu's Jungle Retreat too?"

"Yeah, I just came up from Mumbai yesterday," I said.

"Arre! That's fantastic, yaar! Totally great place," she said, smiling. "You know what? This place really, really grows on you, even with the monkeys and all. This is my fifth time staying here, you know."

"Hey, Mina," I said, "would you be interested in showing me around Matheran? I've never been here before, and I'd love to have a guide." I was excited by the possibility of making a new friend, and the affable—and attractive—Mina seemed like the perfect person to introduce me to Matheran.

"Totally!" she said, sliding her rolled-up yoga mat into a sack. "It would be my pleasure. Just let me get changed up, OK?"

Before she left, Juhu emerged from his lair to gruffly address a young boy watering the courtyard's plants, ordering him to fetch a bottle of beer from the refrigerator in the guest house kitchen. The boy extended one of his middle fingers and trained the slender digit upon Juhu, shaking it at the guest house owner before heading off to the kitchen. Juhu, having already turned his back on the boy, was oblivious to the disrespectful gesture, which was probably a good thing, given his hair-trigger temper and the switch he kept just inside his door.

Juhu spotted Mina and me and lumbered down the front steps of his house to join us. Before he reached us, though, a barrage of stones and dung began sailing through the air, one volley beaning Juhu squarely on the side of the head.

His brain rattled, the stocky Indian stood dazed in his tracks as the perpetrators of the crime, the surly monkeys, squawked jubilantly at their launch's successful outcome. Juhu began speaking nonsensically before eventually retreating to the safety of his house to sleep off his dung-induced stupor.

Mina hurried off to her room to change once the commotion in the courtyard had died down. She soon returned to the courtyard wearing a pair of hip-hugging jeans, a black T-shirt, and a baseball cap. She was a pretty girl, taller and more carefree than most Indian women, and she seemed supremely confident, though not full of herself. We headed for the main bazaar.

"Many of the girls who stay at the guest house find Juhu to be quite the stud muffin," Mina said. "He's very high-end husband material," she added, giggling, the sarcasm dripping from every word like oil from a samosa.

I learned on our march to the bazaar that Mina, born in Alappuzha, in Kerala, was currently working as a choreographer in the Mumbai film industry in one of the city's major studios. Her gait, dress, and mannerisms all suggested she identified more closely with girls from the city than those from the village, but a childhood spent in the backwaters of Kerala had left her with an appreciation of modesty, I thought, as I watched her smile at the sari-clad women passing us along the trail.

"They are so beautiful, *na?*" she cooed. "I wish I could wear a sari more often, but the film crowd is full of very hip, very modern people who dress like this all the time," she said, pointing at her clothes.

"But what do the more traditional women think of your Western wear?" I said.

"Don't even get me started, yaar," Mina lamented. "Juhu's mum, for example, keeps giving me the hairy eyeball."

"Just because of your clothes?"

"That, and because I'm twenty-eight and still not married."

"I'm sure she could probably hook you up with Juhu," I said.

"*Uff!* Don't you even dare mention it, yaar!" Mina retorted, elbowing me in the ribs. "I swear, he keeps telling me he's a born-again virgin, many times over. He thinks it's totally funny."

Our first stop of the morning was at one of the sweet shops, where we bought several varieties of *chikki*, a peanut brittle–like snack adored by the locals and many of the Indian tourists. We hadn't walked but a few yards down the trail before Mina was accosted by a monkey, who swiped the package from her hand.

"Achchha!" she said, briefly chasing after the creature. "Come back here, you *chod!*"

The monkey, in less than a moment, had bounded up a nearby tree, shredded the packaging, and begun feasting on the sweet treat. The creature's eyes then grew as large as saucers as the postprandial sugar buzz took hold. Reclining in the crook of a branch with one leg dangling in midair, the monkey let out a loud belch and rubbed its bloated gut.

We caught glimpses of beautiful colonial-era homes along the trail, through the patchy fog of early morning. We also saw a large group of children learning how to rock climb using secondhand harnesses and shoddy, fraying ropes. Vacationing parents, the nouveau riche of India's recent technology boom, periodically encouraged their boys to climb to ever-greater heights while they snapped pictures with newly purchased digital cameras.

It was interesting that while the boys took turns scrambling over the rocks, the girls remained huddled near their parents, as though the girls were somehow unfit for such risky business. I could hear Beth Lewis in the back of my mind lamenting the sexism that still exists in many countries around the world, especially when it comes to athletics.

We rounded a bend in the track. Mina and I looked on in amazement as four unshod men with thin yet powerful hindquarters schlepped a bullock cart carrying a heavy piece of machinery up the steep grade. The men, who were stripped down to their *chuddies*, panted and grunted loudly, their tongues lolling and eyes bulging from their effort.

The men continued huffing their load up to the village as shouts of "*Chalo! Chalo! Chalo!*" rang out from spectators in the wooded grove nearby. Mina and I, exchanging incredulous looks, agreed that the passing blur of sinewy brown brawn was unlike anything we had ever seen. I was impressed by the men's feat of strength and endurance, and I felt lazy just watching them.

We headed for one of the lookout points to get a panoramic view of the surrounding countryside. We soon came upon a young couple from the city and their newborn child, all being held hostage by a particularly ill-mannered and aggressive monkey. The monkey, whose facial features resembled those of a wizened man, had planted its bottom in the middle of the trail and was refusing to budge.

The creature hissed repeatedly. The couple, flustered and fearful, threw small sticks at the monkey, but the creature held its ground. The poor husband looked desperate, helpless, and near the end of his rope. His wife blubbered away behind his back, holding their child close to her bosom. There was no telling how long the standoff had been going on, perhaps for hours.

Mina, with nerves of steel, moved in immediately to shoo the monkey away. It was only after she'd made several threatening roundhouse kicks in the creature's direction, though, that it finally skulked off the trail and climbed into a nearby tree. The monkey ogled the newborn from its perch high up in the tree while the couple thanked Mina. "*Laaton ke bhoot baaton se nahi mante,*" said Mina to the couple; she quickly explained that her words meant that those who were accustomed to kicks would never respond to words.

Mina calmly turned toward the tree-bound monkey and made a slicing gesture at the base of her neck to indicate that should it continue to prey upon tourists in such a manner, the creature would one day be rewarded with a dirt bath. The monkey quickly whipped around and bolted deeper into the jungle.

"I swear, yaar, these monkeys are *really* eating my head."

"I'm pretty sure that that monkey would have eaten that *child's* head if we hadn't come along. Hey, where did you learn that move?" I said, referring to Mina's impressive roundhouse kick.

"I'm a choreographer, silly," she said, smiling. "I do dances *and* fight scenes."

Mina and I finally reached the lookout. We sat down on a rock and took in the incredible view. Sheer rock walls dropped hundreds of yards to the Maharashtrian plains. The plains, brown and scorched and baked like clay in one of Kumbharwada's communal kilns, appeared expansive from our vantage point. It seemed as though the entire subcontinent were on fire, as smoke billowed into the air from numerous sources dotting the horizon. I sat there looking out over India and couldn't help but think that Adriana was out there somewhere. I would have felt incredibly lonely if it hadn't been for Mina sitting by my side. I looked over at her and smiled my thanks.

Mina returned my smile and then leaned in and kissed me. The kiss, while completely unexpected, filled me with excitement and left me wanting more. Part of me wanted that kiss to have come from Adriana, but another part of me wanted to forget about her entirely and just enjoy the moment.

I pulled back slightly after a few seconds of smooching, caressed Mina's face, and dove back in for more. It had been a long time since I'd kissed a woman—so long, in fact, that I'd almost forgotten how good it felt. We continued our lusty embrace, oblivious to the world around us. Neither of us heard the approach of a family, several generations strong, who, once they saw us, announced their presence at the lookout with a loud round of coughs and throat clearing.

Mina and I laughed at the embarrassment we'd caused and bounded back up the trail, into the relative privacy of the jungle, where we continued to explore each other's faces and necks with our lips.

We returned to the village after a long day of exploring and making out, where we dined at a restaurant run by a friendly Parsi man. The restaurateur, who sat in on part of our meal, spoke passionately about the prophet Zoroaster's teachings. When he wasn't with us, Mina and I kept our conversation light, maybe feeling a little awkward after our intense day, mostly joking about our interesting guest house proprietor. When we finished our meal, we thanked our kind host and returned to Juhu's Jungle Retreat, where we found the subject of our teasing sitting on his front steps and drinking a bottle of beer. It was clear he'd just finished devouring a thali.

"So, Juhu," I said as we approached, "how'd you develop your physique?"

He took a big swig of his beer, set the bottle down on his front step, and sparked up a fresh *beedi*.

"In my-my-my youth, I used to be a wrestler. I buh-buh-built my-my-my upper body by performing rep-rep-repetitive *dand*, the Hindu push-up. Here, I shh-shh-show you," he said.

Carefully placing the smoking beedi on one of the steps, he jumped to his feet. He then got down on all fours and formed an upside-down *V* with his body. He slowly lowered his body in a sensual arc, all the while casting a suggestive leer in the direction of Mina. The movement more closely resembled a sexual act than a traditional push-up, but I couldn't deny the chest-building potential of the smooth move. Mina, of course, looked disgusted by Juhu's rendition of the Hindu push-up, and told him to knock it off, saying she had come to Matheran for the peace and tranquility of the place, after all, not for the juvenile antics of a former mobster.

Juhu, not easily offended, offered to show us a few magic tricks he'd been working on in his abundant spare time. In perhaps his finest trick of the evening, Juhu, who possessed a flare for the dramatic, dusted a handful of ashes over Mina's forearm and then gently blew them away. I suspected that Mina was somehow complicit, given that I'd told her my entire life story earlier that day, but what remained on her forearm was, unbelievably, the word *Adriana*. Juhu, intuitive and caring in his own, weird way, looked up at me and smiled. "She is the Shak-Shak-Shakti to your Shiva," he said, laughing softly.

How, I wondered, could I let go of a person who had vanished as easily as the ashes on Mina's forearm? There was nothing to let go of, I reasoned, except a hardwired memory of her, a memory that defined almost everything I knew about love and suffering.

Juhu led Mina and me to his brother's house after he'd run out of magic tricks. We found Bhupendra lying supine on his king-size bed, as Juhu had said he would be, watching a Bollywood movie on a big-screen TV. Bhupendra, absorbed in the film, took only a passing interest in us, occasionally casting us wan looks while waving the remote control like a wand, possibly in a halfhearted effort to make us disappear so that he could return, undisturbed, to the multihour *masala* movie unfolding on the screen. Bhupendra looked extremely ill, and I told this to Juhu once we'd returned to the courtyard.

"He needs to go to the hospital, Juhu, to get properly diagnosed and treated," I said. "Didn't you see how yellow the whites of his eyes were? That's not a good sign, brother."

Juhu nodded his head slowly as he described the sad predicament facing Bhupendra. He explained that his brother couldn't go to a hospital in the city for fear of being arrested for his crimes as a Bombay mobster. With no medical services available in Matheran, except for a natural-healing guru who insisted he could diagnose and treat patients solely on the appearance of their tongues, Bhupendra would be left to languish in his king-size bed as he slid further and further into a state of degeneration.

Juhu, refusing to dwell on his brother's misfortune, suggested we all take a nighttime stroll to the village's edge, to a place where we could breathe in the succulent jungle air and do a little stargazing. With Juhu leading the way, we soon came to a large clearing where the thick jungle canopy gave way to a clear night sky. We lay on our backs, gazing up at shooting stars, familiar constellations, and satellites orbiting the earth while, closer to home, giant fruit bats dive-bombed our temporary encampment. The night sky captured our imaginations, and we lay there for at least an hour without anybody saying a word.

Juhu eventually spoke, and when he did, Mina and I heard a quieter, less boastful side of the man emerge. It seemed that, above all else, he simply wanted to see his youngest child. The mother, after giving birth to their child in India, had taken the infant back to Romania, and would not respond to any of Juhu's recent letters. Someday, he vowed, he would leave his jungle hideout and travel to Bucharest, where he would be a father to his son. I wasn't sure if that would ever happen, given Juhu's lengthy list of felonies and the numerous warrants out for his arrest, but his convictions seemed strong and his intentions pure. Anything was possible, I supposed.

I explained to Mina the following morning, when it was time for her to depart, that I would be leaving for Kathmandu almost immediately.

"Oh my god, yaar," she said. "It's wintertime in Kathmandu. You'll *freeze!* You might as well be in Goa."

"Goa, huh?" I said, mulling over her suggestion.

"I have a friend down there," she said. "Let me give you his name. His guest house is called Hotel Furtado."

And just like that, my plans were set. I missed my friends back in Kathmandu and my family back in Berkeley, but Christmas in Goa sounded like a mighty fine idea.

I escorted Mina to the platform at Neral Junction and waited with her until her Mumbai-bound train arrived. We shared a warm hug and a hearty laugh at the previous day's adventures when the time finally came to say good-bye. Then Mina was gone, and my life was suddenly quiet. I spent the next several weeks in Matheran walking the trails and staring down monkeys. Adriana's abandonment was still smarting, but it felt good to be out in the world; it felt good to be out of my head and away from my worries, if only temporarily.

Goa on the Go

STELLA'!'S THUMPING RETURNED ABOUT HALFWAY TO GOA. I DIDN'T KNOW it at the time, but that thumping was the sound, the death knell, that augured the VW's eventual demise. Stella'! hung on all the way to Palolem, where she died almost immediately upon entering the beach town's main bazaar. I hopped out of the Bus, gathered up my gear, and tossed the keys to a group of four young men who had been drawn toward her by the smoke pouring from her engine.

"She's all yours, boys!"

In a matter of seconds, the young men threw the Bus into neutral, turned it around, and started pushing it away from the main bazaar, presumably to some local garage where the vehicle would be stripped and eviscerated, its parts sold to local mechanics for a tidy profit.

Letting Stella'! go was bittersweet for me. On the one hand, the Bus was a gift from Dr. Singh and had served me well during my time in Kathmandu. The doctor had yielded full ownership of the Bus to me—which meant that I could do with it whatever I chose—but I felt an obligation to care for it with fastidiousness because it was his link with the past and a symbol of the life he'd shared with Margaret. I wanted to respect his generosity and honor his kindness, but my budget was not so robust that it could support a round, or possibly *rounds*, of expensive repairs. And it felt liberating to give up my bulkiest possession.

It looked as if I would be in Goa for some time. *Not a bad place to be stranded.* I rolled up the cuffs of my jeans, kicked off my Doc Martens and my socks, and struck off over the hot sand to find Hotel Furtado.

I headed north along the beach, past a series of low-key guest houses, large wooden boats resting on logs, and countless sari-clad hawkers peddling their wares. Palolem was beautiful, perhaps the most idyllic beach I'd ever seen. Spanning the beach, which itself stretched far to the north and south, countless palm trees, their corrugated trunks and broad green leaves leaning ever-so-slightly out over the sand, shaded a long string of reclining beach bums. The beach, while crowded, looked clean, and the foamy sea inviting. The smell of seafood cooking in many of the local restaurants made my mouth water and my stomach growl. I was in paradise.

I found Hotel Furtado near the beach's northern end, near a rocky peninsula that jutted into the Arabian Sea. The main building, which consisted of a bungalow and an open-air restaurant, was flanked by a handful of cabins all connected with a network of sandy pathways.

I bounded up the front steps, through the breezy restaurant, and toward the reception counter situated at the joint's rear. I was hoping to find a man named Nitesh—who supposedly owned the hotel—because he was Mina's contact and would, she insisted, cut me a deal on the basis of their friendship. Unfortunately, Nitesh was out harvesting coconuts and wouldn't be back until much later, explained the man at the reception counter, but I was welcome to check out a few of the rooms and relax with a banana lassi that he would prepare in the meantime.

It was almost Christmas, and the beach was crawling with Indian tourists from Mumbai, Mangalore, and Bangalore and vacationers from Europe. Fortunately for me, Hotel Furtado still had a few vacancies. I left the restaurant with a set of keys in hand and headed away from the beach and toward the cabins, or *cocohuts*, as the hotel staff called them. The cocohuts, though basic in design and relatively small, were perfect. I liked their rustic charm and the fact that each came with its own private bathroom. I retraced my steps to the reception counter, returned the keys, and said, "I'll take cocohut number seven!"

I slept straight through the evening and the night, waking late the following morning to the sounds of my growling stomach. I changed into shorts, a light T-shirt, and flip-flops, grabbed my beach towel, and headed for Hotel Furtado's open-air restaurant. After a breakfast of muesli and yogurt, I slathered on some SPF-40 and headed for the beach to lounge on my blanket under the warm, late-morning sun. I soon dozed off, only to be woken moments later by a great commotion. I rubbed my eyes in disbelief as an elephant, which had somehow found its way onto the beach, proceeded to scatter the wiry Goan fishermen and scantily clad Europeans in its path.

The great beast slowly sauntered up the beach. A man—who cut the flamboyant figure of a showman—rode on its back. It took some time to register that the man behind the mischief was none other than Nepali Pete. His lanky frame soon became unmistakable against the bright Goan sky. The elephant trundled toward me, and I could see that Pete was wearing the same purple Speedos he'd been sporting the morning I first met him below the Bagmati Bridge. Unfortunately, he still wasn't wearing much else.

One of Pete's arms was wrapped around a vintage ghetto blaster he'd hoisted to his shoulder. "Sex Machine," by James Brown, pumped from the speakers. Pete's other hand gripped the handle of a giant parasol. The parasol was so large, in fact, that it was almost able to shade both man and beast entirely with its ample coverage.

I picked up a shard of a cracked coconut lying nearby and tossed it in Pete's direction. "Hey, Nepali Pete!" I said. "What are you doing here in Goa? Shouldn't you be hunting for treasure in the Kathmandu Valley?"

"Ah, 'ello, mate! Bloody nice to see ya again," Pete said, his broad smile revealing his near-total lack of teeth. "I 'aven't seen you for yonks, lad. This is me annual Christmas trip to Goa. Been comin' 'ere for years. Gives this old, salty sea dog and his arthritic knees—his shabby Robert E. Lees—a wee reprieve from the cold of Kathmandu. I'd stay 'ere year 'round, but I can't afford the bloody expense of the place!"

"Where'd you get your elephant?" I asked, glad to see that Pete was as jovial as ever.

He horked up a big wad of phlegm and spat the mouthful onto the sand next to my beach blanket before continuing in his familiar, gravelly voice. "I just borrowed Tiny 'ere from a game preserve down the street. Cheaper than petrol, mate!" he winked.

Nepali Pete looked ten years younger on the beach. It was as though his longtime abuse of cannabis and other psychotropic substances had been checked by the salubrious effects of the coastal climate. It seemed obvious that Pete used his annual Christmas trip to Goa as a springboard to help get him through the rest of the Kathmandu winter, which, I imagined, could be tough when you were living in a shack by the side of a river. With so much good food around, it even looked as though he had put some meat on his porous old bones.

"Come take a ride on me boat, lad! I call her I Dream of Dolphins. Finest craft in these waters," Pete said. "You can bet yer lily-white arse on it."

"I'm just settling in here, Pete," I said. "How about a rain check? Maybe some other day, if you're around?"

"Sure thing, mate," he said, running his hand back and forth through his long beard. "But don't let them bloody boatmen on the beach trick you into paying for a ride. With Nepali Pete, friends always ride for free. Should be a good day for dolphin spotting, mate," said Pete, scanning the watery horizon with his gaze.

I lay down on my beach blanket again after Pete and his great steed had moved on. I was joined moments later by Nitesh Furtado, the amiable and carefree twenty-nine-year-old owner of Hotel Furtado. Nitty and I hit it off right away, thanks in part to our mutual association with Mina Kaimal.

"How's old Pete this morning?"

"Wait, you know Sri Lanky over there?" I said.

"Of course, mon. Pete's been coming here ever since I was a boy. He always stayed at Hotel Furtado, until this year," Nitty said, his large nostrils flaring and his dark-brown skin glistening in the midday sun.

"Why isn't Pete staying at Hotel Furtado this year?"

"Pity, mon," said Nitty, shaking his head. "For the longest time, we were the only hotel on the beach that refused to play music in our restaurant. Pete liked the peace and tranquility, but it was a bad business move, so we had to bring a sound system online. We attracted more guests with the sound system, but we drove old Pete away. Now he stays in a shack at the beach's far end."

"But Pete *loves* music," I said. "He even claims he wrote the lyrics of Cat Stevens's 'Katmandu.'"

"That's true, mon," said Nitty. "But here at Hotel Furtado, we play trance music. Very popular with the Europeans," he added, "but not very popular with old Pete."

Nepali Pete would stop by Hotel Furtado to hurl obscenities at the guest house staff, according to Nitty. His ravings apparently frightened a number of the female guests, and the local police had to place a restraining order on him, such that he wasn't allowed within twenty feet of the hotel. It was too bad the relationship between Pete and the staff at Hotel Furtado had eroded so much, but Nitty seemed unconcerned. If anything, he was amused by the old hippie's tantrums and viewed them as a cheap form of entertainment.

Nitty, always attuned to his guests' needs, insisted I join him in the hotel's pavilion for a round of banana lassis before my white skin began to burn. So thoughtful a host was Nitty that he had insisted on building the restaurant's chairs himself, making sure the angle of recline was precisely one hundred and twenty degrees to the horizontal, which, he assured me, was the optimal angle for blissed-out relaxation.

Once our drinks had been delivered, Nitty said, "Cheers, mon!" and clinked his glass against mine.

I headed to the local bazaar for a haircut and a shave after finishing my drink. I paused outside a Catholic church on my way to listen to its choir belt Christmas songs through the wide-open front doors. What really drew my attention, though, was a gang of animated young boys clustered near the church's front steps. The boys, their necks craned skyward, jabbered loudly among themselves while repeatedly and emphatically stabbing their index fingers at a statue of the virgin Mary sheltered in a grotto high above the church's entrance.

A rubber ball punted by one of the boys had lodged itself between the virgin's downcast chin and her matronly bosom, looking very much like a holy goiter. The boys, now splayed in attack formation around the virgin and growing bolder by the moment, began pelting cricket balls at the Madonna to dislodge the rubber ball, a spectacle that would have made even the most hardcore nonbeliever squeamish. The church's priest, red faced and with vestments flapping in the perfumed morning breeze, came charging out to investigate the commotion, causing the boys to lose their nerve and scatter across the beach like cockroaches under a flashlight beam.

I entered the shop of barber Naresh Almeida, a close friend of Nitty's, who greeted me warmly. "Namaste, friend," he said, smiling. Even in that first moment, I could see his eyes surveying my jawline to find the most efficient path along which to drag a fresh blade.

"*Ek* minute, please," he said, pointing to a customer with whom he was still working.

I sat on a wicker stool waiting my turn and watched closely as Naresh performed his work. I couldn't help but notice that a haircut in India, or at least a haircut in the barbershop of Naresh Almeida, was more than *just* a haircut. Not only did his customer receive the closest shave I've ever seen, he also received nothing less than a full scalp massage and a therapeutic beating of the skull. Naresh, much to my great surprise, even threw in several textbook cervical adjustments that would have made any chiropractor proud, I was sure.

I continued to watch Naresh, amazed by how different he seemed from his Goan counterpart, Nitty Furtado. While Nitty easily pulled off unbuttoned shirts, free-flowing shoulder-length hair, and formfitting boot-cut jeans, Naresh had found his fashion groove in starched-collared shirts, a crew cut, and pleated dress slacks. Nitty had told me that while both men were successful business owners, Naresh was a conservative entrepreneur while Nitty, who thrived on risk and excitement, was a gregarious entertainer. Rather than clashing, though, their styles were complementary, and even though their approaches to business and life differed vastly, they'd always been close friends and regarded each other with great esteem.

I let Naresh have at it when it was my turn for a trim. It appeared that his scissors never rested from the moment he began until the moment he finished. Even when his scissors weren't in contact with my hair, Naresh's thumb and trigger finger still continued to snip away, at the air. I looked in the mirror and smiled when the dust—or the hair, more appropriately—had settled. I'd had many haircuts in Nepal, but none of them were as fine as the one Naresh had just given me.

"Nice job!" I said with enthusiasm.

"You like, boss?" He sprayed some shaving cream on a brush.

"Best haircut ever," I said, brushing a few small hairs off my nose.

Naresh painted my jaw with shaving cream and began vanquishing my stubble. I could see in the mirror the intense concentration on his face as he slowly dragged the razor over my skin. It seemed clear to me, based on his skill and his attention to detail, that, while he gave excellent haircuts, it was his work around the jaw where ritual and obsession collided.

I thanked Naresh for his services, tipped him handsomely, and told him I'd be back in a few days for another shave.

I sat on the beach and watched the sun set back at Hotel Furtado later that evening. As the fiery disc sank toward the horizon, the puffy clouds above morphed from acoustic to electric, pumping out their own chromatic version of cumulus rock 'n' roll.

I kept a watchful eye on the golden contrails of several jets beating a hasty retreat across the Goan skyscape. I couldn't help but wonder about the stories of the people on board. Where were they going? What forces had caused them to get up and move? Would there be someone waiting for them when they arrived? Or would they, like me during my first trip to India, land in a foreign place not knowing a soul?

And then the jets and their wispy contrails were gone, leaving little trace they had ever been there. With the tide coming in, I retreated to the safety of the palm trees fringing the beach and watched the day fade into the blue-green hues of dusk.

Performing the day's final beach patrol was a small band of uniformed soldiers, whom I'd taken to calling bikini inspectors, due to their incessant ogling of foreign women. All carried lathis. A few of the men even carried semiautomatic weapons, a sight that was jolting and out of place in the peaceful surroundings.

Just then, a trio of Goan swimmers emerged from a nearby grove of palm trees. They tore across the still-warm sand, dove headlong into the salty waters of the Arabian Sea, and with powerful strokes, seemed to head for Africa at a brave two knots.

I packed up my stuff, headed back to the hotel's restaurant, and took a seat at one of the tables. After I scanned the dinner menu, I ordered several items that sounded particularly scrumptious, including the garlic naan and the catch of the day. I also preemptively ordered dessert, something called Hello to Queen, which the menu promised was a sinful indulgence of chocolate melted over graham wafer and sliced banana, topped with a dollop of vanilla ice cream.

Darkness had descended over Palolem by the time my food arrived. Each table in the restaurant was illuminated by a small wax candle, whose flickering flames appeared to groove in unison with the up-tempo trance music filling the evening air. After the evening's main course had been delivered and subsequently devoured, Nitty approached. "And for dessert," he said, "baked...*potato!*"

Seeing the confused look on my face, he laughed good-naturedly before slapping me on the shoulder and pulling a plate from behind his back. "Just kidding, mon. Baked *Alaska!*" he said with zeal. He set the plate on the table, pulled a flask of rum from his back pocket, and doused the sweet treat before flambéing it. The flames, leaping high in the air, nearly singed my eyebrows. "*Bombe* Alaska, technically," said the Goan. "Sorry, no Hello to Queen tonight. Restaurant's all out of chocolate until tomorrow. It's OK, though, mon?"

"No worries, Nitty. It looks great," I said, nodding my head. "It definitely beats a baked potato, I can tell you that."

I dug in enthusiastically and succeeded in getting more of the dessert on my face than in my mouth. I tried to wipe my mouth clean using the restaurant's waxy napkin, the kind that absorbs absolutely nothing, but only spread the treat around my face. I finished the last few morsels and thanked Nitty for his hospitality before hurrying off to cocohut number seven to wash my face and climb into bed.

I stepped onto the cocohut's front porch late the next morning, Christmas Eve day, and thought of my family. I wanted to share the holiday with them, but for the second year in a row, that wasn't going to happen. A telephone call that I would place later that afternoon would have to suffice.

I wandered down to the beach, scooped up an abandoned volleyball, and made my way toward the net fronting the hotel's restaurant. I began bumping the ball to myself in the hopes of drumming up some interest in a game. A game of three-on-three broke out before I knew it, much to the irritation of restaurant patrons who were forced to guard their breakfasts from the errant bumps and spikes that routinely sailed their way.

We formed a motley crew on the court, including me; a young IT consultant from Bangalore; an overweight Californian businessman of Indian origin and his scrawny, fourteen-year-old nephew; a pretty woman from Omaha, Nebraska; and a middle-aged Sikh man dressed in black from head to toe: black turban, black knee-length shirt, and black trousers.

It became apparent as the morning progressed that the Sikh gentleman was the best player on the court, serving up a vicious underhand serve that baffled opponents and impressed onlookers. The man, who ran a confectionery stand in Mumbai, joked that any Indian businessman worth his Salt Satyagraha should be adept at such "underhanded" matters. We all laughed heartily at our friend's good-natured and self-effacing humor.

The game finished shortly before noon. I grabbed my beach towel, found a shady piece of sand beneath a palm tree, and plunked down. I loved watching the beach life in Palolem because it was so fascinating. It was a place where different universes temporarily intersected. The humble lives of fruit sellers, fishermen, and sari-wearing hawkers were juxtaposed against the relative affluence of Indian visitors from the city, local hotel owners, and flesh-baring European tourists. It was a place where white people tried to be brown, and brown people tried to be white.

I lay on my side with my gaze locked on a nearby fruit seller and spent several minutes studying his routine. "Pineapple-a-watermelone-a-coconit?" he would say to nearby sunbathers. If he sensed a sale, he'd approach the interested party and point his bony index finger to confirm his or her interest. "Pineapple? Watermelone? Coconit?" he would ask. "Mango?" Once the customer had selected his or her preferred fruit, the seller would use his knife or cudgel, depending on the fruit, to shave clean its flesh, carve it into slices, or crack it wide open.

An energetic Nepali Pete, not far behind the fruit seller, huffed his way up the beach on his morning constitutional, his head down and his arms furiously pumping. On his left wrist, he wore an expensive-looking watch, which he periodically checked to measure his progress up the beach. I could also see that, on each finger, Nepali Pete sported rings of varying size and gaudiness, rings, like his watch, that clearly had been appropriated from Bagmati corpses.

Nepali Pete deviated from his path along the water's edge and ran straight toward Hotel Furtado—right up to the boundary imposed upon him by the restraining order. He then performed his customary daily saber rattling, hurling a string of insults and obscenities at Nitty and the guest house staff.

"Biggest cock-up you ever made, mate!" he said, pacing back and forth like a crazed animal. "Bloody trance," he muttered before kicking some sand at the hotel.

Then, in a clear violation of the police restraining order, Nepali Pete climbed the steps leading into the restaurant and dipped his thumb into a guest's Hello to Queen before dabbing the chocolate mixture on his own forehead.

"Sorry, luv," he said. "Chocolate tika. For good luck!"

Nitty, who was sitting at the bar with his arms folded across his chest, shook his head in amusement. Nepali Pete leaped from the restaurant and resumed his march up the beach as though nothing at all had just happened.

I dropped my towel off at cocohut number seven after I finished sunning myself, threw on a loose-fitting shirt, and headed toward Palolem's main bazaar to make my phone call home. I tripped over a piece of driftwood about halfway down the beach, however, and lost one of my flip-flops.

When I stooped to retrieve the sandal, I was immediately besieged by three female beach hawkers, who displayed their jewelry and trinkets and regurgitated the same lines I'd already heard a thousand times. "Sir, looking is free. If you no like, you no buy," said the first, her eyes wide with expectation. "Sir, you are my first customer today. I do you good price, you do me small business," implored the second, scrunching up her forehead. "Please, sir, it is afternoon; I give you good morning price. How much you pay?" questioned the third, bobbling her head from side to side.

I was forced to sit down and collect my thoughts, my head reeling from the onslaught of unsolicited solicitation. The women, dressed in colorful salwar kameezes, took my sitting as a cue to spread their small blankets around me and display their entire collection of cheap souvenirs. Crouching around me and speaking simultaneously, they pummeled me with their pitches. As my headache grew, the women's dickering doubled in intensity.

Naresh Almeida, appearing as though by magic, charged across the beach toward me, flapping his arms at the women, in the hopes of scattering them. Their resolve was strong, though, and they clung to me like swimming briefs on a European beachgoer. The women knew I was in a weakened state and would do just about anything to get rid of them, including making a purchase if it bought me my freedom. So they stayed by my side, willingly weathering the disapproving scowl and harsh reproach rendered by Naresh.

"Uh, how about that bracelet over there?" I said, pointing to a cheap-looking bracelet on one of the women's blankets.

"Very high quality, sir. Only six hundred rupees."

It looked as though the barber would explode in a fit of rage. The veins on his forehead bulged dangerously as he narrowed his eyes and scolded the women. "How *dare* you start your asking price so high. Your silly attempts at commerce make you look desperate," he said, "and that is *very* embarrassing for you!"

"Naresh, brother, it's OK," I said. "It's just money."

Naresh, his upper lip twitching in spastic convulsions and his head bobbling furiously, made the women lower their initial asking price to three hundred rupees. I was grateful for Naresh's support and business savvy, and I thanked him with my eyes.

"One hundred rupees," I said, punctuating my statement with an emphatic nod of the head.

"Oh dear god, sir. Are you trying to kill us?" one of the women moaned, feigning a heart attack before discussing the offer with her colleagues. They came back with their next offer. "Our cost price is best price for you: two hundred seventy rupees, yes?"

I learned long ago that one of the best bargaining strategies to employ in Indian business transactions was that of indifference. If you simply didn't want the item in question but were forced to negotiate for it, you didn't feel any shame in offering an absurdly low price.

"Fifty rupees," I said, my voice full of defiance. My offer caught the women off guard, as they expected my next bid to land somewhere between one hundred and two hundred and seventy rupees. "If two hundred and seventy rupees is your cost price for that bracelet," I added, "then you got ripped off, my friends."

Nepali Pete, in the meantime, had made his way back down the beach and was leaning in to watch the bidding war unfold. A none-too-shy Pete—who didn't exactly toe the line when it came to the use of appropriate social graces—said, "This deal smells about as sour as Yeti's nuts, mates! Bollocks to these slippery broads."

Naresh agreed with Nepali Pete and stepped in to broker the sale for me. He spoke with the women in what I believed to be Konkani before paying them thirty rupees for the bracelet. He handed the jewelry to me with a "Happy Christmas!"

I was grateful for his generosity. Not only did he come to my aid and offer his assistance with the transaction, potentially saving me hundreds of rupees, he also forked over thirty rupees for the bracelet itself, which was the exact amount I had paid for my haircut the previous day, not including tip. I thanked him profusely before strolling into the bazaar and placing my phone call home.

I spent several hours catching up on e-mails at a local cybercafé after the phone call. Scanning my inbox, I was touched by the number of e-mails I'd received from friends back in Nepal who wondered how my journey was unfolding. Seeing that great outpouring of love and support made me realize what a good thing I had going back in Nepal and what a fool I'd been, in hindsight, to throw it all away. Once someone ET'd, he or she wasn't allowed to return to that country in a Peace Corps–volunteer capacity within whatever time remained of the original service period. The likelihood of my ever returning to Nepal as a Peace Corps volunteer was extremely low.

It struck me that, for all I knew, somebody else might already be preparing to fill the vacancy I left in Pepsicola Townplanning, and that realization filled me with jealousy. I could go back to Kathmandu, but I would never be able to duplicate my experience of the past year. I left the cybercafé in a foul mood, angry at my decision to leave the Peace Corps and Nepal.

Christmas Eve celebrations were just getting under way back at Hotel Furtado. Nitty had decided to throw a huge customer-appreciation bash as part of the holiday festivities, inviting his guests and a few of his Goan friends to the hotel for a night of excessive feasting and moderate alcohol consumption. Despite the considerable revenue he was forgoing, Nitty insisted that it was the one night of the year where he could truly show his patrons just how appreciative he was for their business. Besides, he explained, most of that lost revenue usually found its way back through generous gratuities from guests and word-of-mouth referral to guests' friends back home in Europe, Australia, and North America. It was a win-win situation for everybody, he insisted.

The party itself attracted a diverse array of guests. Most of the thirty or so people staying at Hotel Furtado showed up, as did a sizable number of Nitty's Goan friends. Standing in marked contrast to the cultured civility of the well-off Europeans, however, Nepali Pete sneaked in, and did not hide. Gorging himself on the food at the buffet table, he would pause between mouthfuls to announce something crass to the group before laughing fiendishly at his own jokes. Nitty, however, didn't seem to mind Pete's presence.

I didn't either, because his noisiness took much of the pressure off me to socialize. I wasn't feeling very social, though at one point I suggested to Pete that we head down to the beach to mingle with the guests at the fringes of the party. Pete drunkenly descended the restaurant steps and stumbled across the sand, eventually propping himself on the shoulder of an Englishman who hadn't bid me the time of day since I arrived in Palolem.

The man, sensing an opportunity to stroke his ego in front of his friends, immediately asked Pete, with mock curiosity, what he did for a living. Pete explained to the group that when he wasn't searching for treasure in the Kathmandu Valley, he often busied himself as a painter. "Oh, do tell," replied the smarmy man, his right eyebrow slowly inching toward his receding hairline. "Just what kind of painting do you do, old chap? Acrylic on canvas? Oil on wood panel? Watercolor on cheesecloth?"

"No, brother," replied a proud Nepali Pete after taking a belt of whiskey from a flask he had tucked in his back pocket. "Commercial: water-based latex on concrete!"

It was all I could do to keep from bursting into laughter. Pete simply smiled and slapped the man on the back with a well-timed blow that nearly caused him to choke on the olive from his martini. When the man recovered, Nepali Pete plied him with further libations from the bar and scrumptious morsels from the tandoori grill. The man, embarrassed by Pete's kind gestures, quickly excused himself and slunk away down the beach.

Nitty invited a few of us, including Nepali Pete, to join him for midnight mass at the nearby Roman Catholic church after the party had run its course. Nitty steered me toward a brick wall into whose cracks were stuffed countless pictures and letters from the faithful. He explained to me that people from all around the world came to this church to heal their emotional scars and put the problems of the past behind them.

"It's simple, mon," he whispered over the sound of the opening hymn. All one had to do to access God's healing power was place a memento of pain in the wall, light a candle, and say a prayer.

Something in the wall caught my eye as I was about to turn away. "It *can't* be," I gasped aloud. There in one of the cracks was a dog-eared picture of me. It was one I'd given Adriana while we were at UC Berkeley. I felt a conflicting series of emotions rising within as I took a good, long look at the picture. I was sad and embarrassed I had done something so horrible it required the hand of God to mend. But I also was happy that Adriana had tried to put the past behind her and move on with her life.

"*Chroist!*" said Nepali Pete, upon seeing the picture, drawing disapproving looks from a group of nearby parishioners for his blasphemous outburst. Nepali Pete paused, looked up at a nearby crucifix, and quickly made the sign of the cross over his chest in repentance. "That's *you*, mate!" he whispered forcefully into my ear.

I told Pete and Nitty my entire story after we stuffed ourselves into a nearby confessional. I told them about Adriana, and Dharavi, and the Peace Corps. I told them about my insatiable desire to make things right between us, and how she'd fled each time. I found it painful to rehash the events of the past, but I received only words of support and understanding from my friends in the confessional.

The beach population shrank noticeably over the following week as the Christmas and New Year's holidays ended. Even Nepali Pete headed back to Kathmandu, tanned and ready. For the first time since I arrived in Palolem, the beach was silent. And that's the way it remained for the subsequent three months, while I continued to rest and play, and do some chores around the hotel, which Nitty assured me covered my room and board during these slow months.

And then I was finally ready to take on the world again. I just had to tell Claire. It was Wednesday, and since my weekly breakfast with her was the one appointment I still made and kept, I decided to tell her about my travel plans right away.

Claire Mendelbaum, whom I first met on the volleyball court fronting Hotel Furtado, had become more than just a good friend. On leave from her studies at Columbia University, she had come to India to spend time with her longtime boyfriend, an attaché assigned to a US diplomat in Delhi. When a series of surprising and serious differences in opinion with her boyfriend—now ex-boyfriend—finally got the better of her, she had fled to Goa to drown her sorrows in the deep drink, the Arabian Sea, or in the deep drinking of feni, a Goan liquor distilled from milk or cashews.

Wednesday morning lox and bagels at Rosenblatt's, the local kosher deli, had become a highly anticipated weekly ritual for us both. I reached the entrance of Rosenblatt's, removed my flip-flops, and was immediately greeted by Rabbi Rosenblatt, a retired Jewish scholar who served up a hearty shalom.

"Greetings, Benihana," a smiling Claire called to me over the woody trills of the taped klezmer music, patting my seat at our usual table. We embraced and then, her hands still gentle against my cheeks, she spoke. "Please," she pleaded, tossing the bangs of her short brown hair away from her eyes, "no goyish bagels this week, OK?"

"Not even blueberry or cinnamon raisin?" I laughed.

"Ew." She curled her upper lip in disgust. "Everybody knows that lox should only be eaten with sesame seed or poppy seed bagels. Maybe garlic or salt," she added. "Only a *meshuggener* would eat lox with cinnamon raisin!"

Rabbi Rosenblatt—who was known as much for his blintzes, chopped liver, and corned beef sandwiches as he was for his rabbinical services—brought us an appetizer of pita, olive oil, hummus, and *za'atar*, a spice combination to purportedly open up the mind. I took the sign and opened my mouth to tell Claire that I would be leaving soon.

But Claire spoke first. "I think I'm getting cabin fever. I'm feeling the urge to get out and explore Goa. How about you?"

"That sounds like a great idea," I said. "Any thoughts on where to go?"

"Well, it's market day in Anjuna," she said, "and neither of us have seen that."

"Yeah, OK," I said. "Why not?"

There was a glint in Claire's eye. "The buses around here are sketchy and slow. Why don't you talk with Nitty to see if we can borrow his bike? Look, I'll meet you at noon at Hotel Furtado, and we'll go from there, OK?"

"You know what, let's invite Naresh too," I suggested. Naresh and I had started hanging out outside the barbershop, catching a televised match together whenever Nepal or India played cricket or football. And we had come to realize that we knew the same Claire too—she and Naresh had so often run into each other in the coffee shop that they decided to make shared sipping a regular planned gathering.

After we dined, Claire retreated to her beach hut, and I headed for the restaurant, where I figured Nitty would be. Sure enough, there he was, jiving with a guest to Emraan Hashmi's, "Tu Meri Shab Hi." The song immediately transported me back in time to the Durga Darshan Drive-in Theater in Kathmandu where, alongside Nepali Pete, I'd heard the tune for the first time.

And with Kathmandu on my mind, so was Raju Shrestha. I shuddered as his limp body was dragged across the doorstep of my memory. I couldn't help but wonder if Raju suffered any complications from his gunshot wound or, worse yet, if the shot had been fatal. One of my first priorities upon returning to Kathmandu would be to check up on the cakehouse owner.

"What's up, mon?" A still-bouncing Nitty startled me out of my reverie.

Nitty agreed without hesitation to lend me his bike for the day. His bike, I recognized when he unlocked and pried open the storage shed door, was a Royal Enfield Bullet 500 cc, the same make and model favored by Yarone and Shil for their romps around Kathmandu.

"Nitty, it's really generous of you to lend me the Bullet," I said. "You've been an incredible friend."

"No worries, mon," he said. "Cheers!"

Under a dusty blanket, which Nitty snapped away with a flourish, sat a vintage wartime sidecar, complete with driving goggles and a clearly nonfunctioning machine gun. The sturdy sidecar, shaped like the nose of a rocket, was pockmarked from the battering of bullets that had apparently found their mark.

"This thing has a lot of character," I said, running my hands over the sidecar. "It still works?"

"I'm not sure, mon," he laughed. Nitty eventually succeeded in attaching the sidecar to the Bullet using the skills he acquired as a mechanic before he became a hotel owner.

We lifted our heads from our greasy work to see the beautiful Claire, thin and elegant like a palm frond, standing before us in a purple salwar kameez and shawl. The loose-fitting tunic and trousers, while not entirely successful in hiding her feminine curves from the leering eyes of Indian men, protected her modesty well.

Not long after we met on the volleyball court, I'd begun having feelings for Claire. I was enamored by her small chin and ears and her large, doelike eyes—eyes the color and shape of almonds—but I was also taken by her gentle nature and her ability to listen with empathy and offer sound advice.

The thought of finding love again hadn't even crossed my mind after the great disappointment in Mumbai and again at the church in Palolem, but with Claire I found a renewed hope in the possibility of love. I also found a lover and a friend, and in our state of mutual attraction, we'd fallen into each other's arms on numerous occasions over the past three months. We both understood that her return to America would make it difficult for us to continue our relationship, but we resolved to enjoy our remaining time together and not talk about the future.

"Claire, you look great," I said, pulling her close and kissing her on the cheek.

"Oh, Benny." She batted her eyelashes. "Flattery will get you every-where!" Turning toward the motorcycle and sidecar, she cocked her head to the side and said, "So who are we gunning down?"

"That depends on who gets in our way, I suppose."

In the meantime, Nitty had hopped onto the Enfield and brought the craft to life. Thick clouds of exhaust coated the nearby vegetation. He turned the bike over to me after revving the engine several times. Claire, donning her Gucci sunglasses, obligingly hopped into the sidecar and wrapped her shawl around her head to keep the wind from tousling her hair. We roared off down the narrow alley, the entire craft sashaying with the acceleration. I could see Nitty clapping and cheering us on in the bike's rearview mirror, through the enormous dust cloud that had been kicked up in our wake.

I wasn't exactly sure how I was going to persuade Naresh to join us, given that he almost never left his barbershop during normal business hours, but I had a plan I hoped might work. Naresh was a real prankster, for being such a conservative guy. He was constantly coming up with new and better ways of pranking me ever since I arrived in Goa. The practical joking had become a two-way street, though. I'd snuck into his barbershop at night one week earlier and replaced his shaving cream with whipped cream, only to find my bed short sheeted and several alarm clocks hidden in my room a few nights later. I didn't have that sort of relationship with many people, and I was grateful for Naresh's presence in my life.

Foreigners and locals alike scattered for cover as our pseudo weaponized trike entered Palolem's main bazaar and rolled toward the barber's shop. "Just play along with me," I said to Claire. I pulled up in front of Naresh's shop, killed the engine, and called Naresh out into the street. "Naresh Almeida," I said in a booming voice. "Please come out of the building with your hands in the air." Naresh stepped into the doorway, wiping his hands on a towel. Claire trained the nonfunctioning machine gun on him.

"Dear god," he finally said, shaking his head from side to side as he walked toward us. "You call *this* a prank?" He slapped the barrel of the sidecar's machine gun. "Amateurs."

Claire and I couldn't hold our laughter in any longer. "Naresh, Claire and I would *love* for you to join us on our trip up to the market in Anjuna. What do you say?"

"OK, boss." He shrugged his shoulders, one move I'd never seen him make. "Why not? Business is slow."

"Carpe diem!" whooped Claire.

He climbed onto the bike behind me after locking up his shop, and we zoomed upstate toward Panaji, Goa's sleepy capital.

I turned to smile at Naresh and noticed that his face was veined and verdant, like the leaves of the nearby trees. I took this as a cue to slow down.

"Thanks, boss," said Naresh over the bike's engine, after I cut our speed.

We reached Anjuna later that afternoon. Our trio marveled at the wealth of goods and the diversity of people milling about the market stalls. We paused at the booth of a *putliwallah* to watch him dexterously manipulate his marionettes into grooving effortlessly to the trance music emanating from an open-air club just down the beach.

When the multisensory stimuli of the market became too much and my eyes had long since glazed over with price-haggling fatigue, Naresh, Claire, and I headed to a nearby restaurant. Our mouths watered at the thought of consuming *vindaloo*, a traditional Goan dish of fiery curry in a marinade of tamarind, vinegar, and garlic.

Claire and I, sitting side by side at the table, came to a mutual decision that it was time to leave Goa. Together we made plans for a trip to Mumbai, the city by the sea that Claire had never visited. I looked forward to our time in Mumbai, but I knew I would never be able to go back to the slum; there was simply too much of Adriana in that place. She'd left a *presence* in Dharavi that would always haunt me. I tried my best to win her back, but I had failed miserably and lost everything, and I knew that going back would only remind me of that failure.

I joined Claire at the Canacona Rail Station the following day, after promising to write my guidebook's authors on behalf of Nitty and Hotel Furtado. Claire and I looked on in silence as the Matsyaganda Express, fresh out of Mangalore, slowly chugged into the station, its hulking mass set to plunge us into Mumbai's maelstrom.

Caught in Transition

I BREATHED DEEPLY THROUGH MY NOSE, DESPITE THE GROWING PAIN IN my stomach, as the Matsyaganda Express pulled in to the Lokmanya Tilak station in Kurla, a Mumbai suburb. "Hey, Claire," I whispered in her ear, rubbing her back to help ease the transition from the dream-world to reality. "We're here."

Claire blinked several times, rubbed her eyes, and looked out the train window at the bustle of life on the nearby platform. Shifting her gaze from the platform to me, she took on a concerned expression.

"Benny, you look *horrible*." She placed the back of her hand on my forehead. "Are you OK?"

"No, not really," I admitted, grimacing with pain.

I had felt just fine for the majority of the daylong trip up the coast, but after I ate the catering service's complimentary lunch, I began having stomach pain. What had started as a minor bellyache had, in the past few minutes, become a full-blown gastrointestinal nightmare. Now doubled over in pain, I held my stomach and rocked back and forth in my seat.

"Maybe you just need to sit on the toilet for a while," Claire said. "Sometimes that helps."

"I think the pain is going to pass," I groaned, downplaying the serious-ness of my discomfort. "Let's just get down to Colaba as fast as we can, find an affordable place to stay, and get some sleep. I think that will help me more than anything else."

"Are you *sure* you don't want to use the squat toilet in the Kurla station?" Her suggestion was no doubt a wise one, but I was all too familiar with the gruesome state of public squat toilets throughout Mumbai. The thought of lingering, even for a moment, in such nasty conditions was enough to persuade me to bear my suffering until I could find a more hygienic place to relieve myself. I suffered a few more moments of intense pain, but eventually was able to get up and move around, albeit slowly.

I had a rough idea of our location in the city, but I'd never spent much time in Kurla. Claire and I, slightly disoriented, waded chest-deep into a swarming cartel of touts, baggage handlers, and taxi drivers who were waiting on the platform. I fended off the men's guileful pitches and non-stop badgering, while Claire fended off their suggestive ogling and not-so-subtle advances. We seemed to see the man in the business suit at the same time, because we both started pushing toward him.

Seemingly lost in his newspaper, the man took a few moments to look up to address us. I was shocked by his unusual facial features, and I took a step back.

His jowls hung low over his jaw—the distended tissue stretching well beyond what I had ever imagined possible—and his bushy eyebrows were set at a steep angle, such that they resembled the letter V. He also had a lazy eye and seemed unable to control his drooling.

Though extraordinary in appearance, he was eager to help us and quickly scribbled a map on the back of Claire's train ticket, explaining that we needed to walk a short distance, cross a footbridge, and hire an autorickshaw that would take us to Bandra, where we would be able to catch our train.

It was a rude awakening to be thrust back into the unbearable pollution and heartbreaking poverty of Mumbai. I missed the blue, brown, and green hues of the Goan landscape; I missed the privacy of my cocohut, whose walls allowed me to escape the reality of India and my situation for as long as I desired.

After reaching the informal autorickshaw terminal and telling the driver our destination, Claire and I shrank into a semiprivate world under the craft's thin canopy, its dark shroud shielding us from the street's roar and lulling us into a false sense of security. We were almost invisible to the world around us, which was a rare treat in a place where a person was so often exposed. That short chance to sit and observe the street's happenings without feeling like a target helped soothe the pain in my gut and gave me hope that I would make it to Colaba.

The autorickshaw itself possessed an aura of decrepitude and gave off the distinct odor of petrol fumes, but it was still strangely charming. The driver, who cast furtive glances in all directions to monitor nearby vehicles, had decorated his brave little machine with numerous blinking devotional ornaments and a Britney Spears air freshener. I felt an incredible amount of respect and admiration for the man as I watched him work the craft's controls. The skill set required to navigate the streets of Mumbai must be mind-boggling, I thought. I watched him weave in and out of traffic—at times feathering the brakes, at other times twisting the throttle—with the grace and poise of a ballerina.

Claire and I hurried to the platform after we arrived at the Bandra station and caught the first passenger train bound for Colaba. We sat quietly by a window as the train pulled away from the station and watched with curiosity as a street child, a boy of no more than seven years old, hopped into the compartment and proceeded directly to my side.

"I think he wants you to give him some money, Benny," Claire said.

The boy continued to stand next to me, looking up at me with his big, doleful eyes. I explained to Claire my reluctance to give handouts to kids. The boy, becoming increasingly agitated with my seeming lack of sympathy for his plight, furrowed his brow and began speaking in Hindi. Then he started to slap the pockets of my jeans, each slap producing an incriminating jingle from the coins resting within. An older man sitting in the same compartment, aware that I wasn't going to give the boy alms, addressed the child in a stern voice before giving him a one-rupee note and banishing him to another car. I gave the man an appreciative glance and a sheepish smile after the boy left the compartment. The man, smiling and wiggling his head in return, then fell asleep as the train hurtled toward Colaba.

Just when I thought I too could drift asleep, waves of nausea swept over me. I wasn't going to make it to the squat toilets at Churchgate, the end of the line; I needed to go *now*.

Little is worse, for any human, than having the need to defecate when there's no place to do so. A feeling of complete helplessness overcame me as I staggered toward the nearest exit. Claire, who understood exactly what was happening, moved to join me near the compartment's breezy opening and rubbed my back. Hunched there, with one hand on the railing and the other on my stomach, I realized I was getting worse by the moment, with every lurch of the train bringing me one step closer to the ultimate embarrassment of filling my pants. An upbeat young man standing nearby sensed my discomfort, and with blithe unconcern offered a few words of encouragement. "Don't worry, sir," he said, smiling. "This is India. Shit first, ask questions later!"

I had seen plenty of people in India squat near railroad tracks to do their business, but some psychological barrier buried deep in the recesses of my brain refused to allow me to shit in front of others. I'd been raised to believe that defecation should always be a private act. I tried to focus on the graffiti scribbled on the car's walls. Decades' worth of humorous political diatribes lampooned India's larger-than-life politicians for their incompetence and corruption, from what I could tell by dates, names, and drawings.

Claire and I hopped off the train as it slowed on its way into the Mahim Junction station and scoured the platform for a public restroom. I spotted a concrete building at the platform's far end and hobbled toward it—relief at last.

Urinals. The bathroom only had urinals! I stood there dumbfounded. Hating myself for what I was about to do, I slunk toward the most remote urinal, turned around, and undid my belt. I looked straight ahead and was shocked to see a wild-haired, toothless, crippled vagrant lying on his side in the opposite corner. The panhandler, shooting me a horrified look, furiously rattled the coins in his tin cup to attract the attention of other men entering the building.

The man's actions had an unexpected calming effect on my bowels, and I suddenly felt better again. I quickly pulled up my pants, fastened my belt, and dropped a few coins in the man's cup, which he again rattled furiously.

I hurried back over the platform toward Claire, stopping a man along the way to ask him where I might find the nearest squat toilets. "Churchgate station," he said. All the stations between Mahim Junction and Churchgate had facilities for urination only, according to the man.

"I hate to say it, Benny," said Claire, "but things aren't looking too rosy for you. I *told* you that you should have used the squat toilets at the Kurla station."

"Noted," I groaned in response.

Claire and I jumped aboard the next train entering the station, opting for the less crowded men's first-class compartment. We received curious stares from a group of three teenage boys. It was rare, I knew, for a woman to travel in the men's compartment. Women could ride there, but most kept to their own compartment, where men were not allowed; if men tried to enter, they would usually be beaten back by a barrage of purses, shoes, and other accoutrements.

Blasting along the tracks through the steamy Mumbai evening, the train heaved and sighed as it released and imbibed passengers at the Dadar, Elphinstone Road, and Mahalaxmi rail stations. The train wheeled into Mumbai Central, and the teens in our compartment bolted from the passenger car and tore off down the platform. *That was odd.*

Several gruff-looking, uniformed men entered the car. One of the men, the apparent leader, used the overhead stability straps to pick his way through the remaining crowd with the slow, labored determination of a giant sloth, mouth breathing—heavily—the entire time. I'd ridden Mumbai's commuter trains many times before, and not once had I ever been approached by a security detail. I tried to think of some legitimate excuse for not having a pass but came up empty. Now was not a good time to be delayed, given the unpredictability of my gastrointestinal problems.

All three men carried lathis on their belts, bamboo batons that they fingered menacingly as they demanded to see our first-class tickets. With nothing to show for ourselves but the bags under our eyes after a long day of travel, Claire and I were escorted off the train and reprimanded harshly by the head of the security detail.

"Tsk, tsk. You people are all the same," he said. "You think you are above the law." The man, whose sense of self-worth oozed from his greasy pores, led us toward his office on the concrete platform. "Not only did you sneak onto train," he said, "but you snuck into first-class car. Very serious offense." He looked over his shoulder at us, bobbling his head in disapproval. "It is *worst*. Very steep fine."

There would be no banks open from which to withdraw funds at such a late hour, and neither of us knew where to find an ATM. We would be spending the night on the streets of Mumbai if the six hundred rupees we had pooled went to pay a fine. We stepped into the guard's office to find six more men waiting around a shoddy, rectangular table. I got the distinct feeling that Claire and I had just stumbled into a prickly thicket of Indian bureaucracy, that we were two chickpeas now mired in a sticky batter.

The head of the security detail—whose belly was plumper than the pakodas I'd consumed in such vast quantities at the Pepsicola Community Hospital—settled in behind his desk, leaned back in his chair, and put his hands behind his head. He used great effort to hoist his chunky legs so that his boots rested on the desktop. His body language—torpid, mocking—typified that of a classic sadist, of an interlocutor who derived extraordinary pleasure from presiding over others' suffering and humiliation. His accomplices looked Claire and me over from head to toe, sneering.

The overweight official wriggled in his chair to find the most comfortable position before indulging in what was perhaps the single loudest fart I'd ever heard in a public setting. I observed the reactions of the other men in the room. All those within earshot of the trumpeting seemed quite pleased to have such a talented man in their midst. I, however, was not nearly as impressed.

"You are guilty of trespassing on property of Indian Railways," he said, rocking back and forth in his chair as he picked at his nostril with the thumb and index finger of his right hand. "You are subject to four-thousand-rupee fine. Pay now or we will arrest you."

I swallowed hard. That was more scratch than Claire and I had ever carried, even combined. "Look, brother," I said. "We weren't trying to cheat the system, OK? We just spent the entire day on the train from Goa, and all we want to do is make it down to Colaba to find a place to crash for the night. If you could just let us go, we'll promise to buy the correct tickets from now on, I swear."

"No. You must pay fine. You don't leave here until you pay." He slammed a fist against his desk. His other hand kept working at his nose. He soon extracted a large booger, which he pasted against the side of his chair. I could see from my position that the booger—a slippery nougat the color of charcoal—was simply the latest deposit in a long, vertical line of snot caked to the chair's side.

"Look, there's no need to be difficult," I said, trying not to gag. "The truth is, we can't afford the fine. We've only got six hundred rupees left between us, and we need that money to pay for tonight's hotel room."

"Then you will leave passport with us until we receive balance of fine."

Claire, who loathed confrontation, had slipped into a state, pale and slumped against the shack's wall. Her eyes were filled with tears and seemed to beg me, *Do something!*

I tried appealing to the official's heart, which I knew was every Indian's weak spot. "You've got to be kidding!" I said, my voice now full of alarm. "Are you going to put *her* out on the street tonight? Would you put your own daughter out on the street?"

"Only if it would help her find a decent husband, a man better than the chod she's going with now," he said. "The law is the law. Where you put up is your own problem."

"I think you're making up the law to suit your needs," I said. Several of the man's peons reached for their lathis, but he waved them down. "I think you're a manipulative xenophobe who derives pleasure from taking advantage of unsuspecting foreigners! I'll...I'll tell the CIA about you!" It sounded like a grasp to me, but I hoped it would instill some amount of legitimate fear.

I continued to try to shame the man. I explained to him how the countries of the Western world had opened their hearts to the vast numbers of Indian immigrants who had chosen to settle in countries like Canada, the United Kingdom, the United States, and Australia, even though I knew this to be a lie. I understood perfectly well the intolerance and prejudice some immigrants faced in their transition to Western lifestyles and customs. But in my desire to spring Claire and myself from our sticky situation, I insisted that a little reciprocal hospitality on his behalf might do diplomatic wonders between our two nations.

The official sneered derisively after I finished my speech and dismissed my words with a simple wave of his hand. "You must pay, *now*."

"Please," I said. "Find a little forgiveness in your heart. Or, if you insist on taking all our money, maybe you wouldn't mind if we stayed at *your* house tonight?"

"Most certainly not!"

Then, as if things couldn't possibly have gotten any worse, my gastro-intestinal distress returned, stronger than ever. I was truly trapped this time, and the mass movement was coming. I sprinted toward a garbage can near the official's desk, dropped my pants, and relaxed my bowels. So urgent was my need to go that not once during the act itself did I think about how humiliating it was, focusing instead upon the rapidly dissipating agony of my gut.

Not a soul except for Claire and me remained in the shack by the time I finished. "Claire, don't watch," I said, out of my stupor and now too embarrassed to look her in the eye. I searched for something to use as toilet paper and pulled a handful of rupee notes and the morning's train ticket from the front pocket of my jeans. We needed the rupees for the hotel room, that much was for certain, but the thought of desecrating a country's currency—especially that which bore the image of Gandhi, casting me a curious sideways glance through his small, round spectacles—in that most heinous of fashions easily tipped the scale in the ticket's favor.

I was mortified by what I'd done in the official's office, but I felt remarkably better overall. I pulled up my pants, fastened my belt, and hurried, alongside Claire, toward the platform and a departing train.

We slung our packs over our shoulders and jumped into the outstretched arms of the men near the closest train-car door; they then doled out punitive blows upon the official and his men who were trying to chase us down and apprehend us. I'd always been fascinated by the Indian public's tendency to favor the underdog, even if this went against the local authorities.

Standing a full head and shoulders above the aromatic grove of armpit hair belonging to our new friends—all of whom clutched the train's overhead straps for support—Claire and I felt protected and enjoyed safe passage all the way to Churchgate.

Claire and I explored Mumbai over the next few days. We visited rooftop gardens, the Haji Ali mosque, and restaurants such as Indigo and Basilico that were popular with Western tourists, expatriates, and moneyed locals alike. We took a short trip to Elephanta Island to view the elaborate stone carvings and visited the Bandra Bandstand to eat *kulfi* and watch the sun set over the Arabian Sea. And then we were in Delhi.

I never had to leave Claire; instead, her time in India ran out first, and I put her on a plane back to the States and her studies. I heard from her several days later, after she had settled back in to her New York apartment, but already she sounded distant, as though she were on a different planet.

A Return to Pepsi

My decision to return to Kathmandu, while finalized only days before my departure from Goa, was not a snap decision. I had hoped for a cathartic moment or an epiphany to help guide my life after three months in Palolem, after three months of solitude and thoughtful reflection by the beach. But such a moment had never come.

Instead there had been only the slow realization that my future, at least my foreseeable future, was in Nepal, among the people I came to know and love during my days with the Peace Corps. I was no longer working with the Peace Corps—whose support I had always considered a cornerstone of my success in Nepal—but I knew I possessed the tools to serve and serve well.

But beyond that, something Dr. Singh had said about the people of Nepal was what really rekindled my ambition and mobilized me from my beachside retreat. The quality of their character, he said, *compelled* him to devote his time and energy to the betterment of their lives. The quality of this people's character—their integrity and their fighting spirit in the face of almost impossible odds— ultimately drew me back to Nepal and Kathmandu to lend a helping hand wherever I could.

I rode in trains and taxis and buses to get back to Kathmandu. I even rode on an Indian army officer's back in Gorakhpur after rolling my ankle while stepping off the train; the barrel of his loaded gun dangled precariously close to my face during the entire ten-minute trek from the station to a nearby cycle-rickshaw stand. "Ho, Pepsicola, Pepsicola, Pepsicolaaaa. Ho, Pepsicola Townplanninnng!" sang the fare collector for my final bus, and I jumped on board.

I wondered how people would view my return to the city. Would they be angry, confused, and unapproachable? Or would they be happy, excited, and eager to see me? I'd left the city on decent terms with everybody, but there was a big part of me that felt I'd abandoned my Peace Corps friends and the people of Pepsi. I was sure there would be wounds to patch up, and I resigned myself to the fact that I would have to win back people's trust, and that that would take some time.

I automatically assumed the worst, but then I remembered something Dr. Singh had said before I left for India. He told me, if you're going to make a mistake, make a really big one, and be proud of it. I had made a huge mistake in leaving the Peace Corps to chase Adriana, but why not be proud of my Himalayan blunder? I'd done something unconventional, something unexpected, and it hadn't paid dividends. Big deal. I had spent plenty of time beating myself up over it, but I resolved to give myself absolution and let myself move on with my life, guilt-free.

It was springtime in Nepal, and under the dazzling glow of a waxing moon, the fields interspersed with the growing network of roads and houses around Pepsi had never looked more beautiful: aesthetically pleasing works of agrestic art tended to with the loving affection and pride of those whose very lives depended upon their bountiful yield.

I'd been gone for only about four months, but as I walked through the fields, I saw that several new concrete buildings had already popped up in previously vacant lots. I wondered what the farmers thought about the continued plundering of their land. I also wondered if they had been fairly compensated for their loss by the ambitious landowners. It seemed to me that within a few years, there would be no more farming in Pepsicola Townplanning, the men and women of the fields driven off to other parts of the valley by the rapid and seemingly endless development of the neighborhood. I felt sad for those farmers, not only because their way of life and their means to a livelihood were being threatened but also because their work seemed insignificant in the face of developers' goals.

I knocked lightly three times when I reached the front door of Shruti's house. The door opened. Shruti, her eyes bulging, flung her arms around me and welcomed me home. Little Annu, rising from bed, squealed in delight as she ran toward me and hugged my leg.

We talked in Nepali over a hearty meal, and then Shruti insisted I get some rest. She'd kept my room just as I left it, she said, in the hopes that I would one day return to Pepsicola Townplanning and resume residence at the Bhupani house.

I walked over to the Pepsicola Community Hospital to catch up with Madhu, Arjun, and Kabita late the following morning, after a meal of dal bhaat with Shruti and Annu. I approached the clinic and saw, off in the distance, a stately looking Madhu standing in the middle of a dusty street next to a statue of Nepal's late King Birendra. I didn't know it then, but word of my return had already spread throughout the neighborhood, and Madhu was expecting me.

I continued marching toward the small hospital with the warm sun at my back. Children, boisterous only a few minutes before, grew silent, except for a few snorts and giggles that they quickly stifled when I looked their way. It had been months since anybody in the community had seen me. What had once been a usual sight was again a novelty.

I saw a giant smile creep its way onto Madhu's face as I approached, and the closer I came, the more furiously his head wiggled. Madhu sprang forward when I finally reached him and hugged me with a strength I hadn't thought he possessed.

"Oh, daai! I am so happy for your coming backs!" he shouted, refusing to loosen his grasp. "Too long it is being since we are last seeing your fine and handsome self!"

When I had gently pried Madhu from my body, we headed to the hospital, where we found Arjun and Kabita sunning themselves on the clinic's front steps. They too welcomed me back to Pepsicola Townplanning with a level of enthusiasm comparable to that of Madhu's. Arjun and Kabita then quizzed me about my recent adventures in India, especially those concerning Adriana.

I chatted with the trio for several hours before heading to the city to visit my good friend Raju Shrestha. It had been months since the night of his shooting in Sunauli, and I wondered how his recovery was progressing. If I knew anything about Raju, though, I knew that he wouldn't let a round of hot lead slow him down. But I had to see him for myself. I had to hear, in his own words, why he'd chosen such a risky, and potentially lethal, occupation.

I ducked inside the cakehouse and strode toward the counter. I asked the man at the cash register—the Chinese man who preferred wearing leisure suits—where I might find Raju. Without uttering a word, he scribbled a message on a scrap piece of paper and handed me the note before dancing off to the kitchen. It read, *Bir Hospital, physical therapy wing.*

At Bir Hospital, a nurse led me up several flights of stairs. I knocked lightly on the door of the room we stopped in front of.

"Aaunus!" said a gruff voice from within the room. "Come!"

I entered and found Raju with a fully loaded barbell resting on his shoulders, in the middle of a set of squats. A handful of nurses who were scrutinizing his form with intense curiosity took one look at me, blushed, and then scampered off to some other part of the hospital. Raju, with his rock-star charisma and his Bollywood good looks, was "man lovely," and I sensed that he received more than his fair share of attention from the female staff assigned to the physical therapy wing.

He set the barbell on a rack after completing his set and grabbed a towel to mop his sweaty brow. "Ahh, hello, my friend! It is most good to be seeing you again."

He had a slight limp as he walked toward me to shake my hand. Instead of making him look weak, however, the limp only made him look tougher. Here was a man who wasn't afraid of being shot, a man who was willing to deal with the long-term consequences of a gunshot wound so that justice could prevail.

"Sabin-ji is telling me you were being there that night, in Sunauli," said Raju, who had dropped to the floor to stretch his left quad.

"Yeah, I was there," I said, "in the room next door. I saw them drag you away after you'd been shot. *Jesus*, Raju, I thought you'd been killed."

"Just a flesh wound," he said in a matter-of-fact voice. "*Nothing* that could ever stop the Great Raju!"

"I had no idea you were an undercover cop," I said. Not wanting to just stand around while Raju did all the work, I picked up a set of dumbbells. "You had me totally fooled. How long were you working on that case?"

"Many months," he said. "This time was necessary to build the trust, you could say. Only then could I be putting that *chikuwa* away for good." Raju ambled over to a water cooler and filled a paper cup to the brim. Taking a big swig, he swished before spitting the water into a nearby sink. "Thanks to Damodar Sankar Singh, MBBS, and my three-times-weekly PT sessions, I am being almost back to 100 percent function," said Raju.

"Dr. Singh is your physician?"

"Yes, he has been helping me a great deal with my injury," he said. The physician usually joined him for at least part of his physical therapy sessions, according to Raju, although he hadn't yet come to visit today.

Several moments later, a great wailing arose from the nurses' lounge down the hall. Raju bolted for the door with me following.

"What is going on?" Raju demanded of the nurses we found in the lounge. Their bodies were heaving in grief.

"It is Doctor-ji," said one of the nurses. "He has…expired." The nurses, between sobs, explained that Dr. Singh's body had been found earlier that day in his study, according to one of the doctor's friends, who had ringed the hospital to deliver the bad news; Dr. Singh was the victim of a catastrophic heart attack that was attributed to his pack-a-day smoking habit. The pages of his handwritten memoir had been scattered over his desk beneath him.

Raju immediately sank to his knees and joined the women in their wailing as he questioned the logic of the gods for having taken life from the dedicated healer. "Why must the good men die while the bad men live? Take the pimp, take the murderer, take the drug dealer, but for the fuck's sake, don't take the men who are making the world a better place!"

The news of my friend's death sucked the wind out of my lungs. I ran out of the room, down the stairs, and out into the street. I hopped over a cement barricade and continued to run. I ran all the way to Thamel. With tears and snot finally choking my breath and with my body a powder keg of emotions, I slowed to a trot and eventually walked all the way to Swayambhunath and then all the way to the top of the temple's steps.

I let my grief wash over me like the incoming tide as I looked out over Kathmandu.

It didn't make any sense. He was so active and vital, and he had so much more life left to live. *How can he possibly be gone?*

My grief consumed me, but I still found room to be furious with myself for not coming back to Nepal sooner. I could have at least told him how his belief in the goodness of the people had inspired me to come back to Kathmandu and devote myself to them, if I'd been even one day earlier. But now all was lost. The doctor, my mentor and friend, was gone. I couldn't believe my misfortune.

News of Dr. Singh's passing traveled as quickly as all other information did throughout the Kathmandu Valley. Shruti, Madhu, and everybody else associated with the hospital had already heard the news by the time I arrived back in Pepsi later that afternoon. Shruti said she'd learned of the doctor's death from the crowd that had gathered—informally, spontaneously, each person drawn by fear, confusion, and sadness to join others—under the people tree. A funeral had been arranged for the following day. It would be open to all those who wished to attend.

I hired a taxi for Shruti, Annu, and myself late the next afternoon to drive us to the burning ghats at Pashupatinath, where Dr. Singh's body was to be cremated. I'd borrowed a gray suit and purple tie from Manfred for the occasion, although I felt a little conspicuous among the other attendees, most of whom were wearing white.

We climbed out of the Maruti Suzuki and joined throngs of mourners entering the temple grounds. A lone cow chewing its cud at a leisurely pace was the sentry by which we all passed.

I glanced downstream, beyond the muddy waters of the Bagmati, and saw what looked to be the entire sukumbasi encampment walking toward the ghats. Leading the group was none other than Nepali Pete himself.

The eccentric Englishman made his way to my side and placed a bony hand on my shoulder. He whispered in my ear, "It's a bloody shame, friend," he said. "A real blow to the community, if ya ask me."

"How did you know the doctor?" I whispered back.

"The doctor and I 'ave been on friendly terms for aeons, mate. Never seen a bloody week go by without the man showing up in Camp Cornelius for some reason or other. Free shots for the wee ones, medicine and nutritional advice for the infirm—the man was a bloody saint!"

The Milk Baba emerged from his hermitage across the Bagmati, traipsed around a troop of monkeys, and made his way across the bridge toward the burning ghats, where he would recite the final prayers and set the funeral pyre ablaze.

Madhu leaned over and whispered in my ear, "Yesterday, I am forgetting to give it to you, this envelope," he said, handing me a small brown envelope that had my name written on the front.

"Who's this from?" I said, failing to recognize the handwriting. I held the envelope in my hands, running my thumbs over its smooth and shiny exterior.

"I am not knowing it, this person." Madhu furrowed his brow and shrugged his shoulders. He straightened up and turned his attention back to the Milk Baba, who circled the funeral pyre multiple times while holding a burning sheaf of straw. The guru then set the pyre ablaze, the flames leaping high into the air as the conflagration consumed the doctor's body with its fiery licks. A mild wind suddenly kicked up, carrying juniper-scented air.

I'd seen bodies being cremated on the ghats at Pashupatinath before, but I'd never known any of the deceased personally. I knew it made perfect sense to burn the body after death, but seeing the doctor's body slowly disintegrate on the pyre was extremely difficult for me. Death in Nepal is very raw and very real. Death in Nepal is not something that people hide from.

I watched the dancing flames and was suddenly struck by something that Dr. Singh had told me that night in New Baneshwor, over four months earlier. He said that a candle loses no light when it passes its light on to others. It was a brilliant notion, and it helped me realize that even though a great man had fallen, his legacy—the way in which he had touched others and improved their lives—would always live on in some capacity. How many people had he passed his light on to during his lifetime? How many lives had he affected in a positive way? I believed that his spirit would live on for a long, long time to come, if the number of people attending his funeral was any indication.

The Pepsicola Community Hospital crew gathered for a meal at Shruti's house after the funeral. We each shared our finest recollections of the doctor over several rounds of food; the group laughed heartily at my description of our hot-air-ballooning accident in Kathmandu's Durbar Square.

The crew dispersed throughout Pepsicola Townplanning when the stories had been told and the doctor properly remembered. Work would start again, in some capacity, the next day.

I walked to the people tree, where I sat down on the short brick-and-clay wall encircling its base and extracted from my pocket the envelope Madhu had given me earlier. *Dear Ben,* the note inside began. *You're probably wondering why I'm writing to you now after all these years.* Already I could feel my pulse quicken.

As I continued reading the letter from the woman I'd loved and lost, I could almost feel her beating heart growing stronger. I could feel her coming back to life for me, and that renewal made me the happiest person alive. We'd been dead to one another for so long, and now, all of a sudden, thanks to her letter, there was hope for a future between us.

Distance and time, Ben. Distance and time. These are the only things that have helped me heal. I still see the ugliness of your words in my mind's eye, but I've been able to transcend their hurtful intent to see just how badly you were suffering when you wrote them.

Ben, I want to apologize for the way I treated you so long ago. I want to apologize for shutting you out of my life and for any pain that resulted from my evasiveness. You have to understand that my original departure from Dharavi was necessary to protect my sense of self-worth. To have met you in that time and place would have been disastrous for both of us, of that I'm convinced.

You also have to understand that it wasn't just you I was running from. As you know, my parents' demands can be...unreasonable, and I was running from the obligations they'd forced on me, especially that whole arranged marriage bit. It just wasn't a good fit for me. The thought of marrying somebody I didn't love was just too depressing. I hope you can understand the complexities of my situation and find for me a place of forgiveness in your heart.

Even though our paths never crossed during your first trip to India, I was happy, on some level, that you'd met and befriended the people of Dharavi, and that you were able to experience aspects of Indian life few Westerners ever get to experience. I can only hope that your time in Dharavi stayed with you and helped you prioritize your life. I'm assuming that this was the case, based on your decision to join the Peace Corps.

Concerning your most recent trip to Dharavi, let me state that I never intended to disappear on you. I didn't know that you were coming, and if I had I would have welcomed your presence. My colleagues at Chota Sion and I were attending a public health conference in New Delhi then, and we returned to Dharavi about a week after you left. I spoke with your dear friends, the Panchals, who gave me your thoughtful postcard and told me that they thought you'd already left for Kathmandu. It turns out that you had changed your plans.

Ben, I can't tell you how touched I was by your desire to see me, by your desire to resolve the suffering we've both endured. I was so touched, in fact, that I decided to come here, to Kathmandu, to find you.

The Panchals told me that you'd recently left the Peace Corps, and even though you were no longer working for the organization, that small piece of information was all I needed to track you down. After consulting a few of the Peace Corps Nepal administrators, I was directed toward Dr. Singh.

After speaking with Dr. Singh on the phone, Adriana had headed to Pepsicola Townplanning, where she spent time wandering around the neighborhood, trying to get a sense of the life I'd lived there as a volunteer with the Peace Corps. It had been clear, based on her conversation with Dr. Singh, that I hadn't yet come back to Nepal, so she'd written a note to be given to me upon my return. She'd entrusted that note to Dr. Singh, who in turn had handed it over to Madhu for safekeeping. She left Kathmandu for Dharavi, where she planned to spend several more weeks finishing up research for her master's in public health. Considering the letter's date, I understood that she'd long since left India and was probably back home in Fremont.

Adriana talked about her conversation with Dr. Singh in the final few paragraphs of her letter, about how impressed she had been by him and all the wonderful things that he said about me. *Ben, he believes that you have an incredible capacity to help others,* she wrote. This encouragement to put my skills to good use lent me all the support I needed to fully commit to an extended stay in the Nepali capital. Just as one of my major pillars of support had been knocked out from underneath me, another had emerged to take its place.

I continued to grieve the loss of Dr. Singh and celebrate the return of Adriana into my life over the next several days. I also began giving serious thought to what I would do next. I still had no idea how I would find my niche, but I had the unmistakable feeling that everything would work out for the best.

Not long after Dr. Singh's funeral, I bumped into Madhu during a walk around the neighborhood. He wondered if I would be interested in joining Rakesh and him on a weeklong trip to his native Tarai while administrators at the Pepsicola Community Hospital figured out what to do about the loss of the doctor. I agreed without hesitation. Madhu had been eager to show me around Nepal's ricebasket since I'd joined the clinic's staff, and now that we were finally going, he was beside himself with joy. "We will ride it the big elephants in Chitwan, visit Janaki Mandir temple in Janakpur, and then, after you are liking it the Tarai so very, very, very much, we will be eating it like three little piggies in my village!"

Madhu, Rakesh, and I headed for Gongabu bus station, Kathmandu's principle bus terminal, early the following morning. It took at least two hours for the bus to fill and for everybody's belongings to be stowed on the roof, and when we finally did get rolling, a thick fog and bumper-to-bumper traffic slowed our departure from Kathmandu. I showed Madhu and Rakesh several of the magic tricks I'd learned from Juhu in Matheran, but for the majority of the drawn-out trip, I just sat next to the window, watched the striking Nepali landscape roll past my eyes, and thought about Dr. Singh.

Residents were rightly concerned about what his loss meant for their long-term health and well-being. It was true that all the staff members of the Pepsicola Community Hospital had contributed to its success, but Dr. Singh alone had been the wellspring from which all healing in the community had flowed. He'd often taken patients under his wing and made their personal welfare his personal responsibility. And I couldn't help but wonder what events had comprised his final days. I thought it was unlikely he had resolved the problems of his past, but I hoped he had, through the writing of his memoir, found peace.

The weeklong stay with Madhu's parents and eight siblings in the Tarai passed quickly. My friend had been right—I would have missed a key part of Nepal had I never experienced the blend of quiet contemplation and sightseeing opportunities possible at every moment in the Tarai region. But nothing could prepare us for the shock of what we found in Pepsicola Townplanning upon our return.

Standing side by side on the road after our taxi sped away, our bags still in our hands, Madhu and I stared in horror at the pitiful remains of the once mighty Pepsicola Community Hospital. Speechless, we looked at one another before dropping our bags and moving in for a closer inspection. We circled the building in the hopes of finding something familiar in the rubble, but we found nothing but what we could see from the road: a charred shell, its flame-seared walls blackened beyond recognition.

"It is a *most* horrible," wailed an inconsolable Madhu, his watery eyes as large as thali trays. I died a small death inside listening to Madhu's wavering voice.

It wasn't long before Shruti, Arjun, and Kabita appeared. Arjun looked the worst of the three, his face full of cuts and bruises, his right eye black and grotesquely swollen.

"Your face, daai!" said Madhu. "It is looking like baboon's rear end after it is beaten with bamboo cane!"

"What happened here? And *how* did this happen?" I asked, examining Arjun's eye.

"Goondas," said Arjun, a scowl appearing on his face.

"Goondas? *Paakaa ho?*" I asked. "Here in Pepsicola Townplanning?"

"Paakaa ho," nodded a somber Arjun. "It is so."

Shruti explained that while we were in the Tarai, a group of men wearing ski masks had forced their way into the clinic. Militant addicts bent on pilfering the minimal yet potent stash of seminarcotic drugs locked in the clinic's dispensary, they threatened Arjun, who was the only one at the clinic at that time of night. The men beat him, bound and gagged him, and threw him into a nearby field after he unlocked the dispensary.

Theft was not enough for these goondas: the thugs broke windows, smashed chairs, and destroyed most of the clinic's medical equipment. The men even knocked down walls. Not that any of that mattered in the end, since they then torched the place. Stray dogs gnawed on anything that might have been salvaged, and for days we would continue to receive reports of dogs scattering pieces of the clinic around Pepsicola Townplanning.

"But surely people heard the ruckus?" I asked, incensed by Shruti's description of the clinic's demise.

"Too scared for life," said Arjun, explaining that while many people in the community knew what was going on, understandably few were willing to put their lives on the line to stop the clinic's destruction. "Ke garne?" he asked, wiggling his head. "What to do?"

I was devastated by the loss of the clinic. But the people of Pepsi, of course, had lost much more: the only means to affordable health care for many and a source of employment for some. I had occasionally been accused of being cynical and suspicious about life—especially because of my belief that life demanded too much from people and gifted them too little in return—but deep down, I was an optimistic person. And I wasn't about to let a few goondas ruin everything that Dr. Singh had worked so hard to build.

During my undergrad days at UC Berkeley, I volunteered several times to help build houses with Habitat for Humanity, so I had a decent idea of how to coordinate and carry out such an endeavor. This project would be different and would present its own unique challenges, but I felt confident that everything would go well, that the spirit of volunteering would see us through to the clinic's completion.

I described my idea to the clinic crew, and we quickly decided that we would build a new clinic—a clinic that would honor Dr. Singh's life's work, built by his friends' and coworkers' very own hands.

I made countless phone calls and visited numerous contacts around Kathmandu over the next few weeks, continuously explaining the unfortunate circumstances surrounding the clinic's destruction. The majority of people I spoke with, including my Peace Corps friends and many of the people who had attended the doctor's cremation on the ghats at Pashupatinath, expressed sincere interest in helping raise a new clinic. Several Kathmandu contractors also volunteered their time and expertise to the project.

With a capable team assembled, we solicited donations of building materials from local suppliers. We wanted the clinic to reflect Dr. Singh's belief in sustainable development, so the materials had to come from local sources and be as ecologically sound as possible. The clinic also had to reflect the doctor's preference in design aesthetics and would therefore need to meld the quaintness of the past with the functionality and hygiene standards of modern medical facilities.

Once we secured the necessary materials, we formally invited the entire community of Pepsicola Townplanning to help with construction. I was excited to start building the new clinic, and I looked forward to the camaraderie such a project would generate within the community.

When the day finally came to start building, Shruti, Annu, and Kabita busied themselves in Shruti's kitchen preparing a massive meal of dal bhaat tarakaari for volunteers. Nepali Pete appeared for the first time since Dr. Singh's funeral. "*Chroist*, friend," he murmured, eyeing the ruined hospital. "You've been burrrgled!" He thought for a moment and then asked where he might pitch his tent. "I'm planning to stay onsite until we finish 'er off, mate," he said. Nepali Pete: treasure hunter, commercial painter, and now, security guard.

The morning progressed, and so did our eager, helpful crew. In came the Nigerians and a whole hoard of Aussies; in came Yarone and Shil on their retooled Royal Enfield motorcycle; and in came Beth, Bronte, Manfred, Laura, and Taka.

"Fool, what kind of trouble did you get yourself into here?" said Bronte, looking at the hospital and shaking his head in disgust. "This part of the valley ain't no place for a fine and upstanding citizen like myself," he added, dropping his gear near the construction site.

"Thanks for coming, guys," I said. "It means a lot to me."

"No sweat, Baby Bear." Beth gave me a high five. "We're just happy to help."

"And by the way, Benjamin, we're all thrilled you're back in K'du,"

Manfred said, picking up a sledgehammer. "We still meet every Tuesday night at the Rum Doodle, if you're interested."

"I'm there, brother," I said. "Count me in."

We worked hard that first day, demolishing what remained of the old clinic and digging a new foundation.

Later that night, after a third helping of dal bhaat tarakaari at Shruti's, Nepali Pete, the project's self-proclaimed field boss, rose from his wicker stool and rubbed his weary eyes. "I'm right knackered, mate. Old Pete really worked his nuts off today. I'm going to sod off now and get me some rest before we break our bloody backs again tomorrow."

"Hey, Pete," I said. "Before you go, I should warn you about the stray dogs in the neighborhood. They go crazy at night. Do you think you'll be OK in your tent?"

"No worries, mate," he said, laughing. "Old Pete's leathery hide is thicker than chain mail!" And besides, Pete explained, the intensity of his snoring was bound to thwart the advances of even the most aggressive cur.

Our team of dedicated volunteers began laying the foundation for the new clinic early the next morning. Just when I thought our work crew had reached its maximum complement, in walked Raju Shrestha, still limping slightly from his gunshot wound but moving well under his own steam nonetheless.

"I am thinking you could be using my help," he said, lifting a trowel so I could see that he had come prepared. Raju, after years of icing cakes at Slice of Life Bakery, was the perfect man to apply the mud-and-clay mortar between the bricks that would eventually form the new clinic's walls.

I pulled Raju aside later that afternoon and asked if he knew anything about the goondas who destroyed the hospital. "I'm concerned about the safety of people here in the community, especially people like Shruti and Annu," I said.

"Yes, it is a problem." He glanced over at Shruti, who had just delivered a tray of lemon tea. "I am knowing the goondas who are usually working this turf." He put down his trowel and wiped his brow. "They did not do this. Even *they* had respect for Doctor-ji and would not have committed such a crime." Raju guessed that the offenders must have been from outside the community. He was personally going to see that security was beefed up around Pepsicola Townplanning.

"Are you remembering those men we met in front of Hanuman Dhoka many months ago?"

"How could I forget, Raju. I almost wet my pants."

"No, no. You are having it the wrong idea, I am thinking. They are good men. Very loyal. I am thinking you will be finding their methods of determent most effective."

Raju explained that, to get to the bottom of the crime, he would "take it up under the tree." That phrase was a euphemism, I realized, for the act of gathering people from the community under the people tree to discuss who might be to blame and how they wanted to handle the investigation. Raju was convinced that the guilty parties eventually would be "put through the wringer," another euphemism that hinted at a gruesome fate for those who had destroyed the clinic and terrorized the neighborhood.

Our crew made great strides toward completing the clinic over the course of the following week. The clinic's exterior, with its mud-and-brick design, ceramic-tile roof, and ornately carved wooden lintels, sported a classic Newari design; inside, the clinic was almost as modern as Bir Hospital, which had donated an assortment of medical equipment and supplies. All the clinic needed was a doctor.

The Damu Sankar Singh Memorial Hospital opened its doors several weeks later while the community applauded. Madhu performed the ceremonial snip of the large, red ribbon I'd wrapped around the porch posts. I snacked on a celebratory slice of Raju's chocolate cake, and I couldn't help but think how happy Dr. Singh would have been to see the new clinic.

Next, a shaman gathered us all inside the clinic for a traditional blessing. The man, who wore his hair long and his glasses large, explained that this ceremony would draw from the teachings of two great faiths: Tibetan Shamanism and Buddhism. He lit several candles and sparked up incense sticks. He called for three volunteers and smiled his thanks as Raju, Pete, and I quickly stepped forward.

The shaman instructed us to om together to help lift humanity through troubling times and past the tension and velocity of the world's prevailing condition. He arranged the three of us in a triangle formation—our feet shoulder-width apart, our arms at our sides, and our wrists fully supinated—around a picture of Dr. Singh, and we toned, the resonance of our deep voices meeting somewhere in the middle of our tight little triangle. Everybody else followed the shaman around the clinic's perimeter three times as he called upon all those within our sphere—including future colleagues, friends, protectors, and patients—to simply "be with us."

I opened my eyes a crack and saw that both Raju and Pete had extremely serious looks on their faces. I felt a little shy about my own toning in that moment, but I closed my eyes again, stood my ground, and opened up my chest. I let my toning find a frequency that made me lose all self-consciousness. And so I continued to tone, letting the guttural sound rise straight from my navel to mingle with the monosyllabic utterances emanating from Pete and Raju. When the clinic had been blessed, we thanked the shaman, locked up, and headed home.

Pedalers' Progress

I received a phone call from the lawyer in charge of Dr. Singh's estate not long after the clinic's opening. He explained that, along with making sure his attendants would be financially cared for, the doctor had left me a sizable inheritance. For me, though, there was a catch: to collect the full amount, I would need to stay in Nepal for a duration of no fewer than two years and create a nongovernmental organization that catered to the needs of everyday Nepalis.

The physician hadn't stipulated what sort of organization it should be, only that it should serve the people of Nepal in a way they weren't currently being served and that it should be geared toward protecting some of the most vulnerable people in Nepali society. The organization should also include a certain number of Nepali administrators, the lawyer explained, men and women who would assume full responsibility for the NGO's operation once my two-year term as chief administrator ended.

If, after two years of operation, the organization had succeeded in meeting Dr. Singh's stipulations—a decision that would be made by the lawyer and a panel of the doctor's closest friends—the remainder of the inheritance would be released, and I would be free to use the money however I pleased. Until that day, though, he had earmarked a monthly stipend for me to live on and a pool of funds to be used only for the organization's launch and the salaries of future employees, should I choose to accept the

329

challenge. The rest, including the nuts and bolts of the operation, would be up to me to figure out, the lawyer said.

That was just like the doctor to reach out from beyond the grave to positively influence the lives of friends and strangers alike. His plan was crafty, loaded with incentives, and designed to help his Nepali brothers and sisters he so dearly loved. He had willingly let me slip away to India—in fact, he had encouraged it—but it was clear, based on the terms of his will, that he saw a future for me in Nepal, a future that arrived far sooner perhaps than either of us had ever expected. He knew I loved the country with all my heart and would find his challenge irresistible, so he had built a scenario that would put my Peace Corps skills into action and my leadership abilities to the test.

He must have known that I would have accepted the challenge even without the financial stimulus, but I was grateful nonetheless. I didn't know exactly how much had been gifted to me, but I understood that the money would give me plenty of options when my work in Nepal was finally done and that it would help offset the expense of returning to a life in America, if that was the path I chose.

I was honored that Dr. Singh had chosen me as the agent through which his compassion and generosity would continue to reach the people of Nepal. I envisioned creating an NGO to help empower Kathmandu's rickshawallahs—a population for whom I had developed considerable respect and admiration—called Pedalers' Progress, modeled, in some ways, after the wildly successful Porters' Progress. I wanted to create a micro-credit lending program so that men and women could get their own ricks, but this was just one of many details that still needed to be worked out.

I joined my Nepali friends at their new place of work several nights later, after mulling over the idea of Pedalers' Progress. We left the clinic after some lighthearted banter and headed for the Pepsicola people tree, where we sat under the broad, leafy canopy and enjoyed the warm evening breeze. Around us, the sun set in the purple sky and children scampered between rice fields, kicking up dust in their wake. A tuk tuk trundled by, its three wheels coming to a peaceful halt not far from the great tree's base.

Sitting on the short brick-and-clay wall that surrounded the people tree and among its thick, twisted roots radiating in all directions, we

reminisced about Dr. Singh and my time in the clinic. Shruti produced a thermos of lemon tea and six tumblers seemingly from out of nowhere, as was her specialty. We heartily accepted her tea. Arjun, who had volunteered to buy pakodas from the local *pakodawallah*, soon returned to the tree and distributed the tasty treats.

I munched on my snack and glanced over at Madhu, who had kicked off his sandals and was resting, barefoot, between two large roots, his back against the tree's base—the absolute picture of comfort. Dangling one of his legs over a root, and with his head cocked slightly to the side, he had placed one hand on his knee and was using his other hand to pick bits of pakoda from his glistening white teeth. I scratched an itch on my left arm and surveyed the rest of the crew, who were busy gabbing among themselves. A feeling of great nostalgia swept over me.

I looked into the eyes of the people seated around me, the eyes of the overworked and underpaid, and I saw deep and unwavering conviction. I also felt every one of their struggles, triumphs, and tragedies in my own heart. My love and respect for Nepal and its people, especially my friends at the clinic, was every bit as strong and intense as the subtropical sun now setting behind the valley's hills.

I was immediately reminded, as I looked into the eyes of my friends, that the world's wealthiest people are not always the most advantaged, that the world's wisest people are not always the ones with the greatest access to opportunity, and that the world's most generous people are not always the ones with an abundance of material resources to share. I was also reminded that life's most significant accomplishments—the ability to consistently express love, humility, and compassion—could only be achieved when we explored, with honest intentions and a pure heart, *all* facets of the human condition, when we let ourselves be moved in strange and inexplicable ways by *all* the world's people. There was hope in that exploration, and the possibility of being irrevocably altered for the better.

I said my good-byes, left my friends, and headed toward Kathmandu, toward the Rum Doodle and a night of celebration with my Peace Corps friends. But I heard the pounding of footfalls behind me after I'd walked only several hundred yards. I spun around to see a gasping Madhu running toward me. In a matter of seconds, he was by my side, panting heavily after the great exertion of the sprint.

"Here, daai," he puffed, pressing a small flashlight into my hand, a gesture that affirmed his sincere kindness and generosity—both of which were enduring character traits of the nation's people. "Please, you must be taking this to help light your ways."

Claire Mendelbaum and I had stayed in touch on a regular basis since our parting in Delhi. We managed to speak on the phone at least once a week, and we exchanged e-mails on an almost daily basis. I missed Claire badly, but I knew she was happy in New York surrounded by the city's incredible energy and diversity, not to mention its plethora of great Jewish delis. I'd wondered on more than one occasion if she had found a New York Reuben that could rival that served up by Rabbi Rosenblatt in Palolem. She always replied that, no, she hadn't but that she still had several thousand more delis to try. She'd get back to me on that one, she said.

My communications with Adriana following my return to Kathmandu, while less frequent and more emotionally taxing than my exchanges with Claire, were no less significant. We had worked out a number of our grievances over the course of several lengthy letters, although there was still much that needed to be addressed. Adriana was optimistic that, with some dedicated work, we could easily go on to have a long, healthy friendship.

Even though she never explicitly stated it, and even though our most recent communication was cordial, even playful at times, I finally understood and accepted in my heart that we would never be together as more than friends. What we once had, those precious fragments of a relationship, would always remain part of who I was, though, continuing to meld with my blood, bones, and body to forge a more complex and compassionate me, just as they already had started to do. With that realization, I let go of the idea that, if given another chance to win her love, I would somehow swoop into her life and sweep her off her feet, once and for all. And this letting go was…OK. I was a free man with a clean slate, and that meant something in a world filled with regret.

Afterword

WHEN THE PEACE CORPS SUSPENDED OPERATIONS IN NEPAL IN 2004, MANY (including myself) believed that the organization would never return. I began writing what would eventually become *Jaya Nepal!* in 2006, after my own volunteer experience (not with Peace Corps) in Nepal, and the manuscript was completed, more or less, in 2011. The fictional members of N-199 featured in this story were already over five years old when the Peace Corps announced that volunteers would be returning to Nepal in the fall of 2012 and that the first group back would be called N-199. So, now we have a fictional N-199 and a real N-199. It's my great hope that the members of the real N-199 find this work entertaining and enjoy the same tradition of friendship and cooperation with the Nepalis as do the fictional volunteers in this novel.

CPSIA information can be obtained at www.ICGtesting.com
Printed in the USA
BVOW09s1811091014

370135BV00005B/10/P

9 780990 578406